Big Red

OTHER WORKS BY JOHN HAASE

Novels
The Young
Road Show
The Fun Couple
Erasmus with Freckles
Petulia
The Noon Balloon to Rangoon
The Nuptials
Seasons and Moments

Plays
The Fun Couple
Wall to Wall War
Don't Call Me Dirty Names
Erasmus with Freckles

BIG RED

by John Haase

HARPER & ROW, PUBLISHERS

NEW YORK

Cambridge
Hagerstown
Philadelphia
San Francisco

1817

London
Mexico City
São Paulo
Sydney

FIRST EDITION

Designer: C. Linda Dingler

Library of Congress Cataloging in Publication Data

Haase, John.
    Big Red.

    I. Title.
PZ4.H1215Bi [PS3558.A18]   813'.5'4   79–2648
ISBN 0–06–011809–1

80 81 82 83 84 10 9 8 7 6 5 4 3 2 1

Acknowledgments

One wishes at a time like this that one could make a horizontal list rather than a vertical one, so many people shared equally in the writing of this book. Three people, however, belong at the apex: Professor Imre Sutton and his wife, Doris, who spent many hot summers in Boulder City, not only ferreting out fact after fact, but also lending a great deal of imagination and humanity to the project. Virginia Choate was organizer, archivist, right arm and left arm. No one could have given more.

I think of Rhoda Weyr, whose calm and wisdom provided the very necessary sea anchor throughout, of Buz Wyeth, for his consummate and compassionate skill as my editor, and Margaret Cheney, the copyeditor, whose surgical erasures, cool logic, and devotion to the project were always felt.

To Richard Kluger, whose early guidance proved very prophetic. To Helen Barrow for being the perennial healer.

To Jerry Hulse, Max Hall, and Frank Merlo for graciously allowing me time and space in which to work.

To the memory of Gerald Goodstone, M.D., a wonderful friend.

And to Janis whose patience and beauty made all the hours seem shorter.

To all of them, I can only say that which is totally inadequate: you have my profound gratitude.

JOHN HAASE

Los Angeles
May 31, 1979

5

for
RON MARDIGIAN
who kept the faith

Nature understands no jesting; she is always true, always serious, always severe; she is always right, and the errors and faults are always those of man. The man incapable of appreciating her she despises and only to the apt, the pure, and the true, does she resign herself and reveal her secrets.

—GOETHE

Big Red

1

Dawn had always been Frank Crowe's favorite time of day. He loved the grays, the blues, the reflection of the mist as the land once more emerged from darkness. More philosopher than he was willing to admit, he liked the precision of nature, the perfect renewal of another day. Perhaps it was the memories of Vermont, even the end of night, which he did not admit he feared; yet the speculation occurred to him.

He straightened his legs and his torso as he arose from the rattan-covered couch of the washroom of the railway car. He could have afforded a sleeper, his wife had urged him this indulgence, but he had spent too many nights on trains working for the Bureau of Reclamation, pocketing the difference in the allowance for a sleeper against the fare on coach. He was used to fixing his eyes on the washbowl in the corner, the metal basket beneath it holding used towels, the familiar sound of the rattle of the door to the toilet, its hinges mercilessly beaten by the endless, poorly maintained span of track bed.

He stood, washed his face with cold water, combed his sandy hair, and reached for his slouch hat, good felt, shapeless after twenty years of wear. He was forty-four years old, stood six feet four inches, lean and fibrous, a physique that many men would feel was frail.

He was not a physical man in the sense of brute strength or bulging muscles, yet he felt trim, knew that his body could take heat, cold, dampness, rain, that he could sleep on a hard bench, as he had, and dismiss the discomfort with one stretch. He had suffered much exposure to the elements, but it affected him little; there was always a greater purpose which eclipsed the physical discomfort.

He wore denim pants and a beige shirt, knee-high boots, a shapeless jacket, gray flannel, the remnant of some obligatory suit he had needed for some "damn-foolish" event in his long career of supervising engineer.

The green curtain to the washroom parted, and the conductor entered yelling, "Las Vegas, next stop," an automatic gesture. He had almost disappeared into the passageway of the car when he stepped back into the washroom.

"Ain't you Frank Crowe?"

13

Crowe looked somewhat uncomfortably at the conductor, his hair graying, steel-rimmed glasses framing a bulbous nose, his blue uniform as shiny as a polished opal.

"Yes, why?"

"We used to ride together when you were building Jackson Lake Dam. I'm Edward Fast."

"That's right, I remember."

"What are you doing in this godforsaken neck of the woods?"

"Just a trip."

"Come on," the conductor prodded. "Nobody comes to Vegas on a trip. Nobody like Frank Crowe."

It frustrated Crowe. Not only the fact that he'd been discovered, but more that he had not counted on discovery.

"Sit down, Edward," he said, and the conductor did as asked, pushing his cap back from his forehead. The rim had cut edges on his head over the years.

"How long before retirement?" Crowe asked.

"Ten years, Frank, but I'll never make it."

"Why?"

"There's lots of talk of shutting down this line. They're gonna abandon Vegas as a railhead. They'll let twenty crews go. I ain't got that kind of seniority."

"How would you like to make a deal?" Crowe asked.

"What kind of deal?"

"You're too smart, Edward, to believe Frank Crowe is going to Vegas lightly."

"You bet."

"I'm not. I'm coming here to look at Black Canyon. It's not the first time."

"Another dam?" Frank could see hope in the conductor's eyes.

"The biggest dam you've ever seen."

"Jesus." The conductor took off his cap and wiped his forehead with the sleeve of his coat. "When," he pressed, "when you goin' to start?"

"A year, maybe two."

"That may be too late. They're talking about shutting down this run by end of summer."

"I know all about it, Edward. So does the Bureau of Reclamation. They're not going to shut down this run. I know more about it than any other man alive."

"I guess you would," the conductor nodded, "so what's the deal?"

"I've told you something that's none of your business."

"I appreciate it."

"But I want something in return."

"What's that?"

"I want your word as a man that you'll keep this under your hat."

"You got it, Frank." He stuck out his hand and Crowe shook. It was a good hand, firm and roughened from years of turning a brake wheel.

"Wind gets out that Crowe is going to Vegas, you know what will happen. A goddamned avalanche of stiffs will come to this town looking for work."

"I know."

"We're a long way from hiring."

"I understand."

"Got any money saved up?" Crowe asked cautiously.

"Not much, why?"

"Now is the time to buy a little land in Vegas."

"Yeah, you're right. Working for the railroad don't leave much over after the pay check. You just count on that gold watch and retirement at the end."

Frank Crowe nodded, his eyes steady on the conductor. "I know what you mean. It's the same in the Bureau of Reclamation."

"We're here," the conductor said, watching the train pass the water tower, slowing gently.

Frank Crowe rose and picked up the briefcase he had brought. It was of good worn cowhide and two buckled straps held the contents securely. "Don't worry about your job," Crowe said, "and keep your mouth shut."

"You got my word, Frank."

Crowe felt secure in that, stepped out into the aisle and to the rear of the car. The porter had hardly placed the step on the platform when Crowe lighted on it and walked briskly toward the station and entered it. He took out his watch; it was a good Hamilton with a second hand ticking gracefully. He opened it and checked it with the wall clock in the station. Seven-ten. He closed the cover, felt the click of the tiny lock and headed for Mary's diner.

Anyone who had ever worked with Crowe, and thousands who had worked under him, knew that this watch was his master. Punctuality and utilization of time were a fetish with this man. He had been kidded about it, cursed for it, but it was as much of a trademark of his character as his felt hat or his denim work clothes. The latter came from L. L. Bean in Maine, and he liked the sparseness of their cut, like the precision of his watch and perhaps the precision of the dawn. He did not speculate about this as he put distance between himself and the station. He heard the sound of the locomotive as the train

15

pulled out of town. He could not resist turning to watch the engine belch smoke. It was a sight he had beheld since he was a young boy, and he laughed at his constant fascination with the iron horse.

It was seven-twenty in the morning when he arrived in front of Mary's diner, where he was to meet Jack Williams and Tom Wanke. It was ninety-five degrees already, this June day of 1927, and Frank measured the town of Las Vegas briefly.

It was a desert town, raped by mining, short on good soil, depending now almost solely on the railroad shops of the Union Pacific for its income, a revenue in doubt since rumors often precede happenings with greater consequence than the actuality of the event.

Heat and despondency showed their effects. He could see no sign of fresh paint, or a seedling tree, or a crisply lettered sign. Main Street, with half its doors shuttered, mirrored the despair of the dying town's inhabitants. All was yellow and gray, dust and tin cans resting by the side of the road.

There were saloons where the drinking was heavy and humorless, a couple of grocery stores, a garage, several rundown tourist cabins. There were the whores on Block 16, as worn and as poor as their desperate customers.

The evaporative cooler had not been invented yet; people sat on rickety porches, under the faint shade of cottonwood trees, waiting for the day that the desert would swallow them up. "I couldn't raise fifty men here who'd be worth a damn. This merciless heat has seared the will of most of them," Crowe thought to himself.

He entered the diner. Williams and Wanke were seated in the only booth. Crowe was revolted by the odor of the place. It mirrored the decay of the town. Mary's kids sat dolefully on the bar stools playing with a stack of packages of chewing gum, which Mary hoped would be sold when customers paid their bills.

Frank sat down quietly with Williams and Wanke. They shook hands easily and by agreement discussed nothing about their mission.

Jack Williams was portly, of Irish descent. His clothes resembled Crowe's: boots, denims. He sat next to a wooden box, two feet long, a foot high. He wore a leather string tie around his open shirt collar.

"All dressed up, Jack, I see," Crowe commented lightly.

"Yeah, well, Tom and I spent the night here, and thought we'd let the girls know they're dealing with gentlemen."

A waitress appeared and Crowe ordered coffee.

Wanke was almost as tall as Crowe. A studious-looking man, bespectacled, lean, wearing Levi's and a faded sport shirt. "We thought of letting you wait a couple of hours," he said. "Just see how you'd react."

"If you guys think I've mellowed since I quit the Bureau, forget

16

it." He pulled out his watch and opened it. Both Williams and Wanke laughed.

"Okay," Crowe said, "enough bullshit. Let's get on the road."

They walked to the counter and Mary took their money.

Crowe looked at the woman. Perhaps fifty, perhaps twenty-eight, surviving on corn flakes and lemonade, he figured. The features were almost rachitic.

"You wouldn't have a taxi in town," Crowe asked.

Mary laughed. "You're kiddin'. Ain't nobody here's got cab fare. 'Sides, where's there to go?"

"I understand. Anybody's car for hire?"

"I reckon," Mary said. "Go over to Ned's Garage. Might be cheaper to buy one than rent one. This town is full of abandoned cars."

"Thanks very much."

The three men strode purposefully to Ned's Garage, the owner's face so dark from oil it was difficult to guess his age.

"We need a truck for a day. Something that'll hold up in the heat and on some back roads."

"You guys miners?"

"I'm looking for a car not a job," Crowe said sternly. "If you got one I'll pay you cash money."

"The only one I can trust is my own. It's a Ford pickup. Runs good. New tires. Five bucks a day."

Crowe reached into his pocket and brought out a worn leather coin purse. He knew Williams and Wanke were watching him as he carefully reached for a five dollar bill. He snapped it to make certain there were not two bills, and handed it to the garage owner.

"I need a deposit," he said.

"What for?" Crowe asked.

"I ain't giving up that car for five bucks."

"How much do you want?"

"Twenty bucks."

Williams reached into his pocket, took out a twenty dollar bill and handed it to the garage man.

"Give me a receipt," he said sternly, "and fill that thing up with gas."

"Yes sir." He fumbled through a maze of bills, road maps, battery cables, looking for a receipt book and a pencil. It was evident that he was much more proficient with a grease gun and a wrench than with paper and pencil.

The three men piled into the cab of the pickup. Crowe looked at his watch. It was eight o'clock as they headed toward Black Canyon. The Nehi thermometer in front of the Cottonwood Cabins was frozen at 105.

17

2

It took a scant five minutes to get out of town as they left the pavement and hit the dirt road leading to the river.

"Have a good trip, Frank?" Williams asked.

"Like any other, except the goddamned conductor remembered me."

"That ain't good," Wanke said.

"No, but I shut him up. He was worried about his job. I told him to stop worrying about it. He'll be all right. How about you boys?"

"No big deal. We stayed at the Colonial, had a few beers at Charley's Saloon. The locals stare you down, get a few drinks into them, and accuse you of being another damned-fool miner."

"We let it go at that," Wanke said.

Crowe nodded. There was silence, the heat intense in the cab of the truck. Finally Crowe broke that silence, looking ahead, the desert almost liquid with sunshine.

"Jackson Lake, Wyoming, Tieton in Washington, Arrowrock Dam in Idaho, Flathead in Montana, Deadwood . . ." His voice trailed off. In one sense he had chronicled twenty years of dam building, twenty years of brilliant engineering, and twenty years of camaraderie with Williams and Wanke. Williams was the best tunnel man in the country, Wanke the greatest concrete engineer, and Crowe by reputation the ultimate supervising construction engineer.

It was a bond between three men so deep and secure it needed little reminiscing to shore it up. They were, all three of them, basically silent men, tough, organized, weather-hardened, private.

"They say," Crowe continued, "a man has five dams in him in a lifetime."

"I've heard that too," Wanke said.

"This will be our sixth," Crowe said, swerving to miss a boulder.

"As my water boy said at Deadwood, 'I don't cotton to that bullshit,' when I asked him about voodoo," Williams said.

"I agree," Crowe said. "How about you, Tom?"

"I don't go to church or see a palmist."

18

Frank Crowe's single most outstanding quality was meticulousness. His Yankee shrewdness and a solid engineering education at the University of Vermont were combined with twenty years of service with the Bureau of Reclamation. Like a surgeon he had mastered the art of making decisions, vital decisions on the spot, and preparing for these decisions before the emergency arose.

This was Crowe's strength. Time and time again he had proven that the most carefully chosen set of plans, the most detailed researches of stresses, the most stringent estimates of weather were inadequate before reality. Each step he took, though honestly and thoughtfully prepared, would need a counter step and the counter step would need a counter step.

Project after project had proven that on-the-spot decisions by Crowe, although often seeming foolish to other engineers, to theoreticians at the drawing board, were nevertheless right. Dead right. "Six months on the job, ten crises down the road," Walker Young once said, "and Crowe's got them eating out of the palm of his hand." And, though Crowe had worked with Williams and Wanke in the wilds of Montana, the heat of Idaho, the floods, the rainstorms of Washington, he could predict their reaction at the first sight of Black Canyon. He remembered his own, and he would never forget it.

Outside of the sheer canyon walls and the rushing river, which were familiar sights to dam builders, Crowe knew what would hit these men: the nothingness, the vast, vast, unrelenting nothingness.

The Nevada desert, not unlike the moon, is the most inhuman stretch of landscape on earth. In the summer, for days and months, the sun rises full-blown from ragged craters in the east, describes its arc and descends unspent behind the craters in the west. The heat is so intense, so merciless, that everything under it grows painful to the touch. A shovel left unattended resembles a bar of steel emerging from the furnace.

There is no life except for reptiles or vultures, whose black wings swooping over the lower landscape seem like an endless reminder that this is the territory of the dead.

But there is winter. Winds, icy winds whose prodigality is limitless because of the endless playing field, black clouds from which thunderstorms strike furiously, rains so devastating as to almost preclude breathing, frost, floods, all the inclement qualities of weather seem to grandstand in the desert of Nevada.

Frank Crowe knew this desert. He knew Black Canyon. He had traversed it with Herbert Hoover years ago, when Hoover was chairman of the Colorado River Commission; he had surveyed it with Walker Young, with Elwood Mead; and he had camped by the river and lived

19

at the canyon's edge, with his binoculars in his briefcase, his slide rule, his graph paper and fountain pen, his canteen of water, and his poncho.

He knew not only the fury of the weather but also the subtlety of the desert. He knew spring when mesquite bushes sprout with green, yucca raises white flowers, and myriad wildflowers prevail despite the seeming lack of water or the sparsity of nutrients in the soil. It was this annual resurgence, the flowers and the foliage, which gave Crowe courage. He knew the desert *was* alive, but at this moment, at nine-thirty in the morning, temperature at 115, he could predict the reaction of Wanke and Williams.

"Jesus Christ" is all that Williams could manage.

"There's not one fucking tree," said Wanke, a man who rarely used profanities.

The three men stood at the rim of Black Canyon looking at the river eight hundred feet below them, but Crowe prudently would not let them linger long. There was much work to be done this day and endless reflection would only depress his friends.

He sat on the ground, opened his briefcase, and took out his slide rule. The other two men joined him in a tight circle.

"As you guys know," Crowe said quietly, "I'm not a speechmaker. Perhaps they'll say someday that this was the most crucial day in the building of this dam."

He used his slide rule like a baton, punctuating his objective. "I've seen the plans at the Bureau for this dam. They're good. Damned good. Best I've ever seen, and believe me, the best you've ever seen. But, as you know, plans are on paper. Drawn by a lot of kids wet behind their ears, kids who've got a diploma in civil engineering but never owned a pair of boots or slept in a pup tent."

He stopped. "Sure, there's Walker Young, and he's great, and Herbert Hoover, who can't be beat."

"What's troubling you, Frank?" Williams asked.

There was a pause.

"I'm going to build this dam. I am. Not Walker Young, not Herbert Hoover, not the U.S. government or anyone else. I'm going to build that dam. I am, and you are, Tom, and you are, Jack." He looked at each of them for a long time. "I've been over every set of plans, I have read all the data, watched all the projections. . . ."

"Where's the hitch?" Wanke asked.

"To build it I need to know two things. I need two answers, and you can get them for me today. You, Jack, have got to get four tunnels through this rock in less than a year. Four tunnels fifty-six feet in diameter, fully lined, as pretty as the Taj Mahal."

"Fifty-six feet," Williams shouted.

20

"Fifty-six feet," Crowe reiterated. He looked down at the Colorado. "The locals call that river Big Red, and it's the toughest, meanest river in the world. It can rise seventeen feet in four hours, gouging out tons of earth and making that tame river down there look like flowing red lava. It tore out the Grand Canyon, it built up a riverhead of silt a hundred feet above sea level. It will make every other river we have dammed look like a spring creek."

"Fifty-six feet," Williams repeated, obsessed with the enormity of his job.

"Well, we've all done this before." Crowe looked at them and they nodded. "I want you, Jack, to go to the end of Black Canyon and blast test holes. Now. I don't have to tell you what to do.

"And you, Tom, you take the truck and find a gravel bed. The best gravel, the closest, and the greatest quantity. The Bureau claims it's five miles north of the Arizona border. Check it out.

"And, while you guys are cavorting in the beautiful desert, I'm going to make my last set of determinates. With all their plans, the Bureau has made one fatal error."

"What's that?"

"They want to bring the dam in at 560 feet. My figure, and I have figured it over and over, is 726 feet."

"One hundred sixty feet will add another year," Wanke said.

For the first time Crowe smiled. "Not the way I figure it. Get off your ass. I'll tell you all about it at dinner. Right now it's academic."

After twenty years of working with Crowe, both Williams and Wanke knew the conversation was over. Wanke jumped into the truck and said to Williams, "I'll take you as close as I can to where you're going."

It was deathly quiet when the sound of the pickup faded in the distance. Crowe set up his tripod and transit and slung a pair of Zeiss binoculars around his neck. Carefully he wiped the lenses of the binoculars, adjusted the sights, and slowly he moved along the canyon wall across the river until he found the faded red markers he had staked out years ago. He spread out his graph paper and ignored the heat and the buzzards overhead.

He worked methodically, plotting, shooting, writing. Occasionally he heard the blasts of Williams's dynamite far down the canyon; once he sighted Wanke's truck. The sun was almost set when both men returned to Crowe's perch above the canyon.

"Got everything you need?" he asked.

They both nodded their heads.

"What do you think?"

"I'll get through the canyons," Williams said. "All fifty-six feet of them."

21

"I'll give you all the concrete you need," Wanke added. He threw a handful of pebbles at Crowe's feet. Crowe picked up several, inspecting the lowly rocks like an aging jeweler examining a diamond.

"You got plenty of this?"

"Enough for five dams."

Crowe nodded. "I'll buy dinner. I know a good place."

Williams drove the pickup and Crowe slept on the way back to Vegas.

3

Dominick the Greek, as he was called in Vegas, owned a restaurant called Poppa Joe's. It was one of those quirks which bothered no one in town, least of all Dominick, who, in the mining days, had built up a flourishing family restaurant proud of an oak-carved bar, which had come around the Horn, a trellised dining room, festooned with straw-covered wine bottles, fake grapes, dusty Italian flags. There had even been stories of gambling going on upstairs, but now Poppa Joe's merely hung on, the miners gone, the residents too poor to eat out, and Dominick too stubborn to move.

Frank Crowe asked for a private booth and he, Williams, and Wanke sat heavily on fragile woven-cane chairs. Crowe ordered a bottle of red wine, Dominick brought an ample plate of antipasto—salami, olives, peppers, garbanzo beans—and soon the three men settled down to a heavy, pleasant meal of pasta, meatballs, Italian sausage. The talk was easy, discussions of deaths and births, promotions and firings, other projects, other days. Neither Williams nor Wanke pressed Crowe, knowing he would divulge his plans sooner or later.

Another bottle of wine arrived.

Finally Frank began to talk about those plans.

"As you know, I quit the Bureau two years ago and joined Utah Construction Company."

"We heard about it," Jack Williams said. "We wondered too."

"Twenty years I'd spent," Crowe said. "Built five dams, just like you, and what do I have to show for it? A house worth maybe forty-eight hundred dollars, a beat-up Chevy, arthritis in my right shoulder, and the prospect of getting three hundred eighty a month for the rest of my life."

Williams nodded his head in agreement. "It's gone up to four ten now, Frank."

"Very generous. Finally it came to me that every son of a bitch that graduates from engineering school has three choices: he either works for the Bureau, or for a big company, or he buys a truck and a cement mixer and is in business for himself.

"Look at Barnes, Edward Chapman, Henderson-Andrews, they're no better engineers than any of us, and where are they? On Nob Hill, in Salt Lake, getting fat. Why?"

"You're right, Frank. I've thought about it too, but maybe that's a decision we should have made fifteen years ago."

"Maybe it was, Tom, but I made the decision at forty-two, joined Utah, and even now make three times what the government ever paid me."

"You're worth it, Frank."

"Sure I'm worth it. What is it they say? Frank Crowe, the best dam builder in the world. Jack Williams, the best tunnel man. Tom Wanke, the best concrete engineer."

"What do you suggest?"

"Join me at Utah. I'll double your salary. Soon they'll start bidding on the Boulder Dam. Utah is going to be one of the bidders."

"How much are they willing to put up?"

"A million bucks."

"Wow."

"Wow is right. Shaughnessy who owns Utah isn't half the engineer we are, but he's *got* a million bucks. Earned it fair and square, I'll say that."

"It's not that easy, Frank. I could retire soon; so could Jack."

"I know. I know. The government has you by the balls. Three more years and you're home free. Twenty-five years, five dams, maybe six, and you haven't got enough dough to take your wife out once a week."

"You got enough authority at Utah to hire us?"

"Shaughnessy paid for my trip to Vegas to meet you guys. He's even buying this dinner."

Crowe noticed the engineers looking at each other. Things were working fast. These men, sitting across from him, were equally methodical men. Their lives were orderly. Offers like this were unnerving.

Wanke took the initiative. "Look, Frank, I know what's going through Jack's mind, it's the same as me. You're betting on a couple

23

of horse races. *One* is whether the dam will be built, and *two,* whether Utah will get the low bid. Goddamned Arizona will never ratify that pact."

"You're right," Frank said, "but you've forgotten a third factor."

"What's that?"

"Whether Hoover will make President."

"I never considered that," Williams said.

"I *have*," Crowe answered. "I went to Palo Alto and talked to Hoover. I went right to his house. Perhaps the greatest day in my life. He was humble, honest, brilliant. He told me he would run, he would win, and he'd build the Boulder Dam."

"Did you ask him about Arizona? It takes seven states to ratify that pact."

"It does *now.* I asked Hoover about it. He said, 'Frank, when I'm President, it will take six states out of seven. It's as simple as that. I can do it with the stroke of a pen.'

"I'll never forget that statement. Hoover laughed. Said yes, just like that. 'Bet you never learned that at the University of Vermont.'

" 'No sir,' I said.

" 'Well, Frank, you learned all there is to engineering and I hope to hell you'll get to build that dam.' "

"I'll say one thing," Williams countered, "you sure been getting around."

"That's not the only place I've been. Where do you think I've spent most of my days these last two years?"

"Where?"

"At the Bureau. Right next to Walker Young's drawing board."

"What about the others? The others who will want to bid on the dam?"

"The Bureau's offices in Denver are open. It's a government office. They're just as welcome there as I am."

"I'm not so sure about that."

"Well, let's say I'm on home ground," Crowe adjusted.

"One thing, Frank," Wanke added seriously. "When we were at the dam site, you mentioned something about one hundred sixty extra feet."

"Right. Five hundred sixty feet of dam can't hold twenty million acre feet of water behind it. It'll wear out the spillways in two years."

"What does Walker Young think about that?"

"We've argued and argued. I've worn out three Keuffel and Esser thirty-dollar slide rules but he's stubborn."

"Maybe he's right."

Crowe looked at Wanke quizzically. "Maybe he is."

"You've got to bid on *his* plans."

"That's right. His plans aren't finalized yet. He listens to me, and if I can't make him see the light, one person can."

"Who's that?"

"Hoover. Walker idolizes the man."

"Okay, okay," Wanke said. "It'll still take one extra year."

"It won't."

"Why?"

"Because I plan to bring that dam in two years early."

"How?"

"I'll work twenty-four hours a day instead of eight."

"Jesus," Williams gasped.

"What difference does it make to you, Jack? You'll be underground *day* or night."

"It doesn't make any difference to me, but what will the government say, the unions, the Wobblies."

"Three shifts a day means a payroll three times as large. What politician is going to argue against employment?"

"It's ingenious," Wanke said.

"It's secret," Crowe retorted. "Up to this minute, the only man who knew about this was *me*. Now you both know."

"That's no problem," Williams said.

"I know that."

A dark-haired girl, probably Dominick's daughter, delivered three brandies, courtesy of the house. Williams commented on her good looks. She blushed and left.

"There's one more thing," Crowe continued. "The way I've been watching the plans, the computations I've made, I *know* I can bring in the low bid, I *know* I can come in two years ahead of schedule, and I *know* we'll be in the black."

"I trust your figures, Frank."

"Thanks, Tom, but I also know this will be *my* last dam, and your last dam. Before I take this job, I'm going to demand ten percent of the profits."

"That's pretty steep, isn't it, Frank?" Wanke asked.

"Very steep. But I intend to give each of you twenty percent of my share."

He noticed both men trying to accept the reality of it all.

"You're better with figures than I am, Frank. What kind of profit do you project?"

"About $3 million."

"So you're talking about $300,000 for yourself."

"I am projecting $180,000 for myself and $60,000 for you each." He watched his friends trying to cope with those figures. "And I'll make one more projection. You'd have to live to the age of 190 to

25

get that kind of money in pensions from the Bureau."

"When did you figure that out?"

"On the train coming here."

There was silence in the room. All the three men could hear was the dishwasher working. Frank drank his brandy in one swallow.

Finally, Frank Crowe said, "I never deal with anybody after booze. Let's all get a good night's sleep and take another run up to the site tomorrow. You guys talk it over. I'll see you at seven at Mary's."

"You wouldn't want to make that seven-fifteen?" Williams suggested, laughing.

"Seven o'clock," Crowe said, also laughing.

"I wonder," said Wanke, "what time Henry Barnes gets up?"

4

Once more they had traced their way to the dam site, standing on a promontory later to be known as Observation Point. Familiarity with the site did not bring affection. The utter desolation of the area reminded Wanke of a deserted battlefield, one in which the battle was really about to begin.

Yet, here in this wasteland, nature somehow managed to survive, thin-leafed aspens were replaced by water-filled cacti, animals had skin which not only concealed but protected, and the river, far below them, had a life which awed them all.

"Well, what did you boys decide?" Crowe finally asked.

"I've got some questions," Tom Wanke said. "So does Jack."

"I bet." Crowe knew they had spent most of the night talking.

Wanke with binoculars around his neck directed Frank to raise his own. He spoke carefully. "I want you to raise your glasses and follow this canyon wall east until we come to a ridge about five miles upstream."

"I'm with you."

"Now cross the river with me—straight across."

"All right."

"You see a level area there?" Wanke asked.

"Yes."

26

"Just beyond it is the gravel wash."

"That's what the Bureau figured."

"Well, they were right. I'm going to need a bridge across here, Frank, a good trestle railroad bridge that can take two tracks with a maximum load of forty gondolas filled with concrete, not counting the engines."

Crowe retraced the river in his glasses. "That'll have to be a hell of a bridge."

"You bet."

"You'll get it. What else?"

"I want some of that new high-carbon steel for the trackage. The lime has a way of eating steel. You remember Deadwood."

"I do indeed."

"Is that bridge coming out of our pockets or the government's?" Wanke asked.

"The government's."

"No wonder you're not worried." All three men laughed.

"I'll build my hi-mix plant at the west bank and my lo-mix plant along the river. I've got to figure how many consists I'll need. Do you think you can still get Elverson to run the railroads?"

"He's ready for retirement," Crowe said. "I talked to him last week. He said, 'Just give me four hours and I'll be packed.'"

"Good," said Wanke. "He can keep an engine going with spit and Wrigley's gum."

"I know," Crowe added, then reflected. "God almighty, I was at his wedding in Montana."

"Yeah," said Williams, "twenty years ago."

"What else?" asked Crowe, feeling the men were with him.

"That's all for now."

"And you, Jack."

Jack Williams sat on the ground and spread out a rough drawing. Crowe hunched beside him. "I figure roughly I've got to blast one and a half million yards of rock for those four tunnels. I'll blast a twelve-foot hole first starting at each end and then increase to fifty-six feet."

"What's this rig?" Crowe wondered.

"This will be known as the 'Jack Williams Special.' It's a rig three stories high. It will be on tracks. There will be six stations on the first level, six on the second. I'll have twelve men drilling twenty-foot holes at once, stick in the dynamite, pull back and BLOW. Then the muckers can haul away the rock."

Crowe studied the drawing carefully. "It's ingenious."

Wanke had joined the circle now and was equally impressed with the invention.

"What else?" Crowe asked.

27

"One thing," Williams said carefully. "What about the inspectors, the canaries, the usual crap?"

"No problem."

"You say, 'No problem,' Frank. You *know* Arizona isn't going to sign that pact. What if they plague me with their safety men?"

"Arizona won't have any jurisdiction. The entire area will be declared a federal reservation. If any state inspectors show up we'll give 'em a bottle of bourbon and a broad in Vegas. If that isn't enough, I'll keep 'em off the reservation."

Crowe remembered Deadwood. He knew what Williams's fears were. Williams was the best tunnel engineer because he attacked a wall of rock the way Crowe would attack the Colorado River, with a vengeance. No one in the business was more aggressive or fearless than Williams, but tunneling has inherent dangers, not the least of which are noxious fumes caused by the use of dynamite. He well recalled an obstreperous inspector in Montana who held up a caged canary to prove to Williams that he was ordering his men back into the ground too soon after blasting. Canaries supposedly have an oxygen need similar to men's. He waved the dead canary in front of Williams's nose until Williams with one swoop of his arm tossed the cage and canary out of the inspector's hand. He turned to his tunneling crew and yelled, "What are you guys, men or canaries? Get back to work." Very few men disobeyed Jack Williams in a tunnel.

"All right," Williams said, "no state inspectors. What about the government? All those bright young college boys in Denver you were telling about. What about them?"

"I'll handle them," Crowe said.

"How?"

"I'll tell you something, Jack. Walker Young is older than I am, so is Herbert Hoover. They're from *our* school of construction. Walker Young wants that dam built just as much as I do. He wants a cabinet post."

"Good man," Wanke said, "Walker Young."

"Right," agreed Williams.

"And Hoover?"

"Hoover, Tom," said Crowe carefully, "Hoover wants that dam for two reasons. The first one is because he's an engineer. He knows that building that dam will save the Imperial Valley, create jobs, produce energy. The second reason is because Hoover, like the rest of us, is human. He knows this thing will bear his name. *Hoover Dam.*"

"I'll be goddamned," Wanke said. "You've got the Jack Williams Special, Hoover will get the dam, what glory do I get?"

"We'll name the shithouse after you," Williams said.

28

"Yeah." Crowe laughed. "The Tom Wanke Federal Relief Facility."

It was at this point of levity that Crowe asked the question he knew he did not have to ask. "Well, are you guys in?"

"We're in."

Crowe and Williams and Wanke, three men with buzzards over their heads and a rampaging river below them, shook hands solemnly. There would be no papers drawn; there would be no legal eagles involved. Heavy-construction men, like firemen or sailors, men pitted against the elements, would shake hands and that was their word.

"I've got a couple of questions for you boys," Crowe said.

"Shoot."

"I've got to bring in power from California. Two hundred miles from here." He pointed west. "I'm worried about these California boys. I've led 'em before. They're soft."

"Get Higgins or Jones. I don't know any tougher foremen."

"Good idea. Maybe I can get them both."

Wanke was almost speaking to himself. "You're going to light up that whole dam site."

"Yup," Crowe said. "Every inch of it."

"That's going to be quite a sight."

"I figure it would be. Might even invite Edison to look at it."

"Fine," Williams said, "and you'll have to wear a suit."

"Yeah, I forgot about that. Scratch that idea, I'll have enough trouble with all those lard-ass senators and congressmen taking their jaunts."

"A little concrete on their blue suits will discourage that soon enough."

They were poised to leave when Crowe took one final look upstream. He looked at that silvery breast of water and said, almost like a soliloquy: "The Colorado River starts at the top of the slopes of Longs Peak in north-central Colorado. It flows into Grand Lake, picks up dozens of Rocky Mountain streams, the Williams, the Blue, Roaring Fork, Eagle, and Frying Pan. It joins the Gunnison at Grand Junction. It picks up myriads of mountain streams and then the Green three hundred fifty miles down in Utah. The Green from the Grand Tetons has picked up the Uinta and Price before it joins the Colorado. The Colorado picks up the Muddy, the Fremont, the San Juan. Then it picks up the Little Colorado coming from the White Mountains, gathers Kanab Creek on the north, Havasu Creek on the south, picks up the Nige from Zion Canyon, which holds the waters of Meadow Valley West and the Muddy River and finally the Vegas Wash. That's what we've got here. *Right down here.* The drainage of 167,800 square

29

miles, which cover parts of Wyoming, Colorado, Utah, New Mexico, Arizona, Nevada, and California." He paused, but then he said, "If I tame that river, it will still have its monument: the Grand Canyon. Two hundred and seventeen miles long and from four to eighteen miles wide."

Crowe turned toward his partners, almost embarrassed by his speech.

"You forgot the San Rafael," Wanke said. "It flows into the Green."

"You're right," Crowe said, almost relieved to break the solemnity of his speech. "Guess you've done a little thinking about this river too."

"One question," Jack Williams asked. "Do you *hate* this river, Frank?"

Crowe thought for a long time. "Right now," he said, "I respect it. Before we're done I might hate it."

Williams kept his eyes on Crowe and said nothing.

They drove back to Vegas in silence, returned the truck, and ate a final meal at Poppa Joe's.

"When can I expect you in Salt Lake City?" Frank asked.

"I figure a week," Williams said. "I'll give notice tomorrow."

Crowe laughed. "Construction stiffs. God damn. We're all construction stiffs. No roots. A week is all it takes to move your gear."

Williams and Wanke took Frank to the train station. They said little as the Salt Lake run approached. Finally Wanke said to Crowe, "Heard you got married, Frank. About two years ago?"

"That's right. Guess you'll get to meet her when we start working."

"Can she cook?" asked Williams, patting his ample stomach.

"That's not her *best* quality."

The men shook hands; Crowe boarded the train and headed for the rest room with its six-foot bench. Mercifully it was empty and he took off his coat and hat, made a pillow out of the coat, and waited for the train to gain momentum.

Twenty years and five dams, that's how long he'd known Tom and Jack. Twenty years in heat, snow, floods, in forests, disaster, fifteen hours, eighteen hours, side by side, seven days a week across the western slopes of the United States. Twenty years of work, hard work, hard drinking, whoring, picking up the weekly check at the Bureau office, shopping for a new pair of boots, bitching about the bums in the crew. And still they were impersonal years. Sure, Tom was married, so was Jack, they had kids, they lived in houses, but above all, it was the job, the mountain, the river, the gorge, the jackhammers and the compacters and the miles and miles of graph paper which held them together. If there was a death, they stopped and had a funeral and

30

if there was a wedding they stopped and got drunk, but these were short beats in a long concerto.

"Heard you got married, Frank," Wanke had said. The first personal remark in two days, as he was boarding the train to go home, and it was natural.

"Heard you got married, Frank." Yeah, he thought. "You didn't marry me," Elle had said once, "you married the Colorado River."

Frank Crowe was asleep before the train passed Searchlight.

5

Herbert Hoover was right. He ran for President of the United States and he won, as he had told Frank Crowe he would in the garden of his home in Palo Alto, and on December 21, 1928, the Boulder Canyon Project Act was passed in Congress and signed by Calvin Coolidge. Arizona had held out to the end, fighting began over the public and private financing, but the act was passed.

Its vital sections read:

For flood control, improving navigation, and for delivery of water for irrigation and domestic purposes, the Secretary of the Interior is authorized to construct, operate and maintain a dam and incidental work at Black or Boulder Canyon sufficient to store not less than 20,000,000 acre feet of water for the Imperial and Coachella valleys in California. He is also authorized to construct, or to cause to be constructed, at or near the dam, a power plant and incidental structures. . . .

If the Colorado River compact is not ratified by all of the States within six months, until it is ratified by *six* of them, including California . . .

Frank Crowe in his office at Utah Construction slammed his fist on his desk when he read this section in the paper, remembered what Hoover had told him: "You didn't learn *that* in engineering school." He ran into his boss's office, and excitedly waved the document in front of him. Shaughnessy had never seen him so emotional or even recalled his ever shoving into the office without knocking.

The Boulder Canyon Act had projected the $165 million estimated cost on the basis of $70 million for the dam and reservoir, $38.2 million for construction of a 1.8 million-horsepower hydroelectric plant, $38 million for the All-American Canal; and interest on the whole sum during the construction period was figured at $17.7 million.

The government projected amortization of the project over a period of fifty years, and before anything could begin it was necessary to negotiate the sale of the projected power to finance the project.

There were twenty-seven applicants for the energy. The City of Los Angeles, the Southern California Edison Company, and the Metropolitan Water District, being the most affluent bidders, got the lion's share. The states of Arizona and Nevada each were to receive 18 percent of the available energy.

When these figures were released Arizona blew its legislative stack once more, claiming that California was raping not only their water but also their power. In desperation the state chartered a paddle-wheel steamer, filled it with armed National Guardsmen, and moored on the Parker Dam site to "defend" it from California invaders. "The Arizona Navy" as it got to be called, stayed for months and effectively won the battle. They left only after Los Angeles agreed to allow Arizona a share of its water.

On June 25, 1929, President Hoover issued a proclamation noting that the Boulder Canyon Project Act was in effect.

Order 436 instructed Dr. Elwood Mead, Commissioner of Reclamation, as follows: "You are directed to commence construction on Boulder Dam."

The conductor of Run 4 of the Union Pacific read the news and smiled. He had managed to buy an acre in Las Vegas. And he had kept his mouth shut. Perhaps soon he would see Frank Crowe again.

Williams and Wanke were in Crowe's office when he returned from his emotional visit to Shaughnessy. Crowe's office was large and meticulously neat. Along one wall were scores of cubbyholes for maps, carefully labeled and obviously delicately handled. Along the wall facing Crowe's desk was a model of the dam he was going to build, ⅛ inch to the mile. It was a beautiful model handmade of balsa wood and papier mâché and correct to every elevation.

Crowe's desk was oak and bare except for a green blotter, an inkwell and pen and a beer mug holding twelve highly sharpened pencils, black, red, green, and blue. There were a telephone and an unused ashtray. Along the last wall was a large drafting table, a map spread over its suface, and triangles and T-squares laid out as meticulously as a surgeon's instruments.

Williams and Wanke brought in two straight-back oak chairs and sat down facing Crowe, who stood. He detested chairs, feeling that it was better for a man to stand when he was working.

32

"Well, Frank," Wanke said, "so far you've called it one hundred percent."

"I listened to Hoover and I believed him. He's an engineer."

"Well, when do we get to work?" Williams wondered.

Crowe walked around the room. He was agitated, unsure of himself, a detestable quality. "I was just as excited as you guys when I burst into Shaughnessy's office with the act in my hand."

"What's the problem?"

"The problem is simple, Tom. Shaughnessy told me that, for a company to bid, the government is going to require a five-million-dollar bond."

"Five million dollars," Wanke shouted. "There isn't a contractor in the West who's got that kind of money."

"Exactly."

"So some Eastern bastard is going to grab the ball and run with it, is that it?" Williams said angrily.

"Maybe," Crowe answered.

"What, maybe? We're through. Finished. Those sons of bitches!"

"The old man said we were not through."

"How come?"

"We'll have to join forces, maybe with Barnes, maybe with Chapman, maybe with both of them, and maybe with more contractors to come up with the bond . . ."

"Sure," Williams said, "they're all thinking the same thing, but what if they decide they don't want *our* million bucks?"

"I'll tell you what Shaughnessy said. He said, 'Sit down, Frank. This is the way I have it figured. I've got a million, I'm not ashamed of it, it isn't chickenfeed, that's that, all that Utah Construction has for that bond. Barnes has a million, Chapman has a million, Mackenzie-Stein has a million, I've been on the phone all morning. . . . But I've got one thing that all of them want.' 'What is that?' I asked. 'Frank Crowe,' he said."

It bothered Crowe to make that speech. All his New England reticence revolted against this display of braggadocio, but he had brought these men in, he had terminated their safe career at the Bureau, he had to give them hope.

"He's right," said Wanke. "The old man is right, but what about our deal? I figured you could swing it with Shaughnessy, but what about the others?"

Frank Crowe picked up his slide rule from his drafting table and sat down on his desk. Somehow, he felt better with this instrument of precision in his hand; he enjoyed the interaction of the highly polished ash, tongue and groove, as he enjoyed the click of his watch case when it shut, the bubble of a level when it centered.

33

"My deal and your deal are the same. Whether I'm up against Shaughnessy or Chapman or Barnes or Stein or all of them. I'm desperate, Tom. I'm shooting craps. I'll get it my way or I'll walk out of this office and build sidewalks in Salt Lake."

"I'll get a wheelbarrow and help you," Williams said.

"I'll carry the water," Wanke followed.

"Thanks, boys," Crowe said, standing. The meeting was finished.

Crowe watched them leave and closed the door behind them. He was still playing with his slide rule. Years ago at the University of Vermont, someone had commented that the instrument was sexual. He had never forgotten that, and detested the fact that the thought would not leave him.

The days grew long before the opening of the bids on March 4, 1931. Merritt and Scott were already building railroads and highways to the dam site, Bureau engineers were all over the area checking and rechecking their calculations, and Crowe, never a desk man, sat caged in his office, waiting, waiting for the money to materialize for the bond. He had persuaded the Bureau to raise the dam to 726 feet, but all that seemed gratuitous now.

He rarely saw Shaughnessy, though he knew that this man was doing what he knew best—wheeling and dealing, figuring as Crowe figured elevations and stresses.

Finally in November, Shaughnessy, a short energetic man, called Frank to his office and handed him a list. "There it is," he said. "Five million bucks."

Frank Crowe read carefully and aloud. *"Utah Construction Company, one million dollars. J. F. Shea of Los Angeles, half a million dollars.* Williams will be happy with them; they're good on tunnels and sewers. *Mackenzie-Stein, San Francisco, one million dollars.* What in hell did they ever build?"

"The Mark Hopkins Hotel," Shaughnessy said.

"That makes them dam builders?"

"They have a million dollars."

"Henderson-Andrews," Crowe continued, *"Edward Chapman,* and *H. A. Barnes."* He put down the list. "That's five million dollars."

"To the penny," Shaughnessy said.

"This Stein," Crowe asked. "He's a Jew?"

Shaughnessy, irritated, answered, "Yes, Stein is Jewish, but he doesn't worry me."

"Who does?" Crowe asked.

"Between us," Shaughnessy said, "Ed Chapman. I used to build gutters next to him right here in Salt Lake City. We used to find a lot of *our* shovels in *his* trucks. At any rate, that's it, Frank. That's three months of work on this goddamned telephone, and the only

34

thing everyone agrees on is that you should be general superintendent, so get to Denver and wait for the Bureau's plans. They should be ready by December 1; then we can get on with the bid."

"Shaughnessy," Crowe said, "you can save that train fare. I know those plans better than the private parts of my wife."

"I believe you, Frank, but those bastards at the Bureau may throw you a last-minute curve and I'm taking no chances."

"I see your point," Crowe answered quietly.

Crowe stood up and started to leave. "What kind of a place is the Mark Hopkins Hotel anyway?"

"It's the most beautiful hotel in the world and you'll never have enough money in your jeans to stay there overnight."

"We'll see about that," Crowe said, smiling.

Crowe picked up the plans in Denver. The Bureau offices had been his second home for years now, and Elder, the Bureau chief, presented them to him personally.

Elder and Crowe had worked side by side for many years; they had shared women and booze and they had borrowed and repaid money to each other when salaries were meager. Crowe had urged Elder to join him at Utah Construction Company, but Elder preferred to remain secure at the Bureau. His wife was crippled with arthritis; he knew his days on construction sites were likely to be few.

"Close the door, Frank," he said, and Crowe did as ordered.

"You know, Frank, that I've worked for the Bureau for twenty-seven years and this job is sacred to me."

"I know, George."

"I want you to get this job because without you I wouldn't have a set of plans to hand you."

"Come on."

"Not a set that's going to work."

He stood up and paced the room nervously. "I know Arundel from Delaware will be bidding. So, I understand, will a couple of other Eastern outfits. . . ."

Crowe knew that Elder was trying to reveal the Bureau's estimate of the Eastern bid. He would be breaking the law.

"Don't say a word, George," Frank said. "Give me a piece of paper."

George handed him a sheet of paper and Frank drew a horizontal line through the center. At the far end of the line he wrote the number 50 and then an arrow down. He showed it to Elder and Elder nodded his head.

Frank picked up a match and set the paper on fire. Both men watched it turn to ashes. Frank took his sheaves of maps and shook Elder's hand.

"Bring up the wife when I get the house. That heat will be good for her arthritis."

"I'll do that, Frank. Good luck."

All the principals of the Big Six Companies met at the Brown Palace in Denver on February 28, and while they represented the cream of builders in the West, some with $30 million of construction on their drawing boards, they teamed up in twos to fill the six bedrooms they had rented. They were all construction men and a buck was still a buck. This was a business meeting, and it came as no further surprise that the council meeting the next morning would be held in one of their rooms, the men sitting on unmade beds, windowsills, dressers, their backs against the wall. It was an atmosphere which made Crowe comfortable.

There were introductions, coffee was passed, and finally Frank Crowe, pointer in hand, had everyone gather around the model of the dam. He was aware that around him stood some of the best engineering talent of the West, and he took pains to be as brief and precise as he could.

He took the job step by step. Tunneling, cofferdams, unwatering the site, cherry picking, pouring the dam, grouting, finishing, housing, safety, labor, materials, wages, food, legalities, hazards. The presentation was so masterful it prompted not one question until the end. Mackenzie asked it.

"What is your bid, sir?"

"The cost," Frank Crowe said evenly, "will be $36 million. The profit you have to decide."

"Twenty-five percent," Old Man Donner said, "in order to cover the bond and pay off the backers. That leaves $3 million net profit."

"Then the bid will be $48 million."

"Hold on, Crowe, hold on," Chapman said nervously.

"Mr. Chapman?" Crowe looked at him.

"My boys have been in the field too, and listening good. The last I heard is that Arundel is going to bid $56 million. You're $8 million under."

"That's right, Mr. Chapman."

"That's one hell of a discrepancy."

Crowe paused for a minute to let the room settle down. "Arundel, to the best of *my* knowledge, and every other bidder is planning to work eight hours a day. I plan to work around the clock."

"Three shifts?" Mackenzie asked.

"Three shifts," Crowe answered.

"What about the Bureau," Stein asked, "the unions? How do you get around this?"

36

"There is nothing in the plans that states we cannot work twenty-four hours a day. The Bureau specifies that no man can work more than eight hours a day. No man will."

"What about the swing shift and the graveyard, won't they demand more money?" Barnes asked.

"I talked with Las Vegas yesterday, Mr. Barnes. There are two thousand stiffs sitting around the lawn of the Union Pacific in the heat, surviving on doughnuts and coffee. I'll have no labor shit on this dam, I promise you."

The room was filled with skepticism. Crowe seized the opportunity. "If my projections are accurate, and God willing, I'll bring this dam in two years early. I'll earn back your bond the first year. The profit will be three million dollars. I have figured and built five dams in my lifetime and come in within ten thousand dollars of my projection each time."

Crowe knew that money talked in this room and today he too could talk money.

Stein spoke next. "Mr. Crowe," he said quietly, "I have an engineering question, not a money question."

There was nervous laughter in the room.

"Do you feel confident that you can pour concrete continuously twenty-four hours a day, year in, year out, without causing too much heat?"

Crowe forgot all the misgivings he had about the man. He thought of the Mark Hopkins Hotel.

"That is a good question, Mr. Stein. Perhaps I did not make it clear earlier that I intend to pour in very definite patterns. Each grid is ringed with ice water, each grid is individually monitored. . . ."

"That's never been done before, has it, Mr. Crowe?"

"No, but before Edison we used candles."

"That answers my question, Mr. Crowe," Stein said respectfully.

Old Man Donner of Shea had known Crowe and admired his skills for years. "Frank," he said, "you know it's no secret that everyone here expects you to be supervising engineer. What is it that you want from *us*?"

Crowe had expected this question for years and knew the answer cold, but now at the point of delivery he could only think of the hills of Vermont, the sparsity of the winter landscape. He had never been taught to ask. But he did.

"I want a salary of twenty-five thousand a year, I want the largest house in Boulder City for my home, I want a number of men on my staff, and ten percent of the profits."

It was the last statement that jarred the room as Crowe had known it would. He stood and headed for the door. "I'll go find myself a

37

beer. You gentlemen can make your decision."

Once Frank Crowe had closed the door everyone started talking at once. Chapman asked Shaughnessy whether he had known of Crowe's demands and Shaughnessy said no.

"The nerve," Barnes shouted. "Ten percent of the profits! Who the hell does he think he is?"

The talk was loud, gesticulations were wild, and finally Stein of San Francisco, the quiet-voiced gentleman, brought the room to order. "There are two questions, as I see it. The major one is whether we can get away with working around the clock. Let's take a poll. Remember that very little opposition will come from the government. Employment is the key word of the dam."

Everyone raised his hand.

"If we can get away with it, as you feel, then my second question is, do you think we can come in at a profit?"

Slowly, but steadily, everyone raised his hand.

"Then it is my conclusion that no one will work harder than Frank Crowe to earn us that profit, and his share to boot."

"I'll second that," Old Man Donner said.

But Barnes was not pacified.

"I'm not going to have some son of a bitch tell me what kind of house he wants and how much I should pay him. I'm putting up a million bucks. What's *he* gambling?"

Shaughnessy was angry now. Visibly. "You put up a million bucks and Frank Crowe puts twenty years and five dams on the line. You can believe me or not, I knew nothing of his demands, they're *his*, not mine, but Frank Crowe works for me and he either gets what he asked for or I'll pull out my stake. That's final."

"Shall we vote, gentlemen?" Roger Stein said, still quietly.

"All in favor of the proposals of Frank Crowe say aye."

They all said aye.

Shaughnessy then spoke: "I request that the conversations which took place in this room remain in this room." Everyone nodded.

"I hope, gentlemen," Stein said, "we win the bid, build the dam, and celebrate as my guests at the Mark Hopkins."

Now Shaughnessy recalled Crowe's smile. God damn, he thought, he might afford a night there yet.

6

Crowe had declined the festivities for the night of his agreement with the heads of the Big Six Companies, preferring to take the first available train back to Salt Lake City. He sat on the green velour seat, looking out the window; he studied the verdant Rockies, the well-irrigated land of the Mormons in Utah, and relished that rare splendor of having for once purchased a ticket for a parlor car.

This would be good country to retire to, he thought, and for the first time in his life the possibility of retirement seemed in his grasp. It was a curious thought, coming as it did at the beginning of the biggest assignment he had ever undertaken, a thought no doubt prompted by his misgivings about taking his young wife, Elle, to Las Vegas.

He had been married five years now, living the tame life of a deskbound engineer, working at Utah Construction Company, departing at reasonable hours in the morning for work and returning at usual hours for dinner.

He closed his eyes and tried to sleep; conferences, negotiations always tired him more than the physical strains of construction.

They had been eventful years, these last five. His decision to leave the Bureau of Reclamation, his joining Utah Construction Company, his marriage, all of them had happened within such a short period of time measured against a span of twenty years of knocking around rootlessly from dam to dam. All this could not help but make him retrospective, a quality he felt was useless and time consuming, still a quality his wife constantly encouraged.

Raised in a small town in Vermont, the son of an optician, he had early memories of snow and cold and loneliness, all of which paled beside the shock of his mother's early death.

She was a warm, bright woman, constantly in defense of her only son, who enjoyed books more than fisticuffs and building ship models more than playing football.

Frank was twelve when she fell sick with pneumonia. He woke one morning to see his father at the foot of the bed. It was six A.M. "Your mother is dead," his father had said coldly, perhaps trying, as

39

he had since Frank's earliest memories, to "make a man" out of him.

They had buried her in a pine box, he remembered. Family and friends had gathered at the graveside, a minister had read the sermon as dutifully and coldly as only a New England clergyman could. There had been cookies and coffee at the house, but discussions centered more on fall and winter than his mother's untimely death, and Frank Crowe disappeared early to his room and cried himself to sleep.

Scarcely six months later, his father introduced him to a heavy-set red-faced woman, who he was told would be his new mother. She brought two older, equally clumsy boys into the household, who promptly shared his room and his books, and took great pleasure in sailing and breaking his carefully built models.

Perhaps Frank could have survived with his father alone, but his new wife, Mary, was constantly suspicious of this child who brought home decent grades from school, who had little interest in his step-brothers. She successfully made him feel like an outcast, and at age sixteen, after writing a respectful letter to his father, Frank Crowe gathered up his few belongings, some clothes, a pocket knife, a watch his mother had once given him, and hopped a freight for San Francisco.

Already six feet tall and accustomed to raw weather, Frank easily found a job on board a Grace Line freighter as a wiper in the engine room.

Unlike other youngsters who became restless in the bowels of a cargo vessel, he found the complexity of machinery an endless puzzle, a puzzle he patiently unraveled with common sense and the help of Earl East, the ship's senior engineering officer. Frank cared little about the ports the vessel was making, what hours of the day or night he worked. He lived in a world of pistons and pressure gauges, of crank-shafts and generators, boilers and relays.

East was a patient, warm man, generous of his time and the few textbooks he kept on board. Crowe easily mastered logarithms, the art of the slide rule; he could soon chart a pressure curve and figure ballast in a hold.

When Crowe turned seventeen the ship was in Hong Kong. East and the junior engineering officers took him ashore. They filled him with tropical drinks and finally stumbled to a whorehouse, where an elderly madam took pains to make the rites of passage as memorable as possible.

The girl was Oriental. She was young, small breasted, thin limbed, and she had enough wisdom and sensitivity to fake some vulnerability toward this green stumbling boy from Vermont, who had only once seen a naked woman, in a burlesque house on Kearny Street in San Francisco.

40

"He velly good," the Oriental girl had said to his shipmates before they departed, a merciful lie which he did not contest. As the voyage continued, his friend East continued to tease him about the experience. "Can't get your mind off that Oriental *poon tang,* can you?" he'd say, patting Frank on the shoulder. He'd blush, but East was right. There were moments before falling asleep when he would remember that tiny girl slipping easily out of her kimono, and his urge to tell her not to rush, not to rush.

The turn of the century was still a good time for a young man at sea, and a boy who applied himself as assiduously as Crowe quickly stood out, although he was totally surprised when he was summoned to the captain's cabin three days before his ship was due in Portland.

He had rarely been topside and never inside the master's quarters. He could not believe the elegance and spaciousness of the dayroom which served both as office and living quarters for the captain. There were heavy carved oak chairs and side tables, a rocker in the corner, an antimacassar spread over the green velvet back. The captain sat behind a desk in a large leather chair. The desk held writing utensils, a pair of binoculars, the captain's gold-festooned cap, a miniature house flag mounted on a brass stand.

"Crowe," he said, pleasantly.

"Yes sir."

"Sit down."

"Thank you, sir."

Crowe sat gingerly in an oak chair, fearful that some of the oil of his overalls might stain the cushion.

"Relax, Crowe, I have good news for you."

"Yes sir?"

"The chief has recommended you for the company's training school, we have wired the company, and your acceptance has been confirmed. When we land in Portland you'll receive your orders, a railroad ticket, and a small allowance."

The news stunned Frank. The ship had been home. His friendship with Engineer East, other officers, and the other men had been genuine.

"I like this ship," Crowe stammered.

"I believe you, boy, and I suspect that it will be hard to leave."

"Must I?" He looked pleadingly at the captain, who tried to avoid the intense blue eyes.

"This company needs engineering officers. Our only source is young men like yourself who show aptitude. If you remain, your talents will never come to fruition. An officer's berth will let you use those talents. You'll like school, Crowe, you'll do well."

"Yes sir."

41

"And you'll return to sea. In due time."

"Yes sir."

Captain Fromm was not an insensitive man. He knew the boy would obey orders but also realized that he could not quite fathom the opportunity given to him. "I went to the school myself. Wasn't much older than you. Good food, good quarters. You'll never get this kind of opportunity again."

"I appreciate it, sir, believe me, it's just that . . ."

"What is it, Crowe?"

Crowe could not bring himself to say what he felt. He stood quickly.

"I accept the appointment and thank you for the opportunity."

"Don't thank me, thank the chief."

"Yes sir."

Somehow, Crowe could not muster the courage either to thank the chief or face him before his departure for New Bedford. He was afraid he would make a fool of himself. A noisy party drowned his farewell in alcohol, at times like these a merciful solution.

Crowe had attended the school in Baltimore scarcely a year when he was called into the superintendent's office. The captain had been right. Both the food and the quarters were above reproach, but the education he felt was cursory—endless lectures by chief petty officers with twenty years of sea duty under their belts, equally endless hours in laboratories and machine shops under the tutelage of substandard professors, who could not make it in the first-rate universities. The students, for the most part, were romantic boys from the Midwest, whose only thoughts were of shipping out, leaving the cornfield, and being met in Samoa by a covey of naked brown-skinned girls.

The headmaster's quarters were spotless but seedy, and the occupant showed more wear from liquor than education. "Crowe," he told the young man, "I have a letter here with a check. It is from your father. The check is in the amount of three thousand dollars and is bequeathed to you by instructions of your late mother. This amount to be handed to you on your eighteenth birthday." He handed Frank Crowe the check.

"I'd suggest that you spend this money wisely. A local bank should be able to pay you decent interest until your graduation."

Frank Crowe accepted the check and realized that yes, today *was* his birthday. He started to leave.

The headmaster blocked the door.

"And happy birthday, Mr. Crowe."

"Thank you, sir."

"Care for a drink?"

"No thanks."

The school no doubt had had much to offer him academically, and his appetite for knowledge was endless. He haunted the library, he spent nights in the laboratories, but that very library, shopworn and sparsely stocked, proved to him that *real* engineering, *pure* engineering, was being taught at MIT, at Case, at the University of Michigan, not here, in this institution whose slogan could well have been, "You'll keep that ship floating and moving, never mind why, mister!"

Crowe did not want applied engineering or didactic answers to theoretical questions, he wanted the essence, and the essence he sought was in the universities. Of course he realized that his decision would probably end his career at sea, and though he loved the warmth of a ship, the feeling of camaraderie that only the sea can evoke, he decided quite coldly that his talents demanded a better education than this school could provide.

It was an unpleasant meeting with the headmaster, who grumbled about the year wasted on Crowe by the beneficence of Grace Line, but he finally gave in and handed Crowe an honest transcript of his year's achievements, which proved to be excellent.

Two weeks later, with his uncashed check and twenty dollars he had saved, Frank Crowe, aged eighteen, headed for the University of Vermont, a school known to teach *pure* rather than applied engineering.

Vermont was not only a match but a challenge to his talents. A succession of great professors tested his mettle endlessly, often cruelly, with unorthodox, highly sophisticated problems, which one of his masters claimed were really the heart of engineering. "First you must realize you have a problem, and then you must solve it. If you do not think you have a problem, you are in error. There is *always* a problem, only sometimes it is more difficult to recognize the problem than to solve it." He had written down this aphorism and printed it carefully with pen and ink. He had carried that little sign with him from job to job.

Frank Crowe had graduated summa cum laude from the University of Vermont with a Bachelor of Science in Civil Engineering, and after a brief and unrewarding visit home he entered service in the Bureau of Reclamation as a junior civil engineer, serving at the pleasure of the government of the United States.

"You should go on," one of his teachers had urged, "get a master's degree, a Ph.D.," but Frank Crowe was anxious to get to work. Somehow now he needed to put away the books, the graphs, the projections, and the lecture notes. He wanted to find the problems and see how good he was at solving them.

43

7

Frank had built four dams and his reputation was growing. Decisions, bold decisions, were made in each of them, decisions which were highly respected by his peers at the university. It was then that Professor Heinlein persuaded Frank to seek his master's degree by correspondence.

As Frank began his scholarly discipline, he was in constant communication with the engineering library and with the junior librarian, a young girl by the name of Elle Solang.

There was no question that the job of supervising engineer was a lonely one, particularly for a man who was unmarried. He was working on Deadwood Dam in Idaho for the Bureau with a work force of three thousand men. Henderson-Andrews from the private sector had won the contract on that dam and Crowe at first angered but subsequently awed Papa Andrews as he brought in huge gas-powered bulldozers, diesel trucks, gas-powered shovels. The initial outlay was staggering, but the speed with which Frank Crowe brought in the dam proved the wisdom of his decision.

Unquestionably there were enough demands on Crowe all day, and most nights, to give him little leisure, but he could not deny the pangs of loneliness.

It was not really until his correspondence began with Elle at the University of Vermont that he realized the void in his life, the need to convey thoughts other than orders related to the project.

At first the letters were stiff. "My dear Elle," he would address her, talking freely about the progress of the job, the weather, the men, his friends, spectacular occurrences, but soon the letters were becoming more personal, a circumstance no doubt initiated by Elle. She had made it plain in one letter that her name was pronounced like the letter *l*, she seemed quite insistent, not *Ellé;* the second *e* was silent.

Crowe soon found that these letters to a girl eighteen years his junior, twenty-five hundred miles away, were becoming a very important facet of his life. He not only instructed the project postmaster

44

to deliver them to him personally, but also ordered him to keep the fact of this correspondence under his hat.

Crowe was by no means celibate. His urges were as normal as any other man's, and when he felt the need of a woman he would visit Aunt Mary's, a brothel just outside the federal reservation gate. There he would find a drink waiting for him, often a second or third, and a faceless girl, usually from the Midwest, who had come to the site seeking at first an honest job, and failing this, had turned to prostitution.

They were cold alliances; they took place in the dark. Crowe rarely spoke. Occasionally if the moon was bright he would catch sight of his naked partner. Occasionally he would have a more experienced prostitute from San Francisco who could make a ceremony of undressing, of teasing her man, and giving him some small illusion of conquest. However, for the most parts the assignations were wordless, bloodless, and rapid, and Crowe would quickly get dressed, pay, and rush into the night air, somewhat ashamed of himself, still unsatisfied.

While Frank had little patience for introspection and philosophizing, he had an even greater resistance to acknowledging his own strong physical desires. It wasn't that Frank was a moral hypocrite. He didn't pretend to be ashamed of his sexuality as did many of his contemporaries. Frank was simply naïve. He had never experienced the bond that links love and sex, and no one was there to tell him that it existed. He had lost his mother at an early age, and his cold, stern father only served to reinforce young Frank's embarrassment over such intimate matters. So Frank learned about sex over the back fence, where his peers elbowed each other knowingly as they shared the latest obscene joke—which, in fact, few of them ever understood. This seamier view of sex was how Frank began his education and how it remained for him, moving from the back fence to the saloons and brothels. The sex act was always something empty, almost degrading; the emotions, the love, that Frank had so little of as a child eluded him now as a man.

Elle, a bright girl, seemed to understand this instinctively. She soon realized that this quiet, brilliant man had much more passion in his soul than he was ever able to admit or convey, but her own sprightliness, her verve, her vitality, her youth, drew out much of that passion from this lonely man in the raw lands of Idaho. She knew full well that the demands of his profession and his tight Yankee background made him shy, aloof, withdrawn, and seemingly humorless to many.

They had been corresponding for a year when Frank Crowe finally had the nerve to ask for a snapshot. He had had the urge often before, but felt no right; it was a letter of Elle's which finally gave him the courage.

"I saw your picture, finally," she wrote Frank. "Someone has sent me a clipping of you and Old Man Henderson at the dam site. I did not know you were so tall and I did not know you were so thin. And where did you get that silly hat?"

Frank Crowe had actually blushed when he had read that letter; he even stood and looked at himself in the mirror of his bathroom. He rarely looked at himself, perhaps briefly in the morning shaving, or combing his short-cut hair, but these were subjective observations, a new experience. For now he had looked at the mirror and he could see that he *did* indeed look gaunt; his strong cheekbones were prominent, his eyes somewhat hollow. Only his tan from the merciless sun had kept a look of vitality around his blue eyes, which were almost violet. He looked instinctively at the foot of his bed where the beat-up felt hat rested, its brim turned down, and he smiled.

Elle had waited for this request for a photograph and persuaded one of her coworkers to snap her in a bathing suit, not because she wanted to portray herself as a lady of leisure, which Frank knew to be untrue anyhow, but studiedly to portray herself as she was, tall, quite tall for a girl, almost six feet, small but firmly breasted, her hair the color of winter wheat, drawn tightly around her head and held by a silver clip at the nape of her neck. She had an impish face, a small well-chiseled nose, high cheekbones, and an ample sensuous mouth.

Elle was Friesian, her heritage the sea, the beaches. Perhaps her outstanding feature was her legs, long and thin and shapely, and she wore the shortest outfit the times would allow, short enough to show her honest assets.

She was playful but careful with words, and told Frank that she felt like a mail-order bride sending the picture and added jokingly that she weighed one hundred twenty-five pounds, used Ivory soap, enjoyed an occasional bubble bath scented with an indecently Oriental aroma, had a healthy appetite and made the best clam chowder in Vermont.

Crowe would not have traded one half of his nearly completed dam for the photograph. He studied it and studied it, unbelieving of the beauty of the girl, finally rationing the number of times he looked at it. He put it in an envelope in his desk and would return to it every night at suppertime like a child hoarding a box of cookies given him for his birthday.

But there was also the letter, and its contents disturbed him. She had referred to herself as a mail-order bride, and he could only focus on the word "bride." She had spoken for the first time of some of the intimacies of her life, which he tried not to dwell on, but this discipline made the thought of Elle in her bubble bath reach the proportions of an obsession.

His outlook on the dam site became noticeably sunny. His gait was sprightlier, his carriage more erect, he even patted an occasional youngster on his head and said nothing when he found some young engineers sitting on orange crates in their offices, a practice which normally would have prompted a swift kick at the object which allowed sitting, an amenity Crowe did not allow anyone except the female help in the administration building.

"What's come over the chief?" people were asking. "He's actually smiling. Always thought he had false teeth the way he kept his mouth shut."

He walked around with Elle's letter for over a week before finally sitting down to write her.

Dearest Elle,

Received your good letter and photograph a week ago and must admit to mixed emotions. If photographs would deteriorate from observation, I can assure you that that snapshot would long ago have disappeared. I have spent so much time looking at it that I now ration myself to three times a day, once before work, once after work, and once before retiring. Needless to say, I think you are the most beautiful girl I have ever laid eyes on. Since you have no qualms about talking about the intimacy of a bubble bath, I shall feel none either about telling you that I have never seen such legs in my life nor can I stop observing that playfulness around the bridge of your nose and your eyes. (Always the engineer.) My ritual is really quite simple. I place the photograph on my desk and reread the letter. There is no need to reread it, I know it as well as the blueprints for the last adit we're building right now. You are beautiful, Elle. Absolutely beautiful, and here the mixed feelings begin.

I have never lied to you in all these letters, as you know, and what began as a wonderful correspondence with a friend, I think you believe, has grown to be a very vital part of my life. But in the letter you refer to yourself (perhaps jokingly) as a mail-order bride, and ever the logician I reduce that phrase with a lot of wishful thinking to the word *bride*. This very possibility has stirred juices in me I did not, as a hard-core Yankee, know I possessed, and though your next letter may well shatter any hope along these lines, I thank you now for the pleasure you have given me thus far and for all the friendship you have extended. If you meant all this to be merely a playful phrase, I will certainly understand and only hope that our relationship can keep at least its platonic warmth.

If indeed there *was* some substance to the reference you made to yourself, then let me restate a few facts which may have become forgotten in our correspondence. I am now slightly past forty years of age, making me eighteen years your senior. I have no family ties, my home at present, and as it has

47

been for almost twenty years, is the bachelor quarters of a supervising engineer. These quarters are ample, but sparsely furnished, and much of the space, like the captain's quarters on a ship I once knew, is more ceremonial than utilitarian.

My habits are neat, to the point of distraction to my underlings. My work pattern is relentless, some of it perhaps to quell an inner loneliness I am not willing to admit. I eat three meals a day because I need the energy, but don't question me about the quality of the food. I rarely notice it. Eating, somehow, has become a necessary distraction and a worn cog in the wheel of momentum which keeps a dam site rolling.

I have never been married, which is not unusual for men in my line of work. I drink when the occasion calls for it, and then heavily, clumsily, and hate myself for it for several days afterward. I am, in short, a middle-aged construction stiff, no angel, no prize, and though professionally I feel very secure, in matters such as this I find myself quite helpless, even afraid.

I won't allow myself to think of all the educated young men you must associate with in Vermont, and your social life at this point is really no concern of mine.

Should you (and I pray you do) think of our friendship as more than that, I would like to ask you some questions.

I am now completing Deadwood. We are eighteen months ahead of schedule and Old Man Henderson has already commissioned a sixty-foot steam yacht being built by Stephens in Stockton, counting heavily on the profits I will deliver on this dam.

Although I am relatively well paid by the Bureau of Reclamation, I am seriously contemplating an offer by Utah Construction Company (I'm sure you've heard of them). These offers always pour in near the successful completion of a dam and I have never seen the need to accept them, partially because I have (to this point) never had the urge for a greater income (I bank almost all of my salary) and secondly because I've never been a desk man.

Shaughnessy, the head of Utah Construction Company, which is based in Salt Lake City, has made me an offer to be supervising engineer of his company, a position which calls for more than twice my present salary, and by nature of the offer an opportunity to live in Salt Lake City for a few years before another project, of which I can't speak now, will mature.

What I am saying, my long-limbed Elle, is that, despite my age, I *can* provide for two quite handsomely and offer the opportunity to live a "normal life" for several years before returning to a construction site.

Besides my age, my spartan habits, you should think about life at a work camp. It is tough, it is lonely, at times frightening. For me, there are no hours, no schedules. There is little time for social life, for *any* kind of life a young woman has a right to expect.

I want you (if you're really serious) to weigh all these factors before you answer me. I will finish this tour of duty in March of next year. At this time, according to Professor Heinlein, I shall also finish my requirements for my master's degree (with no small help from you). I shall leave Idaho to pick up my degree and ask now, four months in advance, for a dinner date or two during my stay.

I know this need not be said, but my Yankee frugality prompts this statement. It is a long and expensive journey by rail to Vermont, and my true reason for making it is to finally meet you. The university could easily mail me my sheepskin.

You *must* believe me that, although this is a long journey, you owe me nothing. I will behave like an absolute gentleman. I feel that we need time to talk to each other, and I know there are things that two human beings cannot convey with pen and paper.

I shall now return your picture to the envelope, and I shall sit on our mail clerk until your next letter arrives.

Affectionately and respectfully,
Frank

It was one-thirty in the morning when Frank Crowe finished writing the letter. It had been the most difficult assignment in his long career. He reached for his hat and walked down the rugged path to the post office to drop it in the mail chute.

The camp site was quiet, an occasional dog barking, trucks coming home from a nearby town, the air cold and crisp. He looked at the sky and saw Orion. That bright constellation had always been his friend. He had learned of it first on the *Santa Maria* when one of the deck officers had taught him the intricacies of the sextant. He had become quite expert at shooting the sun and well remembered the graceful instrument, all curves and mirrors and prisms so well placed in his large hands. He still missed the sea, but less tonight than any other night he could remember.

8

Elle received Frank's letter and cried. A spirited, emotional girl, she sat in the binding room of the engineering library and answered it immediately, explaining the splotches on the paper as being honest tears.

Dear Frank:
The quickness of my response to your letter will not, I hope, brand me as a brazen woman, but the letter was so warm and beautiful I had to stop

in the middle of my working day to answer it while I am still filled with this incredible emotion.

Your extraction of the word "bride," from the phrase "mail-order bride" was certainly warranted. But you must believe me that it came subconsciously—although I am a great believer in the workings of the subconscious. I have loved every one of your letters and have felt a growing warmth in both yours and mine. If you are, and I don't doubt it, such a logician, you should realize that I could have discouraged the growing intimacy of our correspondence early on, but I didn't.

Once again I use the word "brazen," because I *know* that I am a beautiful girl, something I might find easier to write than to say, and though the suffragettes are constantly urging women to state their case more forthrightly, I don't need that movement to prove to me that I am physically attractive. I come from Friesian and German stock, and my family, who are tall and live in Camden, Maine, are blessed with good bodies, healthy teeth, and heads of hair which shine when kept clean and kempt.

I don't know whether to put the cart before the horse and it makes little difference which way I answer your question. Of course you must wonder *why* I am not married or engaged at age twenty-four, and though I can give you some of the reasons in a letter, I can only tell you about other facets of myself when we meet face to face.

Since you graduated from the University of Vermont, I do not have to describe the atmosphere of the campus to you. You must remember that you had some feelings of being an outsider here, living as you did on that small inheritance your mother left you. As at Yale and Harvard, there are a goodly number of young men on this campus from very wealthy families, and I have dated my share of them.

They have, for the most part, been fun, and to a point gentlemanly; however, my position here is unique. I am *not* a student. I am a girl with a high school diploma who has been employed at the library. This is no dilettante job for me, something which other girls handle between studies. For me this job is full time, it is challenging, but it is necessary. The salary is small and barely adequate for my existence.

I receive no help from my family (by choice) and cannot possibly entertain the thought of a college education, since I must work to live, and there are just so many hours in the day.

Being a "working girl" rather than a student puts me into a different category from the usual coed.

I have looks, I know, and poise, I think, but the lack of "good family" (my father is a fisherman), and my somewhat sketchy social graces sometimes give license to the boys I have dated to treat me callously after a period of time. Or, as has happened, when the future is discussed, the social fears of bringing home this fisherman's daughter, who did not even *attend* the university, always seem insurmountable.

Like you, Frank, I have some pride in myself, and the loneliness of which you speak is not an emotion in which I'm inexperienced.

You might well ask the question, *why* seek out these snobs? What's wrong with an earnest young engineering student on scholarship or scraping his way through school?

Believe me, Frank, I am not a social climber or too good for anyone, but the answer lies in the hypothetical question. As you well know, young engineering students are a silent breed. Those on scholarship, those boys working their way through school, have little time or money for women, and if you think back on your days here, you'll agree.

I do have friends, a number of young men whom I like who are in that category, and though we picnic together or I'll make spaghetti or clam dinners for them, their thoughts are not on marriage but on graduation; their horizon is a job in a far-flung project and a life of which you've been a model for twenty years.

I am not only emotional but also impetuous and spoke at length to Professor Heinlein about you. I knew you would disapprove, and I assure you I divulged nothing of a private nature about you, but Professor Heinlein, as you know, is far more perspicacious than the average engineer and asked very few embarrassing questions.

"Frank Crowe," he said simply, "is the most brilliant student we've ever graduated. He is also the most modest man I've ever known." And then he paused. "Modest but stubborn. He is, Elle, the consummate engineer, and what you must consider, and you have to tell me nothing, is whether there is room for you in this consummation."

Dr. Heinlein packed his old briar pipe, his half glasses down his nose, and looked at me over the top half of those tortoiseshell rims. There was a twinkle in his eyes as he said, "Frank Crowe is also a gambler, and a winner. How much of a gambler are you?" I kissed him on the cheek and bought myself a new scarf. I needed it to ward off the cold, but it didn't have to be a bright red, but that color reflected my mood that day. It is hanging at the foot of my bed right now and I laugh when I look at it.

Enough of this drivel, Frank Crowe. Spend that hard-earned money on that trip to Vermont, you skinflint, buy a dozen cornflowers and hold them in your hand as you step off the train so I'll know you, although I doubt whether I would miss you anyway.

Your reassurances about your gentlemanly behavior are accepted with a mischievous smile on this end, and I am writing this to worry you a little, just as I am signing this letter.

Love,
Elle

and that will only give you *one* word to dissect this time.

9

Frank's role at Deadwood was to be finished by that March, and now the time seemed endless. The only thing that kept his sanity was foreseeing and solving the problems which might still arise and cost him delay.

After one of the last inspections by Old Man Henderson, arriving in his chauffeur-driven Packard limousine, Frank Crowe took the liberty to ask for a favor.

"Mr. Henderson," he said as they walked toward Frank's office.

"What is it, Frank?"

Frank was almost nervous as he took out an index card from his poncho. "We're going to finish in eight weeks and I need some new clothes."

Henderson laughed. "Spending your bonus already?"

"Perhaps. I need a suit," he hesitated, "a suit like you're wearing. Gray, charcoal, with a vest. I need some shoes, city shoes, some shirts, a necktie, underwear, pajamas . . ."

"Do you know, Frank, how much this suit costs? It's from Bullock & Jones in San Francisco. More than two weeks' wages."

"I don't care, Mr. Henderson." Frank reached into his pocket and brought out his worn cowhide coin purse.

"No need to pay me now, Frank. You got your sizes on this card?"

"Yes sir." Crowe handed it to him and Henderson put it inside his coat pocket.

"You sure that heat last summer didn't get to you?"

Crowe laughed. "It was heat all right, but not from the sun."

"Goddamn," Henderson said, patting Crowe on the shoulder, "let's look at the site."

As was his custom, Frank Crowe left Deadwood Dam long before its dedication. He was paid off, salary and bonus fair and square. Henderson had his driver deliver the clothes personally, and when Frank tried to pay him the chauffeur handed him an envelope. He opened it and read in the scrawl of the aging successful engineer:

The clothes are on me, Frank, and the 500 bucks are on me too. They're not part of your stipulated bonus, but a token of appreciation from one working stiff to another for a job well done! If you're planning to do what I suspect, bring your bride to the christening of the *Dolphin*, which will come off the ways in August in Stockton. I promise you a party which will rattle your teeth.

Sincerely,
Howard Henderson

Carefully Frank Crowe hung up the suit, unpacked the shirts. He had never seen such material; even the shirts had a chaste monogram "F.C." embroidered on the pockets. He took off his boots and tried on the shoes. They were wingtipped and polished to a fine russet patina. He looked at the neckties, tartan patterns, one he recognized as that of the Black Watch.

He could not resist slipping on the jacket and looking at himself in the mirror. He knew he needed a haircut; the jacket was soft and weightless on his shoulders. It was like Christmas, though he could not remember when last he had celebrated that holiday.

He had contemplated using the washroom for his trip to Vermont, but decided on a sleeping compartment, not because he wanted the comfort but because he feared for the safety of his new outfit. The journey took four days, and most of those days Frank Crowe divided his time between looking at his unworn suit and at the panorama of the country flying past his windows.

And at night he went to sleep in splendor, tucked comfortably between two good-quality Pullman sheets, covered only by a light wool blanket. Most of his thoughts were of Vermont and his new suit and the dozen cornflowers he'd have to purchase before arriving in Albany.

It was seven in the morning when the train entered the freight yards of Albany. Frank Crowe had been up since five getting shaved, dressed, feeling foolish in his finery. He had never owned a vest before in his life, and wondered whether to button the last button or not. He also tried to decide whether to discard his boots and denims that he had thus far worn on the entire trip, but this was a luxury he could not allow himself. He wrapped them carefully and placed them with his hat in the canvas bag he had bought at the company store at Deadwood.

He did not eat breakfast, fearing he might soil his new clothes, but accepted a cup of coffee from the porter, who looked at him in amazement.

"Look at us," he said, "all duded up. You sure you the same feller that got on this train?"

"I look stupid, don't I?" Crowe asked.

"Stupid? Hell no. You look like you own this railroad."

"Well, here's something for your trouble," and Crowe gave him a dollar tip.

"My, thank you. You even tip like a gentleman."

Elle spotted Frank only a car length away. She ran, ran like a gamine into his arms, outstretched at first, and Frank embraced this lithe lovely girl, and she held him tight, kissing his cheek lightly, then buried her head in the warmth of his flannel suit, his face buried in the subtle fragrance of her lovely long, soft hair, no longer tightly pulled off her face but framing it like a good oak border on a delicate etching.

They held each other speechlessly for a long time. It was not a sexual embrace but unbelievably sexual because of its honesty. Frank could feel the girl, like a spring, live and poised and trusting.

Finally they released each other and Elle stepped back as Frank gave her the cornflowers, the worse for wear because of their embrace.

"They're beautiful," Elle said.

"They *were* in Illinois. The porter watered them every four hours. Look at them now."

"I'll press them, Frank. The first flowers you ever gave me. Let me look at you." She stepped back. "Is this the same Frank Crowe I've seen those pictures of? Where are the boots? Where is that hat?"

Frank pointed to his canvas bag.

"These are courtin' clothes, ma'am, as they say out west."

"They look like New York swells to me."

"We got a couple of stores in San Francisco. Even use electric lights now and then."

They walked hand in hand into the station. Frank's eyes could not leave Elle. She was wearing a tweed skirt, a white blouse, a cardigan sweater, and her red scarf tossed artfully around her neck. She wore no hat. Her stride could match his, her face like sunshine, warm and smiling and mischievous.

They took a local train to Burlington, Vermont, and spent most of that hour saying nothing of substance.

"Who gave you that haircut?" Elle.

"Is that the red scarf?" Frank.

"What direction are we going?" Frank.

"The right one, I hope." Elle.

She had rented a room for Frank in the boardinghouse she lived in. It was a dark, oppressive three-story building, with much mahogany

54

and leaded glass; all its original splendor as a townhouse had long disappeared after the owners, fallen on hard times, rented one room after another to hold on to the property.

"Thirteen rooms and ten boarders and one bath," Elle had said.

"When do you find time for a bubble bath?"

"At midnight, and you have to sign up. You're in Room Four and I've penciled *you* in for six-thirty in the bath."

"What makes you think I can sleep that late?"

"You're on vacation, Mr. Crowe. I read about Deadwood in the *New York Times* yesterday. 'Frank Crowe Does It Again,' the column headline said. 'Eighteen Months Under the Gun.' The story said that even Coolidge sent you a wire."

"Well, that's nice," Crowe said. "I hope they mail it to me."

"Imagine, a telegram from the President of the United States."

"Imagine," Crowe said, putting down his canvas bag. "Where can I take you to lunch?"

Elle had picked a small Greek restaurant popular with the college crowd. There were small private booths with velvet drapes on brass rods, and myriad stories of improprieties performed behind them between courses, but all under the benign eyes of Papado Kalins, the owner who cared only about collecting his check, not about the morality of his guests.

It was a blustery day and the restaurant doubly cheerful and warm by contrast. A candle was lit.

"You were right, Frank, what you wrote once," Elle said after they had eaten.

"What's that?"

"You hardly know what you eat. You've just finished the best Greek cooking on the East Coast, but nary a word."

"I tell you, Elle," he blushed, "I've never eaten Greek food."

"How did you like it?"

"I don't know. I'm so busy looking at you, I don't need food."

"That is a very nice thing to say."

"Let me ask you a question. Do you think I could unbutton this vest?"

Elle laughed. "Your first vest?"

Crowe nodded. "I don't know how a man could do a day's work wearing this outfit."

"Not everybody in this world is moving mountains, you know."

"I guess not, but they should try it."

Elle smiled. She smiled and smiled and never stopped smiling. Frank, organized as ever, could not bring himself to confront this girl with questions, options, decisions, answers.

He took out his watch and looked at it. It was three o'clock.

"Let me see that watch, Frank."

He handed it to her.

"You know that watch is legendary in the construction game."

"Don't believe everything you hear. Let's take a walk."

They walked arm in arm around the campus of the University of Vermont. It had been well over a decade since Frank Crowe had seen his alma mater. Seedlings had matured into full-blown trees, ivy tenaciously covered sides of lecture halls where he could remember only a few fledgling branches beginning their climb. He heard the chimes in the bell tower and watched intent students with purposeful briefcases dashing from classroom to classroom. Much had changed and nothing had changed. Elle showed Frank where she worked, she introduced him to the librarian, the cataloguers, and finally they traveled to the lakeshore and sat on its edge waiting for the New England sunset. There were clouds which would enhance it and a ferry, returning from a day's work. Frank loved the staccato of the two banger diesels, the small puffs of exhaust like evanescent rosary beads.

Frank sat behind Elle, she leaning on his chest, her arms around his legs, naturally, unafraid.

"You know, Elle," he said, "you hear a lot of things about a supervising engineer on a big job. Like the story about my watch, which is true, and other stories which are true, and some are myths, but dam workers want them to be true." He stopped. "One of the things that you'll learn about me, or maybe hear about me, is that I make decisions fast, and that they're usually right."

Elle nodded in agreement.

"I know we were going to do a lot of talking on this trip and I will if you want me to, but I have some feelings about all this. When you fell into my arms this morning at the depot I knew I didn't need any conversation. I'm asking you to marry me, Elle. To me it's like building a dam. To accomplish that is to make more right decisions than wrong ones. That's the way I feel now."

Elle thought for a long time. She drew designs in the sand with a twig from a tree branch which had been swept up from the lake. She finally left her repose against Frank and faced him, her back toward the lake.

"I want to marry you, Frank, believe me. I've wanted to since the second letter, the third or fourth, but . . ." she paused.

"But what?"

"There is something you've got to know. I've got to tell you."

Frank's eyes never left Elle's, suddenly troubled now, almost unseeing.

"Tell me."

"It's not easy. It's something I couldn't write you and I *should*

56

have before you spent all that money on the train fare, that new suit."

"Tell me, Elle."

"I wasn't born in this country. I was born in Friesland. It's a small province in Holland."

"I know. I looked it up."

"My father was a fisherman there and did well. Moderately. He knew when the world war started he'd have a hard time surviving in Friesland. He sold his boat, his house, we came to America, to Camden, Maine. He bought another boat, built another house. We're four sisters, three brothers. I'm the second-oldest girl.

"Camden, Maine, is a good town. A pretty town, full of schooners and trawlers, and little inns and restaurants. It's a quiet fishing village, with summer visitors, picket fences, antique shops, but it's not like Friesland, where everyone is Friesian, where families date back for generations. There are Yugoslavs and Italian fishermen, and Portuguese fishermen, Chinese, and New Englanders. It is a different world. The New World in essence."

She paused, and looked at him.

"The Blessing of the Fleet occurs every September. Boats are garlanded, festooned, many of them lit up, often carrying crucifixes. It is a day of religion and carnival, much food, much wine."

Elle stopped staring at the strange pattern she had carved in the sand and Frank did not press her.

"I was tall at sixteen, as tall as I am now. A little skinnier, a lot dumber. School was out that day they blessed the fleet. There was much drinking, dancing. An Italian fisherman, perhaps thirty, danced with me, once, then again, and finally took me on his boat to show me his decorations."

Elle looked at Frank intensely. "I drank some homemade punch for the first time in my life. I admit that, and I was euphoric, I'll admit *that*, but I did not expect what was coming. There, between coils of rope, boxes of fish hooks, between lobster traps and fishing poles was a leather seat, a bunk of sorts, and Tony asked me to sleep with him.

"My face drained of blood, I know, I sobered instantly and screamed. I tried to run, I know that too, but Tony raped me. He ripped off my dress, my underpants, he tore off my bra like decapitating a mackerel. I screamed, I fought, but it was no use.

"I ran home finally. My father saw me, blood caked on my face, my white dress splattered with rust-colored stains. I huddled in a corner of our living room, the oak-planked floor scrubbed, polished, never used.

"He called my mother and she finally came, but not before he slapped me.

57

"My mother was equally cold. I was in shock but she led me to a shower. She ripped what was left of my clothes from my body and shoved me into an ice-cold shower. She ordered me to wash, EVERYWHERE, she shouted, finally threw me a towel and then gave me some fresh clothes. I was numb as I watched her throw my dress and the towel into the kitchen stove, and then wash her hands in the sink.

"She said nothing and took me by the hand to the doctor. I sat frightened in the waiting room as she spoke to him privately. Finally he told me sternly to come in. He was Italian too; all I could see was the same swarthy face as the fisherman. He told me to undress.

"'Undress,' my mother shouted. 'Can't you hear the doctor?'

"I did and stood naked in front of both of them.

"'That's more like it,' my mother said. 'I guess you're used to this, aren't you?'

"'Mama,' I pleaded, 'Mama,' and she hit me almost as hard as my father.

"The doctor showed her the door and told me to lie on his couch. It was covered with the same black leather as the one on the fishing boat.

"I watched as he dripped chloroform onto a mask, slowly, studiedly, watching me at the same time.

"'Don't,' I screamed, 'don't do that.'

"'Shut up,' he yelled, 'and spread your legs.'

"I felt the mask on my face and a roaring in my ears and a pain so severe I passed out.

"I almost hemorrhaged to death, and the doctor, who had been paid twenty dollars by my mother, no longer wanted me on the premises. He took me to the hospital, where a second operation followed. I stayed there five days. No one came to see me except my brother Mike, who told me he would kill Tony.

"Mike came to see me every day, and when I told him I would *never* go home again Mike brought me here, to this town. I worked for a professor and his wife as a mother's helper for two years until I got the job at the library."

It was an incredible emotion for Frank Crowe; it surprised him more than he knew. He leaned forward and cupped Elle's hand gently in his large hands.

"What are you trying to tell me, Elle? Are you trying to tell me that you hate all men?"

"No, Frank. I did. For a while. I was afraid I could never get that vision of Tony out of my head. I would wake up screaming at night. But I'm over that."

"Then what is it?"

"I can't have children, Frank. I cannot ever have children."

Frank Crowe now bent down and kissed Elle on the mouth. A

full kiss. Finally he traced the outlines of her open lips with his fore-finger.

"Children don't belong on dam sites anyway, Elle. I've got no reason to perpetuate myself."

"You *do*, Frank Crowe. You do. You *should* have children, children that can be proud of their father."

Frank Crowe leaned back. "I'm forty-two years old, Elle. Wifeless, childless. I've got a decent bank account, a suit from Bullock & Jones, four monogrammed shirts, several pairs of boots and assorted gear. Not much for twenty years of work, is it?"

"You've got a wire from President Coolidge. How many engineers have a wire from President Coolidge?"

"Yeah," Frank said, "that and a nickel will buy you a cup of coffee for sure."

The sun had set and neither of them had realized it. They ran along the lakeshore to shake off the cool air which had crept into their bones. They found an almost empty restaurant near the lake. Elle sat next to Frank in the small booth.

"Perhaps there are some things you should know about me, Elle. Do you realize that at the age of forty-two I can say I've never made love to a nice girl in my life?" He stopped and fixed his eyes on a grandfather's clock against the wall. "I'm frightened, Elle. They say on the dam site that Frank Crowe can handle six thousand men, but he's got trouble with one woman."

"They say that to your face?"

"Hell, no."

And now Elle put her arms around Frank, oblivious of the waiter, the busboy, the gawking short-order cook peering through his little window.

"If you want me, Frank Crowe, we'll show them."

For the first time Frank Crowe felt tears in his eyes. He could not remember feeling tears since the night his mother had died. He felt no shame. That was strange. He did not feel emasculated. He reached into his pocket and pulled out a small crudely wrapped present.

"This was my mother's," Frank said. "I loved her very much. She died when I was twelve."

Elle unwrapped it. It was a small silver pocket watch on a silver chain. The brass backing showed through the thin plating and Elle knew that it had been in Frank's pocket for many years.

"I would have bought a ring," he said, "but that would have been presumptuous."

Elle hung the watch around her neck and watched it settle into the cleavage of her bosom. "Not only presumptuous, Frank Crowe, but imprudent for a man from Vermont."

"I'm beginning to get the feeling," Frank Crowe said, pointing the finger to the top of her nose, "that between that nose and those ears there is some pretty good brain matter."

"When do you want to get married, Frank?"

"At ten in the morning."

Elle laughed. *"Ten in the morning?* You think I can get ready that fast?"

"All we need is a church and a minister."

"We need a best man, Frank, and I want Professor Heinlein to be your best man."

"I'd like that."

"And I want Professor Smith and his wife at our wedding. They were good to me."

"And when can we do all that?"

"Tomorrow at six, Mr. Crowe. On the nose. How is that?"

"You know I hate delays, but I'll manage. Is there a good library around here?"

"I know of one, but it's just got mostly engineering books."

They both laughed.

Elle was more ready than Frank had suspected. She had a small trousseau which she had slowly for the last two years accumulated from her meager salary. A good crisp linen nightgown with a small bit of lace, some underwear which had a look of indecency, a wedding dress, a new wool coat, a couple of dresses, a decent pair of pumps, a new purse, even a veil, a slight flowing veil like windblown mist on an incoming wave.

Reverend Abernathy performed the ceremony. It was simple. Professor Heinlein gave Frank the ring he had purchased that morning. The Smiths held a reception, small but warm, and Frank and Elle checked into the bridal suite of an inn by the lake. Frank expertly built a fire in the small Franklin stove in the corner of the room. He watched the wood catch hold and was almost unaware that Elle had disappeared and reappeared in her nightgown, the lace of its neckline plunging close to the nipples of her breasts.

She moved like a girl aware of her height; she sat crosslegged, or often had her legs astride as if trying to make herself more diminutive. But for Frank Crowe she was a vision so beautiful and chaste it overwhelmed him.

He fell soundly asleep after they had made love, but Elle, lying next to this man, this good, gaunt, gentle man, listened to the evenness of his breathing, and she knew that Frank's fears of a woman were well founded, but she knew, also, that it was a challenge she could live with. When Elle fell asleep, the last thing she saw was Frank's watch by his bedside. The cover was open and the dial was facing him.

10

They had left Vermont for Salt Lake City. Frank noticed her very meager belongings and he approved. A few inexpensive leatherette suitcases, a small vanity bag were all it took for her to move from one part of the country to the other. Still the genuine tears and the warm embraces at the train station attested to the fact that she was loved and would be missed by all who came to see them off.

Frank had purchased a good two-story frame house on the corner of South Street and Holladay Boulevard in Salt Lake City. There were an ample porch in front, a large foyer, and a handsome stairway leading up to the master bedroom on the second floor. Two other bedrooms had been converted into workrooms for Frank, housing his drafting table, his surveying tools, and a well-chosen engineering library accumulated over the years.

There was a large yard with healthy trees and fertile soil. The considerable age of the house had been evident at first, but it gave Frank ample opportunity to use his physical talents on weekends and evenings while being deskbound at Utah Construction Company.

Elle never failed to be amazed how simply and gracefully Frank handled tools and materials and how seemingly without effort he slowly brought back this shabby frame house to its original dignity. Walls were stripped and re-wallpapered. Bannisters were sanded and varnished. The house was painted and a new roof was put on. The good hardwood floors downstairs slowly came to resemble the teak decks of an elegant yacht; an old iron stove in the kitchen was restored to its utilitarian handsomeness. Frank could build cupboards and reroute plumbing; he was as adept at electricity as he was at irrigating and cultivating the soil in their back yard.

Of course there were the usual squabbles about furniture which Elle wanted and Frank thought he did not. There were arguments over the cost of yardage for drapes and bedspreads, Elle's insistence on purchasing a good brass double bed. But these were minor storms typical of a young marriage.

Elle was not only a good cook, a good seamstress, really quite frugal herself, but she tried slowly to instill in Frank the idea that this was their "home," and not his "quarters." Even the "gewgaws," as he referred to knickknacks (planted pots of ivy, an ornamental kerosene lamp, pictures, a wreath of dried flowers), were just as essential as a bed, a chair, and a table.

Frank's tightfistedness was quite real, but he also knew that the more attractive and warm their new house became the greater would be the contrast of moving to a construction site.

"You don't know what it's going to be like, Elle," he had told her over and over again. "There will be days without lights, days without running water, months before we have hot water. The summers will be mercilessly hot and the winters equally cold."

Elle just smiled when Frank gave her these admonitions.

"Don't smile, Elle. It's not just where we'll live, but how we'll live that worries me."

"Why does it worry you, Frank?"

"Here in Salt Lake I'm just coasting. I don't do a damned thing all day but shuffle plans, do my arithmetic, spend hours on that goddamned creation the telephone. I come home and I am full of energy. I can't wait to get to work on this house; part of me needs that physical outlet. But when we're at the dam . . ." his voice trailed off as he thought of the utter loneliness they were facing, the relative poverty of the workers, the inherent coarseness of existence, which was indigenous to heavy construction.

"I won't have any hours. I may not be home for dinner five nights out of seven. I'll never be home for lunch. I'll get to sleep and be back on the job a half hour later. I won't wash a dish or help you with a bedspread or fix a leak in the kitchen sink, and judging from past experience I'll come home and fall asleep in an armchair before you have the supper on the table."

Elle still smiled. "Just who do you think you married, Frank Crowe? Do you think I have no marrow in my bones? Do you think I need *this* house to be happy, and that bunch of flowers to exist? We are *married*, Frank, do you remember what the man said? for better or for worse. Don't you think I can keep my end of the bargain? Have I been such a burden?"

"No, Elle, no. No, I . . ." he stumbled.

"Say it," she shouted.

"Darling, all right. These have been the best years of my life. . . . ."

"And you think it will end when we move to Vegas?"

Frank did not answer immediately.

"Well, do you?"

"Elle, please try to understand. I am not really worried about your physical needs. I've known you long enough now. You're a tough young girl. Good stock, my father probably would say. It doesn't matter

what pictures I paint of our existence, because you'll never know until
we move to the camp site, but there are things I *have* misgivings
about."

"What kind of misgivings?" Elle said, now more gently.

"I'll change. I know."

"How?"

"Building a dam is like fighting a war, except you have not one
enemy, but many. The river, that's the biggest foe, the weather, bu-
reaucracy, my bosses, the unions and the Wobblies, and the six thousand
men I'll have working for me."

"Why should they be *enemies,* Frank? I can understand the elements, but why the men?"

"Perhaps that's not a good word," Frank admitted. "You have to
understand something, you have to *believe* something, Elle." He looked
at her intently. "I am not a vain man, do you believe that?"

"Yes."

"I find no glory in command, I have no urge for that power, really,
but a supervising engineer must *assume* command and he must convey
a feeling of power or he is totally useless to the job. Do you know
who I am quoting?"

"Yes, Professor Heinlein."

"Correct. There will be two factions on the dam site. The government, which will build the roads and the railroads and bring in the
electricity, and perform myriads of jobs, that's one faction. They will
be under the command of Walker Young. I know Walker Young, and
a finer engineer does not exist. Walker Young knows how I feel about
him and I think the feeling is mutual. Walker Young and I will get
along fine.

"And then there is the dam. The dam and Boulder City. That's
my territory and everything that happens there, whether it's an outhouse or a three-hundred-foot tunnel, will be my concern.

"It's tough work. Tough on me and tougher on the men who
work there. A man hanging on the side of a cliff or a man pouring
concrete in a permanent sweat box does not have an easy life or an
easy job.

"The average pay will be three-fifty a day for the average stiff.
The Big Six Companies plan to house and feed them for a dollar sixty
a day, so a man's take-home pay will be a dollar ninety a day."

"That's all?" Elle asked with amazement.

"That's all, and that's twenty cents an hour above the national
average income. At a dollar ninety a day a man has just so much of
a stake in the dam. I will feed them well, I will build the best company
town the budget will allow. The married men will have houses. But
after five years, or six, or whatever it takes, I have taken those years

from these men and all they will have to show for it is the fact that they haven't starved, that they've had some beer money, some whore money, and hopefully some pride that that dam was part of *them*."

"But why must you pay them so little?"

And now Frank Crowe smiled as he fondled her chin.

"That question, my dear Elle, is a perfect example of the type of question you will *not* be able to ask."

Elle thought for a long time, and then she said very simply, "I understand that," although she was really unaware how weighty Frank's statement was.

Elle had brought in two glasses of whiskey from the kitchen. She drank rarely, but her instincts were usually right about such acts.

"I've worked around engineers before, Frank."

"I know."

"I've never been married to one."

"I hope not."

"I *do* understand what you've told me. I can sympathize with the fact that your authority has to be unquestioned. But what about *us*?"

"What *about* us?"

"Are you trying to tell me that you'll be a robot on that site, that you'll be a body that needs to be covered, and fed, and sometimes satisfied in bed, is that what you are saying?"

"Essentially."

Elle drank more quickly than she did normally. She sat crosslegged on the floor near a good open fire Frank had built on their brick hearth.

"Has marriage to me changed your life at all?"

"Why ask such a question, Elle?"

"I don't mean physically, I mean spiritually."

"I love you, Elle," Frank said.

"Good," said Elle. "Not only the fact that you love me is good, but the fact that you can *finally* say it. That's good."

Frank knew what Elle was driving at.

"Is it possible, Frank, that almost six years of marriage to me will send a different Frank Crowe to Boulder Canyon than to all the other dams you have worked?"

"I don't know, Elle."

"Well, *I* know. Does that frighten you?"

"Perhaps, a little."

"Well, don't let it, Frank. Let me tell you something: I am *not* afraid. I know that while you've been on all these other projects you were in the company of men. Your friends, Williams and Wanke, and they *are* your friends, were men you worked with, day and night.

Yet you scarcely knew their wives, you broke no bread with them, you didn't drink together, laugh together."

"Well, you've changed that."

"You bet I have. Maria Williams in particular has become a warm and wonderful friend. We've talked. We've talked plenty. She's been on four dam sites with her husband. I've asked her, I've said, 'What do you think, Maria, do you think I can measure up?' and she put her arm around me and she said, 'You'll do fine, honey, you'll do fine,' and I cried, Frank, I cried in her arms. You didn't know about that, did you?"

"No, Elle, no I didn't."

"And we've had the Williamses to dinner and the Wankes and we've been to their house and you've survived that, haven't you?"

"Yes," Frank said.

"And I've knit blankets for Eva's new baby and she's taught me how to can apricot jam and we've survived that too?"

"True, Elle. All that's true, and I've sweated every time you've been around their kids because I feared it would upset you."

"It does, Frank. It does. Why should I deny that? But as long as you have that sensitivity to be aware of my feelings I say to myself, 'I love Frank. All my love is going into that man, and that's enough.' "

Frank bent down and kissed Elle.

"I won't question you on that dam site, Frank Crowe. I'll make that vow to you now. You can build the damned thing upside down and I won't question you, but . . ."

"But, what, Elle?"

"I ask you, Frank, I plead with you to let me be your *wife* on that dam, whether it's a day we have, or whether it's an hour. Give me that chance, will you, Frank?"

"I'll try, Elle."

"You're not made of steel, Frank. You're not infallible, you're not a myth, you're a man."

"Then why did you hang up that wire from President Coolidge?"

"Well, maybe there are some questions you can't ask either."

"Maybe there are."

Elle had unbuttoned her blouse. Frank could see her lovely breasts showing beneath the white bra and he watched as she took off her blouse and neatly folded it on the floor beside her, then lowered one bra strap, then the other, the thin straps falling off her shoulders easily. He watched as she brought her arms in back and unhooked the three metal hooks which fastened her bra, and he watched as she took off that bra and her beautiful small firm breasts were illuminated by the warm orange glow of the fire. He watched her nipples, firm now,

65

set symmetrically in the ample areola of her breasts. He bent down to hold these breasts and they felt soft, a kind of softness which never failed to amaze him, a softness and a vibrancy and a symmetry which seemed too good to be true.

Elle reached for the buckle on Frank's belt.

"Don't you think we should go up to bed?" he asked.

"No, Frank, right here. Make love to me right here on the floor in front of this wonderful fire."

Frank Crowe obeyed and felt wicked and wonderful and knew that he held a woman whose strength might well match his own. Perhaps, he thought before he went to sleep, he feared too much or perhaps he feared not enough.

11

Frank was obviously surprised to see Jack Williams at the station when he stepped off the train from Denver.

"What the hell you doing here?" Crowe asked.

"What the hell you doing riding a parlor car?"

Both men laughed. "You could get used to that kind of travel," Crowe said. "I always blamed the rails, but now I know it's the seats."

"Well, I didn't bring my limo down here to pick you up," said Williams as he opened the door to his truck, stowing Frank's luggage in the back.

They drove silently the short trip to Frank's house. Williams stopped in front; Frank swung out of the cab and picked up his luggage and headed for the front door.

Elle opened it and embraced him, and then the entire Wanke and Williams families gathered around him yelling, "Surprise, surprise."

Frank Crowe was startled. Elle laughed, saying, "Look at him blush," but soon they were all seated around the dining-room table, eating roast beef, mashed potatoes, corn, peas, string beans, drinking red wine. No one pressed Frank for details of his trip, but after a second helping of tapioca pudding he called the children-filled room to silence by tapping his glass with a spoon.

"I want you all to enjoy this evening, and I thank you for being here," he said. "The time has arrived." He held up his glass. "Black Canyon, here we come!"

There were much shouting and kissing but Wanke and Williams were eager for the details.

"Did they buy it all, Frank?" Wanke asked.

"Lock, stock, and barrel."

"How did it go?"

"They were all there. Chapman, Barnes, Stein, all of them, and they listened very carefully when I outlined our attack."

Elle noticed that word.

"The room was silent," Crowe continued. "Chapman wondered about the low bid, and the first bomb hit when I told them we're working twenty-four hours a day.

"Stein, whom I'm beginning to like, asked the only engineering question. The second bomb fell when I told them what I wanted.

"You should have seen Barnes's face when I mentioned the ten percent profit. I think he shit right there. Sorry, ladies.

"I left the room. Fifteen minutes later they summoned me. I got everything I asked for."

"Son of a bitch," Jack Williams said, and then turned to his wife, Maria. "Go out and buy that couch from Monkey Ward," and then he looked at his four children, "but none of you sit on it, understand?"

Wanke was still serious. "We still have to sweat out the bid," he said.

"I'm not sweating," said Frank. "Edward Chapman, that sneaky bastard, got wind of Arundel's bid. They are eight million above ours."

"Eight million dollars," Wanke said, "in my business is a safe tolerance. I think I will put some neat's-foot oil on my boots."

After everyone had left, Elle did not clear the table immediately, but steered Frank into the living room. She brought two extra glasses of wine.

"This is a great tribute to you, Frank," Elle said.

"It's all talk now. Let's see whether I can build that dam."

"You'll build it, Frank."

"I'll try."

"And when it's finished you're going to be a rich man."

"I hadn't thought about that much."

"I know," Elle said, "and neither have I."

"I believe you, Elle." He loosened his necktie and sat back on the sofa.

"This is hardly the time to celebrate. In two, three months it all begins."

"You can't wait, can you?"

67

"No, I can't. You know, Elle, I asked for and I got the biggest house in Boulder City."

"Why?"

"Another question you shouldn't ask, but don't worry, it won't be that big or that fancy."

"I'm not worried."

Frank Crowe was stroking Elle's hair. "You know, you're going to be the youngest and the prettiest wife of a supervising engineer that's ever graced a dam site?"

"That's a lovely thing to say, Frank."

"It's just the truth."

Elle kissed him, and now Frank Crowe was unbuttoning her blouse.

"Hadn't we better go to the bedroom?" Elle mimicked.

"Forget it," Frank said, smiling. "This young wife of mine is teaching this old dog all sorts of tricks."

12

Elle had prevailed. Although Frank Crowe had intended to sell their house in Salt Lake City, Elle fought desperately to keep their first dwelling.

"There is so much of you in that house," she said, "I don't want anyone else to own it."

"I can't be thinking about a house when I'm on the dam."

"We'll rent it. I'll find some decent people." And Elle did after Frank relented.

They boarded the train for Las Vegas on March 15, 1931. A good part of the way they rode in silence, Elle noticing the lush landscape of Utah slowly eroding into the desert browns and yellows of Arizona and Nevada. Trees were getting sparse, the heat intensified, but she made few comments to Frank, who seemed lost in his own thoughts.

All big construction sites drew drifters, loners, adventurers, men who spent their whole lives living out of a gunny sack, their only home a tent, a truck, perhaps a room in a railway hotel with facilities down the hall. Many of these men were good, honest workers who had chosen rootlessness as a way of life, but here at Boulder Crowe knew he faced a new situation. Never in recent history had the country been in such a state of poverty. Factories were hardly producing, farmers fought drought and dust, venture capital had almost dried up. Banks were failing or near failure, and Frank knew that secretaries of the Big Six Companies had answered countless applications for employment with a form letter stating, "We regret there is nothing we can offer at present, nor can we hold out much encouragement to you. . . . In view of the many hundreds of men now there . . . we strongly advise against anyone coming on the chance of obtaining work." Still Crowe knew that they would come, no matter what, like soldiers going into battle never quite believing that they might not survive.

The train was coming close to Las Vegas. Frank could see the familiar signs. Trucks and cars clustered around shade-poor cottonwoods, clotheslines were strung with bleached and tattered cotton shirts, pants, underwear. Children, frail and languorous, were playing with equally listless dogs, and men were sitting on runningboards, their elbows on their knees, their eyes staring at the cracked earth, some smoking, others arguing, all of them swallowed by the unseasonal heat and the vastness of the desert. They looked up briefly as the train went by and knew it marked another benchmark in an unfilled calendar. Frank squeezed Elle's hand.

Walker Young, the supervising engineer for the Bureau of Reclamation, was a well-built, immaculate man, shorter than Crowe and six years his senior. His reputation like Frank's was solid, both as an engineer and an administrator.

It was he and a driver who met Crowe as the train stopped. The men shook hands formally and Frank introduced Elle.

"Welcome, Mrs. Crowe," Young said, "and congratulations. Always thought Frank was married to a slide rule."

"He still is," Elle said. "I fit in occasionally."

Young steered them through the station, and Crowe could scarcely believe the changes since his last visit. The waiting room was filled with men and women, most arriving, some departing. But outside the station, which only two years ago had been an empty square, almost a thousand men, women, and children sat on the grass, some sipping Cokes, others half dozing, swinging lamely under the shade of a few elm trees. It was almost like a tidal wave which seemed to arise from this mass of humanity as men and women rose and engulfed Walker and Crowe and Elle.

"That's Frank Crowe," somebody yelled. "Sure enough," someone else shouted, and suddenly a chant, an almost frightening chant began: "How about a job, chief? Hey, chief, need a good worker? Here, chief, look at my work papers."

Crowe and Young slowly pushed toward Young's car, Elle between them. Finally the driver managed to open the door and the three of them sat in the back seat of Young's Hudson, but the wave of humanity pressed on. They shouted, screamed. "Hey, chief, hey, chief."

"Get going," Young ordered his driver, who put the car into gear. At first the men tried to stop the vehicle physically, but slowly the engine overcame its initial inertia and they started moving. Scores of men ran alongside the car, but finally they were clear of the runners and headed down Main Street.

"Stop the car," Crowe ordered, and the driver obeyed. Frank opened his window and shouted at a heavy-set older man leaning against a telephone pole.

"Hey, River Joe," Frank shouted, and the man looked up and spotted Crowe.

He walked over to the car, smiling broadly.

"*Mr.* Crowe," he said. "Well, I'll declare."

"How you been, River Joe?"

"I been standing here for three weeks waiting for you to pass."

"Still got some work left in you?"

"You kiddin'? I'll outwork three of them kids, Mr. Crowe."

Frank laughed. "See me at my office in the morning."

"Yes, Mr. Crowe. What time would you suggest?"

"Six-twenty."

"Six-twenty it will be."

Frank rolled up the window and turned to Walker Young.

"Feel better already. Had that man on every job I've been on."

"I know," Young said, "and you've bailed him out of jail every Monday morning."

"That's right," Crowe said. "Got as hard a grip on the bourbon as he does on a shovel."

They stopped at the Palm Hotel at the western end of Main Street. Walker got out first, helped Elle out of the car, and the three of them entered the lobby, its floor covered with white octagonal tile. Two worn leather couches faced the window, several dusty palms in pots somehow survived, an aging clerk was framed by a tier of mahogany boxes containing keys, some letters, an old Big Ben alarm clock.

"These are Mr. and Mrs. Frank Crowe," Young said. "I've reserved 2A and B for them."

"Right this way," the clerk answered, without bothering with the formalities of checking in.

They walked up the one flight of worn stairs, the carpets fraying on the edges, and down a narrow hall. Elle could smell the cooking of food, but finally the clerk opened the door to a room and waited for his guests to enter.

"Just like you ordered, Mr. Young. Two corner rooms facing west. Ain't much of a view but it's quiet."

"This will do just fine," Crowe said. The driver arrived with the luggage and Crowe told him to leave it in the parlor.

"We live here too," Walker said. "I want you to meet my wife, Emma, Mrs. Crowe. She's in Boulder fretting over our house. The way it's going, we'll have the dam up before it's finished. I guess you'll go through the same thing."

"I'd like to meet her, Mr. Young."

"You will, you will," he said quickly, uncomfortable really in the role of host. "Guess Frank and I better get to work." Walker Young also had a pocket watch on a chain and he studied its face quickly.

"Let's go to Boulder. The Big Six Building is almost done. I'll show you your office, Frank."

Crowe reached for his hat and placed it on his head. "Let's go," he said, and the two men left the room without any pleasantries.

Elle looked at the parlor. It was stifling and she opened a window, but it only increased the heat so she closed it again. There were a mahogany sofa covered in yellow velvet and a side table with an oak mirror over it. She walked to the bedroom, which was small and equally hot. There was a good-size double bed, its mattress soft, covered by a thin bedspread. There were a dresser, several vile oil paintings of cacti and sunsets, a radiator, and a door to the bathroom, which had an enamel tub, a sink with permanent brown drain marks, a soap dish without soap, several thin bath towels, and a light over a mirror framed in pine.

Elle unpacked both her and Frank's clothes, filling a small closet with their meager wardrobe. She stowed her underwear, her stockings, and nightgown on one side of the dresser and neatly placed Frank's underwear and handkerchiefs and socks on the other. She lined up their shoes on the floor of the closet and finally put a photograph taken on their wedding day and framed in silver next to her side of the bed on a small marble-covered night table.

It had taken her perhaps fifteen minutes to accomplish all this, and she finally sat down on the sofa in the living room and put her face between her hands and closed her eyes.

It was true, it was all true what Frank had told her about Vegas, only she realized it was one thing to be told and another to experience actuality.

She would never forget that wave of men and women, desperate and lean, engulfing them at the depot. She had known and she had seen poverty in her life, but somehow, in New England, even the poor had overcoats, hats, the women's cheap woolen coats sometimes with fake fur on the collars.

She had never seen poverty in this climate. She had noticed several women hanging on the car, their sunbleached cotton dresses almost transparent from washing, their breasts bare, their nipples hard and dark, almost frozen in rigidity. She knew that theirs was not an act of exhibitionism, but simply pure, unadulterated poverty, which now even stripped them of modesty.

But there was more that she thought of. The forced cordiality of Walker Young. The curtness of his orders, his reticence toward any real warmth or camaraderie, and further the easy acceptance of all this by Frank, who this day, at eleven-ten (she had seen Young's watch) began the biggest job of his career and left their parlor as if he were going to mail a letter.

"You will be lonely," Frank had said, and already she was, and she had barely been alone one hour.

"No, damn it, Elle," she told herself. "No damn it. Fight it. Fight that feeling." She stood up and looked in the mirror. She reached into her purse and withdrew a comb and combed her long hair, found the room key, and walked into the lobby and out onto Main Street.

She had walked two blocks, perhaps three, when she found herself suddenly surrounded by several poorly dressed women, who seemed to have appeared from nowhere. One of them, blonde, perhaps thirty-five, walked right in front of Elle, almost tripping her, and put her arm against the side of a brick building, blocking Elle's way.

"Excuse me," Elle said, trying to get past the woman, but she stuck out her arm and forced Elle to stop. Quickly the other women came up; one of them fondled the sleeve of Elle's white crepe de chine blouse; another pulled the back of her bra and let it snap.

"Ain't we all pretty and gussied up," one of the now faceless women shouted.

"Out for a little walk on the town."

"Let me go," Elle shouted, and the girls and women laughed.

"Ain't you Frank Crowe's wife?"

"What business is that of yours?"

"What *business*," the coarse blonde shouted.

"What *business*," she repeated, and they all laughed. It was almost an animal laughter.

"We're starving, sister. There's no jobs for men and more whores than buyers."

"I don't want to discuss it," Elle said and suddenly felt a hard slap against her face. She fell and she felt someone kicking her, and then she heard a stern voice saying, "You're under arrest." She straightened her skirt and stood up. Some of the women scattered in all directions, but the policeman, young and tall, held on to two of Elle's accosters.

72

"Line up against the wall," he shouted. Neither of them obeyed.

"I'll give you ten seconds or I'll blow your head off." He raised his pistol and the women obeyed. He pat-frisked them without any regard for modesty and then ordered them to face him. Quickly he slipped a pair of handcuffs around the arms of each of them and told them to march ahead of him.

He turned to Elle and said, "I'm sorry, but you'll have to come along."

"Why?"

"To swear out a complaint."

Elle said quietly, "I don't want trouble, officer."

"You hear her," one of the handcuffed girls shouted.

"Shut up."

"I saw the whole thing, miss. You've *got* to come along."

It was only a short walk to the city police department. The two girls were quickly behind bars, yelling at their arresting officer, "You know who that bitch is? Frank Crowe's wife."

"Jesus," he said, and Elle watched one of the jailers hit the woman across the mouth. "Shut up."

The young officer was visibly nervous and asked Elle to follow him. She was glad to leave the jail area and found herself in the anteroom of the office of the chief of police. There were a hard oak bench; several FBI photographs of wanted men, head on and profile; a brass spittoon on a gray rubber mat. The young officer knocked and entered the chief's office, and after a few minutes came out to usher Elle in.

"Pitt is my name," the chief said, extending his hand. He motioned her to a wooden armchair, then sat behind a cluttered desk. He was a man in his fifties, his face tanned, with close-cut gray-blond hair, very blue eyes, a marksman medal gracing the pocket of his well-cut shirt.

"This is a terrible welcome for you, Mrs. Crowe. I apologize for Las Vegas. Did you get hurt?"

"Not really," Elle said, feeling the swelling on her face.

"We've got the best police force in the West," he said, "but all I've got is ten men and three thousand hungry people."

"I don't want to make trouble, chief."

"You won't have no trouble, ma'am. Those ladies will be out of town before the sun sets and so will their friends."

"That's what I mean, chief. I don't want to sign a complaint."

"You've got no choice."

"This is my first day in town. I should have known better. It's also my husband's first day. He doesn't need my troubles. Not now."

"Mrs. Crowe, this ain't your husband's territory. It's mine."

"I know that, chief. I'm only asking you for a favor."

73

"How old are you, Mrs. Crowe?"

"My name is Elle."

"How old are you, Elle?"

"Thirty."

The chief leaned back in his chair and looked at the ceiling. "Well, you're thirty and I'm nearly twice your age, so I'm going to tell you something. *One* crime in this town that goes unpunished just leads to more crime and more, and Lord knows we've got enough."

"The people are poor," Elle said. "You can't blame them for being poor."

"Ain't blaming them for being poor. We've got soup kitchens, the Red Cross, the Salvation Army. There's a big difference between poor and mean and you'd better learn it. Those ladies, and I use the word loosely, are going to have the meanness taken out of them. I can assure you of that. Now simply sign this complaint, and that's that."

"You won't tell my husband?"

The chief stood up. He was taller than Elle imagined. "I ain't gonna say a word, believe me, but this is a small town and folks got more time than money. Your husband will know about it soon enough. And when he does, and if he finds I didn't do my job, I might not *have* a job at all."

"You said this wasn't his territory."

"That's what I said. Starting today, Elle, all of Las Vegas, half of Nevada, half of Arizona is Frank Crowe's territory. Come on, I'll drive you home."

"There's no need."

"There is *every* need. After today you can walk any alley in this town without a fret."

Once more they passed through the jail. Elle did not look but she could hear fists pounded on flesh and a raw voice screaming, "Who were the other bitches, who were they? I'm just getting warmed up."

She sat silently next to the chief as he drove her back to the hotel, and thanked him.

"I'd put some ice on that face, if I were you."

"I will."

"Just tell Henry at the desk; he'll send it up."

There were tears in Elle's eyes as she ran toward the lobby. She asked for some ice and ran toward their rooms. She took off her shoes, a boy came with the ice, and Elle wrapped a bath towel around it and lay on her bed. She must have fallen asleep. It was almost dark when she heard a knock on her door. She quickly straightened the bed, put the wet towel in the bathroom, ran her hand through her hair and expected to welcome Frank. A slight gray-haired lady in mid-years stood patiently in the hall. She held some wildflowers in her hand.

"I'm Emma Young. Walker's wife."

"Please come in."

Emma stepped into the room. It was almost dark.

"Did I wake you?"

"I'm afraid so. Let me turn on a light."

"I can come back another time."

"No," Elle almost pleaded, "please stay. Please."

Emma looked at Elle and noticed the bruise on her cheek.

"What happened to your face?"

"I ran into a door," Elle lied.

"Mistake number two," Emma said.

"What do you mean?"

"Your first mistake was to walk on the street by yourself and your second mistake was to lie about what happened."

"You *know?*" Elle asked.

"I know, Walker knows, your husband knows."

"Oh *no!*" Now Elle really cried. "The chief *promised* he'd say nothing. I didn't want to swear out a complaint."

"The chief said nothing, Elle." She came over and put her arm around the girl. "He didn't have to say anything."

"But how would Frank *know*. So *fast?*"

"Poor Elle," Emma said, sitting down. "There are lots of things that happen on dam sites that you'll never have explained."

"Frank told me about that."

"Well, he's right. There, put these flowers in that vase and come on over and I'll give you a little sherry."

"How many dams have you been at, Mrs. Young?"

"Call me Emma. Five, and I wasn't much older than you when I came to the first one, but I wasn't as pretty." Elle blushed.

"Do you know Maria Williams?" Elle asked.

"The tunneler's wife?"

"Yes."

"Sure I know Maria, why?"

"She told me back in Salt Lake City, never ask your man where he's been, what he's done, and when he's coming home."

"That's good advice," Emma said.

Elle drank some sherry and said, "What time do you think Frank will come home?"

They both laughed and Emma put some ointment on Elle's face.

75

13

The $165 million allocated by Congress for the building of the Boulder Dam was divided unevenly between the Bureau of Reclamation and the Big Six Companies.

The Big Six Companies' $48 million bid was for the building of the dam, and this was Crowe's bailiwick; it was the responsibility of the government to supply the site with roads, electricity, rail service, personnel, and countless other services.

Walker Young was in charge of the government end. Crowe and Walker had worked alongside each other on a number of projects; there had never been serious differences between them. On Boulder their aims were the same, to build the dam, and though Crowe's motives might possibly be said to be more financial, and Young's political, at this stage of the game it was really the job that counted. There was no time for arguing about overlapping authority or personal egos; the river, the gorge, the weather, everything which had to be overcome, overshadowed any competition of command.

It was with considerable pride that Young was able to show what he had accomplished the last few months. The macadam road which they now traveled had been built by him.

"The first freight train," Young said, "rolled into the interchange yard at Boulder City on January 31. Carried a load of lumber for Le Tourneau, who are building the road from Boulder to Black Canyon. We opened the line up full blast on February 5."

They stopped at a hillside near Boulder City.

Young pointed west. "I've started twelve hollow-tile houses, one of them yours, one of them mine. I've got a warehouse going, pumps for the water supply, and I expect Lewis Construction Company to finish the railhead to the dam site in May."

"When in May?" Crowe asked and Young laughed, but Crowe did not mean it as a joke.

The Six Companies had erected a headquarters construction camp near the interchange yard at Boulder City, and Walker Young had his driver take them to the administration building, a medium-size frame structure painted white, which contained a number of offices, a stenographic unit, and a large drafting room upstairs. Crowe's office was the largest in the building, and its furnishings resembled those of his office in Salt Lake City. These had been his orders and as he walked around the room he was satisfied with the results.

"Well, Walker," he said and closed the door to his office. "I'm sure you've got some questions, and I'm sure I've got some answers."

"I've only got one," Walker Young said. "How do you expect to come out on that low bid of yours?"

"Simple," Crowe said. "I'm going to work around the clock."

"Jesus Christ," Young shouted, pacing the room. "Jesus H. Christ, I should have known. Old Overtime Charlie, isn't that what they used to call you at Deadwood?"

"They called me a lot of other names too."

"Three shifts, eh?"

"Yup."

"How are you going to see at night?"

"I'm going to light up the dam site."

"Who's paying for the lights?"

"We are."

"I'll be a son of a bitch," Young said. "I know, I know," he held up his hands, "there's nothing in the contract that forbids it. Right?"

"Right."

"What about the labor punks, the pinkos, the Wobblies? What about the goddamned reporters? What are you going to tell them?"

"Nothing," Crowe said. "How far along is your fencing?"

"Almost finished."

"Good. So this is a government reservation, right?"

"That's right, Frank. No booze, no firearms, but I can't fight your labor battles for you."

"I'll handle it, Walker."

"It might be tougher than you think."

The door opened, a young engineer entered. "Can I speak to you for a minute, Mr. Crowe?"

"Speak up."

The engineer looked at Walker Young. "It's private."

"Bullshit," Crowe said. "I've got no secrets from Mr. Young."

The engineer hesitated, and finally stammered, "It's your wife. She was attacked this afternoon."

"Attacked, by *whom*?"

"A bunch of women."

"Is she hurt?"

"They bruised her face."

"They get the women?"

"They got two. They're sweating them for the rest."

"That will be all," Crowe said, dismissing the young man.

The blood had drained from Crowe's face as he drummed the edge of his desk.

"There's your answer, Walker. There's only *one* reason they'd attack Elle. They want jobs for their men. They're desperate and they're hungry and they're sweating and there'll be no labor shit on this dam. I told that to the Big Six and I'm telling you. You saw that horde this morning. Well, there'll be work. Lots of work, but every stiff better give me eight hours of his sweat or I'll have another one in his place before he can take a leak."

If Walker Young had any reservations about Crowe's married state on this dam, they were in this instance wiped out. He thought of offering Crowe a ride back to Vegas to see his wife but kept the thought to himself.

"We've been here eight months now, Frank, and we've had no problems. Take my advice, and hire a good share of men from Arizona. They're just as hungry as Nevadans or the Okies. The more of them we've got on the payrolls the less trouble their state house will give us. They vote too."

"I've thought of that, Walker. What about the power?"

"It's almost here."

"That's good. Did you have any trouble with those California boys?"

"Not much. Lot of starving farmers from Imperial, Coachella. They want that dam as much as we do."

"I bet." Crowe took out his watch. It was six o'clock in the evening. "I've got a meeting with Williams. Thanks for picking us up."

"Quite all right," Walker Young said.

Crowe could hear his car drive off and answered the knock on his door from Williams.

"Well, Frank," Williams asked, "how did Mr. Young take to your twenty-four-hour schedule?"

"He invoked the name of our Savior a great deal."

"I bet."

"He had to be the first to know," Crowe said.

"Of course."

"His biggest worry was the light bill."

"That figures."

"Well, what have you got, Jack?"

"What do you want first? Men?"

"Men is fine."

"I'll need twelve to fifteen hundred men."

"Reasonable," Crowe said.

"I'll drill three headings. Twelve feet in diameter for the first, thirty feet for the second, and sixteen feet on the river. I'll alternate at the adits. Blast and drill one side and muck the other. Equipment," Williams said, and all from memory. "I'll need eight shovels, one-hundred-ton electric with three-and-a-half-yard dipper."

"Wow," Crowe said.

"Fifty-six feet, Frank, less than one year."

"I know, go on."

"Five drilling Jumbos."

"The Jack Williams Special."

"Yeah."

"Why five?"

"One in reserve."

"That's good," Crowe said.

"Twenty-five trucks on each side of the river, fifty trucks on the upper portals. I'm having these built on special bodies holding fourteen cubic yards. I'll need bulldozers and cowdozers.

"For ventilation I need Roots blowers through eighteen-foot pipes at the rate of eight thousand cubic feet per minute."

"How soon after blasting are you resuming work?"

"Five minutes," Williams said forcefully. "The first truckload goes out fifteen minutes after the blast."

"In some kind of hurry?" Crowe teased.

"One year you gave me."

"I know, Jack, I know. There's one thing that's very vital to us."

"What's that?"

"What kind of dynamite are you using?"

"Forty percent gelatine dynamite."

"Where are you storing it?"

"I'll have a central magazine. From there the stuff will be hauled by trucks to smaller magazines near the points of use, and finally it goes to the tunnels. The primers will be prepared by powder fitters, working in isolated stations, and carried into the tunnels in specially designed containers. I'll set the primers from no delay to fifteen, giving me sixteen delays. I'll use a four-forty-volt circuit with locked safety switches outside the tunnels for detonating."

Crowe was taking notes while Williams spoke. Finally he looked up. "You've got four stations that handle powder, right?"

"Right. What's bothering you?"

"That's too many, Jack."

"I've got every powder fitter back from Deadwood."

"That's good, but you still have too many magazines. Cut it down to two. One on each side of the river, close to the tunnel. And code your powder *daily!*"

"What are you so nervous about?"

"I'll tell *you* this, Jack, and I'll tell Wanke and that's all, but I think I'll have more trouble with labor than I figured. Those stiffs have been sitting in Vegas for months now and their brains have been cooked. They'll go for any crawling labor bastard who promises them the moon."

"It looks ugly in Vegas," Williams agreed.

"I want you to know where every stick of dynamite is at any given minute. Understand?"

Williams nodded.

"What about labor? What do you want?"

"On the Jumbo I'll need twenty-two miners at five-sixty a day. I need twenty-one chuck tenders at five dollars a day, three rippers at five dollars a day. I'll need a safety miner and a drilling foreman in each tunnel on each shift. Two crews of fifteen drilling the wings on either side of the top heading."

"What about the muckers?"

Williams continued. "I'll need a shovel operator at ten bucks a day, an oiler and a pitman at five dollars each.

"I'm still working with the superintendents, the electricians, the pump men, the power men."

"Those figures you'll have when?" Crowe asked.

"Tomorrow by four."

Crowe looked at the figures. "What did a shovel operator get at Deadwood?"

"Eight bucks."

"Give 'em nine."

"All right," Williams said. "There's another thing."

"What?"

"The beer."

"Beer *chits*. They can use them in Vegas. You'll get them."

Frank Crowe stood up but Williams did not.

"There's one more thing, Frank," Williams said.

"Shoot."

"You remember when we were up here two years ago and I blasted those test holes."

"Sure."

"The rock felt good to me, but I kept some samples. I sent them to the Colorado School of Mines. You want to hear the report?"

"Sure."

"'Dear Mr. Williams,'" Jack read. "'The rock you will encounter in driving the diversion tunnel is, in the opinion of this laboratory, *ideal*. It is volcanic in origin (ardesite tuff mecia). It is easily drilled, and when properly loaded breaks so that it may be conveniently handled by shovels. This rock is in our opinion dead and you should encounter no water or seepage. Sincerely, etc.'"

"That's good news, Jack."

"Yeah. Here comes the bad news. The bill. One hundred dollars for laboratory testing." He handed Crowe the bill.

"Well," Crowe said, penciling and circling a "1" on the invoice, "here it is: Invoice No. 1. Top drawer, attention Mr. Barnes."

Now Williams rose. "You want a lift back to town?"

"Hell, no," Crowe said. "I've got a meeting with the draftsmen in four minutes."

Williams left. Crowe paced his office, then sat behind his desk and looked at the figures. Nine dollars for a shovel operator. He could remember when they were happy with three.

It was eleven o'clock that night when Frank let himself into the parlor of his suite. Elle was sitting on the sofa, reading. He could smell a stew cooking somewhere on a hot plate. He walked slowly toward her and gently touched her bruised cheek. Then he kissed her.

"You know," she asked.

"I know."

"I'm sorry, Frank."

"About what?"

"About being dumb."

"Why were you dumb?"

"I shouldn't have left the hotel."

"You're a big girl. I'm the one that's dumb. I should have warned you. I didn't think things were that bad."

"I didn't want to press charges, Frank. The chief made me."

"The chief was right. They got 'em all. All ten of them."

"What will they do to them?"

Again Frank stroked Elle's swollen cheek. "Kill them, I hope."

"Come on, Frank. They were desperate. Hungry. So they hit me."

"They not only hit you, Elle, they hit the wife of the supervising engineer. What's for supper?"

"Stew. Frank Crowe, I love you."

14

Unlike Edward Chapman, who started with a wheelbarrow and a shovel in Salt Lake City, or Howard Henderson, who they say was born with a filled leather tool belt around his waist, Henry Barnes was not a self-made man, although he did much now to perpetuate that myth.

His father had been a builder developing many of the cheap-jack three-story apartment houses on Howard Street in San Francisco, and Henry's marriage to Hortense Dubois, a member of an old-line family, only added to his holdings. Max Dubois specialized in brick buildings on the fringes of Chinatown, Filipino town, Stockton Street, Kearny Street, even sections of Sutter and Post.

When both Henry and Hortense came into their full inheritance in their late twenties, the total land holdings were substantial, and the same San Francisco *Examiner* which once heralded their marriage now questioned a number of disastrous fires in their buildings both on Mission and on Stockton streets, the latter killing forty Filipino men, who had a habit of sharing rooms in large numbers. Barnes shrugged off the stories at the Bohemian Club as the product of some new Eastern Jew reporter, an explanation eagerly accepted at this segregated club, and Henry's practice of handing ten-dollar bills to fire inspectors continued, this being more expedient than repairing stairwells, purchasing fire extinguishers, or "any such damn foolishness" as he called it, which no one should expect paying four dollars a month for the privilege of sharing a room with three other souls who paid the same rent.

It was to Henry Barnes's credit, however, that he had not made his life one of property management, but rather he had pursued engineering and graduated with honors near the turn of the century. He founded a firm and, unlike Chapman and Henderson-Andrews, quite unlike *most* of his competitors, realized early that initial investment in heavy equipment not only paid off handsomely but allowed him to bid on jobs ranging from Chile to Alaska. It was one philosophy which he shared with Frank Crowe, whose favorite saying was that you can't get a two-by-four through a one-by-two opening.

One foggy morning in summer, 1931, Henry Barnes was driven to his office on Montgomery Street near California and he hardly said a word to his Chinese chauffeur. Unlike the Zellerbachs or the Wertheimers, the Barneses did not dismiss any of their servants during the depression, although they stopped paying them. These unfortunate souls, most of them Chinese, many of them elderly, had little choice but to remain in exchange for room and board rather than face the soup kitchens on Mission and Howard streets. They lived in tiny quarters in the large and ornate Victorian mansion on Nob Hill, the windows of their cells barely reaching street level, while the rest of the home, turreted and gingerbreaded, enjoyed one of the most breathtaking views of San Francisco Bay.

Barnes's first stop was the barbershop of the St. Francis Hotel. There his shoes were shined, and his hair trimmed, he was shaved, his face bathed in alternately hot and cold towels, scented with bay

82

rum, while his nails were being buffed by Ida, a petite French manicurist who worked her customers' nails close to her ample bosom and overlooked any small intimacies during the process. There were the usual boys at the St. Francis barbershop: Kelish of the Bank of Italy, Steinberg who owned the municipal railway, Baker of the shipping company, and Sorres who managed the St. Francis Hotel.

Shaven, barbered, shined, and fondled, he proceeded to his office, an inauspicious two-story brick building holding large drafting rooms, a library, a minuscule reception area. An accounting office behind glass and steel bars was presided over by Mr. Ganz, who stood daily like a statue at an old oak desk, sporting a vest, his sleeves pulled back by black elastic bands, wearing a green eyeshade and gold-rimmed glasses. "Mr. Ganz," Barnes used to say, "has *never* been off one penny," and his books balanced meticulously each evening as he put away his pen and returned the ledgers to a large black wall safe whose combination was known only to Barnes and himself.

Barnes's office was elegant: paneled in oak, the floors covered with Oriental rugs. Several jade lamps and other Far Eastern appointments had been foisted on him by Hortense after she had seen the offices of Walter Groper, president of the California Bank, who was in charge of her personal holdings.

Perhaps the most utilitarian piece of furniture in Barnes's office was a large leather couch, tufted and well worn, which he used indiscriminately to screw frightened girls from shipping and receiving, accounting, or the mail room. They were most of them products of South of the Slot, their fathers streetcar conductors, sewer workers, managers of small corner grocery stores.

Barnes was a good engineer but he was also a realist. He not only found Hortense headstrong and militant, but for the last twenty years of marriage he had found her totally unchallenging in bed. Although he considered divorce, he considered it lightly, for even though Hortense had little influence over his personal habits, she held tightly to her own property, and any ventures she entered with her husband were always carefully spelled out legally and the documents kept in her own strong box.

There were other reasons for his legal propriety of staying married to Hortense. They had three children and he was becoming a respected, powerful member of San Francisco society. He belonged to the Bohemian Club and the Mechanics Institute, and was high on the list to be received in that most august body the Pacific Society, whose portals almost across the street from his house led not only to the city's most opulent public rooms, but to a third floor that reputedly contained some of the most elegant hookers in the city.

Barnes *did* work. He made decisions. He walked about the drafting

83

room, cajoling one draftsman, lauding another. He would go over proposals, cost analyses, he had an eye for overtime, for items labeled "misc." which *had* to be explained, and he would storm into the stenographic section waving a manila envelope in the face of a mail clerk demanding to know why this piece of mail had to go to New York *air mail,* when regular mail would certainly suffice.

At twelve-thirty he promptly left for lunch. It was only a short walk to Tadich's, not only California's oldest restaurant, but the best fish house on the Pacific Coast.

He joined Edward Chapman today in a reserved booth, lit gently by fifteen-watt bulbs in tulip shades, the wood of the booth a well-varnished mahogany: it all resembled a good compartment on the Orient Express.

Charlie, their regular waiter, dressed in black with a crisp white towel wound around his waist and the inevitable white napkin over his arm, said simply, "The usual, gentlemen?" as he piled fresh French bread and butter on the table, and both men nodded approval.

Lunch consisted of small Olympia oysters in tomato sauce, rex sole, thick slabs of French fries, asparagus with hollandaise sauce, several water glasses filled with Chablis, an order of zabaglione, a half loaf of Laraburu French bread (delivered hot at eleven in the morning), several brandies and a good cigar from Cuba.

The men spoke little during the lunch; there was simply too much food to give them time for conversation, but once their waiter had cleared the table of bread crumbs and fish bones, they sat across from each other, their brandy glasses looking as small in their massive hands as the Oriental girls they saw occasionally in the evenings.

"I hear Crowe's got them working on the dam before the contract is signed," Barnes said bluntly.

"Couple of hundred workers," Chapman shrugged. "He's anxious to get to the tunnels."

"Shit, Ed, you know those goddamned politicians. What if they change their mind? We're out on our ass. And he didn't hire a couple of hundred workers, we've got three hundred fifty on the payroll."

"I'm close to Washington," Chapman said; "there'll be no problems."

"I'll take your word for it, Ed," Barnes said, belching loudly, "but we've got to watch that Crowe."

"How many cranes can you get to Boulder?" Chapman wanted to know.

"Thirty," Barnes said.

"How many stiff-legs?"

"Twenty at least."

"Good," said Chapman. "I can match that. I should get finished on that Oakland Estuary any day now."

"How did you come out on that job?"

"Better than I thought," Chapman said. "We used a lot of niggers over there."

"Never knew you could get any work out of them."

"Surprised the hell out of me. But niggers get hungry too."

"Try any of that dark meat while you were at it?"

"Well," said Chapman, smiling, "they're no slouches in bed."

"I know," Barnes agreed. "I spent some time in Barbados. Jesus, those bitches are wild."

The waiter came with the check, he was paid and tipped, and Chapman gave Barnes a lift to the Bohemian Club, where both men, ensconced in massive leather chairs, were soon sound asleep behind the headline-filled *Examiner* giving the latest unemployment figures.

Barnes arose at four. He went to the bathroom and Charlie Chan, as the porter was called, brushed his overcoat, offered him more bay rum, and his chauffeur picked him up at four-thirty to take him home.

Barnes entered the large entry hall and strode north through the house to get his daily view of the bay. The sun was slowly making inroads on the fog, and he could see patches of blue water in the distance. There were Sausalito and Tiburon bathed in sunlight, Alcatraz rose like a rock whale from the waters, a Matson liner headed out the gate toward Honolulu.

He heard the front door open and Hortense and their two daughters, Sybil and Brenday, fourteen and sixteen, entered the parlor and dutifully kissed their father.

"We've been shopping," Hortense said, a statement made every evening at the same time.

"Yes, and Mommy keeps buying me these ugly bloomers, Daddy, when all the other girls at Hamlin's have lace underpanties."

"I think," Barnes said, blushing slightly, "there'll be plenty of time for such nonsense," a statement he did not really believe, since both of his daughters were blessed with the worst genetic selection of their parents, and it would only be their ample dowry which would get them out of the house. Their underwear would matter little either now or later.

Barnes picked up a small silver bell from an octagonal table by the window, and several minutes later Chang, the butler, appeared with a martini for him, a sherry for his wife. Hortense waited prudently for Henry to gulp the first martini and watched as he poured a second from the chilled silver pitcher.

"Young Henry will be joining us for dinner tonight," she said calmly.

"Henry, now? He's in the middle of his summer course, isn't he?"

"He phoned this morning and said he had to discuss something with you."

"Why couldn't he phone me?"

"You know how you are about long-distance phone calls."

"I don't like it," Barnes said, gulping his second martini and pouring his third.

"Why don't you wash up for dinner? Young Henry should be home any minute."

Henry Barnes sat at the head of the large Duncan Phyfe dining-room table, his son to his right, his daughters to his left, and Hortense at the other end. The table was well set. Candles burned in silver candle holders, a bouquet of flowers formed the centerpiece. A roast beef on a massive silver platter waited to be carved.

Young Henry Barnes was the apple of his father's eye. He was tall, good looking, somewhat of a rogue.

"Well, Henry, what brings this surprise visit?"

Henry hesitated and Hortense said, "Right now we're having dinner. Afterward you men can go into the study."

Barnes did not like the obvious conspiracy between mother and son, but finished his meal posthaste, lit a cigar, ordered a brandy, and finally sat with his son in his book-filled study, books which had been bought more for the beauty of their leather bindings than for their contents. There was a world atlas on a stand.

"I have a letter for you, father," Henry said, handing him a crisp envelope bearing the crest of Stanford University. Barnes opened the letter.

Dear Mr. Barnes,

This, as you must surmise, is not an easy letter for me to write considering both our personal friendship and your past generosities to your alma mater.

Your son, after much consideration by the campus police, the Academic Senate, and finally even *more* careful consideration by myself, has been dismissed from the university.

The act which prompted this action I would not like to detail, since we are both gentlemen. However, let me assure you that it took all the authority I possess to keep your son out of the hands of the law, who were eager to press charges.

I am mindful, sir, that your name and your position work both for and against you, and I brought all the evidence to light which would allow your son to escape imprisonment. This I accomplished, but the price was high. I could save you and your son the miseries of confinement and public lawsuits, but I could no longer retain him as a student at Stanford. You, as a distinguished graduate, can well understand this.

It was the consensus of the Academic Senate to strongly urge you to seek psychiatric help for your son, and after a thorough period of treatment, I am sure he may resume his studies at some public institution, such as the University of California. We cannot *ever* readmit him to Stanford.

As a father myself, I can appreciate the shock this letter may be to you, however, you may be assured I served your interests with all my tact and knowledge.

Best personal regards,
Charles Wagner
President, Stanford University

Henry Barnes the elder dropped the letter and envelope on the floor. He faced his son, white and tense.

"Did you kill anybody?" he asked.

"No, father."

"What did you do?"

"They said I raped a girl."

"Who said?"

"Her parents."

"Who are her parents?"

"The Andovers."

"Jesus Christ."

Barnes shot up from his chair and approached his son. "Stand up," he yelled, and the boy obeyed.

Barnes shot a fist at the boy's face which belied both the man's age and physique. The boy flew across the room, shattering the glass front of a bookcase.

He rose and put up his fists. "Hit me again and I'll hit back. I can kill you."

Barnes, senior, laughed. "You can kill me. *Kill* me? You dumb son of a bitch, can't even get a piece of ass without raping some goddamn society cunt."

The son had rarely heard this type of language from his father. He knew of his work in heavy construction, but that was far off, in distant countries, other cultures . . . At home, with the influence of his mother, the charade of gentleness had always prevailed.

"I've done everything you've wanted me to do, father. I didn't want to become an engineer."

"Who asked you what you wanted?"

"*You* never asked me."

"You mean I didn't get permission to spend thousands of dollars to send you to the best university in the West? I didn't ask your permission to give you a brand-new Ford roadster, new clothes, spending money . . .?"

Barnes reached down and picked up the letter and waved it in his son's face.

"Well, you're going to be an engineer, whether you like it or not, and if you're so tough, so tough that you think you can kill me, we'll see how tough you really are."

"What do you mean?"

"I'll get you off this rape charge and then I'm calling Frank Crowe and you're going to work on the Boulder Dam. That's where you're going to learn how to be an engineer, and I hope to Christ you're as tough as you pretend to be."

The door flew open and Hortense looked at the two men standing toe to toe. She noticed the shattered glass from the bookcase on the parquet floor, her son's face bleeding above his lip, under the eye.

"What have you done?" She stared accusingly at her husband. "The boy is bleeding."

"Bleeding," Henry Barnes said tauntingly. "Ask your son about bleeding. He's an expert." With that he stormed out of the house.

He did not have to tell his chauffeur where to go. He took his master straight to Rosie Randolph's Parlor on California Street, and it was Rosie herself, half madam, half medicine man, who finally drew the story out of her client.

They had sat in her overstuffed Victorian parlor for hours, Henry drinking heavily, until Rosie finally got him to admit that his primary anger was at the boy's need to *rape* at all, and secondarily at the stupidity of picking an Andover girl at that.

"Does old man Andover still come here?" Henry asked Rosie.

"No." She shook her head. "They've gone uppity. I've got to send the girls down to his office."

At two-thirty in the morning Rosie felt the time was right to summon Yvonne, her latest protégée.

The booze, the tensions, the endless day, had made Henry Barnes impotent. He stood naked in front of a mirror and looked down on the shiny blond head of the equally naked, well-formed shape of Yvonne.

"Get it up, god damn, get it up, you French bitch," he yelled, but he mercifully passed out a few minutes later and could not remember his chauffeur's dressing him and returning him home.

15

Promptly at six-twenty in the morning River Joe appeared at Frank Crowe's office and was received as promptly as he had arrived. The men shook hands and Crowe asked how River Joe felt.

"Fit as ever."

"Save any money from Deadwood?" Crowe asked.

"You know me, chief. Went on a big binge in San Francisco, had a fancy room, a fancy lady, well . . ."

Crowe nodded. "You ready to go to work?"

"Just show me where to dig."

Crowe laughed.

"How many men back from Deadwood, Tieton, Jackson Lake, Arrowrock?"

"Couple of hundred, maybe more. Seen a lot of faces in Vegas that look familiar. The Smith brothers, the Kanekis, the Wilder boys . . ."

"Well, I've got nothing to dig yet, Joe, but you're going on the payroll today."

"Doing what?"

"Check out a truck and go around town and round up all the old boys. Tell them I want to see them at the Bureau office tomorrow morning at eight."

"That'll be good news to a lot of boys. It's been a tough winter here, waiting."

"So I've heard."

"One thing, chief."

"What is it, Joe?"

"I ain't going to drive a truck on this job, am I?"

"How old are you, Joe?"

"Fifty-six."

"And you'd still rather use a shovel?"

"You bet."

Crowe laughed. "Well, as soon as I find a shovel."

River Joe left and Frank paced the room. He liked a purist and slapped his hands together, then rubbed them. Work all day and drink all night. Maybe the formula worked. River Joe hadn't changed in twenty years.

Frank bounded up the flight to the drafting room. It was a large well-lit room. Sixty drafting tables were in six lines, ten deep, like school benches, and sixty men, mostly in their twenties and early thirties, bent over them, each with his set of tools, T-squares, dividers, rulers, drafting paper, parchment, sharp pencils. Some were draftsmen, others engineers, and they represented some of the best talent the universities could produce by 1931.

Crowe walked to Harry Donovan, the chief section engineer, gave him a perfunctory greeting, and then slowly walked from table to table. At least a year's work was projected on these drawings. Power-houses, generators, roads, adits, cableways, bridges, railroad yards, storage yards, water lines, gas transmission pipes, housing units, screening plants.

89

Crowe walked slowly from table to table and studied the work before him. There were no introductions, no formalities. The ritual at each table was almost identical. He gave each man the dignity of studying the work and if necessary he asked questions. Sharp incisive questions, without sarcasm or rancor or emotion. "Where are you drawing this power from? What is the width of this housing, what is the grade on this turn? How much square footage do you have in this shed? What's the average tension on this cable? How many men will this monkey slide hold? Will this insulation hold up to 135 degrees?"

At times the answers were satisfactory, at other times they were not, and then Frank Crowe brought out his grease pencil and he drew, he modified, he restructured and redesigned.

"I need an extra twenty feet at this turnout." He drew it. Sometimes he would question a young engineer. "Where do you think a twenty-ton truck will spin out?"

"Here," the young engineer would answer.

"Wrong," Crowe said. Drawing a curve again. "Here. This is where the driver will lose control." He marked the spot with an X. "This is where he'll swerve." The boy nodded.

At the next table the young engineer argued successfully with Frank. "This is a housing for a cable shed?"

"Yes sir."

"Where's the roof?"

"There is no roof, except . . ."

"Except what?"

The boy pointed to his drawing. "I've indicated canvas. If I put a corrugated tin roof on this shed the temperature will rise to one hundred thirty degrees. If the operator wets his canvas four times a day he'll keep the temperature down to ninety."

Frank looked at the boy; he was one of the first whose physiognomy he had really taken the trouble to study. He was tall and raw-boned. Farm boy, Crowe thought. Reddish-blond hair, good long fingers, freckled and already work-hardened.

"What if there is a rainstorm?"

"He can wear a slicker."

"What about the machinery? What's going to keep that dry?"

"If there isn't enough grease on that cable drum to withstand the rain, it's not a well-functioning drum."

"So far, mister," Crowe said, "you've been right on every count. What's your name?"

"Stubbs, sir."

"Where did you go to school?"

"Iowa."

Frank knew he hadn't been far off.

90

"See me at two-forty in my office."

He continued his rounds like a visiting professor in a hospital ward. He had spent four and a half hours in the drafting room, drawing and redrawing plan after plan; a number of them like those of Stubbs he marked okay, drawing a circle around it and initialing F.C. within the circle.

Finally he returned to Donovan's board and handed him the red grease pencil, almost down to its nub.

"This country is really going to hell," he said. "They can't even make a decent grease pencil anymore." Then he left.

There was silence in the room as they all watched Crowe leave and heard his heavy boots as he descended the wooden stairs to his office. They heard the door shut.

"Son of a bitch," one young engineer said, almost to himself. "I was stuck and he had *three* answers, each more logical than the last."

"Have you ever seen a man draw like that?"

"All freehand."

Donovan had seen this performance many times before, and he would see it endlessly before the dam was finished. He only added, "They say he can draw a perfect circle freehand, now let's get back to work."

Wanke was waiting for Frank Crowe when he returned to his office. Smoking his inevitable pipe, his steel-rimmed glasses framing a narrow face, Wanke had been nicknamed "the professor" a good many years ago on a dam site, not because of his pedagogical qualities, but because of his innate sense of aesthetics, his calm, a mixture of decision and philosophy, the inevitable bookcase above his desk no matter how raw nature was outside his office.

Unlike Williams and Crowe he rarely enjoyed the ribaldry of heavy construction; he hardly drank, he seemed devoted to one wife and several sons, and like Crowe was known to be a tight man with a dollar. It was said that he had made wise investments over the years, slowly buying a series of small stores in Denver, which could easily support him after his construction days were over.

Crowe was aware that Wanke was a different type of engineer from either him or Williams, both of whom attacked a problem with gusto and guts, using their voices, their fists, their endless stamina to get the job done. Wanke was a chemical engineer; he had taken not one sample that first day they all had visited the dam, but returned and picked up hundreds. Then in the laboratory of the Bureau of Reclamation in Denver, he had studied that rock as a pathologist studies a slide which might reveal cancer. He had studied rock size and texture, lime deposits, the proper ratio of cement to gravel, of cement and gravel to water, until he had been satisfied. He had the same approach toward his men. He had his staff well trained. There were few orders by voice; a hand signal would usually suffice. At times of reflection, which were rare, Crowe had to admit that Wanke's method was equally effective, but this was hardly the time for reflection.

Wanke unrolled his plans and opened them on Frank's drawing board. The sand and gravel screening and washing plant to provide the aggregate was to be the largest in the world. It would be able to process that aggregate, and make it ready for mixture with cement and water at the rate of more than 16½ tons per minute.

Crowe scanned the plans minutely for ten minutes, then rolled them up and placed a rubber band around them.

"You didn't skimp," Crowe said.

Wanke drew on his pipe. "I'll give you all the mud you need."

"I can see that."

"When the hell is that railroad bridge going to be completed? I'm hauling everything by barge and that's slow!"

"You'll have your bridge by December. Can you get any lumber on the Arizona side?"

"Sure, but the bastards are doubling the price on it."

"Goddamn them anyway," Crowe shouted. "Why in hell did they ever admit that state to the Union?"

"Should have given it to Mexico."

"Couldn't agree with you more."

"How are things going upstairs?" Wanke asked, pointing toward the drafting room.

"Not bad, considering half of them have never been on a dam site before."

"Yeah," Wanke said, laughing. "Every dam we expect twenty-five-year-old engineers with twenty years' experience."

"Isn't that the truth." Crowe paced the room; finally he said, "I told Williams something and I'm going to tell you something and that's as far as it goes. There's going to be more labor trouble than I expected."

"Things look mean in Vegas," Wanke agreed. "Old Hoover may be a hell of an engineer, but I don't think he gauges the depth of the depression. He feels it demeaning to give charity to a grown man," Wanke said. "Un-American."

"I agree with him," Crowe said, "but there *are* kids starving, *women*, and I can't hire the men fast enough. I can't put men to work when I can't feed them or house them."

"Have you seen Rag Town yet?"

"No," Crowe said.

"Ought to take a run down there. It'll turn your blood cold."

"I've got a meeting' with de Boer this afternoon; maybe I ought to see it before I talk to him."

"Who's de Boer?"

"City planner from Denver."

"Pretty fancy," Wanke said. "All you need is a place to sleep and a place where the shit runs down."

"This is 1931, Mr. Wanke," Crowe said sarcastically. "The nobility of the working man has to be respected."

"Yeah," said Wanke, about to leave. "I wonder if Lenin ever held a shovel?"

"Your plans," Frank said, "are fine, as usual. The only thing I want you to watch is security. How many people know the proportion of your mix?"

"Ten," Wanke said.

"Keep it that way. Have you got a safe for these plans?"

"No."

"Well, keep them with you and I'll get you one. I need one myself."

"You think things are that bad?"

"I don't know how bad yet, and I haven't got my boys together."

"I understand. That's it?" Wanke asked.

"That's it."

Wanke left.

The motor pool had finally completed a small truck for Crowe. All Frank demanded was a pickup without doors, roof, or running-boards. The head mechanic brought it over, proud of his work, especially the carefully stenciled letters spelling "The Chief" on both sides of the hood.

Crowe inspected the vehicle, started its engine and listened to it for a minute, shut it off, apparently satisfied, and said: "Get rid of those letters on the side."

"Handpainted them myself, chief."

"Well, get rid of them. I don't like to say things twice."

The man did as ordered, brought back the truck, and Crowe headed for Rag Town, a flat stretch along the Colorado River before it entered Black Canyon.

There were tents and shacks as thick as manure in a racing stable. Under every rock, mound, and mesquite bush, whatever offered a particle of shade, were people in pup tents, cars, portable houses, or camping nakedly under the sky, their bedrolls neatly rolled, the wash hanging on frayed lines. There were open fires and women cooking, children darted back and forth from the river like evening flies, and above them in every draw and arroyo were the contractors' tents, neat and more sheltered, and workshops equally efficient, their presence a physical and symbolic omen of work to come—at least it was the only hope for those in Rag Town, who bought water for ten cents a gallon, or drank from the Colorado if they didn't have the dime.

There was a general store and the office of Deputy Wardell Murphy, known affectionately as Murph, since he had a reputation of being more a servant to his community than an enforcer of the laws.

"Any trouble?" Crowe asked Murph as he sat in his small office.

"No legal trouble," Murph answered, "just heat and hunger. When you throwing up Boulder City?"

"I'm starting tomorrow," Crowe said. He pointed at the area below him. "Those people on the ground."

"Yeah?"

"Get some wood slats for them." He wrote a requisition on a note pad. "Draw it from Big Six, keep count of it, and return it to me. I'll give you some trucks."

"Much obliged, chief."

"What about sanitation?"

Murph shrugged his shoulder and pointed at the river.

Once more Crowe scanned the flat area below him.

"Dig some latrines. Over there, and fill them with gravel. Put ten men to work. Don't want a goddamned epidemic before we start."

"Ain't my fault," Murph said. "No money from Big Six. No money from Nevada."

"I didn't blame you, Murph. Now get to work."

He swung into his truck and returned to his office.

"That was the chief, wasn't it?" one bearded man said to another, watching Crowe's car enveloped in dust.

"Yup. Maybe things are beginning to happen."

"Maybe."

16

Civil engineers, Frank Crowe included, had a basic instinct about the profession of architecture. "If you can't draw a hundred-foot span bridging a gorge, mister," he recalled one of his professors saying, "maybe you can draw a doorway to a whorehouse." To utilize tools and logic to build objects which only pleased the eye rather than to design objects of great use seemed foolish in most engineers' eyes. Though Crowe admired Monticello and the Acropolis and the Cathedral at Rheims, after studying photographs of them, and was fully aware that his prejudices were ill founded, he knew they were still there. S. R. de Boer, standing in his office, wavy gray hair, a well-cut suit, a small trimmed mustache, physically qualified for all of Frank Crowe's disdain. But de Boer had come well recommended, he was a man at the top of his field, and his plans which he took from an expensive leather case were as meticulously drawn and as carefully thought out as the combination of the man's shirt and tie.

"We chose the site," de Boer began, "by placing recording thermometers at various locations in the desert, and the chosen area, an alluvial fan, was selected because it constantly read ten degrees lower than any other area."

"Good," Crowe said.

"The plan," de Boer continued, "was drawn to fit the site."

"Here," he pointed, "are the government buildings, and from here will fan out the town. As you will notice, everything is built around great open spaces. Here," he pointed to the east, "I plan a fast-growing belt of trees to separate the town from the desert. You can see that the residential area is laid out in such a manner that it will be possible for children to reach a playground from any part of the town without having to cross a street. Your house, Mr. Crowe, will be located here. . . ."

Crowe studied the plans; he reached for his ruler and his grease pencil. "How long do you expect this project to take, Mr. de Boer?"

"Several years."

"There is no English word 'several.' "

"I don't understand you."

"Several? One? Two? Three?"

"That depends on you, Mr. Crowe. How many men can you allocate to the project?"

"Not many," Crowe said. "In my estimation Boulder City according to your plans should be completed about the same time as I finish the dam."

"You must be joking."

"I am not joking, Mr. de Boer. We will dedicate this dam in 1935."

"Four years; you're mad."

"Perhaps," Crowe said, now drawing on de Boer's plan with his grease pencil.

"What are you doing?" de Boer shouted. "These are *my* plans."

"According to my knowledge," Frank said calmly, "you were paid handsomely by the Bureau of Reclamation for these plans. They are not yours, they are *mine*." Now Frank drew on those sacred plans and showed de Boer his intentions. "This area will be warehouses, and this area will be stores. There'll be no sweeping graceful streets because I can get more houses in a block system."

De Boer grew red in the face. "You have no right, Mr. Crowe. Dr. Elwood Mead has seen these plans himself."

"I'm sure he has, Mr. de Boer, but I am building a *dam* and not a monument to *de Boer* or Dr. Elwood Mead. If you want to take a look at Rag Town or the slums of Vegas you'll be the first to agree that I need housing fast, very fast. I've got no time for trees or lawns or playgrounds."

"What you will do, Mr. Crowe, is build another slum."

"Maybe so, Mr. de Boer. But at least it'll have a roof over its head."

De Boer started to leave, but Frank said, "Wait, don't forget that fancy leather case."

De Boer grabbed it and waved it in the air. "Dr. Mead will learn about this, you can be assured."

"Get out," Crowe said. "I've got work to do."

De Boer left and Frank saw Stubbs, the young engineer, waiting outside. He motioned him into his office. "I saw your plans today, and you talked straight to me, boy. How well did you do in school?"

"I did well, sir."

"All right." Crowe paced the room. "I will form a small corps of staff engineers. I want you to join it."

"Thank you, sir."

"You may not thank me before it's over. You'll just work twice as hard at the same pay."

"I've brought in a lot of corn in my life," Stubbs said, and Crowe smiled.

It was ten-thirty at night when Frank Crowe entered his parlor of the Palm Hotel. There was a light on in the bedroom and he could see Elle dressed in a light robe sitting in front of a mirror brushing her long blond hair.

"Hi, Frank," she said, facing him.

"Don't stop," Frank said, "I love to watch you brush your hair," and Elle continued. He sat on the edge of the bed and carefully unlaced his boots, but his eyes could not leave Elle's hair brushed and counter-brushed, like waves of a good clear ocean falling on a gentle beach. His shoes off, he finally stood and pulled her hair back, exposing her very white neck, and he kissed the nape of her neck, his fingers reveling in the cascading hair around his face.

Elle turned and buried Frank's face in her bosom lightly covered by her robe. He could feel the warmth and the beat of her heart and felt her kissing his forehead gently.

"Well," she said, finally pulling his face away with both hands and looking at him, "how was the day at the office, or am I not allowed to ask that?"

"Come over here," Frank said, and pulled Elle down next to him. He put his arm around her.

"Elle, look."

"What is it, Frank?"

"Don't be afraid."

"Afraid of what?"

"Of me. I know I told you a lot of things in Salt Lake, so did Maria Williams, so did Emma Young, and a lot of it is truth. . . . Don't ever be afraid."

"I'm glad you said that, Frank."

"It's new for me too, Elle. It's all new to me, and there will be times when I won't seem a prince. . . . I *know* you're here. I think about you all day long. I can't wait to get home. . . ."

"I'll be okay, Frank. I'll be okay. Look, look what came by train today." Elle jumped up and pulled her husband to the parlor. "My books, my lessons, look at all those boxes."

Frank saw the cardboard boxes, carefully wrapped and tied with heavy twine. He saw the stamp of the University of Utah on the label. Penurious as he was, he felt that any money spent on education was money well spent. Already Elle had spent two years at the University of Utah pursuing her bachelor's degree in library science, and in the desert she would continue this study by mail.

"Do you think," Elle asked, "after buying all these books we could afford a metal card table? I'm tired of sitting on this floor."

"How much do you think it will cost?"

"A dollar."

"A dollar," Frank teased. "For that I can get a woman."

"For a dollar," Elle said, "you can get this woman."

"A deal."

"And if you'd let me, Frank, I'd give you more than a dollar's worth." She knew what she meant and Frank knew what she meant, but it would take a while yet before Frank could conquer his dollar woman's approach to sex. He fell asleep looking at her hairbrush, which had fallen on the floor. He did not even bother to wind his watch.

17

An employment service had set up offices on L Street in Las Vegas. Leonard Blood, its superintendent, had a small glass-enclosed office behind a large oak counter. Most of the room, painted a hospital green, was filled with rows of backless benches. There were ashtrays and spittoons, and broken venetian blinds barely kept the heat out of the building.

It was 6 A.M. and Crowe and Blood discussed hiring practices.

"River Joe," Frank said, "is rounding up the old-timers. They should be here by eight."

"How many men do you expect?"

"Three hundred fifty to four hundred."

"How many men can you put on now?"

"Five hundred at most."

"That'll give me a hundred jobs, Mr. Crowe."

"I know, Blood. Not much. I want single men, mostly. I got no housing for families yet."

"The married men need the jobs the most."

"I know," Crowe said. "I can't get them to the dam and back. Not yet."

"When are you starting Boulder City?"

"Today."

"That's good. Can I give it to the papers?"

"Sure. Why?"

"You don't know what it's like here. They storm this building every morning like a gale. I've got to give some hope. Some picture."

"I understand," Crowe said. "What about Vegas, what about Nevada? We're going to make them rich. What the hell are they doing?"

"They're building highways to nowhere, Mr. Crowe. They're cleaning up sewers, they're spending every dime they can dig up."

At eight, River Joe brought in his quarry. It was quite a reunion and Frank knew almost every one of the men by name or nickname. Some of them had worked on one dam with him, others two, others all of them.

There were muckers and drillers and cable men and oilers, water boys and carpenters, plumbers, crane operators, high scalers, and common laborers. They looked lean and silent, and their eyes were red from the sun and the endless hand-rolled cigarettes they smoked. After the room quieted down Frank rose. He hated public speaking, but he had no choice.

"I don't know," he said, attempting levity, "why you guys keep coming back for more, but you got the right to ask me the same question, and so we're all here and that is that." He paused. "I know I've said this on every dam, but this time I mean it. This dam will be a bitch. It's eight hundred feet from the canyon wall to the river and Big Red is no ordinary river. It's going to be hotter than Hades and colder than a nun's cunt, and we'll be working twenty-four hours a day." He noticed a stir in the room."There'll be lights at night, and water and safety men and housing and board by the company as soon as I can get it built. The pay will be three-fifty a day. One-sixty to the company for room and board, fifty cents a day extra pay for men on the canyon floor.

"Special trades get special wages. I'll have a list of your supervisors on Blood's desk tonight, so report to him tomorrow.

"Any questions?"

Frank scanned the room. He knew these men; there'd be no questions and there were none.

"One more thing," Frank said after waiting for questions which did not materialize. "There'll be over six thousand men on this dam when we get going full blast. That's more men than we've ever had. All of you guys have worked dams before, worked with me before, and you know we'll get a lot of greenhorns, and smartasses, and reds." There was venom in the pronunciation of that word. "We've always brought them around and we'll bring them around *this* time, but they're tougher and better organized. I don't have to say any more."

Crowe was out of the room and on the road toward the dam before River Joe could reach the Eldorado Saloon.

Lewis Construction Company had already set up its camp above Rag Town. They were involved in building the railroad along the dam site, and their facilities included a mess hall, which fed 350 men, and a series of tents, each of them housing 4 men. Much grumbling arose from this site about both the poor quality of the food and about the unbearable heat in the tents.

Crowe listened to these complaints and made good use of them. He had a thousand-man mess hall under construction in Boulder City, he was building houses, and though he had rejected de Boer's noble plan for a model city, he still incorporated the best of that plan and added a measure of his own decency. "A man can't work on an empty stomach or without a good night's sleep," he had told Elle one night, and this credo prevailed.

Always a man to kill two birds with one stone if it was possible, he called in Arthur Anderson of Anderson Provision Company to his office.

Anderson was a massive, ill-proportioned man with thick arms and legs and a head which seemed to sit on neckless shoulders. He wore a blue suit for this occasion. He was known to be a devout Mormon, tithing to his church regularly from the healthy income of a well-run farm in the Moapa Valley.

"You come well recommended," Crowe told Anderson, "but I can't feed six thousand men with good recommendations. I need to know the details of your offer."

Anderson, in his mid-fifties, looked in vain for a chair and finally sat down on Crowe's desk top.

"I can feed each man on your dam site for a dollar a day. Breakfast, lunch, and dinner."

"And what will your profit be, Mr. Anderson?"

"Twenty cents a head. Twelve cents for me and eight cents for my church."

"And what kind of meals will you provide?"

Anderson looked at Crowe. "The best."

"Where will you get your meat?"

"In Reno. I figure a twenty-thousand-pound lot twice a week when you're in production."

"What about flour?" Crowe asked.

"From Enterprise and Ogden, Utah."

"Potatoes?"

"From Hurricane, Utah," Anderson answered. "I'll get my vegetables and fruits and eggs from L.A. and Reno, from southern Utah and the Moapa and Vegas valleys."

"Your own place," Crowe said.

"I grow the best, sir."

"So I've heard."

"How about milk?" Crowe continued.

"From the Moapa Valley. Charley Wills will build a dairy."

"How about poultry?"

"I'll get what I can locally, otherwise Reno."

Crowe studied the man, slightly sweating.

"Have you seen the mess hall at Lewis Construction?" Frank asked.

"I have," said Anderson.

"What do you think of it?"

"Not much, sir. I figure they're feeding them at forty cents a head."

100

"Is that the kind of operation you plan to run?"

"No sir."

"That's good," said Crowe.

There was silence in the office. Finally Anderson said, "Well, what do you say?"

"What kind of help are you planning on?"

"White help, some Orientals."

"What about niggers?"

"No niggers."

"What about desserts?"

"Twice a day."

"What about holidays?"

"Turkeys at Christmas and Thanksgiving. Ham on Easter."

Finally Crowe faced Anderson squarely. "Mr. Anderson, the Big Six Companies do not intend to make *one* dime on the mess hall. You will be under *my* scrutiny, under my bosses' scrutiny, under the Bureau's scrutiny. One valid complaint from a worker and you are out."

"I understand." Anderson almost smiled now. "We have a deal then?"

"We have *no* deal yet, Mr. Anderson." Frank paced the room. "I have nothing against Mormons. You are a hard-working, decent people."

"Thank you."

"However, I have no weakness for *any* religion. I will offer you ninety-two cents a head. How you square this with your church is your business. I am in the dam-building business; I am not a Mormon missionary."

Anderson's face reddened. "Ninety-two cents. That's not much for what you ask."

"For that I want an eighty-cent spread. What you do with the twelve-cent profit is between you and Angel Moroni."

Anderson was flustered, clearly. He knew that in his hands was the opportunity to become a rich man, but he pined for the riches he had already counted on. He was also a realist and accepted.

"There is one other thing," Crowe said almost casually. "You Mormons are good irrigators. Do you know the term 'reservoir severance'?"

"No sir, I don't."

"Reservoir severance means that when this dam is built, the reservoir behind it will be flooded. One hundred forty thousand acres of land will be flooded."

"Good lord," Anderson said, "that much?"

"That much," said Crowe, "but it's marginal land—grazing pasture, a little mining, a little archeology. We will inundate St. Thomas and

101

Kaolin and a portion of Overton, all good Mormon communities. And the government is prepared to compensate them fairly for that land."

"You can't put a price on generations of labor on that land."

"That's very true, Mr. Anderson, and you can't put a price on a man who gives half his lifetime building dams."

"Does the government have the *right* to take our land?"

"The government does, Mr. Anderson."

"Why?"

"Because St. Thomas has 247 souls and Kaolin has 100 souls, Bonelli's Ferry has one family and you put that against the thousands of families that are flooded out each year in Coachella and Imperial and you have the right of the government."

"I can't fight you or the government, it seems, Mr. Crowe."

"That's right."

"So why bring it up?"

"Because I need your help. I know you are an elder in your church. The Mormons will fight, the conservationists will fight; already I'm getting letters from sob sisters in Vermont and Maine who've never been further west than Boston, worrying about the flora and fauna of southern Nevada."

Now Anderson took the initiative. "I am a Mormon bishop. I am proud to be a Mormon and honored to be chosen a bishop. I don't care what your beliefs are, or whether you have any. I will deliver your food for ninety-two cents a head. What the Mormons will do about your reservoir severance is your problem, not mine."

"Your case," Frank Crowe said, "is well stated, and I apologize for overreaching the bounds of this discussion."

"Your apology is accepted, Mr. Crowe. I too like a man who dares to say he's wrong."

Anderson left the office. Crowe felt he was a man who could deliver. He was tired and now wished for a chair himself.

"The burdens of command," he had remembered Heinlein lecturing once, "are damnable and lonely, and when that feeling overtakes you, go out and chop some wood or drain the oil from your crankcase."

Frank Crowe did neither, but drove to Searchlight and drank himself into oblivion.

18

Everything was poised at the dam site. Huge electrical compressors, muckers, and shovels stood like mute iron dinosaurs waiting for electricity to reach the dam, and on June 20, Crowe, raising his binoculars, could watch the row of power poles appear over the horizon.

Three days later, Ferguson, the supervisor of Interstate Power Company, reached the dam site and it was a smiling Crowe who clasped the tall man's hand.

"You made it in record time," Frank said.

"We got the word you had your doubts about us California boys."

"I'll have to refigure that one," said Crowe, but he had hardly time for the handshake. With the power he needed he could get to work.

By July 3 Crowe had thirteen hundred men on the dam site, working three shifts. Crowe had flooded the dam with lights, using thousands of large light bulbs in inverted dishpans. Piping systems were run over the Black Canyon cliffs to carry compressed air for the scaling jobs, monstrous electrical shovels started cleaning out the adits of the diversion tunnels while others peeled out the muck along the cliffside construction roads. Building was under way on the first twelve government houses in Boulder City and B. O. Siegfers of Salt Lake City was low bidder for the administration and municipal building in Boulder City. The Big Six announced plans for a clubhouse for recreation and sports and hired Frank Moran, former heavyweight "white hope" boxer, as the director.

It was the first time Frank had taken Elle to the dam site, the night it was fully lit. They both stood in awe as suddenly the canyon walls, the river, the stark black granite shone under the thousands of bulbs.

"It looks like a roofless cathedral," Elle said, holding on to Frank, watching the awesome gorge eight hundred feet below her.

Frank stared himself and was silent for a long time. Finally he said, " 'Cathedral' may be an apt word, Elle. We've already lost twenty-six men on the job." Elle looked at Frank and saw the pain in his face.

"Two from natural causes, five from job accidents, sixteen from heat prostration, one damned fool went over the road drunk, and two drowned swimming in the river. It's those five I've got on *my* neck."

Elle knew of Frank's fetish about safety. Although he drove his men brutally, and cared basically little about the adequacy of their pay, he held their lives very gingerly in his hands.

"Deaths from construction," he said, almost to himself, "are always stupidity. I plan-check every blueprint, I've got safety men, supervisors who should know better . . ."

"Five men is not a lot of men," Elle said. "You can't blame yourself for every accident, Frank. . . ."

"I know that, Elle. There are things I *can't* blame myself for—the heat, the river, a man's constitution—but every shovel that crushes a man, every cableway that snaps, every power line gone wild, that's *my* fault. I can't be over the whole dam site all the time. I keep yelling at the supervisors that flesh and machinery don't mesh. . . . There are a lot of dumb sons of bitches under those hard hats. . . ."

Elle sensed his frustrations and knew she could do little to change his feelings. Finally she said, "You were going to show me our house."

"I shall," Frank said, and helped her down from the canyon wall.

Frank drove Elle to Boulder City. He showed her the mess hall which could seat a thousand men. She marveled at its cleanliness, the well-scrubbed sinks, the fly-screened cooling areas for stores, the spotless cups and saucers and plates of heavy white china.

"This is the greatest killer of them all," Crowe said. "This mess hall."

"Why?"

"We hire some poor stiff in the morning. He hasn't eaten a decent meal in weeks. His first meal is lunch. It's like Christmas. He fills his plate. Three pork chops, one hamburger, potatoes, beans, rolls, butter, pie, salad, soup; he can hardly carry his tray. I can always tell a new man. He eats like an animal. Doesn't look right or left. He *is* an animal, a hungry animal, and then he hits the dam site, a hundred twenty, a hundred twenty-eight degrees some days. The blood drains to his stomach. He collapses. Some come around with ice water; most of them don't."

"How terrible," Elle said. "Can't you stop that?"

"How? I can't put safety men in the mess hall."

"Put up signs. Tag them," Elle said. "Can't you put them with some old-timers?"

"We do, Elle. We try. You can't stop a ravenous man from eating."

"You can stop him from going into the sun."

"The Big Six Companies, Elle, are not in the restaurant business."

It was an answer, Elle thought, not much of an answer, but it was the kind that she now knew had a finality which stopped further questioning.

Frank drove Elle to Government Hill. He passed along a row of almost-completed hollow-tile houses. On a small knoll sat Crowe's house. It was the biggest house in Boulder City. It had three bedrooms and the best view of the valley. Behind it stood the massive water tank which would serve the city.

The house was almost finished but still raw; Elle could barely make out the configuration of the rooms.

"This is the living room, Elle; our bedroom is up there." His flashlight traced a pattern of two-by-fours, and then he shone the light outside the house, searching and finally finding a small seedling pine.

"There it is."

"What?"

"The tree."

"What tree?"

"You see it? A little pine."

"I do."

"That's Wanke's work. Does it on all the jobs."

"How sweet."

"Yeah," Frank said. "The good old professor."

"Turn off the light, Frank." He obeyed.

"Put your arms around me," and he obeyed again.

"It's going to be a beautiful house, Frank."

"Not beautiful. I hate hollow tile."

"Beautiful, Frank."

He leaned down and kissed Elle.

"You got spunk, girl. I'll tell you that."

"I got a roof and a pine and a supervising engineer."

Crowe watched the headlights of a truck searching up the road to his house. The truck stopped and a man got out holding a flashlight in one hand, a gun in the other.

"Who's there?" he yelled. It was Murph, who had come from Rag Town to assume the role of chief of police.

"It's me, Crowe," Frank yelled and Murph trained his beam on Frank's face.

"Hi, chief." He holstered his gun, and puffed up the hill.

"Thought I'd seen some lights at your place. Didn't want nobody to steal yer blind."

"Much obliged," Frank said. "This is my wife, Elle."

"Happy to meet you. Nice place you got here."

"I think so," Elle said.

"When will you finish fencing the city?" Crowe asked.

"Next week."

"Good. One road in and the same road out."

"Yes sir."

"No booze or firearms in the town."

"I know," Murph said.

"And that includes you and your boys."

"No guns?"

"No guns."

"Jesus, Mr. Crowe, sorry, ma'am."

"If they can patrol all of London with a night stick, I think we can manage in Boulder City."

"Whatever you say, chief. I ain't much for shooting people myself."

"I know that, Murph, but some of those young bucks you've got working for you have seen too many Western movies."

"Yeah." Murph smiled. "They're gonna miss those handtooled belts and holsters. How about night sticks?"

"You can carry night sticks."

"Better get on with my rounds. Be seeing you folks."

Crowe watched Murph drive off. "You can always mend a broken skull, but it's hard to plug a hole in the liver," Frank said.

Elle was shivering and Frank put his arms around her, but she was not shivering from the slight breeze which played about the empty house, but from the constant talk of death and guns, of shots and broken skulls, heat prostration, drownings.

"What is it, Elle, you're shaking?"

"It's nothing, Frank, it's nothing."

"I'll be glad when we move up here. That gate down there will give me lots of peace of mind," but even this statement did not help Elle. She was not afraid, she only feared the fears of Frank.

That first Fourth of July in 1931 was a day neither for fear nor for work, but one of celebration. Outside its national significance it was this day which gave hope to the locals and the transients in Las Vegas because news arrived that Congress had finally signed the appropriation bill for the construction of the dam. This meant jobs, for sure, it meant furniture, a roof, an occasional steak, a bottle of booze, a fancy basinette with silk ribbons. A deafening din roared through the town as every horn, whistle, bell, and firecracker went off. Everyone took to the streets. Fremont Street looked like Broadway; the fire department bellowed through downtown, sirens screaming, bells ringing, and though nationwide Prohibition was still in force, it had scarcely ever been observed in Vegas, and today defiance was the theme as saloons were flooded day and night.

The *Review Journal* was full of enticements for Independence Day. The Meadows, owned by the Coruero brothers, offered "Will Cowan and his entertainers and a Spectacular Review." The Shady

106

Spot (one block west of Charleston) competed with chicken dinners at seventy-five cents and dancing to the tunes of Dusty Rhoads's orchestra. Lorenzi Lake Park was having a big celebration, with fireworks in the evening, and the Blue Heaven offered a free barbecue all day and evening. There was the new Pair O'Dice, The Rainbow, The Big Four, and the Las Vegas Club. And in his office was Crowe with Williams pacing the floor.

"How come you're still working?" Williams asked. "It's a holiday."

"I know. Just listen." Crowe opened the window of his office. "What do you hear."

"Firecrackers."

"Right."

"Jesus, it's the Fourth of July."

"You know what they make firecrackers of?"

"What kind of stupid question is that, Frank? Of course I know how they make firecrackers."

"You got your dynamite in check?"

"Every stick. Color coded daily, just like you said."

"Some Wobbly," Frank said, "some red son of a bitch, can put a lot of firecrackers together and give us hell on this dam."

"That's right, Frank, and some other crazy son of a bitch could roll a 120-millimeter howitzer up this hill and blast us out of the canyon."

"I feel it," Crowe said. "I feel something in the wind, Jack. I can't put my finger on it, but there are creaks in this machinery. I've got thirteen hundred stiffs now but it isn't all oiled yet."

"Look," Williams said, "I've got to blast two hundred feet of rock tomorrow. I ain't the supervising engineer, you are. I've got a table at the Vegas Club and I'm taking the missus to dinner and Wanke will be there with his wife, and I think you ought to knock off and bring your wife too. Hardly ever see that little girl."

Frank thought of Elle shivering in his arms the night before, and agreed.

"We'll be there, Jack, we'll be there."

The phone rang. "Crowe here," Frank answered.

"Mr. Crowe, this is Barnes in San Francisco."

"How are you, Mr. Barnes?" Crowe looked at Williams.

"Well, you squeaked by this one. I heard on the radio that Congress finally passed that bill."

"The news even got up here, Mr. Barnes."

"Yeah, yeah, well, I guess it would."

"You ought to come up," Frank said. "It's just a pleasant hundred twenty-five degrees."

"I'll be up, I'll be up. Oh, incidentally, Frank."

107

"Yes?"

"I'll be sending up my boy. Put 'im on as a junior engineer, and kind of watch out for him."

"What the hell is a junior engineer?" Frank asked. "I'm not building a junior dam."

"I'm sending him up," Barnes said and hung up.

"Junior engineer." Crowe spat out the words.

"Who's that?"

"Henry Barnes's little boy. Shit."

"I'll put 'im in Tunnel 4. Might get lost in there."

"There is no room for nepotism on a dam site," Crowe said.

"You guys from Vermont." Williams laughed. "Did they teach you those big words on purpose?"

Elle was dressed in a white blouse and a white skirt; she had a red, white, and blue corsage of carnations pinned to the edge of the collar of her blouse, which Frank thought was buttoned a little too low. She was beautiful. Simply beautiful, bathed in the back light of a flaming sunset and the vitality of enjoying her own good looks.

"And what makes you think we're going on the town, Elle Crowe?"

"There are questions, Mr. Crowe, which even *you* can't ask."

"I see." Frank kissed her. "What is that smell?"

"Eau de cologne. Bought it myself. Worked eight hours at the library and got paid."

"And where did you put the cologne?"

"At all the strategic points, as you engineers would say."

Frank slapped her fanny. "You keep this up and I can get you a better job than the library."

Frank showered, and Elle had laid out fresh denims for him, clean socks, a gingham shirt. Before they left their rooms Frank said seriously, "I've got to ask you a favor."

"What is it?"

"Don't ask me to dance."

"Why not?"

"Because I don't know how to dance."

Elle looked into her husband's eyes. "I'll never do anything to hurt you, Frank."

"I know, Elle. I know that."

The Vegas Club was a barnlike structure, its new beams festooned with red, white, and blue ribbon. Large paper rosettes of the same colors were nailed to the uprights. There were American flags, flags of Nevada, even a faded picture of Hoover looking as serious as ever.

The room was filled with workers and their families, most of them

108

drinking beer, eating fried chicken with their hands, many of them singing, others dancing on a small parquet floor to the music of a loud but poorly coordinated six-piece band.

Whenever Crowe entered a room full of his employees he encountered an involuntary silence accorded an admiral or general, but the feeling this evening was different, because their eyes were all trained on Elle. She was almost regal the way she walked at Frank's side, and yet there was a simplicity about her; her slightly freckled face, her playful mouth softened what otherwise might simply have been a stark beauty.

"That's Crowe's wife," she heard someone say.

"Quite a looker," she picked up from another table. Someone whistled and finally Frank spotted Williams and Wanke and joined them at their table.

"That was quite an entrance," Maria said. "You really wowed them, honey."

Elle blushed and Frank beamed. Why had he waited so long to do this? he wondered. He truly basked in his wife's beauty.

"You see, we showed them," Elle whispered in his ear, and Frank squeezed her hand.

"Bourbon," Frank ordered, "make it a round for the table."

"You sure you're all right?" Wanke asked. "Heat isn't getting to you?"

Frank smiled and Elle thanked Wanke for the tree.

"Well, that's quite all right, except there's a story that goes with it. . . ."

"What's that?"

"If that tree grows big enough to hold Frank before we finish, we'll hang him from it."

Everyone laughed except Elle, who heard that death rattle again.

"When do you figure we'll be moving to Boulder?" Maria Williams asked Frank.

"A week," he said, "without water."

"I'd move in without floors. Somebody at the hotel next to us plays cowboy music twenty-four hours a day."

"Why don't you do something about it, Jack?" Crowe asked.

"Jack can't hear it, he's so deaf from all that blasting over the years, isn't that right, Jack?"

"What did you say?" Jack answered and everyone laughed.

Wanke turned to Elle. "Hear you been working at the library."

"Part time only. I'm studying library science at Utah, by correspondence."

"Heard that too. That's a good field."

"Maybe I could get a library started in Boulder City."

"There it goes," Frank said. "Another requisition."

"You'd be surprised," Wanke said, "but there're a lot of readers in this crew."

"I didn't know that."

"Construction stiffs have always been readers, like sailors."

"I'll buy that," Crowe said. "When I was at sea, the biggest fights started over a book someone 'borrowed.' Well, honey," Crowe said, "as soon as Mr. Williams gets through those canyons, bring up that library idea to me."

"About what time?" Elle kidded, and everyone raised a glass in salute.

"You know," Eva Wanke said, "if I wasn't so busy having kids all the time, I'd like to help you at that library."

Frank studied Elle's face, but she betrayed nothing. "Good," said Elle, "but first I've got to learn the Library of Congress system and then I've got to figure out a way to get some books."

"Write Mr. de Boer," Frank suggested. "Tell him you're building a library in the park."

"What park?" Williams asked.

"The one on his plans. Jesus, I've never seen a more impractical man in my life."

There were more rounds of bourbon and the noise got louder, the music faster, the dancers more raucous. Crowe could feel the eyes on Elle; he watched men half drunk just openly stare, and though his New England propriety told him to punch the son of a bitch in the face, he had to admit that he enjoyed it, that the very cleavage of his wife's bosom, which was distinct, no longer worried him, but gave him a feeling of pride. "This is my woman," he wanted to shout, "mine," and he remembered the cheerleaders at the University of Vermont, those pretty, innocent nymphs, whose skirts always rose well above their knees as they led the yells, and whose affection was saved for football players, for rich young bucks with cars—new cars, even, some of them.

"I want to go home, Elle," he said finally and Elle agreed. They shook hands all around and left, and Frank felt the stares that still followed Elle. He could not remember when he had wanted her so desperately, and Elle could sense it.

They walked briskly the three blocks, Vegas still 110 degrees, the streets packed with drunks and revelers.

Frank almost tore Elle's clothes from her body as she sat on the bed facing him.

"Wait, Frank," she said. "Relax, relax."

"I can't wait, Elle."

"You can, honey. It can be better than you think."

110

"It couldn't be better than it is, Elle."

They made love. Quickly as was Frank's pattern.

Before they went to sleep Elle, remembering the night Frank had not come home, said quickly, "I'm going to shock you, Frank."

"Why?"

"I'll never ask you why you don't come home because that's none of my business. But sometime, sometime . . ."

"Go on."

"Bring home a bottle of bourbon. Bring home two. I'll get drunk with you. Really drunk."

"Elle?"

"And then I might even teach you how to dance." Elle turned over and was quickly asleep, but Frank found it difficult to follow suit.

He looked at her beautifully rounded shoulders, her long lean back divided by her curved spine, he stared at her buttocks, small and firm, and her lean long legs. He ran his fingers gently down her back and kissed it, and then covered her and himself with the single sheet which lay at the foot of the bed.

19

Detroit was still cold in March. The wind from the river went through a man's marrow, and living in a railroad flat heated only with stolen coal, for which there was much competition in 1931, was torture. Hans and Herman Schroeder were the sons of Helmuth and Lisa Schroeder. Hans was twenty-six, Herman twenty-four, and both their parents were dead. Their mother had died of consumption when Hans was twelve, their father was killed at the River Rouge a year ago when he fell under a drop forge. The Ford boys who investigated the accident had claimed he was drunk, and therefore the family was not eligible for death benefits.

Hans doubted that his father had been drunk, knowing that his Germanic background would allow him to drink only on Saturday nights. But where Hans felt only deep anger and hatred for the company, and sorrow for his father, whom he deeply loved, his brother

111

Herman felt the death as symbolic. He needed a martyr for the cause, which was labor organizing. Both boys continued to work at Ford, Hans on engine blocks and Herman as a messenger, which was a difficult job for a boy who had one wooden leg. Though Hans was able to slug his way through the years of hardship and brutal labor, sustained in part by his youth, clean-cut good looks, and a fair share of women and booze, his brother Herman continued to become an inferno of hatred and bitterness.

It was cruel, of course, to be known as Gimpy, as Peg Leg, as "that crippled punk." These were phrases which opened and reopened new wounds daily. Still he found some salvation in fighting the system by immersing himself in books written by men who, for one reason or other, also were like outcasts of the world. He became a student of Marx and Lenin, and read the tomes of Trotsky. He was an easy mark for the IWW, which thrived on men like Herman, since their aim, the destruction of capitalism "by force," matched on a grander scale the same revolt they experienced in themselves.

Nightly Herman would detail to Hans the evils foisted upon them by society, the injustices around them, the murder of their father, but Hans, usually exhausted from a twelve-hour day, would simply say, "I ain't gonna change the world and neither are you."

He would storm out of their three-room flat and drink at Casey's, only to return at eleven seeing his brother still reading, his books spread on the worn oilcloth of the kitchen table. . . . "Just listen to what Marx said," Herman would plead with his brother feverishly, and begin reading . . . but Hans, half drunk, would undress for bed and ignore his brother.

"I don't understand them big words," he'd say.

"Because you're too stupid to listen."

"You call me stupid once more and I'll kick you the hell out of here."

"Force, force, that's all you got to sell."

"Bullshit. I've been listening at Casey's and the Rouge. They don't like you reds, you Wobbly bastards. You know that?"

"Sure I know that. They're afraid. Afraid for their lousy jobs, afraid to stand up to the foreman, the supervisor."

"Afraid hell, Herman. There's a depression. Have you heard? We're lucky we've got jobs."

"The depression is artificial. Old Henry Ford ain't going on them fancy safaris out of losses. . . . ."

"I don't give a damn *where* Henry Ford goes. I'm going to bed."

It was only innate decency that kept Hans with Herman. His father had told him in the emergency room before he died, "Take care of Herman . . ." Those had been his last words in that cold ice-green

112

room before they put a sheet over his head and wheeled him out to make room for the next victim of the Industrial Revolution.

Hans was the first to lose his job. His foreman handed him the dreaded blue slip on Monday morning and he received his final pay that night. Much of it he spent at Casey's, surrounded by other men, most of whom had met a similar fate. But he quickly obtained a job as a night clerk in the Hotel Detroit; the pay was meager but the hours prevented the nightly encounters with Herman, since Hans now worked from six in the evening to six in the morning.

It was only eight weeks after he was terminated that he watched his brother approach him behind the night desk of the seedy commercial hotel on Fourth Street. He knew that disjointed walk like the workings of his clenched fist as he watched his brother in the shadowy street.

Herman entered and stood against the counter behind which Hans worked.

"I've got to talk to you," he said.

"What are *you* doing here?"

"I've been fired." He reached into his pocket and put a red slip on the counter.

"You got a red slip?"

"What else?" Herman said, almost proudly.

"Do you know what that means?"

"Sure, I can't ever work in this town again."

"That's right, you dumb bastard."

The phone rang at the switchboard and Hans manipulated the wires which made the connections.

"So that's what your Wobbly friends did for you, eh?"

"I got another job already."

"*What* job?"

"They want me to go to Vegas. As an organizer. I get fifty bucks a month and expenses. They got thousands of men there, dying like flies. They said the Boulder Dam was ready for a union."

Again the phone rang. Hans yelled, "Hotel Detroit," then, "No, god damn it, I don't have no extra pillows," then he pulled out the plug. He walked around the desk and directed Herman to a stained sofa in the middle of the small dark lobby.

"Sit down," he yelled, and Herman did.

"I promised Pa I'd look after you, and I mean to keep my promise."

"I ain't asking you to come."

Hans ignored the statement. "You keep making a big hero out of Pa, well, I'll tell you he'd turn over in his grave if he knew one of his boys got a red slip."

"Pa never read a book in his life."

113

"That's right," Hans said. "I don't know whether he knew *how* to read, but he took care of us as best as he could and I aim to keep my word."

"There's lots of work on the dam," Herman said. "Don't matter to me if you want to come."

"Lots of work till you red bastards screw it up, is that what you mean?"

"There's lots of work, and when I'm through, you'll get a decent wage."

"Sure. Sure. Herman Schroeder, the Big Labor Hero. Shit."

Again the phone rang and Hans ran behind the desk and pulled out the plug angrily; he took the phone off the hook and smashed it against the switchboard, then opened a drawer with a key and withdrew $2. He left a note. It said, "That's what you owe me," then he placed the note in the drawer and locked it and placed the key on a hook under the desk.

"Let's go home," Hans said.

"You're working till six," Herman said.

"I just quit." He held up $2. "Severance pay. Two dollars."

"How much money is in that till?" Herman asked.

"How do I know?"

"Take it. Take it all."

"Is that what they teach you at them meetings? Get out of here," Hans yelled and Herman stood up. They both walked out of the hotel into the freezing Michigan night. Finally Hans could not stand the sight of his brother and ran off. He yelled back, "I'll see you in the morning." They had just delivered some soft pretzels at Casey's and Hans shared one and a pitcher of beer with Ruthie, who later shared her bed in return.

It was seven in the morning when Hans returned to the railroad flat. A weak sunrise came through the haze and smoke. Herman was sitting at the kitchen table, writing, drinking coffee.

"And how do you propose we get to Vegas?"

"I can buy a truck from the Wobblies for a hundred bucks."

"And who's got a hundred bucks?"

"We'll sell everything we've got."

Hans looked at the two shabby rooms beyond the kitchen. There was a bedroom, a parlor of sorts. Furniture scuffed, curtains torn, naked bulbs on long black wires, a few piles of clothes, Herman's books, Hans's tool chest.

"What have we got?"

"The wall clock, the furniture, the piano."

"Shit," Hans said. "Couldn't get twenty bucks for all that."

114

"Pa's watch," Herman said. "It's gold."

"I ain't selling Pa's watch."

"Then hock it, god damn it," Herman shouted. "You had a whole drawerful of cash last night and you wouldn't take it."

"That's right, and I ain't selling Pa's watch."

"He gave it to *us*. It ain't your watch no more than it's mine."

Hans walked to a commode in the bedroom. In the top right-hand drawer, wrapped in a clean white handkerchief, was the gold watch. Hans took it out and opened the cover. On its inside was engraved, "To Helmuth Schroeder for 25 years of service to Ford Motor Company."

"Here," he said, handing the watch to Herman. "*You* pawn it and *you* better keep that ticket, and when you get your hundred dollars together and buy your car, pick me up at Casey's or you can go alone. It don't matter to me no more." He stormed out of the house.

Promptly at six the next evening he watched Herman enter the speakeasy. He joined his brother outside. There stood a battered old truck, the fenders wired to the chassis, the headliner in the cab torn, the leatherette seats showing more springs than burlap; one headlight was missing.

Hans walked around the miserable little vehicle.

"Who sold you this pile of junk?"

"What did you expect for a hundred dollars? A Cadillac limousine?"

"I bet they're still laughing. Does it run?"

"Like a clock," Herman said."

"Don't mention clocks to me, or watches. Pa's watch *ran*. I know that. I always kept it wound."

"Yeah, the guy at the pawn shop noticed that," Herman said.

"Start 'er up," Hans commanded and Herman choked the engine and the truck did start.

"Son of a bitch," Hans said, his spirit lifting. "Well, Herman," he said, slapping his brother on the back, "I've never been past Flint, Michigan. Vegas, here we come!" He jumped alongside his brother and they drove out of Detroit and headed west. Not once did either of them look back, but both noticed that slowly the air turned purer, the landscape became greener, and Herman was chanting one of Joe Hill's songs:

> *Work and pray, live on hay,*
> *You'll get pie in the sky when you die.*

They drove from Detroit to Chicago that first night, passing Somerset at ten in the evening, stopping in Coldwater for coffee and dough-

115

nuts, again in Michigan City. They could smell the acrid air of Gary, Indiana, before they passed the huge steel mills, many of them idle, and finally arrived in Chicago the following morning at seven.

"Let's look at the lake," Hans suggested, but Herman said, "This ain't no sightseeing trip. I've got to get to Vegas while it's still hot. Can't pull no strike when the weather is good."

"I want to see the lake, god damn it," and they drove toward Lake Michigan. Hans went to the water's edge, took off one shoe and sock and stuck his foot into the murky water. He looked around him at the vastness of this body of water, at the countless multistoried apartments lining the shores. Finally he put back his sock and shoe and returned to the car.

"Bet Pa never stuck his foot in Lake Michigan."

Herman was silent, then said, "We've got to get to this garage. I've got chits from the union for gas. They'll give it to us."

They found the station near the slaughterhouse district and the operator eyed Herman suspiciously when he presented the chit.

"Where you headin'?"

"Vegas."

"In *that?*" He pointed at the truck.

Hans grew impatient. "Just fill it up, dad, and never mind the palaver."

"You pinkos are all the same."

Hans roared out of the truck and stood next to the operator of the station, towering over him.

"Don't call me no pinko."

"Where did you get these?" The attendant shoved the chits into Hans's face.

"My brother is a pinko, I ain't. And wash that windshield."

"How far to Newton, Iowa?" Herman asked.

"Three hundred twenty miles," the operator said, "and you'll never make it in *this* in one day. Try and get to Homestead or South Amana. With a German face like yours, those Amanists'll take you in like brothers."

"Who are the Amanists?" Herman asked.

"It's some German religion. They got a communal farm out there. Probably all sleep with each other's wives when they ain't tilling their fields."

Hans went to the rest room, stole a fan belt on the way back, and the two continued.

After they had cleared the outskirts of Chicago, Hans showed his brother the fan belt.

Herman looked at it and asked, "If you don't mind stealing the fan belt, why leave all that money in the till?"

116

"That man at the hotel never did me no wrong. Used to bring me a doughnut at midnight. Didn't have to, but he did. That son of a bitch in Chicago called me a pinko. Almost busted his jaw."

They rode on, the landscape more pastoral as they passed through Mendota, Sheffield, Wilton Junction. Herman was driving and Hans watched the temperature gauge, which was rising rapidly.

"You got any water in the truck?" Hans asked.

"No, why?"

"Because this engine is beginning to boil."

"Shit. There's nothing around here." Herman pulled the truck off the road and the landscape was hill-less and endless and barren. Steam rose from the engine after they stopped.

"Well," said Hans, "only one thing to do." Hans got out of the car and opened the hood. He loosened the radiator cap with the tail of his coat and waited for a cloud of steam to pass. Then he took off the cap to the radiator, stood on the fender, opened his fly, and pissed into the spout.

"You're next," Hans said, and waited while his brother followed suit. He could not bear to see the top of Herman's fruitwood leg, which he knew would show when he dropped his pants.

It was almost seven o'clock when they reached South Amana and a filling station. They sensed the prosperity of the town: the carefully painted homes, the trim lawns, the abandon with which people used electricity in their homes, their porches. Great stands of trees.

"Need gas?" an elderly man said, carrying a flashlight.

"We need gas and we need water and I need a place to fix a hose."

"Ja, she's steaming pretty good!"

Hans got out of the car to stretch and the old man recognized the strong Teutonic features of the boy's face, the long hard body, the blue eyes.

"You a German boy?"

"Schroeder," Hans said. "Hans Schroeder. This is my brother Herman."

"We're glad to have you," the old man said. "This is a German community."

"So we heard."

Herman had also left the cab and limped toward the old man. He dug his gas scrip from his pockets.

"You take these?"

"What are they?"

"That's scrip for gas. You send it to Detroit and you get paid."

"I don't send *nothing* to Detroit and get paid," the old man said.

117

"Guess we can't buy no gas."

The old man eyed Hans. "You good with tools?"

"Yes sir," Hans answered. "Got my own set."

"You pull that transmission on that Dodge," he pointed to the garage, "and you get her running and I'll give you gas and a water hose and you can sleep in our barn and eat at the church."

"I'll work all night, mister," Hans said, "but I got to eat first."

The old man smiled. "Ja. You're German all right. Always got to fill that belly."

"Ain't eaten since I left Chicago."

"All right. You leave your truck here and walk down two blocks. You'll see our church. In the back is the kitchen. Here, I'll give you a note. They'll feed you like you never et before in your life."

"Much obliged."

The old man had told the truth, for in a simple stark room filled with oak benches and oilcloth-covered tables and graced with pictures of Jesus and a hand-carved cross, several pink-cheeked German girls, stocky and square, fed them roast and potatoes, vegetables as green as a violent sea, blueberry pie, and milk.

Hans and Herman ate silently. It was the best food they had ever tasted in their lives.

Finally they had finished supper and several of the girls who had been watching them, giggling, came over to clear the table.

"You eat like this every day?" Hans asked.

"Ja. You should of come for breakfast. We make the best Apfel Pfannkuchen."

"Sounds good. Maybe we'll get another note from the old man at the station."

"If you don't," the second girl said, "see Pastor Kleiner, he's my father. We never turn down strangers."

"Much obliged," Hans said, and both of them left for the gas station.

"The Amana Society," Hans mused. "Why don't you Wobblies start something like this?"

"Religion is the opiate of the people," Herman said.

"Yeah. I'd like to get that opiate three times a day."

Hans looked around the tidy garage and fetched his tool box. Slowly he disassembled the rusty transmission of the aging Dodge while Herman dipped the parts first in gasoline, then in oil.

"Don't oil them till you've got that rust off," Hans chided his brother. "And lay these parts out in the order I give 'em to you." Herman followed orders, and unbeknown to them the old man watched in the shadows of the garage and finally returned to his well-scrubbed home.

"That's quite a mechanic out there," he told his wife. "Wish I could keep him here."

"Ja, you're thinking of Katie, ain't you?"

"I wasn't thinking of Katie or nothing. Go to sleep."

It was five in the morning when Hans and Herman finished the transmission and the old man, already up and shaved, inspected their work.

"Ja, that's good. That's a good job, mister."

"I'd better get to my hose," Hans said.

"No, you better get some sleep. I'll fix your hose and fill up the tank. After a couple of hours you can hit the road."

They slept on haystacks and it was the most delightful aroma Hans could imagine as he dozed off thinking of rosy-cheeked girls and Apfel Pfannkuchen.

They woke at eight and Hans was the first one out of the barn. He went to the rest room in the station and cleaned up.

The old man drew him aside. "I know about them chits your brother has. They're commie chits, ain't they?"

"They're my brother's, not mine."

"I figured that. Where you going?"

"Vegas."

"The dam?"

"Yeah."

"I hear they got more men there than they can hire."

"Might as well be broke in Vegas as anywhere else."

"I'd give you a job. Good one."

"Appreciate it. How about my brother?"

"No dice," the old man said. "Not because of the leg. Don't want no commies in the society."

"I understand. Much obliged."

Herman came out of the rest room and the two walked to their truck. The old man had filled the tank, fixed the leak, put a five-gallon tank of gas in the truck and a crate of vegetables.

"It's eighty-eight miles to Newton," he said, "but there's lots of detours. I don't know what they're fixin' up all them roads for. Nobody's got money to go nowhere."

Hans shook the old man's hand, and they drove off. He was tempted to stop once more for breakfast, have one more look at those clear-eyed, healthy girls, but the town had been good enough already. He looked at the aspens and the elms and the hundreds of acres of well-tilled, fertile, dark brown soil. Tomatoes, lettuce, alfalfa, hay, corn. South Amana, he thought. I should try to remember this place.

119

20

Iowa showed some of the ravages of drought. They passed endless farm structures abandoned, shutters banging against hollow buildings in the wind. There was much debris of the Industrial Revolution, rusted farm tools baked in the hot sun, untold acreage was abandoned. Many of the roads in Iowa were unpaved, and most of the traffic headed west.

They would end up behind a succession of trucks the size of their own, laden with kids and grandparents, bedrolls, stand-up radios, lamps, even a piano perched precariously on a flat bed.

There was a hollow look in the eyes of the men who drove, wearing farmers' coveralls, floppy hats, their faces a mass of stubble. The women were mostly gone to fat, sweating in the merciless sun, yelling at children, at cows in the road, at other women in the same predicament. They passed Marengo, Brooklyn, Grinnell, and finally arrived in Newton.

Newton, Iowa, which boomed in 1925 when its factories could not keep up with the demand for its Maytag washing machines, had been hard hit after the crash, when women across the country reverted back to scrub boards and bars of homemade soap. There was a town square dominated by a three-story courthouse, faced on all sides by shops, most of them boarded up. The lawn surrounding the once ornately carved bandstand had gone to weeds, and Hans and Herman camped almost in the center of this desolate square. They slept poorly, kept awake by the heat, the mosquitoes, the endless milling of farmers with no land to farm and no jobs in town, who kept pacing restlessly all night.

They found a diner called The Spot the following morning. It looked like all the other diners they had encountered: a black linoleum-covered counter, round stools on enameled iron bases, a range, doughnuts under glass bells, a few pies surrounded by an army of flies.

A young waitress dressed in a black skirt and white blouse pulled out her order pad from her pocket.

"What'll you have, boys?"

"Coffee, crullers, side of flaps."

Both Hans and Herman were still stiff from the poor night's sleep. They stared blankly at a heavy-set cook pouring the flapjack mix onto an unscrubbed griddle.

It was six-thirty in the morning. They heard a truck stop outside and the milkman delivered two cases, which he placed on the counter.

"Hi, Terry," he said and she answered, "Hi, Bill," and opened the register to pay him.

It all happened quickly. The girl had barely closed the register when the cook's red-hot spatula slapped her hand. Hans could smell the seared flesh.

"You son of a bitch," Terry yelled, and the cook, picking up a meat cleaver, ran after her.

"Caught you, you bitch. Thought I didn't see you slip that ten out of the register."

The girl ran around the counter to where Hans and Herman were sitting, and the heavy-set chef, cleaver in hand, tried to climb over the counter with little success.

Hans thought quickly. He shoved Terry out the door, then ran behind the counter. He had noticed a grease pan under the stove, a five-gallon can, half filled with bacon drippings, and he poured it over the stove. Before the chef could reach him a sheet of flame engulfed the range, the flames spreading quickly toward the chef.

"Start the car, Herman," Hans yelled and his brother limped out in a hurry. Hans shoved the girl between them on the seat and they took off. Hans looked back and could see smoke pouring out of the diner.

"How far to Omaha?" Hans asked the girl, who had tears in her eyes.

"A hundred miles."

"Push it, Herman, before they get some sheriff after us."

"What the hell we going to do with this dame?" Herman said.

"You work for the proletariat, why ask me."

Terry was licking her wounds. Hans picked up her hand.

"That's a bad burn. Maybe we ought to put some grease on it."

"Don't touch it, please."

"Did you get the ten?" Herman asked.

The girl fished it out of her pocket, along with her order book. "You want it?"

"We'll need it," Herman said.

Terry handed it to Herman, but Hans stopped her.

"Hold on to it. We might need it. But hold on to it."

"Where you from?" Herman asked.

"Oklahoma."

"What about all your stuff?" Hans asked.

"There ain't much stuff," Terry said, her tears finally dried. "Owe so much money to my landlady she'd never let me take it anyway. That son of a bitch owes me three weeks' wages." They slowed behind a caravan of cars, truckers.

"Pass them, Herman," Hans shouted.

"How can I? There's a curve ahead."

"There hasn't been a car going east for an hour. *Pass them.*"

Herman swung out and passed perhaps ten cars, listening to the abuse of the drivers left behind. "How's the gas holding out?"

"We'll make it to Omaha if the sheriff don't stop us." They passed through Adel, Atlantic without incident. At Council Bluffs Hans took over the wheel. He threaded them gingerly through side streets to avoid the law. At the outskirts they returned to Highway 6.

"I'm much obliged," Terry said.

"Forget it," Hans said.

"I'd like to give you this ten bucks."

"Just hold on to it. We're not in Nebraska yet."

They drove on silently through the heat of the day, Hans concentrating on the speedometer, the temperature gauge. Terry sat slightly dazed and Herman watched her black waitress uniform creeping slowly up her legs. At four in the afternoon they crossed the Missouri River into Omaha, Nebraska.

"We made it," Hans said, a broad boyish grin spreading across his face, and pulled off the road on the outskirts of town. He got out of the cab of the truck to flex his muscles, to straighten his back after the hours hunched over the steering wheel. His brother also stepped out of the truck and motioned to Hans to take a walk with him, while Terry was still sitting inside.

"Well," Herman said, "we got her across the border, so let's dump her."

"Tired of the working people, eh," Hans said. "Bullshit," Herman argued. "I keep telling you this ain't a pleasure trip. We can hardly feed ourselves. Can't keep no dame around."

"Ain't she a human being too?" Hans said. "Just gonna let her drift down the highway?"

"She looks like a drifter to me. Don't matter *what* highway she's on. There ain't no room for her," Herman insisted.

"I seen you watch her legs. You didn't seem too cramped."

"She ain't going, that's all," Herman said.

"I'm gonna talk to her," Hans said, walking toward the car, then seating himself next to Terry. She was crying softly.

"Your brother wants me to get out," Terry said.

122

"Forget my brother. Where you headed?"

"I got no place to go," Terry said, drying her tears.

"Where are your folks?"

"I don't know," Terry said. "We got dusted off the farm. There was twelve of us kids. Some went with my folks to California. The youngest. The rest of us are just on our own."

"You want to come to Vegas? Maybe you could make it to California, find your folks . . . ."

"I'd like to go to Vegas. I don't want to cause no trouble. All I got's ten bucks."

Hans walked back to his brother, now lying in a small hummock of weeds.

"Terry's going with us."

"Sure, and she's gonna be *your* woman." Herman said the words hatefully.

"She ain't gonna be *my* woman and she ain't gonna be *your* woman."

"What the hell's the matter with you, Hans? Goddamned thief, she's probably a good piece of ass."

"I'd like to kick the shit out of you, Herman."

"Go ahead."

Hans looked at his brother. Bearded, unshaven, hair tousled, his wooden leg drawn unnaturally to his side . . .

Hans rubbed his eyes and wiped the sweat off his face with the sleeves of his denim shirt.

"Get in that fuckin' truck," he yelled at Herman.

"Why don't you stay here with the little lady?"

"This is *my* truck too," Hans yelled. "Don't ever forget that."

Hans got in the truck, Herman followed.

Hans started the engine and put the truck in gear. He could feel Terry's leg as he shifted into third. They rode in silence until Hans reached Main Street. He drove slowly, finally parking in front of Eaton's Emporium, a rundown wooden building, more storefront than structure.

"Go in there and buy yourself a dress. Don't spend more than four bucks. Put it on and get back here. And stop sniffling. I ain't driving 'cross the country with a waitress or a sniveler."

He got out and watched as Terry ran into the store.

"Got better use for four bucks than a goddamned dress," Herman said.

"Me too," Hans said, "but it ain't my four bucks." He looked at his brother sharply. "All the Wobblies like you?"

"What do you mean?"

123

"Stealing, robbing, cheating people all the time?"

"I didn't steal nothing," Herman said. "*She's* the thief," pointing toward the store.

"You wanted me to steal at the Detroit Hotel. You'd like to steal her ten bucks. Who are you to call a thief a thief?"

"If I weren't a serf I wouldn't have to steal."

"What's a serf?"

"You, me, everybody outta work 'cause Big Business is choking us."

"Don't start with that shit again."

They both looked up in silence as Terry came out of the store wearing a flowered cotton dress. She had combed her hair, which was short and light brown. She had managed to wash her face, and her dark brown eyes almost sparkled. She was short, perhaps five feet two, lean, but had firm large breasts. Her legs, perhaps a little linear, were tanned. She carried her black skirt and white blouse in one hand.

Hans got out of the truck to let her in.

"Don't remember when I've had a *new* dress. Always got hand-me-downs."

"Very pretty," Hans said.

"Only cost three dollars," Terry said.

"How old are you?"

"Eighteen."

"Least she ain't jail bait," Herman said.

"Well," Hans said, starting the ignition, "I'm gonna make a suggestion to keep peace in the family."

"What is it?" Terry asked.

"You got seven bucks left. We're gonna rent a tourist cabin and we're gonna get us a *real* shower and then we're gonna go out and have a *real* steak, best that Nebraska can dish up."

He put the truck into gear and looked at Terry. "Okay?"

"Okay," she said.

"Okay, Herman?"

"Yeah, yeah, sounds okay."

They found tourist cabins as they had almost finished crossing Lincoln: a series of one-room shacks separated by narrow one-car garages covered with corrugated tin. DELUXE TOURIST CABINS, the hand-painted sign announced, $2 A NIGHT. HEATED. SHOWER BATHS.

Hans drove into the complex, resembling more a series of stalls for horses than human domiciles. He stopped the truck and walked toward the first shack in the row, where he expected and found a small sign saying MANAGER. He knocked on the door and a toothless woman, gray hair piled on her head, answered.

"We want a cabin," Hans said.

"They're two dollars," she said.

"I can read," Hans said.

"And they're for two. Two *married* folks. I seen three of you in that truck. One of them's a girl. We're decent folk around here."

Hans stared at this harridan in disbelief for a minute, then leaned back and spit in her face. Before the woman could wipe off the spittle, Hans had run back to the truck and raced out of the driveway.

"What's the matter?" Terry asked.

"Fuckin' farmers. Hate 'em all."

It was fifty-three miles to York and Hans covered the distance in an hour and a half. They found another cluster of tourist cabins, as shapeless and colorless as the first, only the name had changed to A-1 Cabins.

Hans asked Terry for two dollars, which she gave him. He walked toward the first cabin almost defiantly and knocked on the door.

A man his own age answered and opened the door about a foot. There was a brass chain.

"Here's two bucks." Hans shook the money in the young man's face. "There's three of us. Take it or leave it."

"Don't matter to me how many you got. There's only *one* bed."

"I'll worry about that."

"I wouldn't worry too much, brother. Looks like a cute trick you got in that truck."

"That all you farmers ever do, stare out the window?"

"I ain't a farmer," the manager said. "You the first car stopped in two days."

"Yeah," Hans said. "Things are tough all over," handing over two dollars. He watched as the manager walked to a table, sat down, and wrote out a receipt. Then he took a key from a nail on the wall and handed it to Hans.

"Where's there a place we can get a good steak?"

"Harman's Diner," the manager said, "but it'll cost you."

"How much?"

"Eighty cents."

"Where they at?" Hans asked.

"Down the road, 'bout a mile. Got a big sign. All the truckers eat there."

"Thanks a lot."

Hans walked toward the truck and motioned to Terry and Herman, standing in front of it. He found the cabin, it was number 4, and unlocked the door. The light switch didn't work, but a small lamp next to a double bed managed somehow to illuminate the room. It was painted blue, there was an old commode, a straight-back chair, a double bed covered by a stained bedspread, one door leading toward the shower, another opening to a closet.

"Real cozy," Hans said, patting the bed, and he could see the frightened look in Terry's eyes.

"What is it?" he asked.

She said nothing.

"Come on," Hans said irritably.

"I'm much obliged to both of you and I know what you gotta be thinking."

"What's that?" Hans asked.

"You caught me stealing, you got to figure . . ." she pointed toward the bed.

"Figure what?"

Terry blushed. She stammered, "My folks were poor, but I wasn't raised bad."

Hans stared at her a long time. "Our folks were poor too. We weren't raised bad either."

"I'm sorry," Terry said. "I'm real sorry."

"Get in there and take the first shower, and don't use all the towels."

She obeyed Hans, happy now, almost, to leave the room and the tension in it.

Hans sat on the bed and watched his brother sit on the chair.

They heard the shower being turned on, and Hans could see Herman facing the bathroom.

"Pretty hard on you, ain't it, Herman?"

"Shut up."

"There she is, got her dress off, and her bra off, and she's got her panties off and putting Lifebuoy soap all over them good teats . . ."

"Shut up, goddamn you. Why didn't you become a preacher or something? You make me sick."

"Religion is the opiate of the masses, didn't you tell me that?"

"Just shut up. *Shut up,*" and Hans did. They heard the shower stop and a few minutes later Terry reappeared, her hair wet and shiny, her feet clean and small.

"There's only one towel," she said. "I only used a corner."

Hans got up and went to the bathroom and Herman and Terry listened to the shower starting up again.

"I don't want to cause no trouble," Terry said to Herman.

"I ain't crippled to my neck," Herman said.

"I didn't say you was."

126

"I don't want to talk," Herman said and Terry was relieved when Hans reappeared, looking ten years younger, his blond hair plastered to his head, his blue eyes very blue, his body long, his arms very muscular.

After Herman had showered they drove to the diner and ate the three largest steaks the cook could offer. The boys drank beer, Terry had a cherry Coke and after she had paid the bill she left a ten-cent tip.

"What's that for?" Herman asked.

"The waitress," Terry said. "Do you know I had two dreams come true today?"

"What's that?"

"I got a new dress and I had a waitress wait on *me*. Imagine that!"

"No cause to leave her no dime," Herman insisted.

"Ain't waitresses working people?" Hans asked.

Herman said nothing. They drove back to their room in silence and fell asleep on the small bed, fully clothed. Hans looked at Terry briefly before he closed his eyes, and watched his brother's open eyes on him, but fatigue caught up with him before he worried about the night. They slept like people drugged, the only sound in the room the whoosh of the gas heater in the corner of the room.

Although York was the county seat, a town of 5,700 souls spread over the landscape like syrup on a pancake, its few industries—a brick plant, a tile plant, another which manufactured sash weights and elevator machinery—offered nothing to Hans and Herman for a day's work.

They drove along the endless plain, hitting Grand Island two hours later. There was a freight division of the Union Pacific in Grand Island, and they managed a day's work cleaning out cattle cars and ending up sleeping in one, after a skimpy meal in another greasy diner.

"Some town you got here," Hans said sarcastically to the short-order cook the following morning.

"You talking about Grand Island?"

"Ain't talking about Chicago."

"Grand Island is God's country. We got one of the biggest flour mills in the state, a big creamery, three parks besides."

"Besides what?"

"Slim Peters was born here."

"Who's Slim Peters?" Hans asked.

"Jeesus, you some kind of rube? Ain't you ever heard of Slim Peters? He's a movie star. One of biggest movie stars in Hollywood."

"You don't say. Never go to movie shows."

"Let's get out of here," Herman said irritably to Hans.

"We're going west," Hans said to the cook. "If I see Slim Peters I'll tell 'im we been to God's country."

"Come on!" Herman shouted and the three piled into the truck and headed toward Kearney.

"Why did you give that guy such a hard time about Slim Peters?"

" 'Cause I'm sick of all these smug little bastards in these smug little towns. . . ."

"Ain't his fault that Peters was born there."

"I know, I know," Hans said, grinding his eyes with his right hand. "I'm sick of this goddamn heat and these goddamn roads and this goddamn truck."

"Let's take a swim somewhere," Terry suggested.

"Where you gonna find some water?"

"Just keep looking. There's always a river or a lake or something."

They reached Kearney at four and slept on the well-tended lawns of the teachers college, rose early the next day and rolled through North Platte, Ogallala, Sidney. There, in the Lodgepole Valley, surrounded by high rolling plains, broken occasionally by imposing cliffs, they found a river. It was a slow-moving stream, the waters muddy, but it was accessible from the highway. Hans stopped the truck and the three of them got out and walked toward the bank and watched the sluggish current.

"Got to swim in my underwear, I guess," Terry said.

"Ain't gonna bother us if it don't bother you . . . eh, Herman?"

"Don't wear nothing," Herman said. "Won't get your underwear wet."

Terry slipped off her dress and ran toward the water and dove in. When she stood up in three feet of water the boys could see her dark nipples through the wet brassière, the shadow of her pubic hair under her equally wet panties. Hans first, then Herman, stripped off their clothes and joined Terry. Herman's wooden leg was mercifully covered by the river. They splashed each other, they laughed and giggled and for a brief respite assumed the roles of kids, which they really were, instead of poverty-aged and depression-riddled young adults, which they were also.

Spirits rose in the cab of the truck after the swim, Hans and Herman, still aware of the sight of Terry almost naked, Terry aware of their awareness. They drove all night until they reached Cheyenne. It was a pretty town sitting on a broad plain below the Laramie Mountains. There were green lawns, paved streets, new pressed-brick and steel houses. They sensed a certain prosperity, for Cheyenne was the state capital; it had a sixty-day-divorce law which brought folks from other states, an oil refinery, cattle ranches; but perhaps also they felt

128

for the first time the spirit of the West. Faces were less hard-bitten, people were unafraid of the sun, they looked tanned and healthy, and though they had their shares of troubles from the depression, the warmth and beauty of the landscape seemingly softened their hardships.

Even the foreman at the refinery who gave them two days' work conditioned his offer on putting Terry to work in the cookhouse.

"While you boys clean them drill bits, I'm gonna keep my eye on this filly."

Terry blushed.

"Look at her blush," he said, taking his hard hat off his suntanned head, showing a generous bald spot.

"I can cook," Terry said, "but . . ."

"But what?" the foreman asked, a slight smile on his face.

"I don't need no help peeling potatoes."

"Okie kid, ain't you?" the foreman asked.

"Yes," Terry answered.

"All the same," he said, "all the same, got that streak of the Lord right down their spine." He put on his hard hat again. "Enough palaver. Let's get to work."

They worked two days, Hans and Herman scrubbing drill bits, Terry washing down tables in the company mess hall. They were fed well, they slept in their truck, they earned fifteen dollars between them and liked the spirit of the oil workers, intense, hard-working, good-natured and playful. They pushed on the following morning, the drillers and muckers waving them on, shouting, "Sure you don't want to leave little ol' Terry? We take mighty fine care of little ol' Terry . . . ."

Little ol' Terry, Hans thought, feeling her warm body next to him, aware of every contact as the truck swayed, and Herman's thoughts were much the same, except they were more erotic.

They passed Ilamo, a coal-mining camp, a town covered in soot, the coal chutes, the mine dumps, even the hillsides, with their shadowy houses with green roofs. It was in Parco, set in a monotonous sagebrush plain, that they first noticed grimy tenements giving way to bungalows, more grassy plazas, a Spanish-style hotel.

Hans pointed to the stucco building. "Boy, look at that," he said. "That building wouldn't stand up to one winter in Detroit."

"I'd like to stay in one of them fancy hotels once," Terry said. "Looks like pictures I seen of California."

"You know something, Herman?"

"What?"

"The further west we get the harder it's gonna be for your revolution."

129

"Wait till you see Vegas," Herman said. "These towns are hanging on, but Vegas gets every drifter from the States."

"They're getting three more in a couple of days if this tin lizzie holds up."

"She runs, don't she?" Herman said.

"She does, I'll say that, but I'd like to find the son of a bitch who put that spring right under my ass. . . . I knew some of them guys that made seats at the Rouge. Real pissheads, all of them . . ."

Herman turned to Terry. "Hans used to work on engine blocks. They looked down on everybody."

"Least it's man's work," Hans said. "Better than stamping out radiator caps all day."

"Old Henry Ford really knew how to run that line," Herman countered, "making every idiot feel he had the best job and screwing them all collectively."

"Here we go again, Terry," Hans said. "Wobbly talk."

"Fuck you," Herman said.

"What was this shit all about anyway? This guy Marx?"

Herman said nothing.

"I ain't sore," Hans continued. "*Tell me.* What kind of guy was he anyway?"

"I been trying to tell you for years," Herman said.

"Sure, when I'd get home from the Rouge, beat up after twelve hours of work, aching to get to Casey's. . . . I ain't doing nothing now but driving. Tell me."

"Karl Marx," Herman said, didactically, "had this idea that every man has only so many hours of work in him in a lifetime . . . don't matter whether he was cleaning shithouses or doing brain surgery . . . ."

"Go on," Hans said.

"And he figured that every man should get the same reward for giving that stretch of his life."

"You mean you'd pay a shithouse cleaner same as a doctor?"

"That's right."

"That's dumb," Hans said. "You know how long it takes to become a doctor."

"Sure, I know," Herman said, "and only rich kids can become doctors in this country."

"So how are poor kids gonna be doctors?"

"The state sends them."

"What state?"

"Russia, for Christ sake."

Terry was puzzled, but happy. Anything that would break the tension in the cab was welcome.

130

"So why don't every kid in Russia become a doctor?"

"Because not every kid in Russia is smart enough to become a doctor."

"And all the others clean out shithouses?"

"No, they become farmers, and workers, and lawyers, and mechanical engineers, same as here."

"And they all get the same pay?"

"That's right," Herman said, " 'cause the doctor treats the shithouse cleaner for nothing and the shithouse cleaner cleans the doctor's shithouse for nothing, and everybody takes care of everybody else."

Hans drove silently for a few minutes. It was a lot to digest.

"That's in Russia?"

"Yeah."

"And everybody's happy as a clam in Russia?"

"They're all working. They all got free medicine, they ain't starving like here. . . ."

"So if it's so good in Russia, why don't we have it like that here?" Hans asked.

"Because dumb bastards like you just call us pinkos and Wobblies and never try to *understand*. . . ."

"Understand what?" Hans said, ignoring the dumb bastard remark, avoiding a pothole in the road.

"They used to have the czars in Russia. They owned everything, the land, the mines, the factories, just like Henry Ford, Rockefeller, like Jay Gould, like Stanford . . . and finally the workers who were starving and dying like us *revolted*. They had a goddamn revolution and they killed all those bastards who owned everything."

"You gonna kill Henry Ford? I seen his place once. You can't get within five miles of it. All fenced with broken glass on top."

"You can't kill Henry Ford. I can't kill Henry Ford. But there's more of us than Henry Fords. Millions more."

Again Hans was silent. There *was* some merit in this argument, he knew, but there were gaps also, he thought.

"What about Herbert Hoover?" Hans asked finally. "What about him? He's a smart fellow, ain't he?"

"Depends on what you call smart."

"Well, he made a million bucks for himself by the time he was forty and now he's President of the United States. . . . You can't be dumb to get in the White House."

"I didn't say he was dumb."

"So why don't he run this country like Russia?"

"Because he'd have to give up his million bucks and all his friends would have to give up their million bucks . . . and he wouldn't live in the White House."

131

"Who would? Some shithouse cleaner? Yeah," Hans said, "the country would be run by a committee. A shithouse cleaner and a farmer and a soldier. . . . I can't see no shithouse cleaner in the White House, can you, Terry?"

Terry had fallen asleep in the heat and Hans laughed as she woke and said simply, "What?" then yawned.

They entered Rock Springs and Hans looked for a stand of trees to shelter their truck for the night.

"If it's all so great, why don't a lot of Americans go to Russia?"

"They just hired one thousand American engineers," Herman said, almost proudly

"No kidding, and they're gonna pay 'em like shithouse cleaners?"

"Yeah," Herman said, "and that's better than getting no pay at all."

"I got to think on that," Hans said.

Rock Springs was quite a town. Large gray staff houses, black smokestacks, tiny shacks, and fine homes, lots of buildings with false fronts, a coal mine owned by the Union Pacific, a good town to get started for hunting or fishing in the Rockies, the Wind Mountains. . . .

Terry had made up the bunks in the back of the truck, using a few old blankets, a piece of rug, some canvas salvaged along the road.

Herman had built a fire, and Hans was plucking a chicken he had managed to run over not totally by accident an hour ago. When Terry had finished making the beds, Hans handed her the half-plucked chicken and said, "I'm goin' to town and try to get some bootleg," and even Herman agreed to the luxury. It took almost two hours for him to return.

"Where the hell you been? We've been stoking this fire for hours," Herman said.

"Jesus, you ought to see this town," Hans said excitedly. "They got a Chinatown and a Jewish street and a Greek candy store here," he said to Terry, giving her a small bag.

"What is it?"

"Candy, all the way from Greece. Boy," he said, "you ought to see all them Chinks running around in their pajamas. . . ."

"Let's eat," Herman said. "I keep telling you we ain't on no pleasure trip." But even Herman mellowed after tasting the crisply fried chicken, drinking his share of whiskey.

In the half darkness Terry was giggling quietly.

"You do much drinkin' in Oklahoma?" Hans asked her.

"Moonshine only. My pa had a still. . . . We used to siphon it when I was a kid. Feel real good."

"Yeah," Hans said, "my old man would slip me a whiskey once

in a while when I was a kid. Remember, Herman?"

"Yeah, I do," he said. "You know in a couple of days we'll be in Vegas?"

"Kind of gettin' used to this traveling, don't know whether I'd like staying put. My ass is so sore now don't matter if we'd go to China."

"We ought to make Salt Lake tomorrow," Herman said before falling asleep, and Hans nodded his head and then looked at Terry, who was shivering.

"What's wrong?" Hans asked.

"I'm scared," Terry said.

"Of what?"

"Of Vegas."

Hans put his hand on her cheek. He felt the moisture of her tears.

"Can't hurt us in Vegas," he said, and turned and fell asleep. Terry watched his easy breathing, wiped her tears and dropped off herself.

They reached Salt Lake City at two the following day, but its cleanliness and orderliness frightened them. Streets laid out neatly in grids, all of them tree-lined; the Mormon Temple, the Tabernacle; the purposeful citizens all had an air of severity which made them feel unwanted. They pressed on to Nephi, a hundred miles south, still Mormon, but rural. They were almost out of money and ate doughnuts for dinner. Around them was the desert, irrigated and fertile somehow, the farmhouses solid and well painted.

"Don't seem right," Hans said. "We're eatin' doughnuts with all that corn around."

"You been doing some thinking," Herman said.

"Yeah," Hans said. "I been doing some thinking of stealing some corn."

"Don't ask for trouble," Terry said. "We're almost in Vegas."

"Yeah," Hans said, "wish these Mormons were like those Amanists."

"Who are they?" Terry asked.

"If I told you, you'd just fall asleep."

"Yeah," Terry answered, too tired to argue.

They camped by the road and watched truck after truck and car after car roll south.

"Looks like everybody's heading for Vegas," Hans said.

"Yeah," Herman said. "The more stiffs they get, the lower the wages."

They rose early the following morning. It was only five but the heat was already unbearable. No one felt like eating, sweat rolled off all of them like rivers, Terry's light dress was dark from moisture.

Hans and Herman had stripped to the waist and Herman suggested that Terry follow suit. She gave him a dirty look.

In the afternoon they drove through St. George, passed another Mormon church, stopped to buy some orangeade and pushed on. The land was getting drier. The earth cracked; there was little foliage and less humor in the cab of the truck. They stopped behind a truck parked beneath two scrawny elm trees and got out of the truck.

They walked toward the family, three generations, eating a sparse supper of bologna and bread. A pot of coffee was brewing over a small wood fire.

"Mind if we sit?" Hans asked.

"You can sit," a woman in her forties answered. "We ain't got nothing to share."

"Don't want nothing," Hans said. "Too hot to eat."

"You going to Vegas?" Herman asked.

"Yup," one of the men answered. "How about you?"

"Vegas," Herman nodded. "Heard there's no work."

"Heard the same," the man answered.

"So why you going?" Herman asked.

"*You're* going," the man answered. "Why you asking dumb questions?"

Hans laughed. "You tell him, paw. That's a good one."

Herman stared at his brother, but Hans shrugged it off. He spotted a baseball and asked one of the boys, perhaps eleven, lean and intense, wearing old overalls, no shoes, whether he'd like to play catch.

"No," the boy answered.

"Don't like baseball?"

"Like it all right."

"So let's play catch."

"I'm tired, mister. Got no cause to run around."

"Yeah," said Hans, rising to his feet, "everybody's tired."

He motioned to Herman and Terry and they got in the truck.

"See you in Vegas," he said to the assembled under the tree. "Good luck."

"Yeah," the man said. "We'll need it."

Hans drove off. "Son of a bitch," he said finally, "this country is really on its ass when a kid's too tired to play catch," but no one in the cab wanted to argue with him.

"That was a scene," the mother of the children said, still sitting under the tree.

"What scene?" her husband asked.

"Them three, coming up like that. Two boys and that girl. Did you see her dress?"

"I seen it."

"Yeah, I bet, and you seen her nipples stick right through it too, didn't you?"

"Shut your mouth."

"You *seen* it, didn't you?"

"*Yeah*, I seen it. I ain't blind."

"And you *liked* it, didn't you? You liked *staring* at that goddamned tramp."

"I said shut your mouth, woman."

"And all the children seen it too," she continued in her high-pitched voice.

"Ain't much the children ain't seen since we hit the road."

"Yeah, and it was all *your* idea, leaving the farm . . . headin' for Vegas."

"Can't feed them kids dust, can't wait forever for the rain. . . ."

An elderly woman spoke up, looking at the screaming woman. "Shut your mouth," she said, "like your husband told you or I'll slap you right across the face."

"You do that, ma," the woman said, "and I'll leave you in this desert to die."

The old woman's hand flew across her daughter's face with the sound of a pistol firing. The screaming woman collapsed in tears, her gray shirt and her faded blue skirt a rumpled mass like a wilted corn-flower.

"Got to cut this shit, Hank," the old woman said to her son-in-law. "I'd a talked like this to Grandpa he'd a beat the hell out of me."

"Yeah," Hank said, taking off his canvas hat and once more wiping his sweaty forehead. "I'm so tired, couldn't even beat up Danny."

The boy looked up at his father.

"Didn't do nothing," he said.

Hank put his arm on Danny's shoulder. "I know, Danny. You didn't do nothin'."

The boy managed a thin smile and Grandma stood up. "Let's go," she said. "This ain't no Sunday church picnic."

They packed their gear into the truck and drove on in silence.

Hans and Herman and Terry reached Mesquite at dusk. It was a pleasant Mormon town along the Virgin River. They found a small cove of the Virgin River and Terry made up the bunks a few feet from the water.

"Don't bother to go into town," Herman said to his brother. "Them Mormons don't sell no booze."

"No," Hans asked, "what do they do?"

135

"They don't drink, they don't smoke, don't even drink coffee."

"They got lots of wives," Terry said.

"How you know that?" Herman asked.

"I heard."

"How many wives?" Hans asked.

"Some got ten, twelve," Terry said.

"Jesus," Hans said, "no wonder they don't smoke or drink."

"You know, it's funny," Herman said. "There's nobody hates the Wobblies more than the Mormons, and they're almost commies themselves."

"How do you figure?"

"Give ten percent of all they make to the church. They got warehouses of food and clothing . . . take *real* care of their own."

"You show me one of them warehouses and I'll get us a meal."

"Yeah," Herman said. "Them Mormon boys would whip your ass."

"You'd think they'd be all tuckered out with all them wives."

"I wouldn't put no bets on that."

They ate a candy bar each, then washed in the river and were asleep not long after the sun had finally set, but none of them could sleep soundly. By three in the morning they were back in the truck. It was only eighty-five miles to Las Vegas and they arrived at dawn.

For days now and for nights, all these endless driving hours, each of them had tried to visualize Vegas. Whatever they expected had been colored and drawn by strangers on the road heading for the town, and though they thought they would recognize every inch of it, reality was something else.

There were miles upon miles of trucks and cars stretched over the landscape, some housing families, others just men. Everything from tarps to flour bags was stretched over wooden frameworks to ward off the merciless sun.

There were endless signs advertising real estate, gambling casinos, restaurants. Surveyors' flags dotted the landscape like the wildflowers in the Rockies, but there were no flowers, and no tilled fields, and no well-paved streets or gas-lit lanterns. Downtown was a welter of humanity, men drunk on benches at six in the morning, cowboy music blaring from bars, people sleeping in the open around the train station in front of the city hall.

All three of them rode in silence through Las Vegas, each feeling the impact personally, all of them awed and frightened.

Herman pulled up to a gas station and asked the attendant where Boulder Highway was.

"Go down one block and turn left, mister. You can't miss it. It's the only road to the dam site."

Herman fidgeted with his ditty bag, which he always kept by his side.

"Lookin' for Alma's fruit stand," he said.

"Alma's fruit stand." The boy scratched his head. "There's fruit stands all the way to Boulder. All got different names. Don't know no Alma's."

"Thanks anyway," Herman said and they followed instructions and hit Boulder Highway.

It was a new, well-paved road and the traffic heavy. Trucks, endless trucks, and government cars painted khaki, and roadsters and people walking alongside the road.

There were fruit stands, scores of them, and restaurants and brokers' offices, and gas stations and hawkers selling painted pots and Indian blankets.

They scanned each sign, one more crudely lettered than the next, SUPER FRUIT STAND, MORNING DEW FRUIT, FRESH FRUIT HEAVEN, JODY'S, ALFRED'S. They finally saw Alma's, looking almost more impoverished than the rest. It was an orange stucco building, windowless, its front open, an array of fly-specked apples, pears, grapes displayed crudely in wooden crates, a hanging scale, a cigar box which served as a cash register, a gnarled woman in her sixties bronzed almost negroid, sitting on a wooden stool.

Herman stopped and walked toward the woman and said, "I'm lookin' for Devere."

"He's in back," she said. "Been waiting on you. Get your truck off the road and park behind the bushes. There's a door in back."

Herman swung the truck behind the building and the three of them got out wordlessly, Hans and Terry following Herman, who knocked on the door. It was opened slightly.

"Who is it?"

"Herman Schroeder."

The door opened and Herman and Hans and Terry entered.

It was a barren, windowless room illuminated only by a gooseneck lamp sitting on an oak desk. An oak rocker was behind the desk, there were cardboard boxes stacked against one wall, a collection of wooden chairs of assorted vintage spread throughout the room in random patterns.

Devere was a man in his mid-thirties. He wore blue denims, a white shirt; his face was well chiseled, with a beard in a Vandyke cut. He wore dark tortoiseshell glasses, his hair was graying early, and his hands, Hans noted, were small and soft and his fingers nicotine stained.

"You're late," Devere said.

"It's a long way," Herman half apologized.

"And I wasn't expecting three, I was expecting one."

"This is my brother Hans," he said.

"Who's the dame?" Devere asked harshly.

"Terry," Herman said. "We gave her a lift."

Devere eyed Terry coldly, then said, "Where's the money?"

Herman dug into his ditty bag and handed Devere an envelope. Devere tore it open. It was filled with bills. Tens, fives, twenties.

Hans could not believe it when Devere counted the money on his desk. He had never seen that much cash money in his life. . . .

"Five hundred," Devere said. "Least you did that right. Sit down," he ordered them, but Hans stood and walked toward his brother.

"You had all that money all the time?" he asked his brother.

"What's it to you?"

"You had *all* that money and you hocked Pa's watch for twenty bucks?"

"What's all this bullshit?" Devere asked.

"Just bullshit," Herman answered, feeling his oats suddenly in the presence of Devere.

"You can sit or get out," Devere said, looking at Hans, and Hans headed for the door. Terry stood up and followed him. They walked toward the truck and sat in it.

"I don't like that guy," Terry said.

"I don't like any of it," Hans agreed, and put his forehead on the rim of the steering wheel.

"Welcome to Las Vegas," he said without raising his head.

Terry stroked the back of his neck. It was the first time in all the days on the road she had touched him.

21

Jack Williams, as Crowe knew he would, was attacking the tunnels in his own way. He had to blast through 16,000 feet of rock and had one year to do it. Williams knew that he could not simply start his four tunnels upstream and merrily blast until he reached the downhill side.

That would take much too long. In order to blast out tunnels fifty-six feet in diameter one had to attack the mountain in as many areas as possible. He would blast upstream, and he would blast downstream. Then he would blast from the side, creating narrow shafts known as adits to reach the center of each proposed tunnel. Once he had reached that imagined spot in the bowels of Black Canyon, he would be attacking each tunnel from four sides—upstream, downstream, and from the center again upstream and downstream. It was no mean engineering feat, since his calculations had to be absolutely on target and he would have four crews working simultaneously in each tunnel. With four tunnels being worked on, that meant sixteen crews per shift.

As he said to Maria, "If you multiply the crews by three shifts, you've got a lot of stiffs to point in a lot of directions, and pity the stiff who looks back." Tunnelers were used to being driven, and Williams was a man whose drive was well matched by his mastery of invective.

Crowe, standing beside the Nevada adit one morning, wondered what manner of man wanted to work in a tunnel. The dangers were as great as those of the cherry pickers on the canyon walls, the heat worse than in the bottom of the canyon, yet most of the men of this key group worked with Williams on dam after dam.

Were they afraid of being buried alive? Were they men who secretly coveted the darkness? Was there a womblike quality to a tunnel? Was constant drilling and blasting an outlet for some deep-seated hostility? He watched the mucking trucks leaving the adit, the men dust-covered, their faces the color of putty, their hard hats dented from endless falling rock, their shoes shapeless and unbending.

He dismissed his thoughts and rode on the runningboard of the next truck going into the adit. He passed under light after light, like a seedy string of pearls, he smelled the acrid smell of tunnels under construction, nitrate fumes, sulfur, and sweat, and finally reached the heading three hundred feet into the mountain.

Out of the corner of his eye Williams saw Crowe arrive, but made no move to welcome the chief. Crowe wanted it that way, Williams knew that.

"Pull back," Williams ordered after inspecting the dynamite once more. The crew had already pulled back, the trucks had backed down, and finally Williams returned to the blasting line and gave the signal. Crowe was used to the roar of the dynamite, but somehow could never get used to the blast of air, like a giant wave engulfing him. Air filled with dust and rock, blinding, biting air seeking an outlet from the explosion.

Williams seemed hardly shaken by the blast as he asked Crowe what he wanted.

"This adit is slower," Crowe said.

"I know," Williams said. "Why the hell do you think I'm here? I've got forty-eight crews blasting and this one has never won a case of beer."

139

"How do you figure it?"

"Can't," Williams said. "Not yet. Got my best foreman here. Doing everything but whipping these bastards with a cat o' nine. Maybe the rock."

"What's wrong with it?"

"We're going more transverse here than the Arizona adit."

"How transverse?" Frank asked.

"Eight degrees."

"You think you ought to timber?" Crowe knew this was a delicate question.

"Timber, shit," Williams said. "This rock is tough. Damned tough, that's why it's hard to get through. Might make these bastards work even faster. Put some steam in their asses."

"You're ahead of schedule on every other heading," Frank said.

"So what? Ain't helping me on this adit."

"It isn't, is it?" Crowe said and left. He stood on another running-board of another much-laden truck and watched slowly as the pinpoint of daylight at the entry of the tunnel became larger, watched as the light became brighter, and quickly found himself at the rim of the canyon breathing the hot pure air.

Frank and Elle's house was spacious by Boulder City standards, but far from opulent. Except for the brass bed which Elle had shipped from Denver, there was hardly any furniture. They had a dining-room table, four wooden chairs, a sofa, and an easy chair. There was a rickety table in the kitchen; Frank's drawing board was in one of the bedrooms. There were no rugs, no lamps, no hot water. There were no towel racks or medicine chest, no night tables, no bookshelves. But Elle made do. She had promised herself and she had promised Frank to take it as it came, and though she had the diversion of her studies and a few close friends, she was aware that little might improve over the years, since Frank had neither the time nor the inclination to make this house a home.

She felt at times that he thought comfort was debilitating, that anything which did not contribute to the building of the dam was extraneous, and she even admitted to herself that it was hard to argue with twenty years of living on a dam site.

That night Frank had gone into his study, where he kept a duplicate set of the plans he used on the dam site. They were meticulously stored and catalogued and Frank studied the drawings of the Nevada adit.

"Can I watch?" Elle asked quietly.

"Come in, honey," Frank said without looking up. He pointed to a spot between two lines on the map. "This is where Jack Williams is. Right here." Then he advanced his finger by an inch. "This is where

140

he *should* be." Frank scratched his temple with his pencil. "He's having trouble with that crew. I don't know why. He doesn't know why. . . ."

They heard a car approach the house, the headlights playing through the uncurtained windows. The car was driven hard and braked hard. They heard a knock on the door.

"Who the hell is that?" Frank said, walking toward the front hall, Elle behind him.

He opened the door. A boy, perhaps twenty, tow-headed, good looking, well dressed, had his arm perched on the door frame, his body angled slightly. Frank looked at him, at a new Ford roadster, the top down, the lights on, a radio blaring music.

"I'm Henry Barnes, Jr. My dad told me to see you."

Frank Crowe said nothing for a while and Elle noticed the tension build in him.

"How did you get into Boulder City?"

"I told the guard who I was."

"Who are you?"

"I'm Henry Barnes. *Barnes*," he repeated. "My dad is the head of this project."

"Your dad is what?" Crowe snapped.

"He's your boss," the boy said, almost innocently, "isn't he?"

"You son of a bitch. Take your hand off my door frame and stand up straight."

The boy did as ordered, stunned, looking frightened now.

"Your father, Henry Barnes," Crowe spit out the words, "put up a million-dollar bond for this dam. So did a number of other men. He's not *my* boss on this dam site. Nobody is. You got that?"

"Yes . . ." there was a pause, "sir."

"If I ever hear you throw your name around again on this project, I'll kick your ass out, you got that?"

"Yes."

"You see personnel tomorrow about a job, and the next time I meet you, all I want to see is your ass and your elbows."

"But . . ." the boy managed.

"But, shit, now haul ass and turn that fucking radio off. There are working people here trying to get a night's sleep." He slammed the door and returned to his study.

"I'll change," Frank had told Elle, before they reached Las Vegas. She remembered what Frank had said and decided to go to bed without saying a word, but before falling asleep she heard Frank on the telephone.

"Crowe here," she heard him say. "You on this shift? What's your name? Spell it." There was a pause. "Did you let in a kid without a pass? Of course I know his name. You got instructions to make exceptions? Have you? I don't pay you to think, you prick. See personnel in the morning. At six-thirty." He slammed down the phone.

Elle was still awake when Frank came to bed. She put her arms around him and tried to ease the tension.

"Can I ask you a question, Frank? You told me not to be afraid."

"Ask," he said, still tense.

"I hated that boy," Elle said. "Reminded me of a lot of boys at Vermont."

"Little bastard," Frank said.

"But you're going to fire that guard."

"That's right."

"He didn't know."

"That's right, he didn't know."

"So why fire him?"

Frank Crowe sat up in bed. Elle still felt his anger.

"I'm going to explain this to you *once*, Elle," he said sternly. "This dam is like a puzzle. A great big puzzle, all little pieces that somehow fit together slowly, carefully. Every stiff on this dam represents a piece of that puzzle. At three-fifty a day we don't give him much of a piece. We tell one guy, 'Dig,' and we tell another guy, 'Blast,' and we tell a third guy, 'Muck,' and on and on and on. Every stiff's got *one* job. I don't pay 'im to think—I pay him to dig, to muck, to scale, whatever." He paused. "*I* get paid for thinking. But when *they* think, like that dumb bastard did, for which I don't pay him, we're in trouble, because I *think* better, and that's *my* job." He was quiet. Somehow more relaxed. "I know you shivered in this half-finished house a few weeks ago and I know why you shivered."

"Why?" Elle asked.

"Because I talked about death on this dam site."

"You're right."

"Well, every time we have a death it's because some son of a bitch doesn't follow instructions. *He* thinks, instead of letting *me* think, and I got another life on my conscience.

"Some goddamned Wobbly could have told that guard his name was Barnes and blown us straight to hell."

Elle sat up. "You're right, and I'm glad I asked you, but for a whole other reason."

"What's that?"

"I'm glad you know why I shivered the other night. . . . I love you, Frank Crowe."

"I guess I use a lot of words they don't use in the library," he said sheepishly.

"I didn't marry a librarian."

142

22

Devere was a well-qualified radical. He had followed the classic pattern: a few years in college, some years at the Rouge; he had been injured twice in violent strikes at Ford, been jailed, and was one of the most violent lieutenants in the Wobbly movement. He thrived on strife and tension, his mind filled with slogans, theories, to the point where he subconsciously no longer remembered *what* cause he was fighting, or why, or at what price. He was a political eunuch, the best kind of radical, who moved, when told to move, no matter what the cost or what the unreality. He had lost his testicles in World War 1. Now he survived on cigarettes and whiskey, and for the most part, hatred, like Herman Schroeder, who sat before him.

"Can you still fuck?" Devere asked Schroeder.

"What do you mean?"

"I mean can you fuck? How much of you is wood and how much of you is man?"

"I can fuck," Herman said almost proudly.

"You got a hard-on for this broad?"

"What broad?"

"That Terry, what's her name."

"Another broad . . ." Herman said lightly, not very convincingly.

Devere said nothing, eying Herman coldly, then continued. "You brought the money. That's good, and I got a letter saying you'll hold up. That's good too. . . ."

"Let's go to work," Herman said, and Devere scowled.

"Go to work, you make me laugh. . . . What the hell you think we've *been* doing, sitting on our ass?"

"I didn't say that," Herman said, but Devere ignored him.

"This dam is tough. Crowe is tough. He hates us as much as I hate him. Figures with all these stiffs storming the gates he can go on paying shit to the workers on the dam. . . ."

"Where's the weak spot?" Herman asked.

"Good question, kid, good question." He reached behind his desk and pulled out a map. He spread it carefully on his desk, keeping the corners down with cigarette tins.

143

"Right here," he said, pointing at the identical spot Crowe had shown Elle a few nights ago, "the Nevada adit. I've got eight of our boys in there. Sand in the engines, ice picks in the tires. Goddamned Williams can't figure it out. Not yet, anyhow. We've cost him eighty feet already. He's driving his crews like a madman."

"What's the temperature?" Herman asked.

"One twenty, one twenty-five, some days one hundred thirty. Another two weeks I can pull the strike. The five hundred bucks you brought ought to feed those guys for two months. I'll have Crowe eating out of my hand."

"What about the rest of the dam?" Herman asked.

"The rest of the dam isn't worth shit unless Crowe gets through those tunnels before the river rises. Crowe knows that. Williams knows that." He paused. "And *I* know that. . . . You smoke?" He handed Herman an open tin of Chesterfields.

"Thanks."

It was eight o'clock and still hot and light. Hans returned to the truck behind Alma's fruit stand and found Terry sitting on the running-board.

"Any luck?" Hans said, sitting beside her.

"No," Terry said. "Keep gettin' the same story. 'You don't want to work here, honey. Girl with your looks ought to try Block 16. You could get rich.'"

"Son of a bitch," Hans said.

"How about you?"

"Nothing," said Hans. "Some days I can't even get into the hiring hall, and if I do the line's a hundred men long. They hire one, maybe two, and close the window."

Terry leaned her head against Hans's shoulder.

"What'll we do?" She was crying. "I can't stand living off Herman. You don't know how he *looks* at me."

"I know."

"He's worse since we got here. I swear he can stare the clothes off a girl. . . . Can't we leave, Hans, take off? Please?"

"I'm going up to the dam site tomorrow," Hans said firmly.

"You'll never get in."

"I'll get in," Hans said.

"Don't get hurt." She clasped his arms as Herman left the back of Alma's fruit stand to join Hans. Terry didn't change her posture. She kept her head on Hans's shoulder, her hands around his arms.

"She ain't gonna be my woman and she ain't gonna be your woman," Herman said.

"Shut up, Herman."

144

"Well, did you find employment from the almighty Big Six Companies today?"

"Just quit it."

"Did that brilliant President Hoover give you a job today?"

"What do you want, Herman? What is it you want?" Hans almost pleaded.

"You're eating pinko food and you're smoking pinko smokes. . . ."

"I'll pay you back, every cent. I'll pay you back."

They cooked a stew, half beef, half rabbit; they all stared into the fire and finally collapsed in the back of the truck.

At the crack of dawn Hans rose, washed, shaved, and headed on foot toward Boulder City. It was a long trek, fourteen miles, and he felt the heat, the dust, and the lack of food these past days.

Two miles outside of Boulder City he approached a trucker at a gas station.

"Give you a buck if you take me inside," Hans told him.

"A buck's a buck," the trucker said. "Get behind them generators; nobody'll see you."

Hans handed him a dollar and thanked him, jumped into the body of the truck, and wedged himself behind the generators. Twenty minutes later the trucker stopped and said, "This is as close as I can take you. We're inside the gates."

"Much obliged," Hans said, jumping off the truck.

"Boulder City is straight ahead."

It was normally quiet in the mess hall. Filling it only to one-third of its capacity, the men who came to eat filed silently through the cafeteria and seated themselves and ate. There were cliques in the room, to be sure. Tunnelers ate with tunnelers, railroad people were clannish, cherry pickers were off to themselves. Though there was a "Blue Room" reserved for brass, Crowe never used it. He sat at an ordinary table with Williams and Wanke and several staff engineers.

Men not only ate for sustenance, but basked in the relative comfort provided by the evaporative coolers. There was little time for conversation or for tomfoolery.

Hans Schroeder sought out the mess hall. He watched men stealing scraps of garbage from huge corrugated cans behind the kitchen and wondered how *they* had gotten onto the dam site.

He entered the mess hall and stood in line. He could scarcely believe the quantity and quality of food spread before him. Salads, meats, potatoes, vegetables, sauces, dressings, celery, carrots, dessert. He filled his plate with one of each, doubling up on meat, on dessert, and finally arrived at the station manned by a slight aproned Chinese.

"You chit," the Chinaman said, and Hans said, "What?"

145

"You chit?"

"What shit?"

"Chit. No chit, no eat."

A burly crane operator behind Hans fueled the fires.

"Come on, buddy, haul ass," he said. "Give 'im your chit."

"I don't have a chit," Hans said.

"Guess you won't eat."

Hans looked at the Chinaman, at the crane operator.

He asked, "You ain't gonna let me eat lunch?"

Again the Chinaman said, "No chit, no eat," and Hans took the aluminum tray, raised it above his head, and smashed it on the floor. There were food and broken crockery, and the entire mess hall became still.

"I'm an American citizen, goddamn it," Hans yelled. "I ain't eating garbage out of garbage cans."

Frank Crowe looked up when he heard the crash. He studied the boy's face. He listened to his strong voice. . . .

He told one of his engineers to bring the boy over to the table. It was Stubbs; he walked over to Hans and told him to follow him.

Hans, still defiant, followed and stood before Crowe.

"You as big with your shoulders as you are with your mouth?"

Hans stared at Crowe. "Try me," he said.

Crowe looked at the Chinaman and nodded his head. "Eat lunch," Crowe ordered Hans, "and report to my office."

Hans was stunned and returned to the line, refilled his tray and ate his lunch in silence at an empty table, knowing that all eyes were on him and on Crowe.

He finished before Crowe and asked a man at another table who had ordered him to his office.

"You're kiddin'," the man said.

"I ain't kiddin'."

"Well, kid," the worker said, "that was the chief, Mr. Frank Crowe. His office is just down the block. You can't miss it. There's a big American flag on top of it."

Perhaps it was the fact that Hans had nothing to lose, perhaps it was the feeling of paternalism which somehow exuded from Crowe, but Hans, his stomach filled, went toward Crowe's office and waited respectfully outside.

When Crowe returned from lunch he told Hans to follow him into his office.

"You know how to drive?" he asked.

"Yes sir."

"I mean *really* drive."

"Just came across the country. All the way from Detroit."

146

"Work at Ford?"

"Yeah, the Rouge. So did my dad."

"German?" Crowe asked.

"Yes sir. Born in America."

"Wait outside," Crowe ordered, and the boy left the room.

After an hour, Frank Crowe appeared in the hallway. He waved to Hans and steered him to his truck.

Hans jumped into the driver's seat and started the engine.

"Boy," he said, grinning, "this feels good after what I brought 'cross country."

Crowe looked at him but said nothing, then curtly, "Head up the road, toward the dam."

Crowe's truck was open, the heat beat mercilessly on its seat, its steering wheel was searing hot, the very metal of its touch seemed like an oven, but Hans drove toward Adit 1 and waited, toward the railroad junction and waited, to Boulder City and waited, all the time in the broiling heat. The temperature an even 128, Crowe ordered another run to the dam site. Hans complied, taking the curves easily, passing slower vehicles with expertise. Suddenly he stopped the car and got out, his mouth filled with vomit. "Guess I ain't the man I said I was," he barely managed to say.

Crowe watched as the boy rushed to the side of the road and collapsed in a pool of vomit.

Frank flagged down a truck behind him. He told the driver to pick up Hans and take him to the infirmary. "Tell him to show up at my house in the morning at five-thirty."

The truck driver obeyed and watched Crowe drive off toward the dam.

23

Frank Crowe had a select group of workers; some had worked with him at Deadwood, others at Tieton, and most of them had worked with him on all his dams. Among this group were muckers and carpenters, high scalers, concrete men, railroad workers—every working segment of the dam was represented. These men were Crowe's eyes and ears in the ranks; he relied on them heavily for any signs of discontent, violence, or strikes. Over the years they had developed a method of communication. Not one of these men was ever allowed to visit Crowe's office. For their information, and for the services these men performed, they were paid one dollar above their regular wages. This money came out of Crowe's personal operating fund and would not show up in General Bookkeeping.

Frank Kelly was Crowe's operative in the beleaguered Nevada adit and on July 9, with the temperature a steady 120, Crowe met with Kelly during the shift change. He was a man older than Crowe, heavy-set, balding, still muscular and known to be a good drinker.

"The fuse is getting short in this tunnel," Kelly said. "We've got one 'accident' after another. Trucks blow tires, sand in the gears, I don't have to tell you. . ."

"What about Williams?" Crowe asked. "Isn't he aware of it?"

"He's aware, sure, but you know Williams, he's such a goddamned driver he don't stop to *think*, meaning no disrespect. . . ."

"Can you point the finger at the bastards?" Crowe asked.

"No, I can't, but I can tell you who's behind them."

"Who?"

"Devere. Feller called Devere. I've heard his name in the tunnels and I've heard his name at the river camp."

"Devere," Crowe repeated. "Any idea where he hangs out?"

"Yes. Behind Alma's fruit stand on Boulder Highway."

Crowe looked at Kelly. "Go to Searchlight. The Reno Café."

"Are you kidding?" Kelly smiled.

"Drink your heart out tonight. Take off tomorrow. I'll square it with Williams."

"Much obliged, chief."

Crowe ordered Hans to drive him back to his office. "Go like hell," he told the boy, but Hans had learned in his few weeks of employment that that was a standing order and he had learned to maneuver Crowe's vehicle past any obstruction. Fortunately, Crowe's truck was well known on the dam site and everyone gave it a wide berth when they saw it approach.

Crowe rushed into his office and closed the door. He picked up the phone and called Police Chief Pitt in Las Vegas.

"Crowe here," he said, "how are you, Jack?"

"Busy . . ." Pitt answered. "You want to build me a new jail? We're up to capacity."

"Well, make room for one more."

"Give me his name."

"Devere," Crowe said, "Alma's fruit stand. In back. Labor punk."

"What charge?" Pitt asked.

"Vagrancy," Crowe said.

"We've tried that," Pitt said. "Those Wobbly bastards all have five bucks sewn in their jeans. We pick 'em up and they bail themselves out an hour later."

"I don't have to tell you how to do your job," Crowe said. "As long as you can keep him, sweat him."

"How much?"

"Keep it legal," Frank said. "I don't want a fucking martyr."

"Got you," Pitt said.

Crowe hung up the phone and paced his office.

Police Chief Pitt, a man in his fifties with twenty years under his belly, thrived on crime as a department store relies on Christmas, only now it was Christmas every day. With pimps and whores, thieves and drunks and gamblers, his jail was like a mint. Length of detention was in inverse proportion to ability to pay one's way out, and crime was not a moral issue with him, it was a source of income. There were rumors that he was the richest man in Vegas, but most of the rumormongers were sooner or later in Pitt's clutches and their propensity for gossip was carefully squelched.

But Jack Pitt was also a realist. He could well remember the lean years in Vegas, and he fully realized that it was the Big Six Companies and the dam which brought the largesse; and the fountain of all this was Frank Crowe.

On Mondays, Crowe would regularly show up at the jail and bail out "his boys" who had gotten drunk or boisterous. It was Crowe who set and paid the bail, and there was no argument from Pitt.

This phone call from Crowe was important, Pitt knew that. He would pick up the man himself but ordered four officers to follow him in another car.

They drove quickly to Alma's fruit stand. The chief jumped out of his car and knocked on Devere's door. It was opened by Devere himself.

"Hello, Pitt," he said. "What took you so long?"

Pitt was surprised at the openness of the man.

"Want to come in? Have some coffee?"

Pitt entered carefully, his aging eyes adjusting slowly to the darkness of the room.

"Keep the door open," he ordered.

"As you say, chief," Devere said, ushering him to a chair. "Sit down."

Pitt sat and saw three other men, younger than Devere, about the barren room.

"I ain't here on a social call," the chief said. "You're under arrest."

149

"What charge?" Herman Schroeder shouted excitedly.

"Shut up," Devere cracked back. "Vagrancy. That right?"

"That's right," Pitt said.

Now he turned to one of the men in the room and said, "Call Levy, have him spring me in two hours, call Waner at the *Age* and tell him to get there right away. I'll give him the story of his life."

Devere stood. "You want to handcuff me?"

Pitt looked around the stark room. "There won't be no need. Let's go."

Pitt and Devere drove toward Las Vegas. There was silence in the car, but finally Devere said, "I'm in one business, you're in another. I appreciate the fact you came yourself."

"No sweat," Pitt said.

"Yeah, well," Devere finished, "I want to talk to you about sweat."

"Go on," Pitt said.

"I'm gonna tell you everything I know, and maybe more than you want to hear, but you don't have to beat it out of me. . . ."

"We'll see," Pitt said, coldly.

"We'll see nothing," Devere said. "You know damned well that vagrancy charge is phony."

"So why you coming along peaceable?"

"Because I ain't gonna fight your vagrancy charge. I aim to tell you everything."

Pitt stopped the car suddenly and faced Devere. "Look, mister," he said, "you might as well know that I don't like you commie bastards and my boys don't like you commie bastards. There's work on the dam. Why fuck it up?"

"They aren't workers," Devere said, "they're slaves."

"Well, before the dam, there wasn't *no* work at all."

"I'll grant you that," Devere said. "I also said we're in different kinds of work. You in the war?"

"Hell, yes, the military police," Pitt said.

"Me too. Infantry. Got my balls shot off fighting for Old Glory."

Pitt looked at the man. "Different kinds of work." He thought about it, and finally started his car and took Devere in to be booked.

Frank Crowe read about it all in the Las Vegas *Age* the following morning. The headlines read, IWW GROUP AT DAM REVEALED, and the story detailed the arrest of Devere, age 36, an American citizen born at Phonerville, Humboldt County, California. In his possession, the story continued, were an array of credentials, letters of introduction, membership cards, dues stamps, and a copy of the *Industrial Worker*, official newspaper of the organization. Devere appeared to

150

have no fear of the consequences of his arrest and talked freely to authorities.

Crowe read the paper carefully, very carefully. Devere, the story continued, had recruited twenty-one new members in the last month and had already called one meeting of the IWW at Rag Town. He boasted his membership exceeded three hundred men on the dam. The story read:

When asked by this reporter what his grievances were, Devere stated his principal objection was that not enough cold drinking water was provided the workers. He maintained that for a man working on the night shift there were no possibility of sleeping during the day. Devere stated emphatically that the Big Six Companies were not obeying the Nevada laws with regard to labor provisions. Mr. Devere was released on bail two hours after his arrest. Bail was posted by the IWW attorney, August Levy."

Crowe threw the paper onto his desk and paced the floor. There was a knock on the door. It was Wanke.

"You read it?" Crowe held up the paper.

"I read it," Wanke said. "He's a pro."

"You bet," Crowe agreed. "I played right into his hands."

"You sure did. I don't believe that three hundred figure."

"Neither do I," Crowe said, "but he got it into print."

"Yes, he did."

"Well," Crowe said, "I don't give a shit about the Nevada labor laws, and I can't build a goddamned hotel for the night shift."

"We can get more water," Wanke said.

"Yeah, we can do that," Crowe agreed. "It's the heat, this goddamned heat, *that's* his biggest ally."

Crowe sat on his window seat. "You know what worries me the most?"

"What?" Wanke asked.

"Devere. I talked to Pitt yesterday. He said he's a slick character."

"How many guys you got on security now?" Wanke asked.

"Ten," Crowe answered.

"I'd double it," Wanke said.

"I tripled it this morning," Crowe said. "What is it," Frank said meditatively, "what is it, Tom? Every dam it's the same thing. I've got three thousand stiffs in Vegas begging for work and I've got over a thousand men on the dam fighting for more money."

"It's the system, Frank," Wanke said carefully. "The American system; we teach every kid in school to make the most of themselves."

"I reward performance," Crowe argued.

"Sure you do, so do I, but we have a tendency to forget that

151

half the stiffs on this dam have nothing to sell but their muscle. That's not a very negotiable commodity."

"I don't look down on labor," Crowe said.

"Of course not, neither do I, because where would we be without it?"

"That's pinko talk," Crowe said.

"Sure, that's what you say, that's what I say, but think about it for a minute. I've got an investment in education; you have. The stiff's got no investment except his body."

"Right."

"Can you blame him for listening to every fucking radical who gives him dignity, hope, the promise of more?"

On every dam that Crowe and Wanke had worked on, sometime during construction this conversation came up. Crowe was aware of it, so was Wanke, but neither man ever had the time or took the time for serious philosophizing.

"I've got work to do," Frank said.

Wanke laughed. "We're not sitting on our duffs on the Nevada side ourselves."

"I know that, Tom. Watch out for that bastard with a beard."

"He's got a beard?" Wanke asked.

"Yes."

"Don't like guys with beards. Must have a weak chin."

24

As one single shot killing minor royalty in Austria-Hungary plunged half the world into World War I, so did one minor stroke of the pen light the fuse at Hoover Dam.

Mr. Ganz, still wearing gold-rimmed glasses, green eyeshade, vest, and elastic sleeve bands, had run his totals twice and made his projections. Once more he carefully copied these figures on a sheet of graph paper and went to see Henry Barnes.

He knocked on the door and entered meekly.

"What is it, Ganz?" Barnes asked.

"I've got some figures, Mr. Barnes."

"Let's see 'em."

Mr. Ganz placed his calculations on Barnes's massive desk and stood aside.

"According to these projections," he said, "and I've checked them twice, the tunnel wages are too high. Considering the hang-up in Tunnel Number 3 this operation is running at a loss."

"What do you propose?" Barnes asked.

"There will have to be a wage cut of one dollar a day."

"I see," Barnes said, thinking of the account of his son's reception at the dam site. "I'll take this up with the board," Barnes said. "Thank you very much," and dismissed Ganz. He then placed a call to Edward Chapman and both of them called for a board meeting, which was held at Chapman's office at eleven o'clock that morning.

It was Friday morning, August 7, 1931. The temperature in Boulder City was 120 degrees at six in the morning and would rise to 128 by noon as it had for the past two days. The dust outside Crowe's office was as thick as soup as an endless array of trucks and cars arrived and departed from the headquarters building like bees flocking to and from the comb.

At noon the phone ran on Crowe's desk. He answered it. Barnes was on the line.

"Yes sir?"

"We have just concluded a board of directors meeting."

"Yes?"

"And we're cutting tunnel wages a dollar a day."

"You're *what?*"

"I see no need to repeat what I said," Barnes said coldly.

Crowe was silent for a minute, stunned.

"You can't," he said.

"What do you mean we can't, Mr. Crowe?"

"The tunnel is my most sensitive area. We're having trouble at the Nevada adit already."

"We're aware of that, Mr. Crowe."

"It's been a hundred twenty-eight for days," Crowe almost pleaded. "We just arrested one of the Wobbly heads. He said he had three hundred stiffs working on the dam. He's been *waiting* for such a move."

"Well," Barnes said, "if he's waiting for such a move, I assume you are prepared for it."

"I'm not prepared for a wage cut."

"Then I'd suggest you do your homework. The cut is effective tonight."

Crowe in his position was rarely told what to do. He knew this

153

contributed to his anger, but the illogic of the move was more consuming.

"Is Mr. Donner there?" asked Crowe.

"Yes."

"Let me speak to him."

Barnes handed Old Man Donner the phone.

"Hello, Frank," he said, almost warmly.

"Mr. Donner, do you men know what you're doing?"

"We're here to see that you bring in this dam at a profit."

"So am I, Mr. Donner, but this wage cut could shut us down."

"I've got to remind you of what you said in Denver, Frank."

"What was that?"

"You said, 'I'll have no labor shit on this dam.'"

Frank was silent. Finally he asked Donner, "Did everyone vote for this wage cut?"

"What does it matter?"

"It matters to me."

"Only Mr. Stein voted against it."

"I see," said Crowe. "Tell your boys to pack their bags and plan to come up here."

"You better follow orders, Frank," Donner said. "The cut goes into effect tonight."

"I've never disobeyed an order in my life." Crowe hung up the phone.

He paced the floor of his office restlessly. He had, he thought, projected every possibility of trouble, and he had ample alternatives at his disposal, but he had not counted on a wage cut. Already he could see Devere rubbing his hands at Alma's fruit stand. He opened the door and called Loomis, one of his young staff engineers, to his office.

"Find Williams," he ordered. "He's probably in Tunnel 3, and get him here fast. Use my truck."

Loomis left wordlessly.

Then he phoned Murph in Boulder City. He barked into the phone, "No leaves, no furloughs for you or your boys. No sick calls, no nothing. Report to me at three."

"What's the trouble, Mr. Crowe?"

"You'll know soon enough." Crowe hung up the phone.

He ordered Stubbs to fetch Wanke and asked Hansen to locate Walker Young. To the woman phone operator outside his office he gave the job of locating Elwood Mead in Washington, D.C.

Williams arrived, his clothes chalky gray, his hard hat squarely on his head, the metal toes of his boots rusty. "What's up?" he said before closing the door to Frank's office. Frank saw Wanke approaching and waited for him to enter, then closed the door.

"Just had a phone call from the Bohemian boys."

"Who?" Williams said.

"Barnes," Crowe said. "Then I spoke to Donner."

"What do they want?"

"They're going to cut the tunnel wages a dollar a day."

"They're *what?*" Williams shouted.

"Effective tonight," Crowe stated.

"Do they know what it's like in the tunnels?"

"I've told them. I told them about Devere's arrest two weeks ago."

"Holy Mother of God," Williams still shouted.

"They'll walk out."

"I know they will," Crowe said.

"How much you got in your supervisor's contingency fund?" Wanke asked more calmly.

"Not enough, Tom," Crowe said. "I could support wages a couple of days, that's all."

"Shit," Williams said. "You can't cut wages today. It's so god-damned hot these bastards would walk out if it would kill their mothers."

These protestations of Williams were natural and warranted, and to Crowe as predictable as Wanke's calm. Frank did not have to project these reactions. It had been almost an hour since the call now, and Crowe was working on the equation.

There was a knock on the door. It was Walker Young. Frank let him in and told him the news.

"That's very poor timing," Young said without emotion.

"To say the least," Crowe agreed.

"What are you going to do?" Williams asked.

"I'll tell you," Crowe said, seating himself on the edge of his desk. "I've got three adversaries at this point. The boys at the Big Six, the heat, and Devere." He paused.

"If I cut the tunnel wages, your boys," he looked at Williams, "will walk out. If I don't get through those tunnels, I've got no dam." He walked toward the wall covered with neatly drawn and lettered graphs and projections. He pointed to one set of figures and graphs after another. "We're ahead of every schedule except Tunnel Number 3. I know you're driving like a madman, Jack, but we're short in that tunnel, you know it."

"I know," Williams said.

"There's no need for me to rush ahead on this dam until I get that tunnel into line." He turned to Walker Young. "How secure is this reservation?"

"It's secure," Young said.

"Fenced, patrolled?"

"It's like the Bastille," Young assured Crowe.

"Good."

All three men watched Crowe pace the room.

He looked at his watch. It was one o'clock. "If you announce the wage cuts at two today, Jack, you'll have a walkout by three."

"I know."

"At evening mess I am going to announce that news and I'll tell them that *all* work on the dam will come to a stop."

"They're not *all* going to strike," Wanke said.

"No, but they're all going to be out of work." Crowe watched the impact of this statement.

"You will follow orders," Crowe mimicked Donner, "and so I will. I'll cut the wages and I'll close the dam site. I didn't *get* the last order. That's mine."

"What is your reasoning, Frank?" Young asked.

"I'm going to have a strike in the tunnel. My information is that Devere has a strike fund. Maybe he can feed the tunnelers for a week, maybe two. When word gets around the tunnelers are out, I'll have another three or four hundred stiffs going out on sympathy strike. Maybe Devere can feed them too.

"But if I close the dam site tonight, Mr. Devere will have sixteen hundred stiffs to feed. He didn't count on that for sure."

Crowe looked at Young, who betrayed nothing. "But I'll need your help."

"What kind of help?"

"I need a statement from you that this is a government reservation and an order stating that as of seven o'clock it is closed."

"I can't issue that order," Young said. "Only Elwood Mead can."

"I've got a call in to him now," Crowe said.

"What else do you need?" Young asked, signifying his approval of Crowe's plan.

"Trucks," Frank said. "I'm gonna move out every soul who isn't vital to this dam site. Lock, stock, and barrel, men, women, and children. I'll feed the women and children and I'll let the men starve."

"Sounds like the Phoenicians," Wanke said.

The phone rang. It was Elwood Mead, head of the Bureau of Reclamation, calling from his office in Washington.

After a few pleasantries Crowe outlined his plan. Crowe and Mead's friendship was a long and good one. The Colorado had threaded through their lives for twenty years, beginning when Frank was a surveyor and Mead an engineer. They had risen as steadily in the ranks of the Bureau as had their respect for each other.

"Who gave you this stupid order?" Mead asked.

156

"Barnes," Crowe said.

"Fucking sidewalk engineer," Mead spat out the words.

"Donner," Frank said.

"*He* should know better," Mead countered.

"Can't figure him either," Crowe answered. "Spoke to him myself. Gave me no leeway."

There was silence in Washington. Crowe waited while Mead was thinking through his proposal.

Finally he asked, "How long do you figure it will take to starve out the stiffs?"

"I'm not worried about the stiffs," Crowe said. "It's Friday today. I'll pay them. They'll get drunk this weekend. They'll be starving by Wednesday."

"What are you worried about?"

"The Big Six," Crowe said. "They'll get the news tomorrow. It'll hit them between the eyes in the morning. They'll be up here the next day."

"What do you figure, Frank?"

"I'll need a couple of days. If the weather holds I'll sweat the bastards by Monday."

"I could talk to Hoover," Mead said.

"I know," Crowe said. "I think I can handle it without him."

"Let me know if you can't."

"I'll call you and thanks for the offer."

"Let me talk to Young," Mead said.

Crowe handed Walker the phone and motioned to Williams and Wanke to follow him out of the room. Crowe felt better now. The futility of the morning was turning into concrete plans, but Williams was still fuming.

"Those pricks," he said, as they paced in front of the administration building. "Whose idea was all this anyway? The Jew's?"

"The Jew," Crowe said, very carefully, "was the only one who voted *against* the pay cut," and Wanke smiled.

"Oh, shut up, Tom." Williams scowled.

"I didn't say a goddamn word."

"I want a different crew in Number 3 when they return," Crowe ordered.

"I know, Frank. I've got the list made up already."

"When you announce the pay cut, Jack," Crowe said sternly, "I want you to watch the men in Number 3. Devere's boys will walk out first. Remember their faces! Their names!"

"I'll remember them," Williams snarled, "if anything is left of them before they get out."

"*Remember* them," Crowe said sternly. "I don't want any violence. Do you understand?"

157

"Shit," Williams said. "Do you want me to hand them each a gold medal?"

"I said, *no* violence. *That's an order, Jack.*"

"I heard you," Williams said, starting to walk away. "What a fucking way to build a dam. Nineteen thirty-one. The age of enlightenment for the working man. Shit!"

Wanke and Crowe watched Williams hurry toward his truck and gun it out of sight.

"Don't worry about Jack," Wanke said.

"I'm not worried about him. I agree with the way he feels."

Crowe turned and walked to his office, where Walker Young was waiting.

"When do you want the trucks?" Young asked.

"At six in the morning. I'll make the announcement tonight. I'll give 'em twelve hours to pack their gear."

Young started to leave.

Crowe said, "I appreciate your cooperation."

"You wouldn't get the cooperation if I didn't agree with your plans."

Crowe nodded.

"And Elwood Mead said 'good luck.' "

"Yeah." Crowe smiled. "Good luck. I'll need it."

Murph, the police chief, was waiting in the hallway and Crowe motioned him in.

He outlined his plan to the chief in detail and ended his instructions with one admonition: "I want no head busting or shooting or beating, do you understand?"

"Yes, Mr. Crowe."

"As a matter of fact, leave your night sticks in the station."

"Yes, Mr. Crowe."

"You got a good deputy?"

"Sure."

"Station him on my front door and tell my wife to lock the house and stay home!"

"Yes sir."

"That's all."

Perhaps the only thing which lifted Crowe's spirit that day was that events occurred in the precise order he had predicted, the precision of occurrences matching a set of determinates triangulating a surveyed area.

Williams made the announcement of the pay cut in Tunnel Number 3 at three o'clock. The temperature was 130 degrees. The silence of men dropping their tools, of engines shut off, of air drills ending their cacophony, was ominous.

158

Loeb, a young red-headed mucker, was the first to open his mouth.

"That's it, Williams," he said. "That's the last straw," as he took off his hard hat and threw it onto the floor of the tunnel. The lights and shadows played on his raw, intense face. There were six, seven others who echoed Loeb's sentiments.

Contrary to his instincts, but obeying his orders, Williams merely stood still. He burned the image of the first men to strike into the recesses of his brain, and during the next twenty minutes he watched silently as 125 men walked out of Tunnel Number 3 into the daylight.

There were loyal men in Number 3, men who had worked alongside Williams at Deadwood, at Tieton, but he had his assistant supervisors shepherd them out of the tunnel too. Williams did not follow but remained with Lerner, his chief assistant.

Finally the work site was empty. There was only the sound of the generators pumping air into the shaft, an occasional rock that fell from the tunnel walls.

"I think the Big Six are assholes," Williams said, "and these stiffs think I'm an asshole. And the fucking Wobblies will have the best party in Vegas tonight, only I wasn't invited."

"I'll take you to the Reno Club," Lerner said.

"Good idea," Williams agreed, "and we'll charge the booze to Crowe."

"Now you're talking, boss." They walked silently toward daylight. The safety man stood at the heading.

"Don't let nobody in," Williams ordered.

"I got no gun," the elderly man said.

"There's a whole case of dynamite." Williams pointed to a wooden box painted red. "You know how to use that?"

"Just needed the order, boss," the elderly man said.

"You just got it," Williams answered, then looked at Lerner. "You driving or me? I've got to get to the other headings first."

Devere was in his office with Herman Schroeder and six of his boys when he received the news of the walkout.

He smiled briefly and rubbed his hands. "Now you're going to learn your first lesson in the field," he said to Herman. "The trouble with capitalists is that they're always stupid. Greed feeds upon greed." Devere stood up. "No time for sermons now." He spoke to all in the room. "Get out the placards and the handbills. Get the boys up to the dam site and get some fires going. We'll be feeding stiffs here for days. Move!"

They left the room, and as Devere worked the combination of the safe behind his desk, he wondered how long he could feed these tunnelers on five hundred dollars.

159

Crowe made the terse announcement at five o'clock in the mess hall. He rose and there was silence. He read from a notice which he had typed that afternoon.

"Due to a strike in the tunnels, this is to notify all Hoover Dam employees that the job is closed down until further notice.

"The mess hall will be closed after tonight to everyone except office help and bull cooks and watchmen. Trucks will be available for transportation to town. Pay checks are ready for issue upon the usual checking out with the bull cooks. That is all."

Crowe left the mess hall still stunned and silent and drove off without having anything to eat.

At six-thirty Devere got news of the general shutdown. Herman Schroeder could not contain his excitement. "You did it," he yelled towards Devere. "You pulled it off." He started to pat Devere on the shoulder but Devere shook him off like a bothersome fruit fly.

"I did it, bullshit. Didn't you hear the news?"

"Sure, the whole dam's on strike!"

"The whole dam, you idiot, is not on strike. A hundred twenty-five tunnelers are on strike and Crowe threw everybody off the dam site. How long do you think we can feed sixteen hundred men?"

"I never thought of that," Herman said.

"You never do much thinking." Then he stopped and lit another cigarette. "I never thought of it either. That fucking Crowe. Check and double check."

25

Cessation of work cast an eerie silence over the dam site as Hans drove Crowe from checkpoint to checkpoint. Night was falling but Crowe had ordered the lights kept on. With each security man he had the same conversation, gave the same order.

"Stay on your post," he ordered. "You know your perimeter. If another guard asks for your help, ignore it. You're responsible for this shed, these shovels, these pipes, that's all, but that's your ass. If ever there's going to be sabotage, now is the time. You got that?" They drove all around the dam site seeing each guard, checking each lock, doubling patrol on sensitive areas like the compressor house, the transformer stations, the heavy equipment yard, the engine roundhouse.

It was past ten o'clock when Hans dropped him off at his house. Crowe and Hans noticed the guard stationed at the door.

"Do you want me to come to work tomorrow?" Hans asked.

"I want you here at five A.M."

"Yes sir."

The guard said good evening to Crowe before he entered the house. He saw Elle huddled in a chair in the dining room, a book spread out on the table.

She rose and put her arms around Frank and, abandoning all advice, asked bluntly, "What's going on? I couldn't even go shopping. All I've got is some beans on the stove and coffee."

"Beans will be fine," Frank said, going to the kitchen and opening the cupboard. He reached for a bottle of bourbon and poured half a water glass full of the amber liquid and drank it neat.

"You want some, Elle?"

"No thanks. What's going on?"

"How about those beans?"

"Sure, honey." Elle set the table, handed Frank a plate of beans, some bread, and a cup of coffee.

"Haven't had a meal all day," Frank said, eating quickly.

Elle watched him, drawn and tired, his eyes hollow, still wearing his felt hat, his sweat-stained shirt.

After supper Frank motioned Elle to their living room and she sat at his feet. They could hear the sound of trucks and cars going by their house, an occasional threat or curse carried through the hot night air in their direction. They heard the guard marching around the perimeter of their dwelling, his flashlight on.

"The tunnelers struck today. The Big Six cut their wages by a dollar a day."

"Why?" Elle asked.

"Because *one* little column in Barnes's records showed a minus sign."

"But the whole dam site is on strike," Elle said anxiously.

"The whole dam site is not on strike, Elle. I threw everybody off the dam site."

"Was that Barnes's doing too?"

"No," Frank said, "it was mine."

He looked at Elle, beautiful, distraught, and very vulnerable. There were times when he felt the difference of those eighteen years between them. Now was one of them. He explained his tactics to Elle. It was unusual for him to do this, but he almost relished giving her his reason-

161

ing, step by step, and Elle in turn was pleased that he would confide in her.

After he had finished, he added, "Tomorrow the big boys will get the word and next day they'll be up here. You'll see them in their Buicks and Packards, and their city clothes, and they'll be hopping mad."

"What will happen, Frank?"

"They'll either buy my plan or we'll head back to Salt Lake City."

Elle thought for a long time. Finally she said, putting her hands on Frank's knees, "Whatever happens, Frank, makes no difference to me. Believe me. We can go to Denver or to Timbuktu. What is it going to do to you?"

Frank finally removed his felt hat, which made him look younger, although he did not feel young at all. He said, "You know, Elle, maybe I'm getting too old to build this dam."

"Nonsense."

"Already I've made two mistakes."

"What mistakes?"

"I've counted on every contingency on this project but I didn't count on being undercut by the Big Six boys."

"What other mistake did you make?" Elle asked nervously.

He put his hand on her beautiful head, stroking her hair.

"I wanted to sell our house in Salt Lake."

Elle smiled now and kissed Frank tenderly.

"I told you, Frank. You're not a myth, you're a man, and I'm glad. Hate to make love to a myth."

Hans Schroeder parked the truck by the administration building and hitchhiked back to Alma's fruit stand. It took him longer than usual tonight. Although the traffic was heavy, the drivers were angry, frustrated. Finally an oil tanker picked him up and let him off at the highway outside his home.

His home, such as it was, still consisted of the truck he and Herman and Terry had driven across the country. They had enclosed it with canvas on all sides; Terry had managed somehow to scrounge some carpeting, some candles, a few dishpans and tin cans, which she used to fry their beans, to make them porridge.

There was a tremendous amount of activity around the back of Alma's fruit stand. Trucks and cars were parked helter-skelter all about the desert, a number of campfires were blazing, men and women sitting about them eating stew, drinking coffee, some singing, others quiet, many angry.

Hans found Terry huddled close to a small fire, the color of the flames playing kindly with her young face.

"What's going on?" he asked.

"Don't know," Terry said. "Been like this since four o'clock. People been coming and coming, talking to Devere, your brother, those others he's got hanging around. They've been handing out signs and handbills. STRIKE, they say, WORKERS UNITE. Everybody's angry. Let's get out of here, Hans."

"I can't," Hans said.

"Why not?"

"I can't. I can't now."

"These people scare me, Hans."

"Just stay in the truck. Here," he said, handing her a hunting knife, the blade eight inches long. "Put that under your pillow."

"Where did you get that?"

"I bought it."

"What for?"

"For you."

Terry unsheathed the knife and looked at the blade, the fire reflected in its sheen.

"I don't know how to use this."

"You'll learn in a hurry if you have to," Hans said.

"I tried to find work today," she said, as she had almost every day since their arrival in Vegas.

"I might get a job for you on the dam."

"Doing what? Nobody else's working."

"They ain't gonna strike forever."

Herman entered the truck. He seemed elated. "Boy," he said, "I think we got Crowe by the balls."

At eight o'clock Sunday morning the limousines of the heads of the Big Six rolled into Boulder City. One by one they lined up in front of the mess hall. Frank Crowe had turned the Blue Room, so far unused, into a conference room by placing army blankets over the mess tables, scattering a few ashtrays around, ordering one of the bull cooks to keep the coffee going.

It was obvious that the men had met earlier, perhaps in San Francisco the day before, perhaps in Vegas that morning. There were few pleasantries as they sat on one side of the long table, Donner in the middle, Mackenzie, Stein, Henderson, Andrews, Barnes, Chapman, all of them well dressed. Frank Crowe sat on the other side, flanked by Walker Young, Wanke, Williams, and several engineers from his staff.

Old Man Donner opened the meeting. "The question, Frank," he said calmly, "is one of authority. Yesterday I ordered you to lower the tunnel wages."

"I did," Crowe said.

163

"Yes, but no one ordered you to close the dam site."

"You did not forbid me to close the dam site."

"It never occurred to us."

"It never occurred to me you'd cut the tunnelers' wages."

"So the question really is, *who* has *what* authority, isn't that right, Frank?"

"I thought that was settled in Denver," Crowe said.

"You told us in Denver you'd have no labor trouble, isn't that right?"

"That is right, Mr. Donner, and I'd have none if you wouldn't interfere."

"Who's going to take the losses, Crowe," Barnes snapped, "you or us?"

"I have a stake also, Mr. Barnes."

"Yes, a bigger one than I endorsed . . ."

"Hold on," said Roger Stein. "Hold on, both of you. I see no room for subjectivity at a time like this."

"Listen, Roger . . ." Barnes interrupted.

"Listen shit," Stein snapped back. "This is not an inquest. Tell us, Frank, *why* you closed the dam site. You're not a spiteful man."

Crowe explained his reasoning carefully: his theory about the Wobblies, his fear for the work already under construction; he talked about the extreme heat, the need for housing, the urgency to move workers out of Rag Town.

He summed it all up, carefully, methodically, without passion.

He finally drew out an envelope from his back pants pocket and placed it on the table in front of him.

"In every job," he said slowly, "in every set of plans, in every projection, there are imponderables. I did not, when I presented my plans in Denver, recognize the backlog of poverty or unemployment in Vegas. I did not gauge the depression properly. I felt I had an endless eager labor supply.

"I *do* have an endless labor supply, but much of it is useless. This goddamned depression has squeezed the juices out of a lot of men. Some would just as soon shuffle to the soup kitchen as slave on a dam site. I've never seen that before. I did not, and I admit it, gauge these stiffs correctly. This country is getting weak and the commies are feeding off this weakness. I've got more labor shit than I expected.

"In front of me, in this envelope, is my resignation."

He looked around the silent table. "You have two choices, gentlemen. Restore the tunnelers' wages and restore my full authority on this dam, or get another supervising engineer."

Having said this, Frank Crowe walked out of the Blue Room, the mess hall, and they could hear his truck starting up.

164

Williams rose next. "If Frank goes," he said, "so do I, and so does Tom. Right?"

Wanke nodded and both men and Crowe's engineers left the room. Only Walker Young remained at the opposite side of the table.

The men of the Big Six realized that Walker Young in his role of chief engineer for the government was neither under their jurisdiction nor a man to be tampered with. Much of the success or failure of their dam depended on his cooperation. It was for this reason that they listened respectfully to his words.

"What I have to say," Walker started as dryly as usual, "will be brief and to the point. I could not believe your absolute stupidity in cutting the tunnel wages Friday when temperatures were boiling and the Wobblies were waiting for a flash point, which you so conveniently provided.

"I felt that Frank's handling of the situation was brilliant, as did Elwood Mead, with whom I have been in contact. He offered to call Hoover to intercede, but Crowe did not wish him to do so. The President, however, phoned me this morning. His message was short and to the point. He said that he and the government had the fullest confidence in Frank Crowe and to convey to you that any managerial changes at the dam would be looked at with great disfavor. I need say no more." Walker Young rose and departed.

Barnes spoke first. "That's blackmail, pure and simple," he said, and Edward Chapman agreed, but Old Man Donner took a different tack. "I don't give a shit what Walker says, or Mead or Hoover, and I don't give a shit whether it's blackmail. I happened to listen to Crowe, and what he said about the labor problems is something *I* didn't realize. What he said makes sense, and what he *did* makes sense, and the fact that he said he erred is good enough for me."

"What do you want to do? Restore the wages in the tunnel? Let Crowe run all over us?"

"You got two choices, as I see it," Mackenzie, the Scot, now said, picking up Crowe's resignation and waving it at his partners, "a dam or no dam."

"*I* could build this dam," Barnes yelled.

"Yeah?" Mackenzie countered. "From that window seat at the Bohemian Club? You've sweated right through already, and it's *cool* in here."

The vote which followed was in Crowe's favor.

Mackenzie's chauffeur so informed Frank, sitting in his living room with Elle, Jack Williams, Tom Wanke, and their wives.

Frank Crowe walked to the window of his house and watched the limousines file out of Boulder City.

"Not one of them took a look at Rag Town," he said.

165

26

Devere, after meeting hundreds of workers around his soup kettles, gave the demands of the workmen to the Las Vegas *Age* on Friday night to be published the following day. The workers, he said, demanded:

1. A pay raise from $4 to $5 for surface men, $5.50 for tunnel workers, $6 for miners, and $6 for carpenters.
2. Improvement in the sanitary conditions of the river camp.
3. That all men be returned to their jobs without discrimination.
4. That workers be supplied with ice water until the drinking fountains are installed.
5. That rates for board and room be set at $1.50 flat per day.
6. Strict adherence to Nevada and Arizona mining safety laws.
7. That dry rooms be installed at portals to the tunnels.
8. An 8-hour day from camp to camp.
9. That a safety miner be placed in each heading.

William Donner, president of the Big Six, gave his reply to the Las Vegas *Age* on Monday.

We do not mean to be arbitrary but we will not discuss the matter with the workers. They will have to work under our conditions or not at all. There has been no wage cut and none is intended.

Devere read the terse message and slapped his desk in anger. "The bastards didn't even give us credit for restoring the tunnelers' pay cut."

"We can stay on strike," Schroeder suggested.

"Bullshit," Devere said. "How long do you think our money will hold out? If you thought we were feeding a lot of stiffs yesterday, wait until today or tomorrow."

"Maybe you can get contributions."

"From whom?"

"The workers."

"You idiot. There *are* no *workers* on the dam. Nobody's gonna support *any* cause right now. Every stiff is coming out of his hangover

166

and anxious to go back to work. Frank Crowe'll be standing there at the gate welcoming them back, laughing like hell."

"You can't get it all overnight," Herman said.

"That's right," Devere agreed. "Not this way. I can't hurt them with the labor market."

"How else?"

"Just wait and see. I'm not through with Mr. Crowe yet. Not quite yet . . ."

It was Crowe's turn to use the newspaper. On the following day he stated that he would give a grubstake to workers' families, and the day after the *Review Journal* hit the street with an extra. It was August 12. Big wood type lines proclaimed, BIG SIX ORDERED TO RESUME WORK—YOUNG INSTRUCTS DAM CONTRACTORS TO PROCEED WITH WORK IMMEDIATELY.

On August 13 Leonard Blood, head of the Bureau's employment service, opened a branch in Boulder City to hire workers. Frank Crowe announced that the Big Six would hire no new men "until all the old working employees are back on the job." He said that "old-timers" would be given a reasonable amount of time to return to the job. Next to this announcement in the *Age* was another column announcing, U.S. BREADLINES FOR THIS COMING WINTER.

The following day 730 workers were back on the job. On Sunday, August 16, against Devere's harassing rhetoric, workers from the tunnel voted 68 to 57 to end the strike. By August 18, the work crew was up to 1,381 men, all former workers being hired except known or suspected agitators. Even Boulder City was settling back to normal, and Crowe removed the guard from his house.

27

Harry Watson had always been a modest man, shy, unresourceful, with neither the drive nor the stamina to make a good farmer. He had married Mary, a girl from his high school class in Indio, whose father had deeded them twenty acres of land, on which he cultivated grapefruit.

The acreage and the equipment were barely sufficient, even in good days, to keep Harry and his family of five alive, but a series of breaks in the levee destroyed his crops three years in a row, his in-laws had passed away, the bank foreclosed on his house, and like a good many of his neighbors, he found himself camping beside his truck in Rag Town.

He had been fortunate perhaps, finding work on the railroad being built to the dam site, but even though he was used to the heat in the Coachella Valley he was not used to the endless hours under the broiling sun in Boulder. Farming was hardly easy, but there *were* trees, there was a rhythmical cycle to pruning, fertilizing, harvesting, even the slight promise of a profit, certainly the camaraderie of the church, a square dance, a county fair. Here in this dust-filled ravine, surrounded by misery, by odors from the latrine, by the absolute lack of privacy, his days under that searing sun seemed endless and the nights spent on a hard bedroll laid on the ground were equally unbearable.

At first the promise of the dam had been symbolic. He understood the need for it, and like many of his present neighbors in the same boat, he spoke of going back, of starting up again, free from the fear of the dreaded Colorado floods. But laying tie after tie, still half starving, watching his wife and kids living a rootless existence took all the spirit out of Watson. He had nightmares at night when he did sleep, or would lie motionless in the windless heat.

Perhaps the only relief he found, as did many others, was to run to the river and immerse himself until his sweat became part of the Colorado, and his body temperature returned to sanity. Dripping wet he would return to his bedroll, and without bothering to cover himself, gained a few hours' sleep.

It was after one of these nocturnal swims that a slight wind came up, and Watson became chilled. He found a few small towels and dried himself as well as he could, but he was still damp when he returned to bed. His fever was high the following morning, but he went to work, nevertheless.

His wife found it queer that he ate no supper that night, almost funny that he was shivering in over a hundred-degree temperature. At one-thirty in the morning Harry Watson died. His wife noticed his death, since he stopped breathing. She did not panic. Death was ordinary in Rag Town. One lived with it night and day, and her grief was soon replaced by common sense as she roused several of her neighbors, some in trucks, others in tents.

The men walked toward Watson's truck, felt his forehead, still moist, and one of them said finally, "Pneumonia."

"Don't worry, Mary," one of the other men said. "We'll get him over to the Arizona side."

Mary and her children watched as four men easily lifted Harry up off his bedroll—he weighed very little—and everyone seemed dry-eyed as they watched the procession of four men carry Watson across the waist-high culvert and bury him in a shallow grave, which they marked with a discarded Nehi sign, rusted almost colorless.

One of the wives of the men carrying Watson to the Arizona side stood next to Mary as she watched the proceedings.

"Don't seem right," the woman said, "that Arizona pays fifty dollars more death benefits than Nevada. They never wanted the dam anyway."

"Nothing seems right," said Mary, finally sobbing gently, gathering her children around her. "Fifty dollars," she said. "That's more money than we had in a year. . . ."

Watson's death report crossed Crowe's desk the following morning, as had a number of similar ones during the summer. He summoned Dr. McDowell from the hospital and shoved the report into his hand.

McDowell studied the coroner's report. "Probable cause of death: pneumonia," he read.

"Sounds right to me," McDowell said.

"Probably is," Crowe said sternly. "But does a man get pneumonia and die immediately?"

"No," McDowell said.

"Then how quickly did he die?"

"How do I know? A day. Maybe two."

"That's right," Crowe said. "A day, maybe two. And I've built you a class A hospital, nice and well-equipped, right here in Boulder City, and are any of you sawbones down in Rag Town?"

"We take them as they come," McDowell said laconically.

"You take 'em, sure," Crowe said angrily. "*If* somebody's got the brains or the guts to bring them up the hill to the hospital."

"We got no visiting nurses," McDowell said. "We're an emergency facility."

"Pneumonia isn't an emergency?"

"I didn't say it wasn't."

"How many doctors in that hospital now?" Crowe asked.

"Three."

"That's what I thought."

"One on each shift," McDowell said.

"All right, Dr. McDowell. I'm going to change your hours."

"How?"

"I want two doctors on twelve-hour shifts and one doctor in Rag Town."

"Where you going to put him?"

169

"In a truck, with a stretcher. When he isn't working, he can use the stretcher to sleep. When he's needed he can take the patients to the hospital."

"I doubt," McDowell said sarcastically, "that our contract with the Big Six Companies calls for a man sleeping in a truck."

Crowe looked at Dr. McDowell and opened a filing cabinet. He withdrew a folder.

"You know what this is?" he asked angrily.

"No."

"These are applications from doctors. *Fine* doctors. Old, young, middle-aged. Harvard, Columbia, Tufts, pretty good training. All asking for employment on the dam."

"You say we're not doing a good job?"

"I say, act like a goddamned doctor. Quit sitting in that air-cooled building I built and get out where people are dying."

"The way you've got them living on this dam, you can't keep up with the deaths."

"A good point, doctor. I *know* I need more family dwellings, but *my* next order is an executive lodge. I need an executive lodge like an outbreak of cholera, but those are my orders. . . . Do you understand?"

"I understand," McDowell said.

"And what I just told you are *your* orders."

Crowe put his manila folder back into his filing cabinet.

"I presume we understand each other?" he asked.

"Engineers," Dr. McDowell said. "All you can think of is your precious dam. . . ."

Crowe threw down his pencil on his desk, then pointed an accusing finger at the doctor.

"Ever since I've been to sea, twenty years of working on dam sites, my picture of a *doctor*, a doctor," he repeated, "is a man sitting in a comfortable rocking chair in an office, surrounded by fading degrees and an endless supply of pure alcohol. How many years do you figure it takes to get over the glory of that goddamned degree and reread the Oath of Hippocrates?"

McDowell, red-faced, rose to leave.

"One thing," Crowe said, before he reached the door. "I would consider it a good example for the senior physician to take the first shift at Rag Town. Your truck will be available at the motor pool at five-thirty in the morning." Crowe picked up the phone and McDowell left, slamming the door.

Crowe ordered the young engineers outside his office to stop all calls and visitors. It was four o'clock in the afternoon, traffic still heavy outside the building, the blasts from the tunnels quite regular. He

170

paced his office aimlessly, finally sat on his desk, put his head between his hands and closed his eyes.

Crowe rarely took time to be reflective but now felt the pressure of his constant fever pitch, his short temper, his fear of sabotage and poor performance.

The strike, he knew, had taken its toll, as had the heat, which had persisted for an inordinate amount of time. He tried to rationalize, to reason with himself, but could remember only a plea which Elle had made before he reached the dam site. "Let me be your wife, Frank," she had said, and Crowe looked at his schedule; it was filled until ten that evening: cablemen, government engineers, an assembly-man from Nevada, plan checks, time cards. He picked up the schedule, walked outside his office, and handed it to Stubbs.

"Reschedule all these appointments," he said, "I'm going home. Don't call me tonight unless the dam site blows up." Then he left, and Stubbs looked at the other engineers in wonderment.

"Wonder if he's sick," he said to no one in particular.

Murphy, another young engineer, said, "I wonder how he can hold out at all the way he's going."

Elle, wearing shorts and a loose shirt, was sitting on the back porch of their house on a blanket, a book in her hand, a lemonade at her side. She was startled when Frank appeared.

"What's wrong, honey, are you all right?"

"I'm all right," Frank said.

"I've never seen you home this early."

"You got any more of this lemonade?"

"Sure." Elle got up and brought a glass. Frank drank half the lemonade and sat next to Elle.

"Just thought I'd take my wife out to dinner."

Elle looked at him, perplexed.

"Can't a man take his wife out to dinner without anything being wrong?"

"Most men, yes. Frank Crowe, no."

"Well, there *is* something wrong, Elle."

Elle touched him. "Are you ill, Frank?"

"No, no, nothing like that. It's . . ." Crowe hesitated.

"It's hard for you to talk about it."

"That's right." Frank shook his head, wiped his brow.

"Try, honey. Try it."

Frank looked at his hands. They were sweating. "I'm not pacing myself well, Elle."

"I don't know what that means."

"It means I have sixteen hundred men on the dam right now and it's almost more than I can handle. . . . Before this project is

171

finished I'll have six thousand men, then what?"

"You've got a staff, Frank. Let them help you run the dam site. You can't do it all yourself."

Frank thought seriously about Elle's remark.

"Just an hour ago I chewed out Dr. McDowell. We lost another man from pneumonia in Rag Town. Those poor stiffs are too hot or too stupid to get to the hospital on time. I ordered McDowell to station a man right at the river."

"What did he say?"

"He didn't like it."

"So you blew up."

"Naturally."

"You told me once, Frank, that you had to have some distance from your men."

"That's right."

"I quite agree with that. I also agree with your decision to put a doctor in Rag Town, but why do *you* have to tell McDowell, why did *you* have to fire the guard at the gate? Issue the order and let somebody on your staff carry it out."

"Makes sense, Elle." Frank paused. "Except for one thing."

"What is that?"

"I'm beginning to wonder whether I *enjoy* getting angry."

Elle put her arms around Frank. She kissed him. There were tears in her eyes. "What is it inside you, Frank Crowe? What is this demon of a man on one hand and a counter demon questioning? Why can't you accept the fact that you are very sensitive? Does that make you any less a man? Tell me."

"Those are powerful words, little girl."

"You bet. I'm not reading *True Story* when you're at the site."

"I guess not."

"Sometimes, you hardly seem to know me, Frank. I don't blame you for that. God knows you work twenty hours a day. We got married so quickly."

"What are you trying to tell me, Elle?"

"From the time I was sixteen I lived in academia. I lived with a professor's family, I worked in a college atmosphere, all my contacts were with students, scholars."

"I know that, Elle."

"I know you know that, Frank. I don't like to go around talking about myself, but everybody I knew tried to offer me scholarships, lend me money, help me get an education."

"Why didn't you accept that?"

"Pride, I guess. I knew I was taking care of myself, I didn't want to feel beholden." She paused. "Pride and fear, I suppose. I didn't

172

know whether I could live up to everybody's expectations. But now, since we've been married, since I've begun attending the university, I know I can handle it all. Easily. I didn't know then, and I'm sorry about the years I wasted."

And now Crowe put his arms around Elle. "Thirty years of age." He smiled. "At thirty, my love, you haven't wasted *any* time. You might be a better student now than you would have been a few years ago."

"We weren't talking about me," Elle said. "I was only trying to tell you that I *might* be of some help to you sometime."

"I'm beginning to find that out."

The guard was stunned when he saw Frank and Elle leave Boulder City.

"Off kinda early tonight, ain't you, chief?"

"Is it all right with you, pop?" Frank smiled.

"If I had a wife like yours, meaning no disrespect, ma'am, I'd be outa here at five *every* night."

Frank put the car in gear and headed toward Vegas. The sunset, orange, red, blue, yellow, and Poppa Joe's welcome and a bottle of hearty wine helped him forget some of his troubles, mercifully

28

There were any number of reasons why Frank Crowe hated ceremonies. The first was that he felt them unnecessary and time-consuming, second, it usually demanded his getting dressed for the event, and last it always put him in contact with politicians, municipal officers, so-called "functionaries," whose soft hands and pale faces fortified his feelings that they earned their living in either a dishonest or unwarranted manner. The Big Six Companies, however, felt different; their Public Information Office was an active branch of management. The reason for all this activity was that any good news on the dam site enhanced their chances for further jobs.

There was little Crowe could do when high government officials or one of the Big Six showed up at the dam site; his presence was required and that was that. But the wedding of Ma Kennedy to Whataman Hudson, which took place on Observation Point almost a thousand feet above the river, at high noon, was an event which absolutely infuriated him.

Ma Kennedy was the mother of Aimee Semple McPherson, the controversial revivalist in Los Angeles, who had parlayed her looks, her voice, even her scandals into the flourishing Angelus Temple, which accepted donations on clotheslines strung across the auditorium. She and her mother represented all that was ugly in religion to Frank; Whataman Hudson undoubtedly was a con artist. Still the event took place. The wedding was performed by Justice of the Peace Frank Ryan of Las Vegas at twelve-twenty-five, attended by the Las Vegas mayor and his wife and other guests from Las Vegas. The papers the following morning reported that the "blushing bride" held up her left hand, displaying her wedding ring, and shouted, "Now the birdies have come home to roost."

Frank Crowe was almost ready to throw up after reading the story the next morning, but his day was made tolerable when Jack Williams came into his office to announce happily that his crew had broken through the first twelve-foot adit in the Arizona bore and had already begun to cut the fifty-six-foot hole.

Frank walked to his maps on the wall of his office and drew some symbols.

"That's good news. Real good."

"Thought you might like to know. They dug one hundred sixty feet in Tunnel Number 3 yesterday. That's a record."

"Looks like you shook out the Wobbly bastards."

"Sure does."

Williams started to leave, but Frank stopped him.

"I know you're busy," he said, "but in your spare time I'd like you to do me a favor."

"What's that?"

"Put some dynamite under Observation Rock and get it off my dam site."

"Yeah." Williams laughed. "The boys were talking about it today. Thought it might be fun to see what a man Whataman is."

"I wish we'd had the dynamite under it yesterday. I'd a blasted them right to kingdom come. Then I'd like to see the mystical powers of Aimee Semple McPherson."

"I heard she was a hooker once," Williams said.

"I heard she was worse," Crowe added, and Jack left.

Kano Iko was Crowe's high-scaling foreman. A well-built man,

174

half Indian, half Eskimo, he had served under the chief on the last three dams.

High scaling, unquestionably, was the most dramatic and daring feat on any dam site, and the men who performed these tasks were half acrobats, half fatalists, suspended from two-inch manila lines over the canyon wall with a hydraulic drill in one hand and a belt full of dynamite wrapped around the waist.

It was their job to peel off loose rocks and boulders from the steep canyon walls before the actual pouring of the dam could begin.

Kano Iko well remembered his first job with Crowe when high scaling had been his first supervisory job. He was at Deadwood Dam and both men had learned some bitter lessons together, but experience taught them that fresh manila was needed at the first sign of chafing, and a four-hundred-pound lead weight had to be lowered on each rope before a scaler could be lowered on that same line. It was necessary for the pulleys to be properly oiled and for the guy wires to be solidly secured.

Frank Crowe liked Kano Iko. He was a simple but reliable man and never once veered from instructions handed him by Crowe. It was one thing, however, to secure the scalers in their precarious perches, another to find men who could perform the task well. They had to drill blasting holes, insert dynamite, clear the area, and wait for the explosive to be set off from the canyon rim controls. The pay was good, the best on the dam, and applications for the jobs ran high, yet over the years both Iko and Frank had learned that only Indians and circus performers used to high-wire work could perform their duties.

Iko rarely came to see Crowe, and Frank realized that his visit must be urgent. He admitted him to his office immediately and Iko in Indian English spilled out his troubles.

"Blood of the Bureau say I need more soldier on job."

Frank knew what he meant. Leonard Blood had complained to Crowe that not enough ex-servicemen were being hired for the job.

"I'll fix it," Frank said to Iko, getting Blood on the phone.

"Mr. Blood, Frank Crowe."

"Yes, Mr. Crowe."

"I wonder whether you could stop by my office to discuss the high scalers' situation."

"Delighted, Mr. Crowe. When would you like to see me?"

"Immediately."

"Fine, I'll be right over."

Then Crowe, winking at Iko, got hold of the chief cable operator.

"Harry? Crowe here. Yes. What's your fastest monkey slide? On the Arizona side? Good. How fast can you let it descend without breaking a man's neck? That's pretty fast. All right. Leave that slide available for me in thirty minutes. No. No safety wires, nothing. Thanks, Harry. Yeah. Iko will tell you all about it."

Leonard Blood was a government bureaucrat in charge of hiring at Hoover Dam. The high rate of unemployment had vastly inflated his ego. He appeared wearing a navy blue suit, a gray felt hat; there was a carnation in his buttonhole.

"We thought we'd take a look at the construction area to show you where the high scalers work."

"I'd enjoy that," Blood said.

Frank walked outside his office and hailed Hans. "I want you to drive me over to the Arizona site and get me to the 4 monkey slide."

"Yes sir."

Blood and Iko sat in back of the truck and Hans drove off. Hans covered the distance to the monkey slide in short order and watched Crowe, Iko, and Leonard Blood get out of the truck.

Blood looked suspiciously at this strange device before him. It was a simple wooden platform twenty feet wide and fifteen feet long. Beneath it were two steel rails, which descended almost vertically from the canyon rim to the canyon floor. The distance was eight hundred feet. Crowe and Iko stepped casually onto the wooden platform, but Blood hesitated.

"Don't you have a rail around this thing?"

"What for?" Frank asked.

"To hold on."

"No worry, Mr. Blood," Iko said. "Momentum—it root you in place."

Gingerly Blood stepped toward the center of the platform, Crowe signaled Harry, and they began their descent.

It took less than a minute to reach the canyon bottom, but it was enough time for Blood to get thoroughly sick, holding on to Crowe and Iko on the way down, collapsing when the platform reached bottom.

Crowe took no notice of Blood's predicament and pointed up the canyon walls which they had traversed.

"You can see the scalers working," Crowe said, pointing at a group of men suspended at various levels on the sheer wall.

Blood, vomiting now, could not force himself to look up.

"I think you'll understand that we need experienced men for this job."

Blood nodded feebly, getting off the platform.

"Is there another way out of here?" he asked, "I mean without taking this goddamned platform?"

"There's a long way around."

"I'll take it."

176

Crowe signaled a truck and the driver halted his vehicle.

"Take Mr. Blood back to the administration building," he told the driver.

"Sure thing, chief. Just got to get this pipe to Tunnel 3."

Crowe and Iko stepped back onto the monkey slide. They signaled Harry and a minute later stood back at the canyon rim.

They both walked toward Crowe's truck, smiling. "I think that ought to take care of your problem," Crowe said, and Iko nodded his head.

"Fix 'em good, chief. Go to work."

Iko walked off and Alfred, the informer from Number 3 tunnel, approached Frank.

"Got to talk to you, chief."

"Shoot."

"Not right here. Take a walk with me."

Crowe obeyed and they walked perhaps a hundred yards. Alfred pointed toward the Nevada side, but the gesture was purely deception.

"Got some more stuff on that Devere fellow."

"Yes?"

"Got a guy working for him, Herman, he's a cripple."

"Go ahead."

Alfred kept pointing toward the Nevada side and Crowe nodded his head in mock understanding.

"Young fellow's name is Herman Schroeder. His brother is Hans Schroeder."

"My *driver?*" Crowe asked, astonished.

"Yeah. There's him and a girl and Herman all living behind Alma's fruit stand in a truck."

"Jesus Christ. Do you think Hans is a red?"

"Can't say. Nobody seen 'im at any of the meetings. Still thought you ought to know."

Crowe sat down on his haunches and now pointed toward Nevada.

"Well, Alfred, the dumbest thing for me to do is to fire him."

"You know what you're doing."

"What's this girl like?"

"A real looker. Young. That's all I know."

"Keep it all to yourself, Alfred," Crowe admonished. "I'm much obliged."

"I'll keep my lines open," Alfred said.

"Do that," Crowe answered, then walked to his truck.

"Take me to my office," he said to Hans, eying the boy carefully as they rode toward Boulder.

When Frank entered his office he watched a pale Mr. Blood entering his car and leaving the dam site.

177

29

When Herman learned that his brother was Crowe's driver, his first impulse was to tell Hans off for being so casual with his information. But his new-gained professionalism as a revolutionary kept his temper in check. Instead he went to Devere, who seemed pleased with this new information.

"I know you've read Lenin," Devere said. "You recall he said that 'constant vigil of the enemy camp will inevitably lead to mastery.'"

"I do," Herman said. "I do remember that passage."

"Well," Devere said, tipping back in his oak armchair, "your brother may be the key."

"How?"

"He's with Crowe night and day. He's got eyes and ears."

"Yeah," Herman said hesitatingly, "but he ain't part of the movement."

"I know that," Devere said. "Why in the hell is he hanging around *here?*"

"Half the truck is his."

"What about the broad?"

"What about her?"

"Is he fucking her?"

"Not that I know of."

"Are you?"

"No."

"Would you like to?"

"Why not. One broad is as good as the next."

Devere half smiled.

"There's plenty of whorehouses around here. We're six miles from Block 16 with the biggest collection of hookers in the country. . . . They're used to cripples."

"I know that," Herman said, staring at Devere. "They always want a dollar extra."

There was almost compassion in Devere's voice. "They're animals," he said to Herman. "Just remember that. They're animals with cunts and teats and that's all they're good for."

"What's all this got to do with Hans?"

"Plenty. I'm gonna need him and I want you to see that he stays here."

"He ain't gonna join the movement."

"I know he ain't. I'm gonna use him in my own way."

"So what do you want me to do?"

Devere reached into his pocket and withdrew his wallet. He opened it and took out a five-dollar bill. "I want you to go to Vegas and get drunk and I want you to get laid and I want you to come back to the truck and brag about this great broad you've found."

Herman took the five-dollar bill.

"And I want you to stop eying that Terry. I've watched you. You've got a real hungry look. Let her be. If she wants to fuck your brother, let her. Leave them in peace. I need them here. Do you understand?"

Herman nodded, and watched as Devere carefully logged the five-dollar expenditure into a black ledger, its edges frayed and colored red.

Hans returned at seven that evening and Terry had her fire banked, a pot of stew slowly simmering; some peeled potatoes lay in a white enamel dish. A coffee pot, made of speckled enamel, blue and white and rusty, sat at the edge of the grate.

It was still daylight, the temperature approaching eighty; a merciful wind came from the west.

Terry was leaning against a cottonwood tree, her dress up to her thighs. She made no move to hide her white panties, which she knew appeared like a triangle to Hans, who was approaching and looking unashamedly.

"I seen Herman head for Vegas in Devere's car," he said, sitting by the fire.

"Can't figure it either," Terry said. "He wasn't even snarling when he washed up and slicked back his hair."

Hans took off his shirt and put it on the ground beside him. His chest and shoulders, his arms were deeply tanned from the constant exposure in Crowe's truck. He liked his work. He liked Crowe, respected him, constantly regaling Terry with stories of his daily exploits until Herman would tell him to shut up.

Hans lit a cigarette and stared at Terry. She too had gotten tanned, her legs shapely and inviting, her thin dress barely hiding her breasts. Terry blushed slightly, watching Hans watch her, but she didn't mind. It wasn't the same piercing look of Herman; perhaps she knew she was staring equally hard.

"Don't you like me, Hans?" she asked.

He looked at her. "Sure I like you."

179

"I mean *really* like me."

"What do you mean by that?"

"I mean, don't you ever want to make love to me?"

"Don't talk about it."

Terry moved closer and put her hand on Hans's leg.

"Why not? Is there something wrong with me?"

"No. There's nothing wrong with you."

Terry's hand moved gently up Hans's thigh.

"Is there something wrong with you?"

Hans smiled as Terry felt his erect penis.

"You, you just don't understand."

"What's there to understand?"

"I gave my word."

"To who?"

"Oh Jesus, Terry, take it easy," but Terry pursued Hans.

"I told my old man on his deathbed I'd watch out for Herman. I told Herman you weren't gonna be my woman or his woman."

"Herman ain't here," Terry said, taking his hand and putting it on her breast.

Hans could feel the warm body, the stiff erect nipple.

"Come inside," she said.

"Now?"

"Now."

"What about supper?"

"Supper can wait."

Terry jumped up and into the truck in one graceful motion and Hans followed quickly. She started to pull her dress over her head but Hans stopped her.

"Not so fast, honey. Not so fast." He pulled her down beside him on his makeshift bed.

"I been staring at you for months now. I've been watching you go to bed and I wake up in the middle of the night and I watch you half-naked under those lousy covers and I . . ."

"Don't talk, Hans," Terry said as she felt his hand go up her leg, slowly, feeling the warmth and softness of her inner thigh. She felt the tug of the elastic as Hans pulled off her cotton panties, then ran his hands up the curvature of her firm buttocks, finally working his hand around her clitoris, feeling the warm sticky moisture of her vagina.

She had pulled down his Levi's, his jockey shorts, and finally they lay next to each other, her large firm breasts against his chest, his arm caressing the curvature of her spine, prominent and moist, and finally they made love, easily, playfully, with all the vigor and grace of two healthy young animals.

180

They lay beside each other for an hour, perhaps longer. It had turned dark when they returned, dressed, to the fire and supper.

"You scared, Hans?" Terry asked.

"No."

"Don't be scared."

"All right."

"It's gonna be between us. Don't worry."

"I ain't worried, Terry, I'm just wondering."

"About what."

"I'm just wondering whether this is going to make it easier or harder."

"Was it good?"

Hans stared at Terry for a long time and finally put his hand on her cheek, still flushed.

"It was the best," he said. "The best ever."

"Good," she said, kissing his hand. "Good, Hans."

"Keep that in your head, will you?"

"I promise."

They ate dinner in silence and fell asleep in their separate bunks easily. They hardly noticed a drunken Herman coming back to the truck in the middle of the night, hardly heard him bragging about his Vegas conquest. They were lost in the dreams and the afterglow of a beautiful moment cut out of the cloth of a very bitter life about them.

30

The news of Jack Williams's getting through Tunnel Number 2 was quickly followed by further news that he had holed through Tunnels 1 and 4. Already his big Jack Williams Specials were hard at work widening the twelve-foot bore to its ultimate fifty-six-foot diameter.

Crowe studied the progress on his meticulously kept maps tacked to the walls of his office, and though he took *some* satisfaction from knowing that every entity of the dam site—the tunnels, the gravel sites, the railways and cableways, the generator plants, the presence of compressors—all of it, was well ahead of schedule, he also knew that as summer turned to autumn, winter and spring would not be far behind.

It was the river now, Big Red, the Colorado, Big Muddy, whatever people chose to call it, that was his biggest adversary. The Colorado River, which could rise seventeen feet in less than four hours, had not yet been tamed and might yet prove the victor.

Prudently he had sent one of his engineers to Grand Junction, to Glenwood Springs, to Alda, all upstream, and instructed him to hire observers.

"I want some men who can watch that river twenty-four hours a day. I want them each to have a phone and I want that phone checked every day. Maybe hire some boys with polio, boys who need the money and can be trusted," he instructed. But even after all these precautions had been taken, Crowe knew that even the fastest news would only give him a sparse few hours of lead time.

It was not only the river, but the weather, and though he looked at that cloudless, deep, deep blue sky above, he knew only too well that within a few months the thunderheads would cover the horizon and rain would come in sheets as solid as steel.

Constantly he harped at the engineers around him about drainage, drainage, drainage.

"Water goes *down*, mister," he would shout. "Water does not go *up*. Where are you draining this road, this spillway, this blockhouse?" and plans would be drawn and redrawn and the surveyors' flags went up and down the dam site like flowers in a cemetery.

Though the strike was over, Frank knew that Devere was not finished. The kind of defeat Frank had handed him would only case harden his steely will; there were times Frank truly questioned his system of government, whose laws allowed these agitators to move about in freedom, when Crowe felt they should be strung up and let dangle so other men could go about their work unfettered. And now he was angry that the U.S. Senate had set up an investigative committee to "study conditions at the dam." He saw faceless men in dark suits peering around his dam site, carrying neat little clipboards and well-sharpened pencils.

J. S. Sheafe of the Sheafe Engineering Company of Chicago was one of the investigators. His comments finally were made public in the Vegas papers:

There is food for all such as I have never seen before. There was so much and such a variety that I found it difficult to decide what I most wanted. There was celery, corn on the cob, pickles, etc. The tables literally groaned. All hands were served in the same splendid dining room from the same supply.

The kitchen is as modern as that of any modern hotel. The "cooler" is the last word. The various rooms where food is handled are all screened and ultra clean. Men live in dormitories having even the most improved ventilating system in each room.

The shifts are short and there is good pay for the hours considering the times. Frigidaire water coolers are down on the job. Electric light everywhere. Tunnels with forced draft from brand new Ingersoll Rand compressors.

Comfortable buses take men directly to their work and back. A hospital with splendid physicians. A clubhouse for the men serving all soft drinks and near beer for a nickel. In the town there is a store with fair prices, a drug store and cigar store also. Sewer system and modern plumbing are almost finished.

Everything that could be put in is there. Boulder City is a hard location but a good place to work for those who want to work.

"And I say, amen," said Elle after having read the story to Frank at the breakfast table. It was five in the morning and the first rays of dawn began to warm their home.

"I'd say, Mr. Crowe, you've been vindicated."

"I'd say," Frank answered, "the government wasted a lot of money."

Elle smiled, leaning over him as he finished his meal, kissing his cheek and pouring more coffee.

"You're a hard man, Frank Crowe."

Elle started to undo her robe.

"Where you off to so early?"

"I'm chairman of the Thanskgiving Committee."

"Is that a fact?"

"That is a fact, Mr. Crowe, and we're going to have a feast nobody will forget."

"Woman stuff," Frank said, standing, wiping his mouth with the back of his hand, but when he saw Elle in her light blue nightgown, its lacy outlines barely concealing her body from the brightening sky outside, he embraced her firmly and quietly.

"Woman stuff," Elle said as he found his hat and left the house. Hans was waiting as usual, engine running.

"Morning, chief."

"Morning."

There was normally little conversation or banter between Frank and Hans Schroeder. This was not because Frank was unfriendly but rather because usually he hurried out of his office with a definite and often urgent mission on his mind, and quite frequently he still worked on the solution of the problem in transit.

There were hours, particularly at the end of the day, when there was some conversation, mostly about the weather, the truck, a baseball game, a prizefight. Frank was well aware of this distant relationship between himself and Hans, and now, when he truly wanted more information about the boy, he knew he would have to proceed cautiously without arousing suspicion.

Today Frank asked simply whether Hans had a girl.

"Sort of," Hans answered, blushing.

"What kind of a girl is sort of?"

"Well, she don't have a job and things are usually tough."

"How old is she?"

"Nineteen."

"Used to hard work?"

"She's an Okie."

"Might get something in the kitchen for her."

"Much obliged, chief."

"Yeah, well, I'll see." They had arrived at the administration building and Frank left quickly for his office, giving a certain lightness to his offer. He knew exactly what he wanted. He wanted his eyes on Hans and the girl. The closer they were the better he liked it, but he would pace himself.

Frank had barely read the night supervisor's report, signed several letters and purchase orders, when he heard the dreaded steam whistle, which signaled an accident on the dam site. It was a high-pitched sound, known and feared by all who heard it.

Within a minute he heard the ring of the phone and he picked it up.

"This is the safety man on Tunnel 1."

"Go ahead."

"We've had a slide. Couple of guys buried."

Frank ran out of his office without replacing the phone on the receiver.

"Get the doctors and medics to Tunnel 1. Get twelve glasses. Get me Red McDonald," and then he ran to his truck and yelled at Hans. "Tunnel 1. Go like hell."

He reached the tunnel in less than five minutes; a mucking truck placed him at the scene of the slide in five minutes after that.

All the drillers, muckers, carpenters, electricians gave Crowe a wide circle as he walked gingerly about the mountain of rock, touching it gently.

"Who's in there?" Frank asked.

"Williams for sure, we're not sure if anybody else was up there."

"Give me a tape," he said and one of the carpenters handed him a metal tape.

Unfortunately this ritual was not new to Crowe. Before beginning of construction he had measured Williams's girth. Jack Williams had been buried twice before and twice before Frank Crowe had rescued him. Crowe knew that Williams would lie as low as possible to gain

184

air and avoid the drill. He had measured fourteen inches on his side the last time and Frank ordered four drillers to begin to excavate at twenty inches from the bottom of the tunnel.

"Drill two minutes and wait," he ordered, "then muck like hell."

He watched as four workmen placed their pneumatic drills and watched as they bored steadily into the rock.

Three doctors arrived, with stretcher bearers; the two-minute excavation time seemed interminable. Finally the drillers ceased. "Put your stethoscopes on that rock," Crowe ordered the doctors. They obeyed. The tunnel was silent except for the blowers.

"Turn off the blowers," Crowe ordered, and it was totally still.

McDonald arrived from Tunnel 4. He was by reputation the best driller on the dam site, and quickly relieved one of the four men as they proceeded on the next round of drilling. After two minutes, again total silence. The air without the blowers was getting thick and unbearable. Twelve glasses arrived from the mess hall and Frank instructed his workers to invert them against the rock. They were not as effective as a stethoscope but more effective than the human ear.

They were on their fifth round of drilling and still no sound behind the boulders. Frank ordered compressed air to be blown into the rock for four minutes, then the drilling started again. He looked at his watch. Fourteen minutes had passed already. He did not look at the other tunnelers. He knew what their faces would betray.

After the sixth round of drilling Dr. Wandowski heard a human voice.

"I hear 'Mother Machree,' " he said, astonished, and a smile came over Frank's face.

" 'Mother Machree' indeed. Let me have that stethoscope."

Crowe put it over his head and adjusted the ear plugs and then he sounded the rock as carefully as a heart surgeon examining a chest. He took off the stethoscope and called McDonald. "Put these on, Red. I'd say four feet at thirty degrees."

McDonald adjusted the stethoscope and listened. "It ain't four feet," he said. "I'd better go up another foot."

Crowe nodded. "Go at it!"

Everyone's eyes were riveted on McDonald, who wielded a drill as a surgeon handles a scalpel. No one noticed the lack of air, the heat; all eyes were on the one driller working, then listening with the stethoscope.

It took four minutes until they reached Jack Williams.

Crowe stepped forward to reach him.

"What took you so long?" Williams asked, and Frank laughed. It was Williams's standard remark, except today there was no humor in his voice.

"There's two of us in here, Frank," he shouted.

185

"Who else?"

"Stubbs, that young staff engineer of yours. I'm on top of him."

"How is he?" Frank asked.

"Dead, I think."

Workers widened the hole with pickaxes and finally Williams stepped out of the excavation. Two stretcher bearers went after Stubbs and finally brought him out. One of the doctors put his stethoscope on the young man's chest, and shook his head.

Frank took off his jacket and placed it over the boy's face and shoulders and watched as they put his body on a mucking truck.

"What the hell was he doing in this tunnel?"

"Checking wiring," Williams said.

"At five in the morning?"

"He was here before I was."

"Son of a bitch."

Crowe left and walked silently behind the mucking truck carrying Stubbs's lifeless body.

He heard Williams shouting at his men: "So let's get our ass in gear, this isn't a paid holiday." Before Crowe reached the mouth of the tunnel he heard the roar of the pneumatic drills again and thought perhaps it was as fitting a dirge for a structural engineer as the mucking truck was a hearse.

Maria Williams was sitting with Elle when Frank reached home at ten that evening. He kissed Elle and Maria kissed him.

"You were fond of that boy, weren't you, Frank?"

"Yeah," Frank said, tossing his hat on a chair. "I don't even know what to write his folks."

"Farm people," Maria said. "They're used to death."

Elle was crying unashamedly and Frank put his arm around her.

"I've got dinner on the stove," Maria said, "and Jack said if you won't come over he'll knock your block off."

Frank hesitated.

"And he's half drunk enough already to do it."

"In that case, we'll go," Frank said, and all three of them walked to the Williamses' house across the street.

Jack had three bourbons in his hands when Maria opened the door and everyone drank quickly and Jack refilled the glasses.

The children were already in bed. No one was really hungry, but everyone ate. Finally Elle joined Maria in the kitchen to help with the dishes.

"What do you say, Maria?" Elle asked.

"You don't say anything."

"Frank loved that boy. I know he did."

"It's happened before. It'll happen again. I hear Jack shout in

186

the middle of the night. He's asleep but he's yelling, 'I can't see, I can't see,' but he lives with it."

Elle dropped a dish and broke it, and started crying again.

Maria bent down and put her arms around Elle. "You got to stop crying, honey. Stop it! You aren't helping your man with those tears. He wants to cry worse than you do, but he can't."

"Why not?"

" 'Cause he's a man."

"Well, did the boys in Frisco tell you about the investigative report on the dam?" Williams asked Crowe in the dining room.

"Not yet. I'm waiting. They made it all sound like a country club. Barnes will probably start cutting wages again."

"If he does," Williams said, obviously drunk, "if he does, tell him I'm short a man in the tunnels. I'd be glad to teach that kid of his the ropes."

"Shit," Frank said. "The last thing that Stubbs said to me was, 'See that car, that Ford roadster?' He was talking about the Barnes kid. 'I'm gonna buy one of those when we finish this dam.' "

"Yeah," Jack Williams said. "Yeah. Sure."

The women returned to the dining room.

"Who broke that dish?" Jack asked sternly.

"I did," Elle said.

"You think just because your husband saved my life you can go around breaking my dishes?"

"Shut up, Jack, or I'll break one over your head," Maria threatened.

Jack Williams instinctively touched the top of his head.

"Try it, it might feel good."

"I know what you mean," Crowe said, and stood.

They left the Williamses and walked slowly around Boulder City. The night was still warm, but the breezes of autumn were more pronounced.

Americans, no matter how difficult the times, or how adverse the weather or the money supply, are basically a communal people, and Boulder City in October, 1931, despite the dusty roads, the vast dumps of materials stacked all around, was already beginning to show signs of being a community.

As Frank and Elle walked about the small town they could see seedling trees barely planted, porch lights still newly brass-finished, glowing, rockers on porches, cacti in pots.

They noticed small hand-painted signs, THE JONESES, THE O'BRIENS, THE LERNERS. They heard the barking of dogs and the blare of radios and saw wash hanging neatly on newly constructed wash lines. They walked past the American Legion post, past the post office, new stores and garages and filling stations, and they passed other residents catching the night breezes. Frank and Elle nodded and the other strollers nodded back and when they finally returned to their own house, both of them felt better.

Frank Crowe had been awake for eighteen hours now, but he sat in his study and began the painful process of writing a letter to young Stubbs's parents.

Dear Mr. and Mrs. Stubbs,

If you feel this letter is a pro forma message, you are wrong. Unlike a general in the field, a supervising engineer is very close to his men, and I was particularly close to Tom, having chosen him for my personal staff at the beginning of the project. This selection was made strictly on merit since Tom was not only an extremely competent young civil engineer, but possessed also that rare talent in our profession, imagination.

Tom was killed this morning at 5:30 A.M. in the California Tunnel No. 1 during a routine electrical inspection. I cannot offer an explanation other than the fact that heavy construction like war makes casualties of innocents.

There is little comfort, I know, in saying that, when Hoover Dam is completed, Tom Stubbs will have played a significant part in its reality; on a personal note I can only say that, if I had a son, Tom would be the kind of man I'd like to call my own.

Please advise me of the funeral arrangements you desire.

> *Respectfully,*
> *Frank Crowe,*
> *Supervising Engineer*

Frank fell asleep in his chair and Elle found him fully clothed, his head resting on his chest. She read the letter and she cried, but heeding Maria's advice she dried her tears before she woke Frank and helped him into bed. He was scarcely aware of the process and Elle lay awake for hours wondering how badly Frank might want a son.

31

The heat was abating. The women in town, even Elle, were getting excited about the approaching holidays. Frank noticed workers walking faster, hammering more purposefully, drilling more rapidly. He realized that winter would soon be upon them, and his race, and Jack

Williams's race, with the river was getting closer to the finish line.

There were a good many hours each week that Crowe had Hans drive him to a remote area on the dam site. During these periods Crowe would use his sextant, his theodolite, his binoculars; he would jot down figures with the inevitable gold Shaeffer pen which he had received from the Bureau of Reclamation for ten years of faithful service.

With these lonely inspections he tried to project every possible curve the Colorado could throw him. He studied the rock walls, the escarpments, the growth pattern of the vegetation which had withstood years of spring runoff. In his office he studied and restudied all of the Bureau's historical statistics on the river carefully assembled by the Bureau in Denver.

He had even more frequent talks with Walker Young, whose concerns for success were different from Crowe's, but equally important.

"Hell," Crowe said to Young, "Williams will hole those tunnels in time."

"If he doesn't, no one will," Young said.

Crowe nodded.

"I think these tunnels should take all the river can give them."

"Then what are you worried about?"

"I don't *know*," Crowe said, quietly.

"I don't either," Walker Young agreed, being honest but nonsupportive. "Your tunnels have always held on all the other dams," Young added.

"Kid stuff," Crowe said. "This is the Colorado."

Walker Young paced the length and breadth of Crowe's office.

"I lose some sleep too, Frank," he admitted finally. "I know as well as you do that all the figures, all the graphs, all the historical data *carefully* put together by the Bureau can be wiped out by *one* fluke from nature. I *know* that."

"That river," Crowe said, "drains one-thirteenth of the United States. Do you know how much water that is? Already I'm getting reports. Early snowfall in Wyoming, Montana, some in Idaho. Every goddamned snowflake is going to arrive here in the spring. . . ."

"If I could help you, Frank, you know I would," Young stated. "I'm older than you. This is my last dam. I don't want to go down in disaster any more than you do."

"I know that, Walker. I'm glad you're on this dam with me."

"Yeah," Young said, picking up his hat, starting to leave, "words aren't going to solve our problems."

"No," Crowe said. "You know something?"

"What?"

"Sometimes I wish I were a religious man."

Walker Young eyed Crowe curiously and left.

189

Elle was busy. Shuttling between the library in Las Vegas and the Thanksgiving Committee in Boulder City, she could hardly detect the more reflective attitude in her husband. As long as she had known him, he had been an intense, decisive man, and though he mentioned approaching winter occasionally, it was no more pressing to her than all the myriad of problems which hung on his shoulders. But finally Thanksgiving arrived and her plans came to fruition.

Elle had ordered all the tables cleared from the Big Six mess hall; her committee had hired the seven-piece Syncopating Syncopators from San Bernardino. The event was sponsored by the volunteer firemen, and a string of 104 cars brought folks from Las Vegas, Tonopah, Reno, and Searchlight for Boulder City's first social event.

Two thousand people crowded into the largest single floor space in southern Nevada.

"You know I can't dance," Frank protested, putting on clean denims, city shoes, a tartan shirt.

"Would you rather that we stay home?"

"Nonsense," Frank said, recalling that strange sensation of bringing Elle into the Vegas Club a few months ago.

"I want to see that new dress you bought. Didn't you say it cost twenty-five dollars?"

"To the penny, and if you'll give me a chance, I'll put it on."

Elle walked into the bathroom and Frank's eyes were riveted to the mirror which reflected Elle's motions, slipping into silk stockings, hooking them to garters, adjusting her underwear, turning to watch herself in the back. He felt ashamed but transfixed as she slipped on a silk slip and finally a black dress, well scooped in front and rear. He could see her pressing in the seams, seams of the dress, her stockings, running her hands over her breasts, adjusting the neckline, lowering then raising it, then lowering it again and finally picking up her hairbrush to put the final shape and luster into her golden hair.

He rose from his perch and stole into the living room. When Elle entered he was almost overwhelmed by her radiance and youth and grace.

"God damn," he barely managed.

"Is that all you can say? God damn?"

"God damn. That's the best twenty-five-dollar investment I've ever made."

Elle put her arms around Frank's waist and leaned back against the strong support.

"You know something, Frank Crowe, I've been wrong about you."

"What do you mean?"

"You're not just myth or man."

"No."

"No. You're myth and man and boy."

Crowe blushed. "We'd better get to that damned dance or I won't get out of the door."

Crowe had not been unaware of the forthcoming festivities. He had to give approval for the use of the mess hall, he had to allocate the kitchen utensils, and he had even taken the precaution of alerting the federal rangers to search every entering vehicle for bootleg liquor.

He had little to fear. People came in good spirits. Daily accounts in the Vegas papers of breadlines, soup kitchens, overcrowded orphanages, and midnight missions did not go unheeded by all the merrymakers. They were working, they were living meagerly but securely, and a dance such as this was as frivolous and welcome as a society ball at the Waldorf-Astoria.

Mr. and Mrs. George Smilarick won the ten-dollar fox-trot prize, Jack Williams and his boys were the fastest and the loudest merrymakers, Tom Wanke danced happily with his wife, and Frank encouraged Elle to dance with Dan Snyder, one of his younger engineers. Standing on the sidelines watching his beautiful wife, Frank felt neither old nor inept, but extremely proud.

However, Elle was not the only girl he watched. He also watched Terry.

"Hans's girl is quite a looker," Alfred had told him at the canyon rim, and Alfred was right, for this little girl in her tight, obviously new red dress stirred juices in Frank that he'd not felt for a long time.

She was short, nearly a foot shorter than Elle. Her hair was dark, so were her eyes. She had a strong, open face and a trim, well-busted body, which fitted into Hans Schroeder's tall and well-built frame.

Frank's eyes followed them about the dance floor, watching the twirling of her skirt, which revealed her well-tanned legs with much abandon. Elle caught Frank's gaze.

"Is there a difference between a whore and a woman?" she asked Dan Snyder, who was ill prepared for such a frank question, particularly from his boss's wife. He had graduated from Harvard with honors; he was a boy from a sophisticated background and not easily shaken.

"Is that a rhetorical question?"

"I did not ask for a classification of the question," Elle said, "but an answer."

"Aah," Snyder laughed easily, "logic seems to run in the Crowe family."

"You're still dodging, Mr. Snyder."

"So I am."

"Why?"

191

"Because you might not believe me when I tell you that I have no statistics on which to base an answer. I am engaged to be married."

"I think that's splendid," Elle said, blushing. "I didn't mean to embarrass you."

"You didn't, believe me."

The dance ended and Dan Snyder escorted Elle to Frank's side.

"When is the happy event to take place?" she asked.

"In June."

Elle turned to Frank. "Dan's getting married in June."

"Congratulations," Frank said. "At least you know how to dance."

"I hope there is more to it than that."

"I wish you the same happiness I have," Frank said, and Elle put her arm around Frank as Snyder left. She felt good and would have forgotten about Frank's roving eye, but Hans stopped dancing in front of them and brought Terry over to meet Crowe.

"Good evening, Mr. Crowe, Mrs. Crowe."

"Good evening, Hans."

"This is Terry."

Terry shook hands with Frank and Elle. It was a solid farmer's handshake.

"So this is the 'sort of' girl," Crowe said lightly.

"Hans never stops talking about you, Mr. Crowe," Terry said openly.

"I understand that's not an infrequent pastime on the dam site."

Hans Schroeder had neither the finesse nor the subtlety of Dan Snyder and pulled Terry back onto the dance floor. "Been nice to meet you folks," Terry said as she whirled out of their sight into the throng of dancers.

"Well, Mrs. Crowe," Jack Williams said, holding hands with Elle, "that's quite a shindig you're throwing. . . ."

"Well, at least I haven't broken any dishes yet."

Williams laughed and said to Crowe, "Come over to the house and I'll make you a real drink." He whispered into Crowe's ear. "Don't know how you can get *real* piss from *near* beer."

Crowe laughed and Maria said to Elle, "Whatever they're talking about has got to be dirty."

The day after Thanksgiving Arthur Anderson appeared in Crowe's office to report that 2,500 Six Companies employees had consumed 2,400 pounds of turkey, 300 gallons of oyster soup, half a ton of candied sweet potatoes, a case of olives, 10 crates of celery, five crates of lettuce, 300 pounds of cranberries, 760 pies, half a ton of plum pudding with hard sauce, and 500 pounds of candy and nuts.

"It was a very satisfactory Thanksgiving meal," Crowe said coldly.

192

Then pointing, "If you look up on my walls you can see that this office is *filled* with statistics, and the ones you have just given me do not interest me in the slightest. If you do not hear from me, which you haven't, you can assume you are doing your job adequately. There is no time in this organization for accolades."

The holiday had obviously passed into history as far as Crowe was concerned, and Anderson left the office wordlessly.

32

Although the heads of the Bix Six were often referred to disparagingly by Frank Crowe, Williams, Wanke, even at times by Walker Young and Elwood Mead, their function extended beyond putting up the original five-million-dollar bond.

All of them, after all, were heads of successful engineering corporations, and in aggregate their past projects, dams, highways, bridges, aqueducts, had done much to shape the West. Their equipment, their machinery, was the bulk of Crowe's inventory and their construction knowledge was far from minuscule. Most of them, like Mackenzie and Henderson, had started with a team of mules, a wagon, and a handful of shovels, and all of them had known the hardship of living on construction sites, of fearing the weather and the wisdom of their bids.

Perhaps it was the exuberance with which they now embraced life in San Francisco, the mansions on Nob Hill, in Pacific Heights, the possession of big cars and yachts and summer cottages at Lake Tahoe, which Crowe, the frugal New Englander, resented, but he knew it was really none of his business.

It is true that San Francisco shared the hardships of the depression with the rest of the country, but this lovely city, its hills overlooking one of the world's greatest natural harbors, perhaps had more spirit than a landlocked equal.

The city was still the gateway to the Pacific, foreign flag carriers entered and left the Golden Gate daily, cable cars added a grace note to the normal traffic of downtown, and Union Square with stores like Gump's, the White House, the City of Paris, florists like Podesta and Baldocchi, whose white-tile-floored showrooms held unbelievable color and fragrance, made even the poorest of window shoppers become confused about the reports of economic collapse all about them.

There were great restaurants like Sam's and Jack's, whose aging waiters took good care of their steady customers, and there were great clubs like the Pacific Union on Nob Hill, the Bohemian Club, the St. Francis Yacht Club, the athletic clubs, whose great glass double doors somehow insulated their members from reality like the rubber seal of a mason jar.

Perhaps it was the earthquake in 1906, and the fire and the rebuilding of the city from the ashes that made San Franciscans tougher. Perhaps it was the great diversity of ethnic groups—the Italians, the Portuguese, the Jews, the French, the Chinese and Japanese—that made the city less stereotyped, less gray, less haggard looking than a mill town in New England or even Chicago which carried the entire burden of the misery of the whole Middle West.

Men like Chapman, like Barnes, Mackenzie, and Stein, like Henderson and Andrews, were *not* hampered by the depression; they were building huge projects with depression labor, and making huge profits.

It was shortly after Thanksgiving that they all met at an office they had rented in the Phelan Building, and Stein, the Big Six treasurer, reported that, if all his projections and those of Crowe persisted, then the government might well be forced to return their five-million-dollar bond at the end of the first year's construction and that Crowe's feverish drive to complete the dam could easily bring them into the black.

This news was well taken by the men. Plans for personal expenditures were expedited, and Christmas would be a jolly time for all. Edward Chapman even donated $1,000 to the Salvation Army, a fact carefully reported to the *Examiner* the following day.

To this point in time of construction, there had been very little contact between Crowe and the heads of the Big Six. They made periodic trips, remained a few hours, and continued home the same day, or perhaps remained in Las Vegas to partake of some of its merriment. The completion of the executive house, well built and lavishly furnished by Sloane's, was not an event which Crowe relished, knowing full well that its use by the Big Six and their friends would not only contribute little to the building of Hoover Dam but, even worse, would inevitably involve him and Elle in a social life he could scarcely schedule, or truly enjoy.

The last carpet had finally been laid in Sequoia Lodge, which became the name of the complex, when Elle waved a chastely written note toward Frank, asking them to be dinner guests there on December 7. The card was signed by Mrs. Stein, who also stated that she and her husband would be entertaining Mr. Daniel Wertheimer.

"Goddamn," is all that Frank could say. "I knew this would start."

"What of it?" said Elle. "It might be fun."

Frank took off his hat and his jacket. "I don't have time," he said, "for all that crap. I don't like to be told to put on my Sunday suit and act charming."

"It's the boy again," Elle said, still laughing.

"What boy?"

"The boy in you. Afraid to wash behind your ears . . ."

"Nonsense, Elle. I told you in Denver there's no room for this on a construction site."

"I don't think you have a choice, Frank."

"Exactly," Frank said angrily, "and I think *you* like the whole idea."

"Why not? Are you ashamed of me?"

"Of course not. I'll stack you up against any of these construction bastards' wives."

"Such hostility, Mr. Crowe!"

"What's for dinner?"

"Discussion ended," Elle said.

"Discussion ended," Frank repeated, but the discussion was resumed in bed after a wordless meal.

"Frank," Elle said, after the lights had been turned off, "are you asleep?"

"No."

"I'm sorry about being so flippant earlier."

"Forget it."

"I'm not forgetting it. I'm *trying* to help you."

"How?"

"Are you ashamed of *yourself?* "

"What do you mean?"

"Do you think these people are *better* than you?"

"Not better, just richer."

"You're not a poor man now, Frank, and I predict you'll be a rich man when this dam is completed."

"Maybe so, but that house in Salt Lake just suits me fine."

"It suits me too, Frank, and I don't really care about your money."

Frank turned toward her. "It's not *my* money, Elle. It's *our* money, and to hell with it."

"Well said, Frank, but it doesn't answer my question. What's wrong with a little socializing? These men aren't stupid. Perhaps you'll like them better over the dinner table than over the phone."

Frank lay on his back and stared at the ceiling. "It's like not knowing how to dance. I left home at sixteen. What few manners I've got my mother taught me."

"Your manners, my love, are just fine. All you have to remember is to take your hat off inside the house."

"It's off, isn't it," Frank said, touching the top of his head, and Elle flung the pillow at him.

"I was right," she said.

"About what?"

"It's the boy in you."

"Yeah, the boy." Frank kissed her. "But I've got a man's work in the morning." She could hear the tick of his watch by the bed.

Francesca Stein was the ultimate hostess, warm, gracious, good-humored, and Elle loved her immediately.

Francesca had married Roger Stein in her early twenties and she regaled the table with endless humorous tales of life with Roger, knocking about California, Oregon, Washington in a small truck, their main possession a compressor and a good length of chain.

She could, and later did, tell Elle more recipes, more ways to light a fire without a match, more ways to make love in the back of a buckboard than Maria Williams had ever dreamt of. She was truly captivating—short, with sparkling black eyes like olives, dark-haired, still slender, and quite pretty.

Even Crowe loosened up on some quality bourbon and really found the conversation easygoing. It was after both women had retired to the kitchen (Francesca having refused the offer of a maid) that Crowe could ask Stein some questions to which he needed answers.

"We get the paper here," he said. "There are two in Vegas. They're not much good and I have little time to read them anyway. Tell me about this Roosevelt."

"Why ask *me*, Frank? I'm probably the only registered Democrat among the Big Six."

"You are? Why?"

Again Roger Stein laughed. "It's not a crime, I hear."

"No," Crowe said, "but where I come from the Democratic party is the workingman's party."

"You may not believe it, Frank, but I consider *myself* a working man."

Frank felt uncomfortable with Stein's answer. "I didn't mean to imply you did not work, Mr. Stein."

"I know and I am not answering your question. I apologize. Perhaps the best way to talk about Roosevelt is to begin with Hoover." Stein pushed his chair back from the table and lit a cigarette.

"Herbert Hoover is a decent, brilliant man—flawlessly educated, scrupulous in business, innovative in engineering. It would certainly seem that I should have nothing but admiration for the man."

196

"Exactly," said Crowe. "I've known Hoover personally for a good many years and I think he's one of the greatest men I know."

"One of the greatest engineers, Frank?"

"That too."

"No, not that too. That first. I feel that everything that Hoover has tackled from his Chilean mines to his Belgian endeavors, his ably run American Relief Committee after the war, to the Presidency— all of it has the stamp of the engineer on it. Efficiency, honesty, a clear-cut chain of command . . ."

"What's wrong with that?"

"The Presidency, particularly in times like these, is not an engineering project. It is a political job, and Hoover is neither a good politician nor even *likes* politics. Wouldn't you agree, Dan?"

Wertheimer, whose family were founders of San Francisco's most flourishing banks, nodded in agreement. "I would. One hundred percent."

"Roosevelt, on the other hand, is a well-bred, equally well-educated squire from Hyde Park who *adores* politics. He's built an organization as governor of New York which is not only progressive but forceful. He sees the needs of this country."

"And Hoover doesn't?"

Stein was a gentle man and did not wish a confrontation; he was nonetheless forceful.

"Hoover does not understand the problems because he does not mingle with his people. He reads the statistics in that bastion the White House, analyzes them, and resigns himself to the cyclical nature of the depression. To him it's like the curve on a hygrometer. He expects it to rise as gently as it has dropped."

"I think there's more to it than that," Wertheimer added. "Hoover has a grade-school primer mentality about America. Work hard, save, go to church, and all will be well."

"I subscribe to that, Dan," Crowe said.

"We all do," Roger Stein said, "in principle, but the Great War has left the world a shambles, including us. We can no longer seal off this big country and play ostrich.

"A shot in Somaliland affects the prime rate in Chicago, a drought in India causes layoffs in Kansas City. . . . Sometimes I wonder whether Mr. Bell or Mr. Morse or Marconi did us a favor with these goddamned inventions."

"God gave us the carrier pigeon," Wertheimer said good-humoredly.

"Yes," Stein said, "but man trained him to fly a mission foreign to his habits."

Wertheimer asked Frank, "Do you play the market?"

"The stock market?"

"Yes."

"Hell, no."

"That's good," Wertheimer said. "I wish millions of Americans hadn't."

"All I heard was that everybody was getting rich."

"Sure," Wertheimer said. "On paper. With a ninety percent margin the only ones getting rich were the New York banks. They floated all that margin at twelve percent. Money was pouring in from all over the world, money, gold, what have you. Millions of Americans were shooting crap with a ten percent investment, just like the Florida land boom, and the bubble busted just like it did in Florida."

"Why blame that on Hoover?"

"Because Hoover just sat back and watched it happen. He figured it was all regulated by the Federal Reserve. Well, you saw what happened."

Crowe nodded thoughtfully.

The ladies joined the men around the table, having finished the dinner dishes, but the conversation continued.

"And how does Roosevelt propose to solve our problems?"

"He's told us," Stein said. "Public works. *Massive* public works. Roads, schools, dams, bridges . . . jobs, Frank. Jobs. He is going to create jobs."

"*Government* jobs," Crowe said.

"Call them what you will, they'll be jobs. Whether the workman gets a blue check from the Big Six or a green check from the federal government matters little. It will put food in his stomach."

"That's socialism," Crowe said, "pure and simple."

"That's right," Stein agreed.

"This country was not based on socialism. Our country never had a need for socialism."

"Not until now," Stein said. "We've been pushing west for two hundred years discovering endless riches, land, oil, gas, water . . . but there's nowhere to go now. The land has been tilled and the ore has been mined and the oil has been struck and we're out of frontiers and out of money. . . . Ask Dan how many venture loans he's making at his bank."

Wertheimer looked at Crowe. "None," he said. "We're desperately trying to hold on to the assets we've financed."

Much was said, and much was said well, and Frank liked none of it. He paced the room unmindful of his actions.

"And socialism will lead to communism, right?"

"It could," Stein said, "but it won't."

"Why not?"

198

"Because Roosevelt is basically a capitalist. He's a tight-fisted Dutchman by heritage, a multimillionaire. I think he knows how far he can prime the pump before he floods the valves."

"Sit down, Frank," Stein said in a fatherly tone, and Crowe obeyed. "You were the first to admit that you'd misjudged the labor market in Las Vegas."

"That's true."

"This is only *one* town, *one* set of circumstances. But this phenomenon of listless, hopeless men is all over the country. Multiply *your* misjudgment on a national scale and you illustrate Hoover's poor strategy."

"Good logic," Frank admitted, "but where does the money come from to finance all this public work. Not from Mr. Wertheimer or from Mr. Crocker or from the Bank of Italy."

"It would," said Wertheimer, "if the government would guarantee the loans."

"With what," Frank asked, "if we're broke?"

"Deficit spending. Roosevelt and his buddies are avid students of the Keynesian theory." There was quiet in the room.

"John Maynard Keynes," Crowe said, "the English baron." He tapped the table and was unmindful of Elle's pride in his knowledge or of the exchange of glances between Stein and Wertheimer.

"I have read Keynes," Crowe said, "and reread Keynes, and somehow there is a flaw in that theory."

"The flaw," Elle said, surprising everyone, "is not in Keynes, but in you."

"Why?" Frank asked, looking at his young wife.

"Because you're a New Englander and the word *debt* scares the hell out of you."

"That's true, Elle. Is that a flaw?"

"You can't feed this country with empty promises and exhortations to work hard," Stein said. "Not if there's no work. If government doesn't create jobs, if factories can't get working capital, the choice, in my opinion, is self-evident. . . . And let me tell you something, Frank. Your fear of socialism, which I share with you, might turn into the tragedy of communism. This depression is fertile ground for these bastards, I don't have to tell you."

"No you don't, Mr. Stein. No you don't."

Francesca interrupted. "I thought we were going to have a lovely sociable evening."

"It's my fault," Frank said. "We get sort of isolated up here. These gentlemen are filling me in on the outside world."

Francesca got up and took a seat next to Frank. "I like you, Frank," she said very openly. "My husband likes you. I like your wife. She's

199

bright and beautiful." She put her arm around Elle, and said, "I like that."

Elle blushed.

"Thank you," Frank said.

"I'm not finished. You've got a monstrous job ahead of you and I know you can handle it, but *enjoy* it. Enjoy your work and your lovely wife and let these codgers," pointing at her husband, at Wertheimer, "let the other boys of the Big Six worry about the economy."

Roger Stein laughed. "Forgive my wife," he said. "She can't restrain herself from mothering people. She does it with everyone."

"I loved what you said," Elle added, "and I thank you for both of us."

Francesca Stein's eyes sparkled. "We've been married thirty years," she said, "and Roger has been trying to shut me up for the same length of time."

"And you can see what success I've had," Stein said.

"Last week I told Mr. Barnes that if they have *one* more meeting at the Bohemian Club, which won't allow my husband on its premises, I would suggest they get another partner."

"Good for you," Elle said.

"My family lived in San Francisco for four generations *before* there was a Bohemian Club and before Barnes built that monstrosity on Nob Hill."

Crowe put his hand over Francesca's. "I'm not a religious man," he said, "but I've found that prejudice in this country is as great a threat as communism."

"Bravo!" Francesca shouted. "Now break out the brandy, Roger, before we get on more heavy subjects. Politics, religion, to hell with it. Let's celebrate the opening of this beautiful lodge and enjoy the munificent evils of capitalism."

Frank Crowe had trouble sleeping that night and Elle sensed it.

"Did you enjoy the evening, Frank?" she asked.

"You want to know something? I did."

"Francesca is a lovely woman."

"She is," Frank said. "She is that."

"You boys were certainly going at it in the dining room."

"I know, Elle. It really bothers me."

"What?"

"I don't know what this country's coming to. There was so much said tonight. It's hard for me to understand how socialism can prevent communism."

"I think you should take Mrs. Stein's advice."

"What's that?"

"Let them worry about it in San Francisco."

"Maybe she's right. She said something about enjoying life too."

"Enjoy, Frank Crowe. Enjoy!"

He reached for her and tucked her lovely head into his shoulder. "You're quite a girl, Elle. You know that? Quite a girl." He kissed her very warmly and tenderly.

Scarcely a hundred yards from Crowe's home Roger Stein was also retiring. His wife was reading, but he interrupted her.

"I don't see much sense in burdening Crowe with our Judaism."

"I didn't burden him, Roger. I spoke my piece. You're the best engineer in the Big Six. Why did they make you treasurer of the organization?"

"They needed a treasurer."

"Sure. Do they still think that Jews know more about money than anyone else?"

"Wouldn't surprise me. God damn it, Francesca, you should be used to antisemitism in the construction business after thirty years."

"I'll never get used to it. When this job is done I hope to hell you can retire. I've hated engineers all my life."

Roger Stein also put his arm about his wife and kissed her.

"Go to sleep," Roger said.

"And shut up," Francesca answered.

"Yeah, shut up." He knew there was a smile on her face.

33

Physically, for Frank Crowe, the change from summer to winter involved simply donning long underwear underneath his denims. He wore the same boots, the same felt hat, at times he donned a rubber poncho. Twenty years of working in the field had made him almost impervious to the elements. They were only something to reckon with in conjunction with his project.

Not all the residents along the dam were so fortunately conditioned. As many had barely survived the ungodly heat of the summer, an equal number were now unprepared for the cold and the rains and the winds.

Although Crowe had set April of 1932 for the closing of Rag Town,

450 souls still lived there. Hundreds of others still lived in their cars, their trucks, and only a few could afford to buy a cottage for $3,000 or rent one for $50 a month, and while a piece of canvas, a sheet of plywood, a length of cardboard would provide a measure of relief from the heat, none of these makeshift measures could stop the rain or the wind. Hundreds of people lived day and night wearing boots, ponchos, slickers, rarely had a chance for decent sanitary facilities, and became almost inured to eating stew or hot dogs as they sat bent over a tin cup, fending off raindrops or dust. There were forty-five saloons operating in Las Vegas now, but not one asked whether customers wanted simply to get out of the cold, or get drunk. If the price of admission to a place of warmth was to buy a beer or a bourbon, it was worth it.

Even the residents of Boulder City, whose houses were plain but sturdy, complained bitterly about the wind. After dark when much of the work force was still laboring on the dam, wives feared those winds which plagued the desert mercilessly. Sand would creep onto windowsills, doorsills, through cracks in walls and ceilings, and these winds, known as one-bucketers, two-bucketers, depending on how much shoveling was required the next day, were frightening. Their voices and their deceptive rattling of doors and windows scared the women, who felt constantly that someone was breaking into their houses. Even Elle felt that fear but never complained of it to Frank.

Devere had ordered Herman to bunk with him in back of Alma's fruit shack, leaving Hans and Terry alone in the truck. It was not an act of charity, but part of his plan to keep Hans on the premises. Relieved to be left alone, Terry made every effort to give some warmth to their tiny living space. She had devised a stove on top of the front seat, where she could cook despite the rains, and they could fall asleep with the warmth and the glow of the remaining embers. Of course their new-found privacy and Herman's changed attitude made cohabitation easier, and being young they explored each other as often as possible.

On December 18 Hans drove Crowe to the Bureau of Reclamation's office in Las Vegas and Elmer Vance handed Crowe a check in excess of a million dollars for work completed during November.

Crowe looked at the blue rectangular sheet of watermarked paper; the seven-digit embossing felt good to his fingers.

"You couldn't endorse this to me direct, could you, Elmer? Thought I might get the little lady something for Christmas."

"I could make it out to both of us," Elmer said. "We could buy half of Mexico."

"The way the paper reads you could buy half the States," Crowe said. "Going to be a cold Christmas for a lot of folks."

"Afraid you're right."

Crowe left the Bureau's office, but not before carefully shoving the check into his shirt pocket.

With this check, he thought, as he sat beside Hans, the Big Six boys would have their bond back easily in the first year. His spirits rose.

"Listen, Hans, I talked to the bull cooks. You bring that little Terry around and they'll put her on the steam tables."

"You mean that, Mr. Crowe?"

"I don't make idle talk."

"No sir. Yes sir." Hans was obviously excited. "Boy, we could get a new piece of winterized canvas for the truck. . . . We sure need it."

"I'm declaring a three-day holiday for Christmas. Why don't you marry her and I'll get you a house in Boulder?"

"Well, getting a piece of canvas sounds lots simpler to me."

Crowe shook his head and said, "Watch the road."

Once in his office, the door shut, he called Barnes and gave him the news of the check he had received. Barnes was pleased and made no objections about Crowe's request for a three-day holiday.

Frank Crowe, who could decide on the spur of a moment to order fifteen hundred men to dig a two-thousand-foot trench, spent almost two hours in Norton's Notions and Gifts in Boulder City trying to buy a Christmas gift for Elle. He sorted through opal-studded silver bracelets, hand-carved ivory figurines, he toyed with a real Swiss cuckoo clock, but his eye was riveted on a slender gold bracelet whose beauty and simplicity so matched Elle but whose price was so high that his puritanism and New England frugality put up a good fight.

"How *much* is that?" he asked Mrs. Norton again.

"It's one hundred dollars. It's from Sweden."

"One hundred dollars. Man's got to work a month for that."

"*Some* men do," she said, somewhat sarcastically, but Crowe did not react.

Frank blushed as he asked, "Do you have any ladies' nightgowns?"

"Cotton or flannel?"

"Neither. Like silk," Frank stammered.

"You mean lingerie?"

"I guess."

"They're over here."

Frank followed meekly as Mrs. Norton gracefully displayed one revealing nightgown after another. He picked one; it was black and lacy; the door opened and a middle-aged woman entered the store.

"Wrap this up," Crowe said conspiratorially, "and the bracelet too, and I don't want a word going around about this purchase, do you understand?"

"I do, Mr. Crowe," Mrs. Norton said, wrapping both gifts discreetly and accepting $110 from Frank Crowe, which he jostled painfully out of the coin purse he kept in his left pocket. He stole into the night like a thief and dashed into his house to hide his presents.

When he returned to the living room he noticed the Christmas tree that Elle had purchased and trimmed. There was a fire going in the fireplace. Elle, dressed in blue slacks and a red sweater, looked festive and young.

"I just came from the mess hall," Frank said. "Gave everybody a three-day paid holiday for Christmas and instructed the bull cooks to pay them tonight."

It was December 23. There were 289 children in Boulder City, 2,800 men collecting pay checks, and this vast forlorn oasis in the Godforsaken Nevada desert might yet turn out to be one of the most festive little towns in a gray depressed country, where Christmas this year would raise more tears than joy, and the eyes of millions of children receiving no gifts at all haunted a greater number of guilt-ridden helpless parents.

Elle had been as enterprising as Frank, and on Christmas Eve after they had finished an excellent duck, a good bottle of wine, some mince pie with hard sauce, they returned to their living room and opened their presents. Elle was delighted and almost in tears when she unwrapped her bracelet, and Frank was equally surprised and pleased when Elle hauled out his favorite rocking chair, which she had had someone bring down from their home in Salt Lake City. A panel on its back was carefully embroidered and the inscription said, "Sit down, my love, sit down."

"Well, I'll be damned," Frank said as he admired the careful handiwork, and then sat in the chair and rocked gently. He knew the genesis of the message.

"There's one more gift," he said, almost sheepishly, "but it has a catch."

"What's that?"

"You have to put it on. Now."

Elle opened the box to which Frank pointed and withdrew the black silk nightgown discreetly sheathed in tissue paper.

She pulled it out, sensuously, to admire its beauty. "It's positively indecent," she said, putting it against her body. "The lace is in all the wrong places."

"That," Frank said, "is all a matter of gender."

204

She kissed him playfully. "Nothing surprises me anymore, Frank," she said, obviously happy. "A man who's conversant with John Maynard Keynes would obviously use a word like 'gender.' "

"A wife who in her tender years also recognizes John Maynard Keynes deserves a word like 'gender.' "

"Well put, Mr. Supervisor, but I have a little gift for you too. Here." She handed him a box. The label was Bullock & Jones. He opened it more quickly and carelessly than Elle had opened her present. It contained a pair of silk pajamas, white with blue piping, a silk robe, a paisley print. His work-roughened hands fondled the lovely silk garments.

"Well, I'll be damned," he said, "two minds in the same gutter. . . . How did you get this?"

"Francesca Stein suggested it and bought it for me in San Francisco. When we were washing the dishes here a few weeks ago she told me quietly, 'You can look like a street cleaner all the day and half the night on a construction site, but go to bed like a prince.' "

Elle left the living room to don her nightgown and Frank sheepishly put on his pajamas in his study; he could not quite bring himself to wear the robe. When he saw Elle in front of the fire, her long lovely body outlined against the blazing mesquite, her breasts barely covered with the gauzelike lace, her open warm smile and obvious delight in her body, it was almost more than Frank Crowe could bear.

He approached her gently, his hand shaking her lovely full-bodied hair, his callused fingers stroking her face, her lovely high cheekbones, her well-chiseled perfect nose. With the back of his hand he felt her cheeks, soft and firm, and then he touched the back of her neck, running his fingers down the long smooth tendons. He kissed her breasts, first through the lace and finally directly as Elle playfully dropped the bodice from her shoulders. His hands grasped her buttocks, small for her size, small and round and solid, and he kissed her stomach, and his hands slid up the inside of her legs from the ankles, upward along her shins and finally upward toward that ever-increasing softness of the inside of her thighs. His face was buried in her pubic hair, sparse and symmetrical and almost childlike. When they finished making love in front of the fire, Frank turned to Elle and said, "I feel guilty."

"Why?"

"Because I'm so unreligious."

Elle said nothing.

"Here it is Christmas Eve. Almost the entire dam site is celebrating the birth of Christ, and here I am, the happiest of men, accepting it all, enjoying it all and paying nothing for all these gifts."

"You're wrong," Elle said. "The love we made, the *kind* of love we made, is simply what it is. I *love* you, Frank, and I think you love *me*. If we bring happiness to each other, it is something we *want* to do. It is nothing we have to thank anyone for. It is our *love*, pure and simple."

"It's more than I deserve, Elle. Much more."

"Why don't you let me be the judge of that?"

"Your judgment, I'll admit, is pretty good."

"But I'll tell you, Frank, my love for you does not stem from this dam or your job or your wisdom. . . . My love for you comes from a strength and sensitivity inside you, that you constantly fight, but I know it's there. . . ."

Frank Crowe said nothing.

"You're not even unreligious, darling. You can't figure out God on a slide rule, so you consider it illogic."

"That's true."

"But you're working on the equation harder than you think, and perhaps it makes you more religious than you're willing to admit to yourself."

Frank put his head on his elbow and looked at his beautiful naked wife stretched out luxuriantly in front of their fireplace.

"That's the best sermon I've ever heard. I'd even donate into the collection plate."

Elle was tempted to ask how much, but she didn't.

"Just one question. Did you put a drop of perfume between your breasts?"

"Ah you lecherous bastard," Elle said. "You *did* notice."

The doorbell rang.

"That's the Williamses," Elle said. "I told Maria I had some gifts for their children."

Frank looked at both of them naked. "What are we going to do?"

"Nothing."

"You mean not answer it? They can see the smoke coming from the chimney."

"That's right, Frank, and they'll figure out that we might be doing exactly what we *are* doing. The burdens of command, Frank Crowe, Professor Heinlein said, are not only lonely, but also rewarding."

"And how do you know?" he said, ignoring the persistence of the doorbell.

"Because I used to type his lecture notes. Let's see if I can find that drop of perfume."

They heard the Williamses depart from their front door and felt conspiratorial and slightly evil and wonderfully young.

There was no room for a Christmas tree in Hans and Terry's truck bed, but Terry had found a cardboard Jesus and a few plastic pine boughs and a red ribbon. Hans had bought her a silver-and-onyx brooch at Norton's Notions and Gifts, and Terry had found a small blue satin pillow tasseled in yellow with LAS VEGAS, NEVADA, embroidered across its face, using the first pay check she had ever received on the dam site for the purchase. She had also bought a veal shank and a bottle of wine and they celebrated their good fortune at not only being together but now both working. They decided after supper to go to church but Hans knocked on Devere's door before they walked toward Vegas in the cold night.

Devere opened the door slightly.

"Merry Christmas," Hans said.

"Yeah," Devere answered.

"Is my brother here? I want to see him."

Herman appeared at the door.

"Merry Christmas," Hans said, handing Herman an envelope.

"What's this?"

"It's the money I owe you, when I didn't have a job."

Herman tore open the envelope and looked at the green bills, ones, fives, a ten and a twenty-dollar bill.

"I'll take it," he said, " 'cause you owe it to me, but it's got nothing to do with Christmas. I don't believe in that shit."

Devere, who feared an argument between the brothers, stood beside Herman. "Your brother is paying back a debt like a man," he said. "Why don't you accept it like a man?"

Herman, caught in the crossfire, said, "Yeah, thanks," and stuffed the money into his pocket.

"You want a drink of whiskey?" Devere asked.

"No thanks," Hans said. "We're off to church."

They left and Terry, Christmas or no Christmas, said, "Your brother is a son of a bitch."

Hans could scarcely disagree with her and they walked to Las Vegas in silence. After church they had two hot toddies at the Boulder Club, and got a ride back to their truck. They made love with less finesse than Frank and Elle, but with no less vigor. Hans placed the satin pillow under his head, feeling warm and fulfilled and relieved that for once he could watch the dawn the following day without having to rise and shower in that ice-cold water.

34

New Year's Eve was celebrated with all the fervor of any community engaged in heavy labor. Las Vegas, because of the conspicuous flouting of laws against gambling, drinking, prostitution, was perhaps merrier and more orgiastic than any spot on earth, and it was a dour Crowe, tired now of endless holidays, who collected a good share of his workers from the Vegas jail, put up bail, and hauled them, like so many cattle, to the dam site.

The year did not start off well for Frank, and the first news from Williams was not the most welcome.

Williams paced Frank's office before he spoke.

"Ain't gonna do you no good to blow up, just a waste of energy, though I wouldn't blame you."

"What's wrong?"

"I'm missing forty sticks of dynamite."

"Shit," Crowe spat out. "All from one place?"

"No. That would be easy. It's a stick here, two sticks there. It's a professional job."

Crowe stared at Williams, then the floor. "You've talked to all your powder men?"

"The reports all coincide. It all happened over Christmas."

"Devere," Frank said.

"Sure," Williams agreed.

"That means you've got Wobblies in your crew."

"I know all that," Williams said. "I'm sure we've got Wobblies on *every* crew. You might have a few in your staff upstairs."

"I might."

"It's just that I've *got* what they *want* right now."

"Dynamite," Crowe said to himself.

"And if I get Pitt to raid their joint, it'll be clean. They know that's the first place we'd look."

"What about the boys you've got working for you? They come up with anything?"

"Nothing. This is the first they've heard of it."

"We could search every man going in and out of the dam site, but those forty sticks, I lay you odds, are still on the site."

"That's the way I figure it," Williams agreed. "I've got to think, Frank. I don't have an answer."

"Just double your guards for now, and thanks for the good news."

Williams left but Crowe continued to pace. He looked at his maps and at the barometer on the wall, which was dropping, but he could not come up with a solution immediately.

He walked to the drafting room, where engineers were working on changes for the canyon wall outlet works, and a decision was made to eliminate the upper valve installations on both sides of the river. These decisions, though weighty, were simple. They were engineering solutions and had no imponderables.

The barometer continued to fall, and on January 12, 1932, all the meteorological predictions proved accurate. A storm, some called it a hurricane, hit the dam site. It began with an eighty-mile-an-hour gale, and a torrential rain razing tents, damaging poorly built frame houses, blowing roofs off dormitories. Construction came to a halt. Those in Hemenway Wash at the river camp lost almost everything, tents, bedding, cooking utensils, and fled to higher ground. The following day snow fell in Las Vegas.

This was an emergency Crowe was prepared for. There were contingency plans for this type of disaster.

At the same time that the weather turned against them, the powerhouse failed. Hans drove Frank to the plant, where Crowe got the final decision from Stephan, its supervisor.

"She's out," he said bleakly.

"Shit," Frank replied, staring at the man's dials; the gauges all rested on the small bar which denoted zero. Frank stared at the finality of these tiny arrows, trying by sheer will to force them into proper place, but his vision blurred. The dials momentarily swam in front of his eyes, and he shook his head to clear his vision.

"Let's go," he said to Hans, and they walked back to the truck. He missed the step onto the cab floor and fell against the fender.

Hans rushed to his side. "You hurt, chief?"

Crowe looked up, slowly standing and brushing the mud off his clothes.

"No, just clumsy. Let's go."

They raced around the dam site and Crowe directed the rebuilding of roads, the resettling of uprooted workers, shoring up walls and digging drainage. Huge power shovels moved earth methodically to build levees in one area and equally hard in others to allow the water to flow toward the river.

"Turn on your wipers," he said to Hans at one point.

"It ain't raining," Hans said, looking at Frank, who was pinching his eyes and then wiping his forehead, which was drenched in perspiration. "You sure you're all right?"

"I'm sure," Crowe said. "Take me to Tunnel 4."

Fighting these elements was extremely hazardous. Huge boards of construction lumber flew through the air like matchsticks, sand-filled winds almost choked a man, but Crowe drove his men like slaves.

The first night Frank came home only long enough to put on dry clothes, and Elle made him sit down while she heated some soup. When she returned from the kitchen she noticed he was asleep sitting up. She felt his forehead, which was warm, and debated about letting him sleep, but knew this would anger him. She put her arms around him to wake him.

"You fell asleep," Elle said. "Your head is warm. I think you have a fever."

"I'm fine," Frank said. "God damn it, I'm just fine." He hardly finished his soup and started out of the house again, putting his poncho on as he ran to the truck, and the cold rain felt good on his hot face.

Terry did not see Hans for days either. Only the lonely cottonwood tree stopped their truck from falling on its side, and at night she slept in the men's hall rather than braving the highway to Las Vegas.

There were trucks all over the dam site, muckers, shovels, cranes, both the Big Six Companies' equipment and that of the Bureau of Reclamation. After the storm had finally ceased, Frank walked into Walker Young's office and thanked him for his assistance.

Young looked as haggard as Crowe. "It's the first storm, not the last," he said. "Don't like the powerhouse going out."

"Agreed," said Crowe. "I've been on the phone to Interstate Power already. Never did trust those California boys."

Frank paced the drafting room above his office. "Practically everything that went wrong these last three days," he said, "was incorrectly designed in this room. Roofs were improperly trussed, drainage ditches were inadequate, highways were poorly graded." Frank paused. "And no one is more to blame than me because no plan left this room without my signature.

"So whether *you're* horses' asses or *I'm* the biggest horse's ass is irrelevant. I want a damage survey and a report on my desk no later than Friday at one P.M. We'll all screw up again, gentlemen, I predict that, but we'll not screw up in the *same* place twice."

He rushed out and down to his own office, wiping his brow, and motioned in McDermott of Interstate Power Company. McDermott waited patiently as Crowe searched his cubbyholes for a set of plans, then opened a file drawer and extracted a contract.

He spread out the plans on his desk and put a copy of specifications on top of it. "Now, McDermott, I'd like to give you a bit of bad news. I have just left the drafting room and taken blame for every bit of damage done to this dam site by the storm."

His vision blurred momentarily and he steadied himself on the edge of the drafting table. McDermott watched, but just as quickly as his vision failed, so it returned, and Crowe went on angrily. "Your goddamn power system collapsed like a house of cards under an eighty-mile-an-hour wind. This dam site has been without electricity for seventy-two hours. Right now we're using our own generators."

McDermott grew red in the face. "It was an act of God."

"An act of God, my ass," Crowe shouted angrily. "You didn't build that powerhouse according to my specifications. I've called up Mountain Electric from Salt Lake and they'll be here this afternoon to rebuild it. I told them to bill you."

"Where do you think we'll get the money?"

"I'd suggest you get in your Packard and go call your board of directors. Meet around some swimming pool or under a palm tree and tell your treasurer to practice *writing* checks instead of banking them."

"I'll see you in court," McDermott yelled.

"I'll see you in jail, you bastard. Get out of my office."

Frank heard the door slam and collapsed on the floor. When he woke he found himself cradled by Dominick, a young engineer who had discovered him passed out on the floor. Several other young engineers stood around.

"Get some coffee," Dominick ordered.

"What the hell is wrong?" Frank asked.

"I found you on the floor—out."

Frank sat up and wiped his forehead.

"You're burning up," Dominick said.

Slowly, carefully, Frank stood, and slowly the floor seemed to level. Someone brought in a steaming mug of coffee, but Crowe pushed it away.

He reached into the bottom drawer of his desk and found a bottle of bourbon, unstoppered it and took a long swig. He passed the bottle to the other engineers, but each declined.

"The only thing wrong with me is that I haven't had a drink in three days," he said. "Man's blood gets too thick."

"You ought to see a doctor," Dominick said, not buying Crowe's self-diagnosis.

"I don't need a doctor, and I don't need advice. I thank you for your concern. I'll leave that bottle here if any of you change your mind, but, gentlemen, I don't want a word of this scene to get out of this room."

211

They all nodded and watched Crowe leave. They looked at his orderly office and the foreignness of that bottle of bourbon on the desk. They looked at each other and shrugged their shoulders and returned to work.

Frank went home and to bed for the first time in three days. He declined dinner and aspirin and a cold towel, which Elle tried to place on his burning forehead. His temper matched his temperature, and when he finally dropped into a fitful sleep, interrupted constantly by a racking cough, Elle put on her robe and ran to the Williamses' house to get Jack.

"He's sick," she cried. "Frank's very sick. He needs a doctor. Talks about getting up at five . . ."

Maria had joined Jack at the door and Jack took command quickly.

"Get one of the doctors," he told Maria, "and Tom Wanke. Then meet me at Crowe's house."

Elle and Jack Williams returned to her house, where Frank was stirring in bed, still asleep. Ten minutes later Maria Williams came with a young doctor carrying a new black bag, and Tom Wanke arrived.

"All right," Jack Williams said to the doctor. "Let's see the patient."

Although a large muscular man, Williams roused Frank very gently.

"Frank," he said softly. "Frank."

"Huh?"

"It's me. Jack."

"Who?"

"Jack Williams."

"What the hell you doing in my bedroom?" He threw his arm toward Elle's side of the bed. "Where's Elle?"

"She's here. I brought the doctor."

"What for?"

"For a poker game, you idiot."

"Don't need a doctor. Got the chills. Be all right."

Jack asked the doctor, "What's your name?"

"Dr. McDowell."

"All right, McDowell, now tell me what's wrong with Mr. Crowe."

"Don't need a doctor."

"God damn it, Frank," Williams now raised his voice, "you'll do what you're told or I'll break your jaw."

Williams left Frank with the doctor and returned to the living room with Elle, his own wife, and Tom Wanke.

They sat silently until the doctor came down the stairs and joined them.

"He's got a temperature of 104, pneumonia, he's a very sick man."

Elle cried and Wanke put his arms around her.

"His constitution is good," the doctor continued. "I've given him a sedative and I'll get an oxygen tent up here. With complete bed rest he should be on his feet in a week."

"A week," Elle sobbed. "He's talking about going back tomorrow."

"If he gets out of that bed tomorrow," the young doctor said pompously, "you'll bury him the next day."

"I'll take care of that," Williams said. "I know all about burials."

The doctor left them with several bottles of drugs, and Elle and the Williamses and Tom Wanke sat in the living room. It was one in the morning.

"Would you like some tea?" Elle asked.

"Don't bother," Maria said.

"All right," Williams said. "I'm going up there and give it to him straight. I'm going to sit in this house until he can *walk* out. Don't worry about anything, Elle."

Frank half-sat in his bed, looking drained and feverish. His eyes, normally clear and blue, were glazed and colorless, his beard, half sandy, half gray, made him look older.

"So did the kid stick the thermometer up your ass?"

"All quacks," Crowe said.

"I know he needed gloves to pull it out. You're running a hundred and four."

"I'll be okay in the morning."

"You'll be okay my ass."

"Get out of here," Crowe said feebly.

"I'm getting out of here," Jack Williams said. "I'm getting out of this room and sitting in a chair in your parlor, and if you make any moves to leave this house I'll kill you. You've got pneumonia and you're going to stay here until you're well."

"Shit."

"Don't argue with me, mister. That's it, so just relax."

Crowe lay back on the bed and stared at the ceiling. He motioned Jack to come closer.

"Listen, Jack, listen good."

"Go ahead."

"That kid that works for me," he groaned, "that Hans."

"What about him . . . ?"

"I don't want him to know I'm sick. I don't want *anybody* to know that I'm sick."

"Okay. It ain't a crime, but nobody'll know. What's so special about the kid?"

"His brother works for Devere. He's *one* guy I don't want to know."

"I got you, Frank."

"Put him under Wanke. Keep an eye on him. Got it?"

213

"Got it."

"Now send up Tom."

"Okay."

Williams walked downstairs and sent up Wanke.

"Hi, Frank," he said calmly.

"Hi, Tom. Listen. I've got Mountain Electric coming from Salt Lake tomorrow to rebuild the power plant. The specs are on my desk. Tell them to follow them or they'll get screwed like Interstate Power."

"I know Mountain Electric," Wanke said. "We should have had them in the first place."

"I know." Crowe coughed viciously.

Tom put his hand on Crowe's shoulder. "For once, Frank, use your fucking head. Stay in bed."

"Yeah. Shit."

Tom Wanke left the room and passed two hospital orderlies and the doctor coming up the stairs. They were carrying an oxygen tank.

Williams explained the situation with Hans to Wanke and Elle was instructed to send Hans to Wanke's office in the morning. "Tell him Frank's in San Francisco."

"Maria," Williams said, "take Elle to the house and put her to bed."

"I don't want to leave Frank."

"There's nothing you can do for him tonight." He looked at his watch. "It's two. Come back at seven and bring breakfast. I'll lie down on the couch."

Tom Wanke said, "I'll have my wife bring breakfast, don't bother Maria." He stood ready to go. "Anything else, Jack?"

Williams said, "Yeah, a couple of things. Get the chief to station a deputy at this house. I don't trust Frank as far as I can spit. He'll feel a little better and go out the back window."

"That's one, what else?"

"See Lerner, my assistant. Tell him I went to Frisco with Frank. Tell him that if those stiffs don't overshoot their records I'll have 'em all cleaning grease pits."

"You don't mind if I put it into my own words?"

"What's the matter, my words not good enough for you? We happen to have the same rank around here, Mr. Wanke."

"But not the same disposition."

"Break it up, you clowns," Maria shouted. "Come on, Elle, let's get some sleep." But Elle was not in the room; she was at Frank's bedside.

Before they put the oxygen tent around him she kissed his hot stubbled cheek.

"Get well, Frank, for me. *For me*. Not for anything else." She put a small bottle of perfume next to the bedside. "There are lots of drops left in this bottle," she said, "and lots of bottles when this one's empty." She left before she heard the rush of oxygen being fed into Frank's lungs, and collapsed on Maria's couch.

She could not sleep, seeing the light in their bedroom across the street and worrying about Frank, and Maria sat next to her and spoke about a kind of camaraderie known to men in this business.

"Do you think it's indigenous to men?" Elle asked.

"Don't know," Maria said. "Never heard of a dam built by women."

"I guess you're right."

They both collapsed finally, unaware that Crowe at first sign of dawn had dressed and inched his way down the stairs, out the door, and almost into the arms of Sergeant O'Leary, who carried him effortlessly through the front door opened by Williams.

"Got any more tricks?" Williams said. "You want me to seal up the chimney?"

Crowe started to answer, but passed out. O'Leary and Williams got him back to bed and under the oxygen tent. Williams called the doctor.

"Now what?" he said.

"What do you mean, now what? You get your ass up here or I'll have my boys thrust a thermometer up your dick and break it in half. Is that clear?"

"Now what?" he said to O'Leary, shaking his head. "Fucking doctors . . ."

35

Although in January of 1932 there were 3,100 men working on the dam site, the absence of only one man, Frank Crowe, was so noticeable that it became quite a topic of conversation.

Hans, hurt and then mystified by his transfer to Tom Wanke's staff, was particularly vocal about the subject, discussing it even with Herman, who quickly passed the news on to Devere.

"That's very interesting," Devere said. "Crowe is in San Francisco. Did anyone see him leave the dam site?"

"I don't know."

"Did anyone see him at the train station? Las Vegas?"

"I don't know."

"*Well, find out—god damn it,*" he shouted, and then called in several of his henchmen to give them the news. One of his other informers told Devere that Williams was in Frisco also, which made the story more incredible to swallow.

"He's either sick or dead," Devere said coldly, "and I'd like to know which. Crowe would *never* leave this dam site with Williams."

But questioning of friends of Crowe's staff was met with absolute hostility. "What's it to you, buddy?" the old man on the day shift said at the gate.

"Didn't you get a postcard?"one of the engineers answered in Crowe's office. "I did," leaving Devere more frustrated and venomous.

Elle's intuition led her to call Francesca Stein and confide in her about Frank's illness and about her skepticism as to the ability of his doctors.

Francesca's response was warm and immediate. Not only did she send the best specialist in San Francisco, but she accompanied him. Laden with candies from Blum's, with flowers, with cakes and French bread and cheeses and wines, she quickly assumed the role of confidante, of truly warm friend.

Dr. Leslie confirmed the local diagnosis, and though his appearance seemed foolish to Frank, his prescription to get out of bed and do some walking was highly welcome. "I'm telling you to get up, Mr. Crowe," Leslie said sternly, "up, but not out. I want to clear that chest cavity of fluids. Do you understand that?"

"I understand it," Jack Williams said, not having left Crowe for three days now, watching him go from delirium to sleep to delirium.

Frank, finally dressed in his brand-new paisley robe, descended toward the living room on Elle's arm and seemed genuinely happy to see Francesca Stein. He shook hands and sat gingerly on his divan as if fearing its legs wouldn't hold him.

"Well, you can tell Roger to dock me three days' pay," he said.

"That was the reason for this trip, Frank," Francesca said. "I've brought the time card."

"How's Roger?"

"Fine. He sends his regards and asks if there is anything he can do."

"There is," Frank said, "as a matter of fact."

"Tell me."

Elle could sense Frank's weakness by his slow speech, but did not comment on it.

"Tell him," Frank said, "that for security reasons Williams and I are supposed to be in San Francisco. Tell him," Frank paused, "to document it. Send some wires to my crew, to Williams's crew, some innocuous orders, and sign our names. He'll understand."

"I'll tell him. I'll phone him tonight."

"Thank you."

"I brought some Blum's cake. How about a piece?"

Frank looked at Elle. "That sounds good."

"You see," Francesca said, "a good sign. A man who eats can't be sick."

Elle jumped up to go to the kitchen.

"That's some wife you've got there, Frank, do you know that?"

"I know it."

"I don't mean that she's beautiful."

"I know what you mean."

"Be sure you do. That's not a little girl you take for granted."

"There's very little in this world I take for granted, Francesca."

"I'm sure that's true."

Elle returned with four plates of cake and Jack Williams had finished his before the others started. "I'm beginning to like this job," Williams said. "Maybe I could learn to become a male nurse. The cake in the mess hall isn't nearly as good as this."

"Why don't you go to work, Jack?" Frank pleaded.

"And give up all these parties? Hell, no. What's for dinner, Elle?"

"I'd like to go to bed," Frank said, "and I want to talk to you, Jack. I've been doing some thinking."

Williams helped Frank to his feet and half carried him to his bed, while Elle and Francesca watched. Francesca had motioned Elle to stay seated.

"Don't pamper him, Elle," she said. "Men hate that. Care for him. Don't pamper."

Elle nodded. "I've never seen him this weak."

"Roger caught malaria in Panama. He's never gotten rid of it. Still gets the chills. Nobody knows the price these men pay."

Frank was settled in bed and obviously pleased to be in it.

"Son of a bitch," he said to Jack. "What *is* this pneumonia anyway?"

"Beats me," Jack said, "but watching you I sure don't want it."

"It's not fun, I'll tell you."

"What's on your mind, Frank?"

"Let me talk slowly and don't interrupt."

"Go ahead."

"If you were Devere, and you had forty sticks of dynamite, where would you use it?"

"At a tunnel entrance," Williams said.

217

"Good thinking, but forty sticks wouldn't really do enough damage there. Where else?"

Williams thought. "I don't know."

"Think of the river."

"I am."

"When's the most crucial time on the river?"

"The day we turn it into the tunnels."

Suddenly Frank rose, pointed his finger at Williams, and shouted, *"That's right."*

Elle ran up the stairs. "You all right, Frank?"

"Fine."

Frank lay back on his bed, smiling. "I'm going to turn that river by dumping rock from the railway bridge."

"I know that, Frank."

"So answer me now. What's the most crucial part of the project?"

"The railway bridge." Williams acted as if a light had gone on in his head. "God damn, God damn," he shouted at Frank, "you're right."

Again Elle ran up the stairs, but Jack stopped her halfway. "We're all right."

"And will forty sticks of dynamite blow up my bridge?"

"It will blow it to kingdom come."

"So far," Frank said, "all the coordinates check. Right?"

"They check."

"The next question is, when will we turn the river?"

"After I finish the tunnels."

"Right."

"You'll have a party, celebrations, right?"

"Right."

"Like sending a wire to Devere: Today's the day."

"Today's the day," Williams agreed.

"Last night, Jack, it came to me. I'm going to let Mr. Devere know when that day is. There will be just one hitch."

"What's that?"

"It'll be the wrong day. Now let me go to sleep."

"Yeah, Frank. You need some sleep."

He returned to the ladies and said to Francesca, "Don't take Frank off the payroll. He's still working."

"I know," Elle said. "Overtime."

36

The Colorado River is far from being the longest river in the world, but has a characteristic unrivaled by any other, namely the ability to change the landscape of the area it traverses. The Mississippi carries a cubic foot of silt with each 1,500 cubic feet of water and has built up tremendous deltas. The Nile carries one cubic foot of silt for every 1,900 feet of water and has literally caused the rise of Egypt. The Colorado on the other hand carries one foot of silt for every 277 cubic feet of water. For eons the Colorado has moved the surface of Utah, Wyoming, New Mexico, Colorado, Arizona, Nevada, and California. For years farmers, with sandbags, with straw dikes, with picks and shovels, had been fighting the rampages of the Colorado, and their fight was always a losing one.

All these facts were engraved on Crowe's mind as neatly as names on a tombstone, and even during his last days of recovery his thoughts never left the river. In the mornings he would get the reports of the usual rock slides, powerline breaks, of trucks skidding off the road, but the progress reports were more heartening.

The railroad from Boulder City to the brink of the canyon was finally finished. The road to the gravel pit was completed, as was the pile trestle eight miles upriver. Wanke in his quiet way provided his modern gravel plant, with its intricate machinery for separating aggregate, shearing and washing sand. Now he was, for the first time, able to ship raw gravel from the pits to the plants.

Blasting of the Nevada spillway was beginning, and Williams's crews were attacking the giant tunnels with their usual ferocity at eight different headings. He was blasting and mucking sixteen thousand cubic yards a day; in early February Tunnels 2 and 3 were enlarged to the final bore of fifty-six feet inside. At this point it looked as if preparations for the diversion of Big Red would be accomplished with time to spare.

But Crowe was barely back on the job, and with that continuous distrust of nature indigenous to engineers he was not surprised by the rampage of the Colorado on February 9, 1932.

For nineteen years, the Bureau's statistics had not shown a flood

219

of consequence during February, but statistics were of little value in a crisis; Frank knew that well.

Far up in the headwaters of the east and west forks of the Virgin River, a tributary of the Colorado which joins the mainstream just above Black Canyon, a heavy warm rain fell, which melted the snow remaining in the surrounding mountains. Both snow water and rain descended together. The flood struck Black Canyon just as the swing shift was coming on at three-thirty. Crowe was at the site in ten minutes. Williams suspended all work on the tunnels and put his men to raising dikes. Hour after hour the waters continued to rise. At eleven-thirty that night the flood endangered the entire project area.

Crowe issued orders for the swing shift to remain and, joined by the graveyard shift which followed, all men labored to stem the flood. There was no need for exhortations. Men worked, worked furiously, and by morning when the water began to recede, the damage was confined to the loss of the trestle bridge, the silting of shops and road and equipment.

Work did not abate as Elle sat home, worried sick about Frank, obviously weakened by his illness, gone from home now thirty hours. The damaged area had barely been cleaned up when Crowe returned to his office to make up his overtime reports. The phone rang. It was two in the afternoon. He had been awake and working for thirty-two hours now. The call was from a gauging station two hundred miles upriver. The same rainstorm which had caused the flood on the Virgin River hundreds of miles to the north had moved to the Little Colorado.

Although the dam site had been pretty well cleaned up from the last storm, the bridge was still washed out and it was impossible for Crowe to get trucks across to the Arizona side to strengthen the dikes for the Arizona diversion tunnels. He sent a large force of men across the narrow suspension bridge 150 yards upstream to try to build up the levee and rescue as much equipment as they could.

The second flood was more vicious than the first. The river rose 17 feet and reached a discharge of 57,000 cubic feet a second. Crowe managed a few hours of sleep in his office before dawn. The flood had receded the following morning and his first inspection was depressing. The receding waters had left a thick deposit of mud, slimy, rust-colored, on pumps and power lines, pipes, drilling equipment, toolhouses, sleds, trackage. The silt was too thin to shovel and too thick to pump. Grimy tired men excavated 200,000 cubic yards of muck out of the diversion tunnels, and no one doubted the saying that on windy days dust blows off the surface of the Colorado.

It took two weeks for Crowe's men, bridge builders, pipe fitters, electricians, and other specialized trades, to make the dam site ready for continuing work. A good many men made overtime. But finally

Frank Crowe, on the insistence of Elle, stayed home Sunday, all day, and rested and wondered what the Colorado would throw him next.

Devere had called a meeting of his closest colleagues. They were seated around his desk drinking coffee, smoking cigarettes. They were all workers on the dam site and represented almost every trade. Some wore their work clothes still, others had changed into denims and sweaters.

Devere tapped the side of his inevitable glass of whiskey and the room silenced.

"First thing I've got to say," Devere rasped, "is that we still don't know where Crowe and Williams disappeared to for ten days. Do we?"

There was silence in the room.

"The two top guys on the dam disappeared and nobody knows where they went."

"Maybe he was sick."

"Maybe he was. What about Williams? Also sick?"

Again there was silence in the room.

"Well, you guys are being paid hard-earned money from the Wobblies and you sit here like a bunch of nitwits. Nobody's got any records from the hospital, the gates, from the phone operator?"

"What the hell difference does it make?" one of the tunnel men said. "He's back. What's the big deal?"

"*The big deal,*" Devere shouted, "is that we're just a few months away from our big operation. If you guys can't keep track of two *key* men, how can I rely on any other information I need?"

"I figure we're about eight months away from holing through," one of the other tunnelers said.

"About eight months. Shit." Devere still yelled. " '*About*' don't tell me nothing. I've got to know the day, the *hour,* the *minute* when Crowe starts dumping rock off that bridge."

"With them storms hitting the dam site, even Crowe probably don't know," one of the electricians said.

"He knows," Devere said. "He knows."

"Why don't we blow the bridge *before* we get finished with the tunnel?"

"Because Crowe will rebuild it, that's why! We tip him off a few days before and he'll build that bridge in no time and we'll never be around here to see it rebuilt."

"What about your brother?" one of the men asked Herman. "Don't he talk to Crowe?"

"Sure, he talks to Crowe, but Crowe don't say nothing. Even if he did my brother wouldn't tell us."

"Can't you put some pressure on him, Devere?"

221

"Let me handle that," Devere said. "Look, you guys," Devere continued, almost calmly now, "the day Crowe turns the river is a big day. I figure it might take him twenty-four hours, maybe thirty. Now Crowe is a very well-organized man. He's gonna need every truck on the dam site, and each truck's got to be working. He's gonna need extra meals and extra chefs. He's gonna marshal his police force. There'll be no visitors on the dam site. Crowe isn't going to organize that overnight. There's got to be orders to Anderson for food and to Murphy for protection and to the motor pool for maintenance. Now for Christ sake, can't any of you get close to the motor pool, the mechanics, the cooks, the cops? I need leads, lots of leads. Just feed them to me and I'll put them together. That's all."

After everyone had gone, Devere asked Herman, "Where *was* your brother when Crowe disappeared?"

"He worked for Wanke."

"How convenient."

"Yeah . . . yeah," Herman repeated.

"They know who your brother is?"

"I guess so."

"Which makes him useless to us." He paused. "Unless . . ."

"Unless what?"

"Unless he can be persuaded."

"How?"

"That little cunt, that, what's her name?"

"Terry."

"Yeah, Terry, always twisting her ass around here. Terry." He put his pencil in his mouth. "There's got to be something more useful for her to do than hang her teats over a steam table all day. . . . Who's that kid that's been giving her rides home in that fancy convertible?"

"Barnes's son."

"Yeah, Barnes's son. I'm thinking he ain't giving little Terry rides home 'cause he's lonely."

"That figures, but Terry wouldn't do nothing. Dumb Okie. You know how they are."

"Yeah. I know how they are. Dumb and Okie. Perfect. I hear that Crowe don't like that Barnes kid too much on the dam site. Maybe we should have him to a little party."

"Don't think you could get him to join the movement."

"Didn't ask him to join the movement. Just like to find out how hot his rocks are for little Terry."

The plot was somewhat convoluted for Herman but he deferred as usual to Devere.

"The next time he brings her home, ask him, do you hear me—
ask him, to come in here for a chat."

"I got you."

Terry and Hans had made love that night and were lying in their
bunks, warm and secure, enjoying the fire of their homemade stove.
They heard the men shuffle out of Devere's office, get in their cars,
and drive off.

"I wonder what the hell they talk about all the time," Terry said.

"Bullshit," Hans answered. "All that Marx bullshit. They're all
working, what more do they want?"

"I don't know," Terry said. "I figured with both of us working
we could get out of this truck in six months."

"Yeah," Hans said. "I'd like that. Sleep in a real room with a real
bed and a cooler in the summer." He touched her hair, but like the
child she really still was, she was sound asleep already. Hans looked
at the red embers crumbling in the stove and they reminded him of
the steel ingots his father had handled at the Rouge. His father had
taken him once and he had never forgotten that red-hot lava leaving
the furnace, traveling down steel rollers, giving off sparks like the
4th of July. He had loved his old man. There was no doubt of that.

37

Crowe was ready to resume work on the dam site on February 16.
Having Wanke's gravel available to him now, he placed two cofferdams
at the outlets of the tunnels, he threw up a dike of muck, all of which
should divert the next flood if the river didn't exceed 90,000 cubic
feet per second.

Henry Barnes, Jr., worked as a warehouse clerk on the dam site,
a job which entailed nothing more than filling endless orders for machine parts requested by an equally endless number of foremen who
shared only one trait, that of being impatient.

All day long the conversation was a monotonous series of complaints. "I asked for a three-sixteenth not a three-eighth, stupid, a dou-

ble angle, not a triple angle, you meathead," and so it went. And though he might never have used his name, his mode of living, a comfortable apartment in Las Vegas, his Ford roadster, his fancy shoes, his carefully laundered and pressed denims set him at arm's length from most of the working stiffs on the site. He made few friends on the dam and only a handful in Las Vegas, where he was known as an easy mark for a loan or a drink.

The boy, six feet four inches, clean-cut and good-looking, was clearly a fish out of water at the dam site. Cursed most of the day by his co-workers, used in his off hours by his buddies because of his money, he felt even at twenty-one that deep gut loneliness of an outcast. He could drown that feeling in alcohol, and he did frequently; he could get mock sympathy from a poor soul in Vegas, as long as he paid for it before or afterward, and he was, as Devere suspected, vulnerable.

It was only a week after his discussion with Herman that Devere saw Barnes's red roadster come to a screeching halt behind Alma's fruit stand, and he watched as Terry slid out of the front seat, waving goodbye to Barnes. The boy was ready to throw his car into gear when Devere hailed him.

"Henry," he yelled, and the boy turned to look at Devere, a man he had never seen before.

"What is it?"

"Come in here for a minute."

The boy waited a moment, shrugged his shoulders, and followed the man into his office. There was no one there; the room looked bleak, deserted, in need of a good sweeping.

"Sit down," Devere said. "Have a drink?"

"Sure," young Henry said.

Devere poured two drinks and seated himself behind the desk, motioning Henry to sit opposite him.

"Been nice of you to give little Terry all those rides home. Long ways from the dam site if you don't have a car."

"Been no trouble," Henry said. "Kind of keep looking for her."

"Yeah, she's a pretty good-looking girl."

"You can say that again."

"Well," Devere raised his glass, "the first thing we've agreed on," and poured down half the glass of whiskey. Henry followed suit.

"Been wanting to talk to you."

"Me?" the boy said, genuinely surprised.

"Yeah. Thought we might have a few things in common."

"Like what?"

"Let's discuss it over dinner tonight. How about Tonopah, the Wagon Wheel, you know the place?"

"Sure."

"At six o'clock. I'm buying."

The boy looked puzzled and hesitated. "Well, the food at the Wagon Wheel couldn't be any worse than Mom's Diner in Vegas. You're on." Henry finished his drink and started to leave. "Six o'clock," he said.

"Yeah," Devere answered. "Don't bother to dress."

He listened to Henry gun his car toward Vegas and opened his cash box to take out $10, then he carefully logged the expense in his notebook.

The Wagon Wheel in Tonopah smelled of booze, Lysol, and urine. There was gambling on worn crap tables in the front of the barnlike structures, dining booths in the back, and prostitution in a series of trailers behind the latrine, which served as a passageway between two avenues of sin. Someone remarked once that every son of a bitch in the Wagon Wheel was forever buttoning his fly coming either from the latrine or the whores. Devere liked the Wagon Wheel since he could talk freely and without being observed in this atmosphere of pure carnality, and no one gave a damn about another man as long as he didn't knock his drink off the bar or wasn't screwing the blonde at the time he had arranged her for himself.

Tonight Devere was in his element, and this boy, this rich man's kid, was like a fly to the tongue of a frog.

It began with drinks, a number of drinks, and a lot of useless talk. Drinks were followed by steak, huge Texas-style hunks of meat, more quantity than quality, and followed by more drinks.

When the boy was finally "mellowed," as Devere thought of it, he began his pitch.

"You still don't know why we're here, do you?"

"No, but it was a great steak and I thank you." His manners had not been totally forgotten.

"Can I talk plain?" Devere asked.

"Go ahead."

"First off I ain't queer. So put that out of your head. I got Wanda lined up in back when we're finished, so that's understood."

"It is," Henry, Jr., said.

"I know who you are," Devere said directly.

"Henry Barnes, Jr."

"Yeah, yeah, I know that. And your old man's head of the Big Six."

"One of the heads."

"Whatever he is. And he's got you here to make a man of you."

"How do you know that?"

225

" 'Cause when I was your age," Devere lied, "my old man was head of Columbia Construction. Probably never heard of it . . ."

"No."

"And he put me on a canal down in Central America which almost killed me."

"Jesus."

"Yeah. Snakes and malaria and niggers with syphilis, and twice a year he'd visit the project and put his arm around my shoulder and say, 'Well, boy, how are things going?' . . . and before I knew it he was on some steamer heading home or whatever he did." Henry just looked at Devere. "You happy here, kid?" Devere asked.

"Hell, no."

"Figures. Owner's son, everybody hates you, whatever work you do don't matter nohow."

"That's right," the boy said enthusiastically.

"Well, I quit," Devere said. "I said fuck it and joined the Wobblies. I hated those rich bastards as much as the workers, and the richest of them all was my *own* father. Well," Devere paused, "I ain't asking you to join the Wobblies."

"Can I buy a round?" Henry asked, obviously fired up.

"Sure, go ahead. Well," Devere said, "I got something you want and you might get something that I want."

"What have you got?"

"Terry."

The boy whistled silently. "She your girlfriend?"

"No. She ain't mine, but she's on my property."

"So how can you get her for me?"

"You leave that to me."

"And what do you want from me?"

"Some information."

"Like what?"

"I'll tell you later."

"And where do you want me to get this information?"

"From Frank Crowe."

"Forget it," Henry said. "He hates my guts."

"Why?"

"I busted in on him one night when I started the job."

"Let me worry about that. Meanwhile, come by tomorrow night. Don't come roaring like you always do. Park your car down the road and come to my office at ten o'clock."

"Then what?"

"I'll give you a preview."

"Sounds interesting."

"Yeah, and wear tennis shoes."

226

Devere disappeared toward the back of the restaurant, and after watching Henry's car disappear into the desert, he got into his own car and returned home.

Herman was already asleep but Devere woke him roughly. Herman rubbed his eyes. "What do you want?"

"I want you to listen and listen good."

"Yeah?"

"I know you been sneaking around that truck of yours at night watching your brother fuck Terry, and don't deny it."

"What's it to you?"

"Nothing," Devere said. "Nothing. They could fuck in broad daylight at the UP station and I wouldn't slow down my car."

"So why bring it up?"

"Because tomorrow night I got a kid coming and you're gonna let *him* watch. Got it?"

"A kid, what kid?"

"Look, Herman, you stupid German bastard, how many times do I have to get it through your blockhead that *I* give the orders, and I pay the checks, and you don't ask no questions."

"I'm sorry," Herman said, and went back to sleep.

Devere, as shrewd as ever, knew that Hans and Terry did not make love every night, but tomorrow was payday, and Devere had watched Hans return on payday before with a bottle of wine and he knew that this forty-cent expenditure was not made in vain. And when Herman pointed out a good place for Henry to watch their lovemaking, the boy was rewarded with the sight of Hans's and Terry's naked bodies undulating gracefully by the light of their makeshift stove.

Herman retreated back to Alma's cottage mystified by Devere's request, but Henry became bolder and more excited as he watched the couple making love, seeing Terry's large breasts, her beautiful heaving buttocks, the fire playing tricks with shadows and lights on her thighs. He was a large boy and clumsy like his father and almost fell through the side of the canvas-covered truck.

"What's that?" Hans said. He rose and jumped to the back of the truck. Henry saw him and began to run. Hans, though stark naked, began to follow, but both modesty and prudence made him finally stop. He watched the stranger reach his car and roar down the highway. He knew that car like the back of his hand.

Hans returned to the truck and watched Terry huddled in a towel sitting on her bedroll.

"What's going on?"

"That son of a bitch," Hans said.

"Who?"

"That bastard that drives that new roadster was watching us."

227

"That kid?" Terry asked innocently.

"You know him?"

"He's given me rides home."

"Go on," Hans said angrily.

"That's all."

"How many times?"

"Three, maybe four times."

"Just given you rides?"

"That's all, Hans. I hitch every night. So do you."

"Don't ever ask you out or nothing?"

"Never has, I swear. Except . . ."

"Except *what?*"

"Something queer happened yesterday."

"Like what?"

"Devere asked him into his office."

Hans put on his tee shirt. "You swear to me nothing's going on between you and that kid?"

"I swear, Hans."

"Okay, okay. You swear. Let me think." Hans was quiet for minutes and Terry watched his intense face.

"Do you know who that kid is?"

"No."

"It's Barnes's son."

"Who's Barnes?"

"One of the Big Six. I've heard Crowe talk about him."

"Jesus," Terry said.

"So why would Barnes's son talk to Devere?"

"Beats me," Terry said.

"Beats me too," Hans said, "but I don't like it."

Again Hans was quiet and finally he said, "I got to tell Crowe. I owe him that. We both owe him."

"For sure," Terry said.

"I'd like to kill that son of a bitch but I got to tell Crowe first, so don't say nothing to nobody about tonight. You got that, Terry?"

"I won't."

"I might just kill him anyway," Hans said before falling asleep.

Routinely Hans showed up at Crowe's house, backed out the truck, on which Wanke had put a canvas roof during Crowe's illness, warmed the engine, and waited for Frank to appear at the front door, which he did precisely at five-thirty-five. Before putting the car in gear and driving Crowe to his office this morning, Hans turned to Frank and said, "I've got to talk to you."

"What about?"

228

"It's important."

"It better be. I got a rough day."

Hans quickly explained his dilemma. He told him of his brother, Devere, the joint ownership of the truck in which he and Terry lived, and finally he told him about Henry Barnes, Jr.

Crowe listened carefully, even told Hans to shut off the motor on the truck. His mind worked feverishly. Everything that Hans told about himself Crowe knew to be true, since he had that information already.

Crowe spoke to himself more than anything else. "Devere needs an informant. He figured on you but you didn't pan out. Now Barnes. Why Barnes? What does Devere have that Barnes wants?"

"Terry," Hans said.

"Yes, Terry," Crowe agreed. "Is she available?"

"No," Hans said.

"You sure?"

"I'm sure."

Jack Williams came out of his house and walked toward Crowe's car. "What's the matter, Frank? Out of gas?"

"No," Frank said seriously. "I'll talk to you tonight." Williams drove off.

Crowe looked at Hans. "What you did, boy, was right, and I thank you."

"Forget it, chief, you been good to me and Terry."

"Yes," Frank said, thinking more than talking. "Now I want you to do another thing for me."

"What's that?"

"I know you want to kill that leering bastard Barnes and so do I, but I'm going to set a trap for him and unless you and Terry cooperate it won't shut."

"What do you want me to do?"

"Nothing. Nothing at all. Neither you nor Terry, except tell me if Barnes shows up again at Devere's."

"That won't be easy, chief."

"I know. The only good thing is that that kid doesn't know that you know who it was watching you."

"That's right."

Crowe looked at Hans. "I'm asking a lot of you and of Terry. If that kid wants to give Terry a ride, let him. Say nothing. Nothing at all, either of you."

"I'll do it," Hans said, "but I won't like it."

Crowe looked intently at Hans. "I can't tell you right now, boy, how vital all this is to the dam. Just believe me that it is, and if I'm right, I'll do right by you and Terry."

229

"You don't owe me nothing," Hans said.

"All right, let's get to work." Crowe looked at his watch. "Jesus," he said, "it's six o'clock. Half the day is gone already."

38

The closer Crowe was coming to the end of tunneling, the closer he was getting to pouring concrete, and although Williams would then have completed the major part of his job, it would be up to Wanke to deliver the "mud." The task for Crowe now was to carefully dovetail the end of one job and the beginning of another, but when he requested Wanke and Williams to meet at his house that evening his mind was not on construction but rather on destruction, and the forty missing sticks of dynamite hung like a dead weight around his shoulders.

He filled in both men on Hans, on Terry, on Devere. "I know where I stand with Hans and Terry," he said, "I know about Devere, but what about Barnes?"

Both Williams and Wanke listened carefully and finally Wanke said, "Look, Frank, I remember you chewed out that kid pretty good when he barged in on you and Elle. And he hasn't been too popular on the dam site either, being the rich man's kid. I think there's more to it than Terry. That kid has no friends. His old man is mad at him, you hate him, everybody is jealous of his money. He's sucker bait for a guy like Devere."

"Good point, Tom."

"So Devere is going to make a spy out of him."

"That's right, Tom," Crowe said, "and I have two choices: either I throw his ass off the dam or I use him. What do you think?"

"Throw his ass off," Williams said.

"Use him," Wanke suggested, and Frank thanked them both for their advice.

Elle, who had been sitting silently in the living room during the discussion, said to Frank, "It isn't right. It just isn't right."

"What?"

"You've got a hard enough time building this dam. I used to be

230

pretty liberal when I worked at the University of Vermont, but watching the Wobblies in action really frightens me."

"You're not alone," Frank said.

"Is there no way to negotiate with Devere? Can't both of you sit down and settle it man to man?"

"Perhaps I could have with Big Bill Haywood, but Devere is not a man."

"What do you mean?"

"He's half a man."

39

Rockabye, Hoover, on the tree top,
When the wind blows, the market will drop.
When the boom breaks, the prices will fall,
Down will come Hoover, Curtis and all.

That was the refrain sung at the annual Gridiron Club dinner held by the Washington correspondents, but the newspapers were gracious enough to report the following morning that President Hoover, as usual, "enjoyed himself."

Herbert Hoover, unquestionably, was a complicated man, whose string of successes brought him to the Presidency. It was at the wrong time in his life, or maybe the time for that job would *always* have been wrong. He was gracious, elegant, honest, in many aspects brilliant, but neither warmth nor compassion was part of his makeup.

Statistic after statistic of the plight of his people left him cold. "We cannot squander ourselves into prosperity," he said more than once, and on another occasion he explained his philosophy by stating that "the back of the depression cannot be broken by any single government undertaking."

But Roosevelt and his followers disagreed. If one dam would create 6,000 jobs right in Las Vegas, and perhaps another 6,000 jobs elsewhere, then ten dams would create 120,000 jobs. Miles and miles of roads, reforestation, rural electricity, national parks, and urban renewal would all create jobs.

If Hoover was not stupid, then certainly he was myopic. His major piece of legislation was the Reconstruction Finance Corporation, whose job it was to help business, and though there may have been some logic in the theory that only business should create jobs, he did not realize that this process was slow and thousands of Americans could not wait for organization, for gearing up, for projected production. Hunger was the evil mistress of the land, and neither projections nor blueprints would stop the gnawing of the stomach. Harry Hopkins said it most succinctly a year later. "People don't eat in the long run. They eat every day."

Elle would bring home copies of the *New York Times* from the library, and Frank somehow managed to squeeze in a little time each day to help relieve the insularity of Boulder City. His dam was absorbing more workers from the town each week, he was no longer faced with the huge frightening breadlines, and local merchants had little to complain about. Still he read headline after headline about financial disasters across the country, tales of personal hardships, the failure of Hoover and his cabinet to turn the tide.

The small library in which Elle worked certainly drew the most literate members of the community—lawyers, teachers, students; even Devere and some of his men made use of the facilities.

"What are they reading," Frank asked Elle, "Devere and those guys?"

"Newspapers, mostly, magazines. Books on economics, agriculture. . ."

"How about engineering?"

"Those too."

"Bastards," Frank said angrily. "My taxes support that library."

"I know, Frank," Elle said. "I sympathize with you, but the opposition can check out the same books, the same material as Devere."

"The opposition," Frank said, "the opposition is *us*. The working people. How much time and energy have they got left to read after a day's work?"

"There *are* men and there *are* women who do find time."

It was a futile argument, Frank knew.

Frank spent hours in the drafting room now, working on the final details of the cofferdams which would rise above and below the tunnels. These were major dams in themselves, and their success was not only vital to unwatering the dam site, but their integrity was essential to protecting thousands of men who would soon be laboring fifty feet below the surface of the river.

Cableways were beginning to be erected. Huge machinery was rooted into the canyon walls, monstrous drums and cranes were carefully put in place, and miles and miles of cable two inches thick arrived from Youngstown, from Bethlehem, from steel furnaces three thousand miles away.

On May 15 another roaring flood arrived, threatening the Big Six Companies' railroad bridge. Frank had followed the reports of his watchers upstream, and worked steadying the bridge with steel cables on either side.

He stood with Wanke all through the night watching the river rise twenty feet, and still the gravel trains continued to roll across, and work continued.

Both men had watched the bridge intently, not only fearful for its survival but trying to decide which end was the most vulnerable. At dawn they took careful sightings of the piers and the abutments, and when they had collected their data independently, they returned to Crowe's office and compared results.

"She sways more on the Arizona side," Wanke said.

"Correct," Frank said. "By four degrees."

"That's what I have."

Devere had also spent the night along the river, and though he and his men lacked the expertise of Crowe and Wanke, they had come to the same conclusion.

Crowe summoned Williams, mud-covered from the night in his tunnels.

"We watched the bridge," Crowe said. "We took sightings this morning. My guess is that if they're going to blow her they'll do it from the Arizona side, but I can't be sure. Would twenty sticks blow the bridge?" Frank asked Williams.

"That all depends." Williams rubbed his stubbled face with a red kerchief. "I'd say it's a question of how well the dynamite is placed."

"Then they could blow it at either end?"

"They *could*," said Wanke, "but they'd have to come from Nevada to do it. We'd spot them before they reached the bridge."

"You *pray*," Crowe said.

"Yeah, I pray," Wanke concurred.

Williams looked at both men, equally worn and haggard from the night's vigil at the bridge. "I use one hundred thousand sticks of dynamite a day. A *day*," he almost shouted. "I'm sick and tired of this shit. Let me take ten men and a hundred sticks, Frank, and I'll blow Alma's fruit stand to holy hell. I'll do it with forty. Yeah, forty. Then we can say they blew themselves up with dynamite they stole. What do you say?"

Frank was silent for a while. Finally he answered Williams, "That's murder."

"Bullshit," Williams shouted. "How many stiffs do you think

Devere will kill if he blows the bridge? It's self-defense. What do you think Tom?" looking at Wanke.

"You just found out," Wanke said measuredly, "why Frank is chief and you're not."

Williams started to leave. He was hurt and angered by the remark, but Frank restrained him.

"I know how you feel, Jack. I know exactly how you feel. The bastards are in Elle's library studying engineering. . . ."

"And *we* sit on our ass and wait!"

"I'm not sitting on my ass waiting. It's just a question who has the bishop and who has the queen."

Williams started to burst out of the room, but stopped. He looked at Frank. "Fuck your bishops and queens. Why don't you try a shotgun or meat cleaver?"

40

It was only three weeks after young Barnes had watched Hans and Terry make love that he found her again on the highway, and following Hans's instructions, she allowed herself to be picked up again, but with misgivings.

She had an intuitive feeling about men, brought up in a family where twelve brothers and sisters were scattered around a small house like fruit salad. She was conscious from the minute that she stepped into the car that the boy had seen her naked and she knew now that he would be looking at her, *through* her, as it were, and she was afraid. She began talking immediately to try to distract him.

"Seen you with Mr. Devere the other day."

"Yeah," the boy said, "we're friends."

"No kidding. How you and him get to be friends?"

"I got lots of friends."

"Seems a lot older than you."

"I got friends older, and friends younger. You want to be my friend?"

His frankness startled her.

"All depends."

"Depends on what?" He took his right hand off the steering wheel and put it on her knee, but Terry pushed it away.

"That's *not* my idea of friendship."

"You weren't born yesterday."

"Didn't say I was."

"I mean you look like a little girl who knows the score."

"I don't want to talk about that."

"Why not?"

"Just don't. Want to let me out of the car?"

Henry liked this girl. She was very pretty and the memory of her naked body was not leaving him. But he did not want trouble. He had also seen Hans, and he had observed that he was a muscular, tough young man. A confrontation would certainly be less gentlemanly than the ones he had had at Stanford, where violence was thought of as low class.

"How about going for a ride with me sometime?" The boy was almost pleading as he pulled up behind Alma's fruit stand.

Terry opened the door and turned to look back into the car. "I ain't saying yes and I ain't saying no. I got to run now."

She waited for Henry to leave, slipped out of her dress, and put on a pair of slacks, one of Hans's sweatshirts. She started a fire and began to heat some water for coffee.

During the night that Crowe had watched the bridge, Hans had been at his side the whole time, and in the morning Crowe wrote out a chit for overtime. It was the first time that Crowe had ever done this and Hans had meant to surprise Terry with this windfall some Saturday evening, but after Terry had told him about her encounter with Barnes, he grew restless. Suddenly the truck bed was closing in on him like the cuddy cabin on a sailor. It was not only the confinement but the exposure. Until the night that the boy had been watching him, he had never really thought much about their vulnerability being parked in the middle of the desert under a shaggy cottonwood tree, but all that had changed.

"Let's go to town," he said. "Let's get dinner and a room."

"Where you getting all the money, mister?" Terry asked. "We bought groceries yesterday."

Hans dug into his jeans and showed her the five-dollar chit.

"Mr. Crowe gave it to me. Working all night the other night."

"You don't think it's wrong spending it like that?"

"It ain't wrong. I earned the money fair and square. Let's go."

"Can't go like this," Terry said, pushing him out of the truck. "Get out of here, I'll put on a dress."

Hans waited patiently outside the truck. It was beginning to get

235

dark, but Terry, wearing her new dress, a navy-blue scarf around her shoulders, her hair combed and face washed, looked truly beautiful.

They had no trouble getting a ride to Vegas. A big steel truck came to a halt and the driver eagerly made room for Terry and Hans.

He shifted gears, gingerly stealing glances at Terry's legs, and Hans watched him watch her, but he was civil and they spoke of Vegas and baseball and he left them off at the Pioneer Hotel, which he told them was one of the nicest in town.

They thanked him and walked into the lobby, partly carpeted, the rustic furniture barely filling the large room.

Hans registered himself as Hans Schmidt and the clerk said, "Ain't gonna register the missus?"

Hans blushed.

"Yeah, sure. Don't stay in hotels much. We live in a truck."

"I understand," the clerk said, almost fatherly, handing Hans a key. "You having dinner here?"

"You got a dining room?"

"Best food in town."

"Sure. Guess so," Hans said.

" 'Cause if you're gonna have dinner here I'll give you this room for a buck. It's a two-buck room, but we ain't very crowded tonight."

"Much obliged."

"Got the best bed in the place, one of them *big* mattresses." Somehow the man said it without salacious connotations and Hans handed him the five-dollar chit and received four silver dollars in change.

They climbed the stairway to the second floor and found the room, No. 17, at the head of the stairs. Hans unlocked the door and let Terry in. There were a large double bed covered by a white candlewick bedspread, a commode with a mirror over it, and several elegant-looking wicker chairs.

Hans turned on the single overhead light fixture and closed the door.

"You know," Terry said, "this is the first time we've ever been in a room alone."

"I know," Hans said.

Terry sat on the bed and bounced on the mattress, then eased her head onto the pillow. Hans looking at her, her skirt almost to her navel, her good tight legs young and inviting.

"You keep this up and I could skip supper."

"No, sir, mister." Terry sat up and straightened her skirt. "We promised the man we'd eat here."

Hans laughed. "Yes, we did. Let's go."

236

The proprietors of the Pioneer Hotel were Swiss, and God only knows how they had landed in Las Vegas, but the meal cooked by the clerk's wife was excellent and ample. They had duck and applesauce, potato salad, fresh bread, a slice of torte, a bottle of beer, and they ate as if they hadn't eaten in a month.

"So fast," the elderly lady said, "you eat so fast."

"It was good," Hans said. "Real good."

"You want another piece of torte?"

"Wouldn't mind."

They happily paid two dollars for the meal and walked arm in arm into the Las Vegas night.

They could see the glow of Fremont Street several blocks ahead, and finally they reached the heart of Vegas, lighted up, noisy, raucous, and infectious. There was club after club, The Four Aces, the Four Deuces, the Lucky Club, the Fremont Club, the Nevada Club, there were Billy's and Al's and Fred's and Joe's, there were the Palace, the Rose Room, the 1890, each of them trying harder to outdo its neighbors in the art of extracting the few dollars earned or the few dollars remaining, each patron with a pair of dice, a deck of cards, a roulette wheel, trying somehow to buy a blanket, a bottle of booze, a new pair of shoes.

Hans and Terry walked into one club and out another, watching the tenseness of a "hot" crap table, listening to the shouts, the exhortations, twenty pairs of eyes focused on two red cubes being thrown against a greasy green felt backboard, rolling, rolling, and stopping suddenly, the final momentum stopped cruelly or blissfully by the tiny cubes.

"Look at that guy," Hans said. "He's got a year's pay on that table." They saw chips and silver dollars flipped with abandon, the stickmen in black pants and black vests and delicately embroidered white shirts keeping the dice in constant motion, the dealers collecting and paying flawlessly, stacking five-dollar and ten-dollar chips with one hand, all without counting. All the personnel around the crap tables wore green celluloid eye shades, as if divorcing themselves from the gaze of the players, a constant chant by the stickmen worked hypnotically. *"Four easy four try the hard way, seven come eleven, the number is eight. Eight is the number, easy six, try the hard way, come. Field, eight the winner made it easy, hot roller double the bets, change, yes sir, drink honey, this gentleman wants a drink. Next roller, next roller, next roller."*

For the heavy rollers, the booze was free. So were the cigars and often the bar girls, who slithered between patrons carrying trayfuls of drinks over their heads.

Terry and Hans had never seen this much energy. They had never seen such jubilation as one patron would carry a handful of chips to the cashier, or such desperation as another dropped from the table, like letting go the side of a lifeboat and drowning in the Vegas night.

At the Four Aces Club an elderly blackjack dealer motioned Hans and Terry to his table.

"Let the little lady try her luck," he said to Hans.

"We don't gamble, we don't know how. We got no money," Hans told him.

"You got a dime?"

"Yeah, I got a dime."

"Well, sit down, honey, I'll teach you how to play this game."

The Four Aces looked like every other establishment: slow-turning fans on the ceiling, gold-speckled mirrors on the wall, lights filtering through cigar smoke, the endless clank of slot machines, of nickels dropping onto metal trays, the clink of glasses, the uninhibited conversation of men, the not infrequent squeals of women, a three-piece band on a foot-high velvet-covered platform playing Dixieland jazz. A long bar with a brass footrest and patrons and bartenders performing a ritualistic ballet of pouring and drinking and sending Chinamen out for more clean glasses and more ice.

And yet, with all the fever and the heat, Terry somehow stood out; her well-chiseled clean good looks, her ample breasts straining at the scooped neckline of her dress, her well-rounded buttocks, her graceful legs, her sparkling dark brown eyes continually made heads turn, and lips purse to whistle.

Perhaps it was Terry's eye-catching good looks that made the dealer call her over to the blackjack table, or perhaps it was charity. Maybe he had a son, a daughter their age, somewhere in Montana or in Maine, and perhaps he hoped that someone would give that son or daughter a break.

It was sleight of hand, pure and simple. Hans gave Terry the dime. The dealer gave her two cards. "Lucky little girl," he said as he dealt her a blackjack and paid her a quarter. Terry was numb at first. She could not understand really what was going on. "All right, next hand. I'll deal you two, I'll deal myself two. Now try to get as close to twenty-one as you can without going over. Twenty, you win. Eighteen you win. Pair of nines, double up. There, put a bet on each one, good— look, you won them *both.*"

In a matter of minutes Terry was sitting behind a stack of chips easily worth twenty dollars. She was radiant, yelling happily each time she won, bouncing up and down on her seat, and Hans behind her was equally excited, nervous, watching Terry, the stack of chips, the dealer. After another five minutes Terry's stack had doubled again.

Hans could not stand it. "Let's go, Terry," he said, "let's go." His German frugality would not let him waste that money.

"Now I'm going to make a gambler out of you," the dealer said.

"What are you going to do?"

He reached into his pocket and pulled out a dime and handed it to Hans. "That's all you wagered, son, is that right?"

"That's right."

"All right, what's your name?"

"Terry."

"All right, Terry. Put up *all* your chips."

"All of them? What should I do, Hans?"

Hans shrugged his shoulders and pocketed the dime.

"I'll draw two cards," the dealer said, looking at Terry. "One for you, one for me. Winner takes all."

Terry hesitated, looking at the stack of chips in front of her.

Terry nodded. "Let's go."

The dealer carefully shuffled his deck. He handled cards as if they were extensions of his fingers. With one hand he cut a deck and recut it, and with an elegant flourish he dealt two cards. He opened Terry's card. It was a three of diamonds. He built suspense, then flipped his card. It was a two of hearts.

"You win," he said, but the words were lost. Terry was shrieking happily; she leaned over with all abandon and kissed the dealer. Hans was all smiles.

"Now listen to me," the dealer said conspiratorially, "will you listen?"

Hans and Terry quieted down.

"Cash in these chips and don't ever come back. Not here, not next door, not across the street. You get lucky once. Maybe twice. But luck is not a habit."

Hans and Terry scooped up the chips. They both needed both hands to carry them to the cashier. They had won $110. It was paid in silver dollars and Hans almost lost his jeans as he stuffed them into his pockets.

One of the managers of the Four Aces came up to the old dealer. "Playing Santa Claus again, Henry?"

The dealer looked at the short, thick-necked manager of the club, his black shirt shiny, his white silk tie wrinkled.

"Fuck you," Henry said. "I can make them go one way or the other or I can go to the Rose Room Club. Which would you prefer?"

"No offense, Henry. No offense." The little manager reddened and disappeared into the crowds.

239

Hans and Terry hurried to their room. They locked the door and Hans poured their riches onto the bedspread. They counted and recounted it. They planned a house, marriage, a trip to San Francisco, purchase of the truck from Herman, and they laughed and made love, and when the clerk rapped on the door at five in the morning, they wakened to the first light of dawn, naked and surrounded by silver, and neither quite believed the verity of their good fortune.

41

Though the Reconstruction Finance Corporation was organized in early spring to help banks, it was Senator Wagner who stated the problem most sympathetically when he asked, "Is there any reason why we should not extend a helping hand to that forlorn American in every village and every city who has been without wages since 1929?" There were scattered strikes and hunger marches on local and state governments, but the people's anger reached its peak as fifteen thousand World War I veterans descended on Washington to collect their bonuses. Senator Patman's bill to legalize payment of the $586 per man was before Congress, and these hungry, angry thousands of men, women, and children, many of them homeless already, began their march across the land. They came from California and Kentucky, the Northwest and the East, and they camped on the Anacostia flats to lobby for the passage of the bill. On June 17, the Patman Bill was defeated in Congress, despite all exhortations, threats, and cajoling of veterans camped at the Capitol steps; the defeat of the bill was final.

Five thousand left Anacostia; ten thousand remained primarily because they had no place to go, and felt better and safer in the company of each other.

The camp was well organized along military lines. The tents and huts were kept spotless, all of them displayed American flags, and the leaders of the dissidents kept radicals away from their men. They were proud that they had kept the reds out of their protest. They were American soldiers fighting for something legitimately due them.

At first, as was his custom, Hoover had simply ignored the veterans. But as clashes between these men and police increased and incident after incident was carefully recorded in the newspapers, Hoover found the veterans an embarrassment to his administration. He resorted to the age-old political trick of labeling the Anacostia exercise a Communist plot. He ordered General Douglas MacArthur, chief of staff of the army, to "evacuate" the veterans and their families.

That had been the order, evacuate, but that is not what occurred. Perhaps nothing is as useless as an army that has no war to fight. There are few promotions, few gallantries, and morale is low because the peacetime soldier is held in poor esteem by his fellow countrymen. Peacetime activity was always welcome to the army, and although no foreign adversary was present, there *was* an adversary, in this case the veterans of World War I. Their brothers.

General MacArthur knew an opportunity like this was rare and he also knew how to make the best of it. He gathered his forces in the vicinity of the White House: four troops of cavalry, four companies of infantry, a mounted machine-gun squadron and six whippet tanks. The enemy was thousands of men, women, and children, unarmed. At MacArthur's side was his aide, Major Dwight D. Eisenhower, among his officers was Major George S. Patton, Jr., whose riding crop whipped restlessly against his thigh, waiting.

The "attack" scheduled for three-thirty was delayed until four-thirty while an orderly was dispatched to Fort Myer across the Potomac for MacArthur's service stripes, sharpshooter medal, and English whipcord breeches. Finally, dressed for the skirmish operation, MacArthur led his troops down Pennsylvania Avenue, which was lined with awed spectators.

He paused long enough to give a historic quote: "We are going to break the back of the Bonus Expeditionary Forces." It was like driving a thumbtack with a sledgehammer.

MacArthur sent his troops across the Anacostia bridge and they reached the flats at four-forty-five. The attack was ruthless and cruel, using tear gas and horses to drive the helpless veterans, their wives and children, from the encampment. Sabers were slashing, bayonets were fixed, as thousands fled MacArthur's troops. They set fire to the encampment. By seven-fifteen the entire Bonus City had been burned to the ground.

The casualties were heavy: two veterans had been shot and killed, an eleven-week-old baby died, there were over one thousand gas casualties, there were injuries from bayonets, a veteran lost an ear from a saber slash. And by nine o'clock that evening MacArthur was safely back in the officers' club at Fort Myer and was asked by newsmen about the unusual cruelty of his men against their soldier brothers. He excused the tactics by suggesting that a mob was about to seize control of the government.

241

Tom Wanke, reading of the events, commented to Crowe that MacArthur had the same mentality as Jack Williams.

"That may be true," Crowe said, "but he got rid of the bastards."

"They were not bastards," Wanke said. "They were veterans of a tough war asking for what was legitimately theirs."

"The bonus will be paid in 1945," Crowe said.

"Sure," Wanke added. "Ask a man to starve for thirteen years."

"I bet the reds were behind all this."

"The reds. Every time there's trouble in this country we blame it on the reds. I think it stinks. Old Hoover better explain this one to me before he gets my vote again."

Hoover, however, in his usual fashion, declined to comment.

Devere had also followed the plight of the Bonus marchers. He sat at his desk and looked at Herman. "I think our man Warner fucked this one up."

"He *tried*," Herman said.

"Sure, he tried. He made speeches. Those boys didn't need speeches, they needed guns. Someday," Devere became excited, "*someday*, we'll march on the White House, on pricks like MacArthur, only *we'll* pick the day and we'll be ready."

42

At the end of May Frank Crowe had completed his field office. It was a simple wooden structure cantilevered from the Arizona canyon wall, overlooking the future dam. Its distinguishing feature was a row of windows on three of its sides, so that the building resembled the fly bridge of a large cruise ship. The windows allowed Crowe to look upstream, downstream, and across to the Nevada side.

There were two reasons for this expenditure. He was tired of running back and forth from Boulder City every time he was needed or felt it necessary to visit the dam site. The second or perhaps the primary reason was that now, at this point, Frank wanted to watch the river. Seemingly for hours he looked upstream. The spring runoff was beginning, and would reach its peak in June. He looked upstream like a ship's captain on the bridge in a fog. Of course he had a radio operator, a forward lookout, as he had river watchers upstream, but like the captain looking through a blinding fog, so Crowe watched a mute river.

He had long conferences with Williams both in the tunnels and in his office, trying to pin down the exact day they would be finished.

"November 5th," Williams said, "that's counting seven days of downtime. We're not through with the runoff yet."

"I agree," Frank said, looking at the river. "November 5th, you say?"

"Yes."

"Where will you be November 3rd?"

"I'll be pouring the last cement around the tunnel entries."

"Is that vital?"

"I don't know that it's vital to the tunnels. It's vital to me. That river is going into an elegant tunnel, not some craggy hole in the wall."

Crowe laughed.

"What's so funny?"

"We all want our signature on something, don't we?"

"Well, it ain't a Rembrandt, but they're my tunnels."

"They are, Jack, and they're superior."

"Thanks, Frank, but why pin me down to a day?"

"Because you will be finished November 3rd."

"I told you the 5th."

"I know you did. On the 3rd I want you to have a barbecue, a day off. . . ."

"I'm with you. . . . When do I get to finish my tunnels?"

"If my calculations are right, the 4th or 5th."

"That queen, bishop stuff again."

"Yes. The queen, bishop stuff."

"You guys from Vermont." Williams left Crowe's office.

Henry Barnes, Jr., sick of working as a parts man, put his jacket on the back seat of his car, lowered the top of his car, and drove back to Vegas. Daily he hoped to find Terry, but she had eluded him. He could not get the girl out of his mind and decided to see Devere.

Devere motioned him into a chair and Henry had difficulty adjusting to the darkness of the room.

"What can I do for you, Henry?" Devere asked.

"You said something about a deal."

"That's right."

"What is it?"

"It's really quite simple. I need the date, the exact date, when Frank Crowe is going to turn that river into the tunnels."

"I guess you'd have to finish the tunnels first."

"*Of course,*" Devere half shouted, then sank back into his role. "The tunnels have to be finished, but *when* will they be finished?"

"I don't know how to get that information. I can't ask Crowe."

"I don't want you to ask Crowe, I simply want you to get closer to Crowe, to your dad. . ."

"Those are the two men I'd least want to get close to."

"I didn't say it would be easy, but you're a bright young man . . . educated . . . clever."

"All right, I'll see what I can do, but what about Terry?"

"What about her?"

"What makes you think I can get next to her?"

"I'll handle that."

"How?"

"You're worried about her boyfriend, right?"

"Exactly."

"Chicken shit."

"What does that mean?"

"My job," Devere said pontifically, "is to organize five thousand men on the dam. *Five thousand* men, Henry. I was trained to do that. You think I'd have trouble with *one* man?"

"All right, you'll get rid of him. What about Terry?"

"She'll just take a little different kind of convincing."

Henry tapped the desk. "I guess you know what you're doing."

"I do. Now I want you to get that date for me. The sooner the better."

Henry Barnes, Jr., stood up, shook hands, and left. As he drove off he could see Terry bending over a camp stove. "Son of a bitch," he said to himself as he roared into Las Vegas and Block 16.

Crowe sat at his drafting board at home; it was one o'clock in the morning and Elle was soundly asleep in their bed. There were many nights like this and his only pleasure was occasionally looking into their bedroom and watching her lovely head framed by a pillow like the folds of a bishop's frock in a medieval painting. Nights like these ending an eighteen-hour day were only briefly rewarded as he slipped into bed beside that sleep-warm girl and felt her instinctively roll into his arms. Then he could feel her slim body fit into his raw-boned frame. He would smell the fragrance of her hair and drop off to sleep.

Frank was planning, playing queen and bishop as Williams had reminded him the other day.

There was no way that he could give Barnes's son the information

244

he wanted without arousing suspicion, but he *could* invite the elder Barnes to spend a weekend at Sequoia Lodge. Stein had spent the night, so had Mackenzie, Chapman, Andrews. That was it! Frank threw down the pencil onto his drawing board. He'd call him tomorrow. He undressed and slipped into bed. He wound his watch. It was one-thirty. He had four hours before Hans would pick him up.

The following morning Crowe placed a call to Barnes in San Francisco. He not only had to take care not to arouse Devere's suspicions but had to be cautious that Barnes suspected nothing. Of all the partners of the Big Six, Barnes's relationship with Crowe was the most strained.

"Mr. Barnes?"

"Yes."

"Frank Crowe."

"How are you, Mr. Crowe?"

"Fine, and yourself?"

"No complaints."

"Some of the Big Six have come up here to Sequoia Lodge, and I'd like to invite you to spend a night."

"That's very kind. What's the occasion?"

"I'd rather not discuss it on the phone."

"I see."

"When could you make it?"

"How about Friday night?"

"That will be fine. What time can we expect you?"

"About five in the afternoon."

Crowe said somewhat sotto voce, "I'm going to ask you a question man to man."

"Shoot."

"Will you be bringing up Mrs. Barnes?"

"No, I won't."

"Just wanted to know whether I should stock the lodge."

Barnes smiled and rubbed his hands gently down his stomach. "Yeah, stock it with something young and live. I like wildcats."

"I'll requisition it for ten Friday night."

"Good man, Crowe. I'll see you Friday."

"I'll look forward to your visit."

"How's the kid doing?"

"Fine. I'll have him up to the lodge for dinner."

"That'll be fine, but just for dinner."

"I understand, sir. Goodbye."

"Goodbye, Mr. Crowe."

Crowe hung up the phone and called for Williams, who entered his office fifteen minutes later.

"Jack, it's all too complicated right now to explain, but I need a hot hooker for Barnes Friday night at ten o'clock."

"No sweat. Who'll be paying for her?"

"The contingency fund."

Williams scratched his face. "I didn't know we had a contingency fund like that. I understand Maria and Elle are playing bridge Thursday night. . . ."

"Get out of here," Crowe ordered. "Wait. I want you and Wanke and your wives at dinner Friday night with Barnes."

"Come on," Williams said. "You know I'm no good at that kind of stuff. Liable to fart right during dinner."

"Just be there."

"Okay."

Crowe walked to his outer office and told one of his engineers to invite young Henry to the lodge on Friday. "And I'm leaving it to you to see he gets there."

"Got you."

That evening he asked Elle to prepare the meal for Friday and act as hostess.

"You, Frank Crowe, are having a dinner party? Are you ill?"

"No, my love, just scheming."

Barnes's limousine parked promptly in front of Sequoia Lodge and he waited patiently for his chauffeur to leave the car and open the door for him. Edward Chapman had taught him that decorum, saying, "Chauffeurs have two functions. To drive and to open and close doors. That's what they're paid for. Getting out of a limousine by yourself is nouveau riche."

Frank and Elle, dressed for the occasion, met Barnes at the front door of Sequoia Lodge, and after Barnes made a few comments about Elle's beauty, he seated himself in the parlor and downed the first of a number of chilled martinis Frank was famous for.

Barnes raised his glass and toasted Frank. "Haven't lost the touch," he said. "Did you get that stock ordered?"

"It'll be here at ten o'clock sharp."

"Very good, very good."

"Your boy's coming to dinner."

"Yeah, how's he doing?"

"He's doing fine," Frank said nonchalantly.

"What's on your mind, Crowe?"

Frank paced the parlor. "Wanke and Williams should be here any minute. I'll wait till they join us."

"Not bad news, I hope."

"It's good," Crowe said, lifting his own glass.

Elle passed a trayful of cheese and French bread. Barnes's eyes followed her every motion and Elle blushed.

"Boy, Frank, if I had a wife like yours, I'd be back building dams."

Frank put his arm around Elle and said, "She does help make life bearable."

"I feel like some prize possession with you two guys. You must have more important things to talk about."

"Spirit, too," Barnes said. "I like spirit."

Elle hated this kind of banter and retreated to the kitchen.

Henry, Jr., neatly dressed, rang the doorbell and was surprised to see the supervising engineer.

"Good evening, Mr.Crowe."

"Good evening. You have a visitor."

It was an uncomfortable meeting for father and son, but old man Barnes quickly lightened the mood in the timeworn manner of his generation and profession.

"Getting enough nookie?"

"I do all right."

"Don't buy the cheap stuff. It can leave souvenirs."

"I understand."

"Need an extra twenty, always be glad to chip in."

"Thank you, sir."

The Williamses and the Wankes arrived according to Frank's carefully scheduled scenario. Maria and Eva retired to the kitchen to help Elle after greeting Barnes, and finally Frank, after serving everyone another drink, spoke up.

"The reason for your visit, Mr. Barnes, is to tell you that on November 3rd we expect to finish the tunnels."

"Jesus," Barnes said, "that soon?"

"I'll finish the tunnel lining on the 3rd," Williams said, holding up his glass, "and I could probably beat that date if I had this quality gin."

"The 3rd will be fine," Crowe said, mentioning the date again.

"I'd like you and the other gentlemen of the Big Six to witness the turning of the river," Crowe added.

"Wouldn't miss it for anything," Barnes said. "Son of a bitch. That's less than six months."

"That's right," Crowe said, "but I have to ask all of you a favor . . . I don't want this discussed. That date is a total secret, and there are people around this dam site that would be very happy to learn about it."

"I got you," Barnes said. "I'll tell the boys and that's it," and looking at his son, "and you keep your mouth shut too."

"Yes sir."

Elle had set an elegant table and Jack Williams didn't have to fear passing gas since Barnes beat him to it.

Everyone left the lodge at nine-thirty. Jack Williams excused himself and walked to the driver of a car parked in the shadows of a street light.

"You got Ginger?" he asked.

"Sure, she's on the floor of the back seat."

Williams drew twenty dollars from his wallet and handed it across the front seat to an outstretched hand.

"Jesus," Ginger said, "what kind of a monster is he?"

"Just feed him two more martinis and you can sleep in that bed alone."

Williams returned to the guests in front of the lodge, and after a few pleasantries everyone headed home.

It was nine-thirty when young Henry Barnes burst into Devere's office. After looking around and seeing other faces he said nothing.

"What is it, Henry? You're among friends."

"They're going to finish the tunnels on November 3rd."

"How do you know?"

"I just heard Crowe say it."

"To whom?"

"My father."

Devere was very quiet, then took out a sheet of paper. He held it up. "This is the day I figured." The sheet said "November 8th."

"That's pretty good," one of his cohorts said.

"You did well, boy," Devere said.

"Thank you. Now how about Terry?"

"What about her? I told you I'd fix it up."

"When?"

"As soon as I know you gave me the right date."

"You mean I got to wait until November."

"Until November 4th, to be exact," Devere said evenly.

"Jesus."

"Come on, kid, at your age you ain't depending on one cunt to keep you happy."

"No, but . . ."

"No buts, that's it," Devere said, standing. "See me then. We're holding a meeting here." Henry Barnes, Jr., walked into the star-filled quiet desert night. He could see the truck where Terry was living. No lights were on. Everything was still. He jumped into his car and drove toward Las Vegas slowly. He thought of his father and of Terry in that truck, and there were tears in his eyes.

Ginger knocked on the door and Barnes opened it quickly. She stepped into the parlor of the Sequoia Lodge and half waltzed about the well-furnished parlor, picking up a piece of jade here, a leather-bound copy of *The Forsyte Saga* on another table.

"Very fancy," she said, "very fancy."

She wore a thin red sateen dress, red shoes, slightly scuffed, and black panties and a bra. Her figure was full but not blowzy, her hair dyed red and the skin under her eyes parchmentlike and bluish, attesting to a number of lean years on Block 16 before the dam building had become a reality and one dollar was considered a fair night's wages.

Barnes sat on the couch and spread his legs.

"We'll start here," he said, pointing toward his crotch.

"Hold on, big feller, hold on," Ginger said. "Ain't you gonna offer a girl a drink? Looks like real Seagram's gin."

"Sure, help yourself."

"How about you?"

"I've had enough for a while."

She looked at him quizzically, poured herself a stiff shot, and sat down next to Barnes on the couch.

Quickly his hands ran up her legs.

"Always curious," he said.

"About what?"

"Whether you dyed your pubic hair too."

"I used to," she said, not resisting his clumsy fingers, "but I shaved it. Sure you don't want a drink?"

"I'm sure."

"I'm in no hurry," Ginger said, putting her arm forward to allow Barnes to pull off her bra.

"Boy, look at those teats," he said, flipping one with his forefingers. "Mighty nice. Well, I ain't in no hurry either, so if you'll sit down between my legs and carefully unbutton these pants. . . . I'd like to rest this cock on this nipple for a while."

Maria Williams was already asleep when Jack turned off the light in their bedroom, and saw the light still burning in Sequoia Lodge He was surprised the following morning to see Barnes's limousine still parked outside, the chauffeur sound asleep on the leather front seat. Later in the day Williams told Frank that Barnes had left the dam site at three in the afternoon. The guard said he was smiling and Barnes tipped him a dollar.

"Good old Ginger," Frank laughed.

"Yeah, good old Ginger. I never knew she had it in her."

43

Frank Crowe had always been a realist about prostitution and liquor on a dam site. These two commodities were as essential as food, water, and housing to men, many of them cut off from their families or girlfriends.

At previous dams this business was usually conducted by middle-aged madams who ran a string of ten or fifteen girls. There was usually an overstuffed parlor where liquor was served, a room filled with the girls scantily dressed in gauzy robes, shorts, and halters, some even half naked. The transactions were good natured and low key. After a few drinks a customer would disappear to the back or upstairs, where a small room, usually containing a double bed, a commode, a chair, a white enamel basin, soap and towels, served all the needs.

The very size of the Hoover Dam, with its thousands of men, had made prostitution big business, and most of the intimate houses were supplanted by large establishments, former hotels, usually under the control of the mobsters of Detroit and Chicago.

There were the usual madams, but they were not in business for themselves. They fronted for the mob, and most houses contained two or three well-armed gorillas who kept the operation in line.

Frank detested the gangsters almost as much as the Wobblies, but since these operations were conducted off the dam site, he had little control. Since he *was* responsible for his men, the stories filtering back to his office became increasingly disturbing. Men were getting laid, it was true, but the mob was not satisfied with taking their two dollars for the privilege. They served rotgut booze, which made many of the workers ill, and the stories of rolling the customer became too frequent to suit Frank. Of course there were fights and retaliation by his men, but they were usually up against the tough armed gorillas of the mob, and a number of men landed in the hospital cruelly beaten.

Aunt Mary was a woman of indeterminate age. Sitting on the window ledge of Frank's office, dressed in a black suit, heavily bejeweled, her gray hair tinged with blue, she might have been fifty, even sixty.

She and Frank had been old and good friends, since she ran the best house both at Tieton and Deadwood, and Frank, then single, not only used her girls, but quite often her parlor and liquor. She was madam, mother confessor—at times informer—and her streetwise knowledge was often sought out by Frank and others on the dams. She referred to her girls as ladies and their behavior in the parlor was expected to be proper. Their performances in the bedroom were expected to be equally fulfilling and honest.

"Well, Frank," she said, looking at his gray-speckled sandy head, "you look a little leaner and a little older."

"It's been seven years," Frank said, "since Deadwood. This one's a bitch."

"How's the new wife?"

"She's an angel."

"That's good news," Aunt Mary said. "I used to watch you leave my houses. You were usually more miserable after you left than when you arrived."

"I wasn't miserable, Aunt Mary. I was just more lonely."

"I know," Aunt Mary said. "I've seen that lots of times. Well," she added, "why did you send for me?"

Frank explained the problems he had with the existing mob-owned houses and the bad blood they were causing among his workers.

"If you could set up a house, Aunt Mary, one I can be sure of, I'd fill it for you in no time."

"I'll tell you something in confidence, Frank."

"You can trust me."

"Well, I may sound like a wise old lady in the parlor, but when Tieton and Deadwood were finished, I was a rich lady. I had fifteen thousand dollars in cash. I moved to San Francisco, bought a house with a little garden. I never wanted to see a whore again. I never wanted to see men buttoning their flies coming down the hallway paying me *two* dollars. I couldn't stand the scream for towels anymore or watch some goddamned quack perform one more abortion in the kitchen. There is a smell to a house which never leaves you. Sweat, urine, perfume, wilted flowers. . . ." Her voice trailed off.

"I met a retired machinist's mate in Vallejo and married him. Good-looking tall navy man, straight as an arrow, but he liked the bottle and the horses. This dress and my valise are all I've got to show for twenty years of work."

She twisted her small lace handkerchief nervously.

"I've got no money to set up a house. I can't compete with those neon palaces the mob has strung up."

Frank looked at Aunt Mary, and the years were becoming evident through the heavily rouged face.

"Can you still get some of your girls?"

"There's no trouble getting girls," Aunt Mary said. "Las Vegas is crawling with Okies, with kids from Kentucky, Tennessee, they make the best girls. Farm stock."

"Yeah, you always had good girls. Well," Frank said, "you line up twenty girls, and I'll get you a house."

That evening Frank held an emergency staff meeting with Wanke and Williams at the Reno Club.

"Well, Frank, what's the big occasion?" Williams joked. "You've bought the two last rounds."

"So I have," Frank said. "The problem is this: I don't like the houses operating around the dam site. They're rolling our boys, selling them rotten booze. The whole thing stinks."

"That's true," Wanke said. "Lot of my boys come back pretty bruised and battered."

"I talked to Aunt Mary today."

"Jesus Christ," Williams said. "Is she still alive?"

"Hasn't changed a bit. Except she's broke . . ."

"What happened to all her money from Deadwood?" Williams asked.

"Some sailor . . . the old story."

Wanke nodded.

"She can get the girls," Frank said, "but she needs a house."

"So what?" Williams said. "We're three engineers, can't we build a house?"

"I was hoping you'd say that."

"If you'll supply the material," Wanke said, "we'll build the home."

"Good. Except it's got to be built off shift. Can you get some volunteers from your crew?"

"What kind of question is that?"

"Well, I picked a spot near Madonna Road in Tonopah, and Aunt Mary said she'd throw the biggest party you'd ever see when it's finished."

"It's Monday," Wanke said. "When will you get the material out there?"

"At seven tomorrow."

"How many rooms do you need?"

"Twenty. A parlor, quarters for Aunt Mary."

Wanke thought for a minute. "Ought to get that done by Saturday."

"Saturday, hell," Williams shouted. "Tell Aunt Mary to get her party ready for Friday."

Crowe laughed. "Not so fast. I'll need two things: a cover for the project and furniture."

"How about calling it the Boulder Retirement Center?" Williams offered.

"Excellent."

"As to the furniture, I'm sure that every God-loving family in Boulder City will do their part."

The waiter came and Frank ordered steaks.

For four nights two hundred tunnelers, carpenters, concrete men, engineers from Frank's office, cherry pickers, and plumbers labored furiously. "A labor of love," Williams said to Frank, amazed at the unbelievable progress of the structure, and by Friday night a number of children in Boulder City found themselves sleeping with siblings, since their beds were gone; chairs disappeared from homes, as did lamps and towels and clothes hangers and night stands.

That Sunday morning Reverend Jotaf praised the unselfish men from the pulpit, speaking of their wonderful devotion beyond the call of duty. Few of the heroes were in church, but sleeping off a party at the new house which Aunt Mary had provided with all her gusto and the proceeds of the sale of her last large diamond.

Frank Crowe sat in the church next to Elle and said a pompous "Amen" after the minister had finished speaking, but Elle detected that small boyish smile which laid bare a fabric of mischief known only to a man's wife.

44

It was nearing the end of June. Williams's tunnels were approaching completion, all moves carefully watched by Devere. Elle had given Frank a book on the art of blasting which Devere had checked out and returned to the library. Frank, Wanke, and Williams tried to detect which method Devere had chosen, but the book was an overall study of the use of dynamite, and they could not ferret out their plans.

Williams, the expert, was the most helpful. "There is only one way you can ignite the dynamite we use. You need Number 4 caps, .048 line, and a detonator. You can glue the sticks to the bridge or tie them, don't matter which. I'd say they'd run their lines out two hundred yards to protect themselves from the collapsing bridge."

"How long would all that take?" Frank asked.

"Placing the dynamite, placing the fuses, and running the lines could be done in less than ten minutes."

"That will give us five."

"How do you figure?" Wanke asked.

"I've checked my books. November 3rd will be almost a moonless night. That's good. Good for them. Good for us. I want to catch the bastards in the act of placing the dynamite. We've got to get them before they set the fuses or run the lines to the detonators. Once they've got the dynamite hooked up they'll blow the bridge, even if they go with it, they're such fanatics."

"So you're going to have your boys around the piers?"

"No," Frank said. "I can't have my boys around the piers. In the dark they might just run into Devere's boys and tip them off."

"Well, where are you going to have them?"

"Above Devere's men."

"On the bridge?" Wanke asked. "Isn't that dangerous?"

Frank unrolled a map of the bridge and the surrounding roads.

He pointed to the Arizona pier on the bridge. "This is where I expect they'll blast. How many men do you think they'll use to set the sticks of dynamite?"

"Five or ten," Williams said.

"Good. Right here," Frank pointed almost to the beginning of the bridge, "I'm going to erect a structure. It's technically a garage, but it will look like a cablehouse. Right below that first pier I'll build another structure. I'll sling a cable from the first to the second. It will be a dummy cable. In the first cablehouse I'll keep two trucks facing backward. They'll be full of sand. The lower cablehouse will have three guys in it. Lookouts. The minute they see Devere's guys appear they'll signal the upper cablehouse. Two trucks will back out and I want your best muckers to reach the edge of that bridge and dump that sand." Frank paced the room. "I'll bury these bastards. Men, fuses, dynamite, and all. That way I'll get the evidence red-handed. Once they're buried, I'll surround them with our cops."

"Very ingenious," Wanke said. "That's very ingenious."

"Why bury them in sand? Why not have Tom fill that truck with rocks and kill the bastards?"

"I don't want to kill them. I don't want any fucking martyrs. They're not gonna be too happy with their lungs filled with sand."

Wanke said, "Frank is right. After they're arrested they'll go on trial for attempting to destroy government property. That's a long rap."

"Exactly," Frank said.

"But what if they don't strike on the 3rd of November?" Wanke asked.

"I've thought of that. I figure we'll start our watches the week before."

"How you going to get those trucks into that garage? Won't that be suspicious?"

"I'm going to erect that structure in a hurry, Tom. It's going to take some gravel. I think I can sneak two trucks in there during the confusion of construction without anyone noticing it."

"It's a gamble," Wanke said.

"Yes. It all is."

Elle served some coffee and sat down next to Frank. "How many people know about your plan?" she asked.

"Right now there are four of us."

"Do the Big Six know all about this?"

"No."

"Why not?"

"In the first place I don't want any more people talking about this than I have to."

"But all the responsibility is on you."

"That's right. That's what I'm getting paid for." Frank said it coldly.

Elle put her hands on her face, then looked at Williams. "Sometimes I like your idea better, Jack."

"Which one?"

"Go down to Alma's fruit stand and blast them to kingdom come. Isn't that what you said?"

Frank was surprised by Elle's statement.

"That's murder," he said, "pure and simple. Besides, the Wobblies have more than one Devere. After that Bonus fiasco they probably signed up five thousand men that would blow up anything that says 'Government Property.' "

After Williams and Wanke left, Frank finished his coffee.

"Your suggestion really frightens me, Elle."

"Why? You think I'm being cold-blooded?"

"Not cold-blooded, just out of character."

Elle sat back in her chair and said very quickly, "Everyone ageed that Devere won't be at the site. That right?"

"That's right."

"But you will be. Right?"

"Sure."

"Sure," Elle screamed. "Sure. *Big Frank Crowe always at the head of the brigade. Always leading the battalion, whether it's a whorehouse or a railroad bridge. My hero, Frank Crowe.*"

"*Elle!*"

"Elle, shit," she yelled. "You were hired to build a dam. That's dangerous enough. You weren't hired to play cops and robbers. *I love*

255

you, Frank Crowe. I love you alive. Do you understand?"

Having made that statement she went to their bedroom and slammed the door, and Frank sat frozen at the empty dining-room table. His inclination was to talk to Aunt Mary, but he stopped himself. He not only had Devere to worry about, and Elle. He also had to turn that river.

45

One hundred and ten dollars was a lot of spare money in 1932, if none of it had to be allocated for food or clothing or medicine, and this sudden windfall of capitalism caught Hans and Terry unprepared. Their first problem was to store it. There seemed no safe place in their truck so Hans finally opened a savings account in Las Vegas, after purchasing a sexy bra and panties for Terry as an indulgence he felt they deserved.

Their next decision was to offer Herman fifty dollars for his share of the truck so they could move elsewhere, but Herman, although eager to get the money, declined the offer after conferring with Devere.

"Where the hell did they get fifty dollars?" Devere wondered. "Maybe that little cunt is doing a little light whoring."

"I can't believe it," Herman said.

"Maybe you don't want to believe it. Like to get your dick into that one, wouldn't you?"

"Shut up," Herman said.

"Yeah," Devere continued cruelly, "that little bitch really gets to you boys."

"Just shut up."

Devere rose and crossed the room to where Herman sat on his couch. He slapped Herman mercilessly across the face. "Don't you ever tell me to shut up, you crippled little Hun. Now get out of here. I'm getting sick of the sight of you."

Herman had been eight years old when he joined his brother collecting coal in the railroad switch yard. It was a miserable job in that drafty, freezing expanse of steel rails as he picked up the black anthracite lying on the ground, and the youth relieved his boredom by jumping ties, four feet apart, a game he had become good at over the past year. But one evening his left foot had not reached the tie but became enmeshed in a switch line. He tried pulling it out, but his foot only wedged deeper into the unbending polished steel. A stray reefer car, unmanned, rolled down the track. Herman could only remember that the railroad car was green, a bright green, and then he could remember the much lighter green of the operating room, where they cut his leg off, the equally sickening green of the ward he shared with twenty other patients, all male, all different ages. He remembered the degrading fitting of the first wooden leg. And he remembered his father's brutal question as he bent over the bedside, "Why didn't you just take off your shoe, boy?"

The sting of Devere's slap was still painful on his face, and with the studied coordination of a man crippled for years he leapt for Devere's desk, opened the top drawer, and withdrew the man's revolver.

With one sweeping motion he pistol-whipped Devere until he saw deep red blood spurting from both cheekbones, then he picked up the bottle half full of whiskey from the desk and gulped its contents and threw the bottle into the corner.

He opened the door and the last rays of sunlight hit Devere, bleeding and groaning in his swivel chair. Herman walked out of the room and approached Terry, bent alongside her evening fire. He waved the pistol in her face as he toppled her on the ground with his left hand, pointing the pistol at her head.

"One move out of you, bitch," he yelled, "and I'll blow your head off."

He pulled up her dress and tore off her panties. He looked at her naked body and almost seemed gentle as he touched her breasts.

Herman rose and walked toward the highway. He saw a huge truck approach. At first it was the size of the palm of his hand, and then it loomed larger and larger. It was green and its markings were yellow. Herman took the pistol and put it into his mouth and pulled the trigger. This time, he thought, he had taken his shoe off.

Hans returned from work and found Terry in a merciful state of shock by the fire. He had heard the sirens and seen the ambulance and the police cars, and there was the frantic trip to the hospital and the frenzy of personnel in and out of the operating room, and the finality of a gray-haired doctor announcing to Hans, "I'm sorry to tell you that your brother is dead."

It was simple grace or womanly intuition of a dumb Okie girl like Terry to say nothing to Hans about that aborted rape attempt of his brother's, and also much to her credit that she offered no objection in spending fifty dollars on the burial. She even watched as Hans went through his brother's meager belongings at the funeral parlor.

His wallet held his IWW card and four dollars and a pawn ticket for his father's watch.

Hans held that little buff ticket for a long time, then replaced it in the cheap wallet and put the wallet into Herman's coat pocket. The undertaker nailed the coffin shut and Hans left the room and followed the slow-moving hearse to the graveyard. He held Terry's hand as he watched the last spade of desert soil cover the wooden box, and they walked slowly back to their truck. Neither Devere nor any of his Wobbly pals had attended the funeral.

Hans walked into Devere's office.

"That's some movement you got," Hans said. "Some movement."

Devere found it difficult to talk through his swollen lips: "Get out. Get off this property."

"Don't worry," Hans said, "you red scum. We're getting out." Then he spat into Devere's face. "Don't you ever cross my path, mister. Don't you ever cross my path."

Terry rolled up the clothesline strung between the cab of their truck and the cottonwood tree and packed the camp stove. Hans started the engine and they roared up the highway toward Boulder City. He could not look at the spot where his brother had fallen into a crumpled heap of wood and flesh and later he could not eat the supper Terry prepared with very shaky hands.

Frank Crowe had heard of the event from the chief of police and roamed the highway between Boulder City and Las Vegas until he found Hans and Terry. He walked over to them, both stunned and silent, and handed Hans a full bottle of bourbon.

"This won't answer your questions," he said, and then softly, "but it will let you sleep." He started to leave but Terry got up and walked up to Frank before he entered his truck.

"Thank you, mister," she said, and Frank nodded his head.

"Take care of that boy," he said. "I'll expect him at five-thirty."

46

There were only three people besides Crowe who knew of his plan to foil Devere: Wanke, Williams, and Elle, but Frank knew he had to discuss his tactics with Walker Young. He asked him to his office the following morning.

Young listened carefully and finally said, "I think that you have fairly accurately guessed their moves, but I do not agree with your counterattack."

"Why?"

Walker Young walked slowly around Crowe's office.

"I don't like the idea of building those two phony structures so you can garage those trucks filled with sand."

"Where should I put them?"

Walker stood in front of the map of the area and pointed.

"This is the Arizona exit of the bridge. There's the road. That shed you're planning will stick out like a sore thumb."

"Go ahead," Crowe said.

"You know damned well every time a gravel train comes off that bridge it holds up highway traffic. It's a bottleneck."

"Agreed," Crowe said.

"I would build an underpass there. First of all it would be useful, and second it would give you an excuse for bringing trucks into the area."

"Very good," Crowe said.

"Start your underpass about three weeks ahead of the tunnel completion."

"That settles the trucks," Crowe said. "What about my lookouts down below?"

"Well, you've got to find *some* excuse to have a crane or a tractor or just a goddamned truck down there, something that can hide a lookout."

Crowe nodded. "I suppose," he said.

"You see, Frank," and he pointed upstairs to the drafting room, "you don't know who the hell you have. *One* of those engineers could be on Devere's payroll. Any *dummy* structure you build has got to raise suspicion. Put in a shithouse for a lookout shelter."

Crowe looked at Walker and shook his head.

"What's the matter, Frank?"

"You're dead right, Walker, dead right. Several months ago I told Elle that I wondered whether I'm getting too old to build this dam. I should have thought of all these things myself, goddamnit."

"You're not getting too old, Frank. The Wobblies have rarely been as militant as they have on this dam. You just have to spend too much time to outguess the bastards."

"That's true," Frank said. "I just hope to hell Hoover wins in November; I'd hate to think what will happen if Roosevelt gets in."

"Well, Hoover isn't having an easy time," Walker said. "I heard he was visiting the dam sometime in November."

"Oh, Jesus," Frank said.

"What do you mean?"

259

"You know me and dignitaries."

"Well, Hoover's seen you in denims before. He'd probably faint if you wore a suit."

"November," Frank mused. "I'm gonna be pretty busy in November."

Walker Young left and Frank paced his office slowly. He was angry because Young was right, all the way, and he remembered Elle's remark, "You're not a myth, you're a man."

There was a knock on the door.

"Come in," Crowe yelled.

Hal Ellis entered, a young, prematurely balding engineer, part of Frank's elite corps.

"What is it, Ellis?"

"One of the cableways snapped. Number 3. They were testing it."

"Anyone hurt?"

"Three," Ellis said. "Cable came back like a bull whip."

"How badly were they hurt?"

"They're dead."

Crowe was quiet, then shouted, "Well, get out your clipboard and get down there. If you ever want to get anywhere in this business then learn how to take charge! Now move, and get me the name of the cable operator."

"Yes, sir," Ellis said, and retreated to the outer office. Before leaving for the dam site he suggested to the others that the chief was not in the best of moods. "If you got anything to tell him, save it for tomorrow."

Ellis left, but was quickly followed by Crowe, who ordered Hans to drive him home. It had been a bad afternoon. Not only had Young shown him up but his outburst at Ellis had been needless and unprofessional. He thought of Stubbs and all the other men who had already given their lives on the dam, and he was grateful that Hans usually kept his mouth shut at times like these as they rode side by side to Boulder City.

He looked at the boy, blond, blue-eyed, tall, tanned, neat despite the most primitive sanitary conditions, his denims pressed, his face slender, his shoes not shined, but wiped; he meant to reach out but was so full of his own problems he knew that silence was the prudent gesture.

Hans drove Crowe to his house and came to a stop at the front door. Maria was just leaving the Crowe home. Elle waved to him from their open front door, but Maria stopped Frank before he entered his house.

"That was a lovely party you had for Mr. Barnes," Maria said sarcastically.

"Oh, shut up, Maria."

"Old Jack was really upset because the lights wouldn't go off in Sequoia Lodge."

"Was he now?"

"Yes. Kept saying something about the contingency fund."

Frank smiled. "Maria," he said, "you're one of the finest ladies I've ever known."

Maria Williams drew herself up. She was from good Italian stock, tall, full-breasted, a lovely olive complexion. The three children had left inches around her waist, as had the pasta and the wine, but there were still youth and mystery around her well-chiseled nose, her very dark brown eyes.

"I know all about your masculine urges, *Mr.* Supervisor," she said, somewhat mockingly, "but *someday* the ladies of construction are going to have their say. You wait. You wait."

"Go tend your stove," Frank said, "beat your kids, I want to get home."

"You're home, Mr. Crowe, you're home," and she pushed him lightly on the chest. "Get out of my way. 'Tend my stove, beat my kids,' hell. I got a bottle of anisette that even Jack doesn't know where it's hidden."

Frank walked up the step and kissed Elle, who had watched Maria's performance, but had not heard the conversation. She kissed Frank and steered him into the dining room.

"I want you to sit down and close your eyes."

"What the hell is going on? Did you girls have a suffragette meeting this afternoon? Everybody is pushing me around."

"Just sit down and shut up." Elle walked to the living room and suddenly the entire house was flooded with the music of Beethoven's Emperor Concerto.

Frank got up and walked to the living room and saw the Victrola, a small stack of records, and an impish smile on Elle's face. She was aware of Frank's love for classical music. Frank had expounded vociferously on the genius of Beethoven, not only because of his musical virtuosity, but because he composed even while deaf. "Imagine," he had told her, "here is a man writing parts for 102 musicians, all of which fit, all of which help to form part of a whole . . ." and Elle had wondered whether he admired only the genius of organization or the pure musicality.

Frank was truly impressed by the recording and sat quietly until the end of the concerto.

"That was magnificent," he said, putting his arm around Elle, "and where did you get this marvelous machine?"

"I ordered it from Monkey Ward's. Why?"

Frank smiled. "I'm really a stingy bastard, aren't I?"

261

"I don't quite know what you mean."

"I mean where did you get the money for all that equipment? I know how little they pay you at the library."

"Well," Elle said, withdrawing herself from his arms and moving to a corner of the couch, "since you've made me bookkeeper of this household I have had some notions."

"Such as?"

"Such as the fact that you get paid a little over two thousand dollars a month and following your instructions I deposit seventeen hundred dollars of this in the Salt Lake National Bank every payday."

"Go on."

"Since our housing is free, our transportation is free, we can, I agree, live very handsomely on three hundred dollars a month. However . . ." she touched Frank's nose with the tip of her finger.

"However?" Frank said.

"Although you feel that life, even for a supervising engineer, should be spartan, lean, I do not think it has to be niggardly.

"We are building a very handsome nest egg in that bank account. We own and receive rent from the home in Salt Lake. I do not think that just because we live in Boulder City we should not enjoy *some* of the luxuries available, like a phonograph."

"What else?" Frank asked.

"A new sewing machine, a washing machine, perhaps a new pair of shorts, very short—"

Frank sat silent for several minutes. "I know I'm a tight man with a dollar," he said finally. "I don't know why really. Perhaps I do. Maybe it's because I've been on my own since I was sixteen, or because I'm from New England where everybody is tight. I've never had anyone to turn to for help. The bank account has been my only security."

"And now you have a bitchy wife who's trying to diminish that security."

Frank looked at Elle. "I don't have a bitchy wife. I have a wife."

"What does that mean?"

"I know it sounds strange, Elle, but even after six years of marriage it's hard for me to believe it, to understand it."

"I know that, Frank. I feel it once in a while."

"How?"

"You still make out lists for groceries, for laundry soap, for one-hundred-pound sacks of potatoes, and then you add a little note, 'And whatever else you need,' meaning things you can't bear to write down."

"Like what?"

"Like Kotex, dummy, or garter belts or brassières."

Frank blushed.

"I'm sorry, honey."

"You don't have to be sorry, Frank. Why the hell do you need to make out the list at all? Don't you think I can shop. Don't you trust me?"

"Of course."

"I'm a woman. I bleed once a month. So what? I have breasts that need brassières."

"They don't," Frank said.

"Look at the hall tree." She pointed. "Four hooks. Poncho, hat, slicker, slicker cap. What about *my* coat? What about my cap?"

Frank pulled Elle into his arms.

"I love you, Elle. I love you, darling. Tell me something honestly."

"What?"

"Do you think I was too old when I married you? Are you sorry, Elle?"

Elle thought briefly and then she cupped Frank's face in her hands.

"I love you too, Frank. You're not too old. I had no right for that outburst the other night when I told you to blow up Alma's fruit stand. I had no right to shut you out. You said, 'That's murder,' and you were right and I didn't even have the decency to come down and apologize. I wanted to, but I'm stubborn too." Elle's eyes were full of tears

She put her head on his shoulder, and Frank put his hand under her dress and ran it slowly up her legs.

"How short will those shorts be?"

"Frank Crowe!"

Frank saw the lightning and heard the thunderclap. Ten minutes later he heard the phone, the damned phone which ended the idyll.

"Chief."

"Yes?"

"It's Ellis. The Vegas Wash is raising hell with the railroad track."

"I'll be right there."

Frank rose quickly, reached for his poncho and rain hat, and was out the front door.

Elle turned on the couch and straightened her skirt.

"Frank Crowe," she said to herself, "needs four hooks like you need Kotex. Buy a hook, stupid."

The Vegas Wash, practically barren of vegetation, sloped toward the Colorado at more than one hundred feet a mile and proved a threat to Crowe every time a storm hit the dam site. Frank had built culverts beside the highway, the railroad, he had built pilings, but tonight the water came down in four-foot waves, picking up tons of rock as it roared. It was more than the trestles could stand. When Frank arrived on the scene several hundred feet of track were hanging in mid-air like an abandoned lonely roller-coaster.

263

The storm lasted only one night but it took Frank three days to rebuild the trackage. During the day he opened the coolers of the warehouse and brought out all the near beer still in stock. At night he had wives bringing coffee and sandwiches, and the following day he paced the drafting room above his office.

"Well, gentlemen," he said. "We know the trestles will hold three-foot waves and they'll collapse with four-foot waves, so build them for six-foot waves. That road and that railroad are as vital to us as the aorta to the heart."

At Alma's fruit stand Devere, still bandaged, looked at Sinsky, his new assistant.

"Well, Crowe lost three days."

"I know," Sinsky said, "but he didn't use any tunnelers to rebuild that track."

"That's right," Devere said. "Wasn't that a beautiful sight? All that track hanging in mid-air. Wait until you see that bridge." He rubbed his hands.

"I wonder where Hans and Terry went?" Sinsky asked.

"Why? You got the hots for her too?"

"No. I just wondered."

"Well, stop wondering. All you guys ever have on your mind is ass." He picked up his whiskey and sipped. It still hurt him to swallow.

Several considerations made Hans finally decide to marry Terry. Although he felt safer away from Devere and his lousy band of hangers-on, their new home consisted of nothing more than another cottonwood tree fifty feet from the Boulder Highway. He remembered Crowe's offer of a house in Boulder City and the remaining fifty dollars of their winnings from Las Vegas, which would more than cover the cost of a minister, the use of the church, and a small silver ring. The following morning Hans asked Crowe if he would be his best man while his wife stood up for Terry.

Crowe said he was flattered but would have to consider it with Elle. "Have you asked Terry yet?"

"No." Hans blushed.

"Feel pretty sure of yourself." Crowe laughed.

And Hans laughed and said nothing.

Frank raised the issue that evening. Elle was delighted and could not understand Frank's hesitancy.

"I've got no time, Elle," he pleaded. "Next thing I know I'll stand up for every son of a bitch on the dam site, be named godfather, be invited to christenings."

"Nonsense," Elle said. "You like that boy. You like them both. I know that. You couldn't turn him down. He's *your* driver. You see more of him than you do of me."

"Goddamned women," Frank said. "I knew I should never have asked."

Meanwhile, Hans, sitting on the runningboard of his truck, wasn't having much better luck with Terry. He had explained carefully to her every valid reason for their marriage and was met by a flood of tears.

"What's the matter?" he said, trying to pry Terry's face from her clenched hands, and finally succeeded.

"Sometimes, Hans Schroeder, you're the dumbest son of a bitch I ever met."

"What do you mean by that?"

"I never said I was some goddamned prize. I got nothin' except three dresses, a pair of slacks, some fancy underwear, and a comb and a toothbrush."

"What are you talking about?"

"I still come from folks. My folks got married. Two of my sisters are married. I don't expect any of them got proposals that just talked about money or a place to stay."

"It'll be better," Hans said.

"I know it'll be better, damnit," and Terry started sobbing again.

"What the hell is wrong?"

Finally Terry looked up and wiped her face with the back of her tanned arm.

"Can't you say you love me? You want me?"

"You know all that."

"Sure, sure, but can't you say it? Just for once?"

Hans Schroeder scratched his head.

"I never asked nobody to marry me before."

"Well, you better not try it again, you stupid bastard."

She kissed him and Hans kissed her back, and they jumped into the back of the truck, and that night Hans heard no noises and cared little who might invade their privacy. But Terry could scarcely sleep after Hans told her he had asked the chief and his wife to stand up with them. "I hope I don't do nothing wrong," she thought.

Frank never ceased to be in awe of his young wife. There were not that many years between Elle and Terry and yet Elle, whose background was no more lofty than Terry's, had carefully learned to make a lady of herself. She had watched the women at the University of Vermont, had learned decorum from Miss Adams at the library, had emulated Mrs. Stein, and gained some intuition from Maria Williams. But, whatever the genesis of her talents, she made Hans and Terry's wedding a beautiful, simple, and moving event, beginning with sewing a chaste white gown for the girl and inviting the Williamses and the Wankes for the ceremony, which was held in their parlor. She had baked a cake and made a punch, and by agreement none of the men dressed since Hans did not own a suit. The minister of the Presbyterian Church, young and handsome himself, made the ceremony light and gay.

Frank and Elle stood watching two people, whose only assets were youth and love, join in marriage in a sunbaked house in the middle of the desert, and Frank kissed Terry, not once, but twice, saying, "This kiss is for you and this one for women." Elle smiled knowingly and everyone threw rice as Hans and Terry, both blushing and reserved, finally dashed to their truck. They headed for Vegas for a night and the following day, which Frank Crowe had given them as a wedding gift. They watched that rickety truck roll down the hill and finally disappear in a cloud of dust.

"It must be nice to be young," said Jack Williams.

"You didn't look so bad before you got that pot." Maria punched his beer belly.

"Let's finish the punch," Elle said, returning to the parlor. "The kids forgot to take their cake."

Tom Wanke put his arm around Elle. "And who is calling a kid a kid?" Frank Crowe loved that remark.

48

Slowly, but methodically, things were falling into place for Devere. The constant exhortations of his men produced all the evidence he needed to give credence to that crucial day in November. Trucks were being serviced with great care, Anderson's company was alerted about mobile kitchens, security guards were placed on special alert. Devere had men in all sections of the dam. The crucial group were being trained to blow up the bridge. They were the youngest, the most radical hotheads, and they took great pride in being chosen for the job.

They had gone over it a dozen times already. Devere's plan was to blow the bridge during the swing shift–graveyard shift turnover, hoping that this usual period of confusion would give greater cover for his men.

"What will we do if there's a train going over the bridge?"

"There's always a train going over the bridge," Devere said. "You'll see a flying locomotive."

"Shit," one of his disciples rubbed his hand. "I don't want no locomotive on my head."

"Those poor bastards," another man said sympathetically, and Devere looked at him sharply.

"You going soft?"

"I ain't going nothing. We ain't fighting the railroads."

"That's right," Devere said, "but every battle has its casualties."

"Just seems like a hell of a way to go!"

"Quit talking about it, for Christ sake."

One could sense Devere's edginess. "We've been sitting in this fucking desert for over a year now while Crowe is getting way ahead of us. We're going to blow that bridge and hurt that man. It will take five minutes. Bam bam. That's it. I'll slow that bastard down to a crawl. He'll lose a year on that project and Mr. Crowe will come begging. *Begging* for peace. I know his kind."

After they left the meeting Devere said to Sinsky, "Keep your eye on that kid."

"What kid?"

"The one with feelings."

"You want me to rough him up?"

"No. Just watch him. Maybe he goes to church behind our backs. That's all I need now."

"What?"

"A Christer." He gulped the remaining whiskey in his glass and refilled it.

49

It was strange for Crowe to be visiting Aunt Mary's place, but even stranger for him to be sitting in her bedroom, rather than the parlor. It was a good-size room, the bedspread made of silk, several rocking chairs, covered in green velour and graced by well-ironed antimacassars, and an Oriental table made of dark teak and covered with ivory elephants and small figurines which were undoubtedly dusted each day. A closet burst with clothes, mostly long dresses, the walls were hung with aging photographs, some in silver, others in oak frames. A madam's bedroom was as sacred as a ship's captain's cabin, her only retreat, her island in an endless merry-go-round of drinking, fornicating men and women in various stages of dress and undress.

Aunt Mary poured a stiff brandy for Frank and one for herself and lowered a paper shade to shut out the afternoon sun.

"Can't stay too long," Frank said. "Don't want to get my driver suspicious."

"Nonsense, nonsense, Frank." Aunt Mary patted his knee. "Been wanting you over since we got started."

"Well, I hear the place is going over with a bang," Frank said.

"A bang and a half," Aunt Mary said, "and I owe it all to you."

"Well, save your money this time," Frank said. "Neither one of us will last forever."

"That's right, Frank. Well," she stood and faced him and put her hand on the mantel of a false fireplace, "you know I didn't ask you for a social call, though I'd like to meet your wife. I hear she's quite a dame."

"She is," Frank said. "More than I deserve. Maybe you could come to the house for dinner."

"Sure," Aunt Mary said. "That would look real great. The madam having supper at the supervisor's house. . . ."

"I know," Frank said, "I'm sorry. I know that Elle wouldn't care."

"I believe that, what I hear about her, but you got your job on the dam, and I've got mine, and that's that."

There was no use to pursue that subject. Both of them knew that what Aunt Mary had said was true.

"A few nights ago we had a couple of bad drunks in here—one was a tunneler, I don't know what the other one does. The usual fight over Heidi—one of my real lookers. I hushed it up fast, but they kept drinking and I kept filling their glasses, hoping they'd pass out, quiet down. One of them kept insisting that he wanted Heidi and I finally tried to convince him that there were lots more nights and Heidi wasn't goin' nowhere and he said there ain't gonna be lots more nights. My ears pricked up.

"'What do you mean there ain't gonna be lots more nights?' He kept wanting to sleep and I kept prodding him, and finally he said, 'In a couple of months we're gonna call Crowe's bluff.'

"'How, boy,' I asked, 'how?'

"He was reeling, but I ordered coffee.

"'We're gonna blow Crowe's little railroad bridge.'

"'No kidding,' I said. 'When you gonna do that, big boy?'

"'We're gonna blow it on the 3rd of November. Bang! Bang. Boy, it's gonna be some sight to see that bridge come down, a whole trainload of gravel flying through the air.'

"'I'd like to watch that, boy. Where should I go?'

"'The Arizona side, but don't get too close.'

"'You take me,' I said, 'I'll give you Heidi the whole night.'

"'No kiddin', you're a real madam, you are,' and then he passed out."

Frank paced the room nervously. "I'm much obliged, Aunt Mary," he said, not looking at her, "much obliged."

"I'm sure this isn't all news to you, is it, Frank?"

"No, it isn't. It's the first confirmation of my tactics."

"Then I've been of some help?"

"You don't know *how* much help. There's just one thing that worries me."

"What's that?"

"What happened when that boy sobered up."

"Jesus Christ," Aunt Mary said, looking at Frank. "What do you take me for? I called Pitt of the Vegas police. When that boy woke up he was sitting in a jail cell in Yuma, Arizona. His trial is slated for March of next year."

Frank slapped his thigh and kissed Aunt Mary on the cheek.

"God damn," Frank said, "God damn, I've always said that . . ."

"What's that?"

"Give me a good tunnel man, concrete man, and an honest madam, and I'll build you a dam in Hades. I'm much obliged for everything," Frank said, heading for the door.

He sat down next to Hans and told him to drive to the office. He half watched the flurries of dust stirred up by the fast-moving truck and half watched Hans. He did not really want to touch the subject, but he had to.

"Take the Bunns cutoff," Crowe said. "I don't want people spotting us on the Madonna Road."

"I got you."

"And keep your mouth shut," Crowe said.

Hans smiled. "I wasn't born yesterday, chief."

Frank did not want to pursue the subject, but Hans felt strangely loquacious. "Somebody was real nice and sent out a glass of lemonade to me. This little trick with real little teats. I never felt teats as little as that . . . sure felt funny."

Crowe shook his head and said, "Watch the road."

When he returned to his office, Wanke and Williams were waiting for him. He closed the door and told Tom and Jack about the news from Aunt Mary.

"That's good news," both agreed, but Wanke wondered about the man in jail in Arizona.

"She's got it all covered," Frank assured him.

"Some Wobbly lawyer will dig him out."

"He won't," Frank assured him. "She knew how to handle this, so did the chief in Vegas. They'll never find that son of a bitch."

"Well, Frank," Williams said, "looks like you're winning at queens and bishops."

"Maybe," Crowe answered thoughtfully. "At least it was *my* move this time."

The disappearance of Charlie Wayne from Aunt Mary's place did not pass by Devere. He had August Levy, the Wobbly attorney, in his office and Devere was in an ugly mood.

"All right," he yelled. "You've been to the jail. You've talked to the police chief. They never saw him or booked him. So where is he?"

Levy shook his head. "You know more about him than I do."

"What do I know? He's from Baton Rouge." Devere looked at an index card. "Organized the docks in New Orleans. Heavy boozer, heavy womanizer, always broke."

"Maybe he went home."

"With what?" Devere yelled. "I've got forty bucks' pay here waiting for him. He didn't go nowhere."

"Maybe he's shacked up with some woman."

"Not likely. He'd be out of dough. No woman around here keeps a man around that's broke."

"I can't produce him out of *thin air*," Levy now yelled.

"Keep your Jew temper," Devere said coldly. "That son of a bitch went to jail. He more than likely went to Aunt Mary's, got drunk, and shot his mouth off. She called Crowe. The two of them are old buddies."

"I'm telling you I've looked at the bookings. There's no Charlie Wayne booked."

"So they booked him under another name."

"Maybe they did. I can't inspect the jail."

"No, you can't. But one of our boys could." He looked at Sinsky. "Where do you keep your vagrancy money?"

"Up my ass," he said.

"All right. Take it out of your ass and go to Vegas and get drunk. Make noise. Get yourself in jail."

"Why me?"

"Because I said so. Are there any other questions, Mr. Sinsky, or Mr. Levy?" he said sarcastically.

It was Levy who spoke up. "Karl Marx was a Jew. Do you remember that?"

"Yeah," Devere said. "I remember. They don't make Jews like that anymore."

"Sure, sure," Levy said. "Only you half-soused Anglo Saxons rule this wonderful world. *Fuck you*, Devere. Fuck you. Why don't you stick your head between your legs? Maybe that will make a man out of you."

Devere threw his half-full glass of whiskey at Levy, but Levy ducked it and stood up. "Go get yourself another boy, Devere. There are others ways to get at Crowe, but you're too sick and warped to understand that."

He walked out the door and left it open. Sinsky and Devere listened to him drive off toward Las Vegas.

"Get me Duncan," Devere ordered, and Sinsky found him asleep in his truck. "Devere wants to see you."

Duncan was tall, heavy set, with crew-cut hair, a small mouth, and a large nose.

Devere opened his desk drawer and took out his small revolver. "Here," he said. "You know where Levy lives?"

"The attorney?"

"Yes."

"Get him out of town."

"Dead or alive?"

"I don't give a shit," Devere said.

271

"Well, I do. I ain't taking no murder rap for you or no one." He threw the revolver back on Devere's desk.

"Don't kill him," Devere said. "Just scare the Jew piss out of him. That won't be hard to do. I don't know how much that son of a bitch knows about us."

Duncan picked up the gun and left the office, leaving Sinsky and Devere.

"What the hell you hanging around for? Didn't I give you an assignment?"

"I got it," Sinsky said, "and I'll do it, but I'm gonna tell you something."

"What?"

"You'd better calm down or you'll blow the whole job."

Devere watched Sinsky leave and sat back in his chair.

He had spent one year in a veterans hospital after the Great War, perhaps the longest year of his life, when he watched his sexual drives channeled into hatred, felt all his hormones turn to adrenaline; for months he could not look at his diminished penis, hanging limply from his groin, its only function to guide his piss to a urinal, and for months he could not look at a woman or a magazine or a newspaper article.

He spent his time drawing, first in bed and then in the sun lounge, sitting in a wheelchair, his feet covered by a dark red blanket with a caduceus embroidered on it. He was talented. He drew other men in wheelchairs, men without limbs, stacks of crutches, rows of dollies, their leather straps hanging from the padded cushions like dead water-snakes. He drew the haunting faces of men in padded cells and vicious portraits of fat female nurses, all bellies and bosoms and charts and thermometers bulging out of pockets of soiled uniforms.

His drawings began to sell in the hospital gift shop and in some of the smaller literary magazines of the day. When he was released from the hospital he had enough money to rent a small apartment in Greenwich Village, and his art continued to thrive on a small scale. His subjects now became pimps and whores and derelicts around the neighborhood, but like George Grosz or even Goya, as one art critic put it, Devere drew with a pen full of tears and charcoal full of hatred.

There was a girl—Lefty was her name; she had posed for Devere a number of times and their friendship grew to a point of accommodation; he was impotent, she a practicing lesbian, doing a little light whoring, writing poetry of sorts. It was Lefty, twenty-three, redheaded and pretty, who gave Devere his first taste of life after the war. She brought him into the Communist Party meetings she attended with friends, neighbors, kids from Columbia, and it was here, at these Tuesday-night meetings full of coffee and borscht, that Devere slowly emerged. He did not join the party at first, but he read Marx and

Lenin at Lefty's suggestion and he drew posters for the Wobblies, strong, frightening posters of fat-bellied capitalists, workers in chains, men standing in soup kitchens.

It was Wobbly leader Warner Strong who gave Devere fifty dollars for one of his posters and an invitation to join the movement. It was perhaps the happiest day in his young life, but even that idyll was short-lived. Lefty was killed outside Detroit as a son of one of the auto tycoons spun his roadster around a tree, killing Lefty and leaving him with a four-inch scar above the knee. It was said he wasn't wearing trousers at the time of the accident.

Devere was paralyzed once more. There had been nothing sexual between Lefty and himself, no more, at any rate, than was possible, but she had been light and gay and beautiful and loved his talent, and maybe even him.

He had gone to see Warner Strong and said he was ready to join the movement.

"Why?" Strong asked coldly.

"I hear you got trouble in Detroit."

"Lots of trouble," Strong said. "I got enough men to storm those gates with clubs and guns. I don't need you for that."

"What do you need?"

"Your pen."

Devere was twenty-six when he faced Strong.

"I got no folks," he said. "I got no balls. All I had was Lefty. You knew Lefty."

Strong said, "Yes. Pretty girl."

"She died because she was sucking that bastard's prick when he wrapped his LaSalle around the tree. I don't want to *draw* him, I want to *kill* him."

Strong looked at the boy for a long time. "I'll send you to Long Island, they'll train you."

"I don't need no training. Just let me at those gates."

Strong took him into the next room and Devere was stunned by the size of the arsenal. Hundreds and hundreds of guns, pistols, machine guns.

"Pick one that will feel good."

Devere chose a Luger pistol, stuffed his pockets with ammunition, and headed for Detroit, complete with letters of introduction, an IWW membership card, and forty dollars in cash.

He needed neither his card nor his letters of introduction. The first day at the gates of Plant 4 he shot and killed two guards. He was a Wobbly hero overnight, but he wasn't out to kill guards.

Grady was the head man of the Detroit Wobbly chapter. He sized Devere up.

"You've done well," he said. "What the hell you after?"

"The one with the four-inch gash in his leg."

"We ain't even through the gates yet, how the hell you gonna shoot him?"

"Just keep giving me ammo. When I see him, I won't miss him."

"Yeah, the boys said you were a pretty good shot. Got both those guards square in the heart."

Devere killed two more men before he was captured. They could not pin the murders on him in the confusion. He got one year in Slattery for inciting a riot.

This time he read Marx and Lenin, not for Lefty, but for himself.

Devere rubbed his face with his right hand. His cheekbones were still tender from the tight, newly-grown skin; his back ached. He felt old and worn. He eyed the half-empty bottle of whiskey. He had learned that even revolutions on a large scale would not bring paradise to the workingman overnight. He poured his grimy glass half full of whiskey, started sipping, and picked up a pencil. He found one of the Wobbly posters next to his desk. He turned it over and started to draw. At first his hand was trembling, his lines insecure, but slowly, slowly he felt some of the surge and finesse return to his fingers; he drew feverishly, his hand returning and leaving the paper with the flourish of a concert pianist finishing a difficult run.

Slowly he watched facial structures develop from a long-forgotten expertise in anatomy, and then the torso emerged and he used his pencil to give depth and dimensionality and he made eyes come alive and lips look sensual, and breasts firm, and his hand steadied as he drew the lines of a leg. His use of shadows and light developed an interplay of muscle and curvature, and he indicated pubic hair with such expertise that the organ it covered came alive and beautiful; even the curvature of a foot, the elegance of a sole, the defiance of a small childlike hand emerged clearly.

Devere had drawn for three solid hours. His whiskey stood unnoticed by his side as did Duncan, who had come back and been watching almost an hour without Devere's awareness. Finally Devere held the drawing out at arm's length and looked at it.

He was surprised by Duncan's presence and his remark.

"Jesus Christ," he said. "That's Terry. It's beautiful."

"It's who?" Devere asked, annoyed.

"Terry."

"Shit." Devere said, tearing up the drawing.

"I didn't know you could draw like that," Duncan said.

Devere nodded without looking at the other man.

"There's a lot of things you don't know." Now he finished his whiskey in one gulp.

274

50

It was late July, a Sunday, the temperature 105, and Elle had asked Frank to take her to the dam site. It had been months since she had accompanied him, feeling happy to have him home the few hours he could spare and knowing that his house was the only refuge he really had. But the previous evening she had questioned him in detail about the turning of the river, and though Frank drew diagrams, explained the engineering flawlessly, he realized that she could not really visualize it all until she saw it in situ.

Perhaps the first thing which struck her was the continuous activity, even on the Sabbath, the endless parade of trucks, of tankers, of caterpillar tractors, which traveled the highway between Boulder City and the dam site. She watched the trains which labored along the canyon walls, the cableways which traversed Black Canyon. There were still high scalers at work on those canyon walls, and she heard the thunder of Jack Williams's dynamite in the tunnels. They passed the huge plant of Babcock & Wilcox, which would build the plate-steel outlet pipes, and Wanke's equally monstrous lo-mix plant. Perhaps what struck her most was that everything dwarfed the thousands of men who were working: the canyon itself, the huge structures, the monstrous cranes, and the behemoth power shovels. Everywhere she looked were shirtless men wearing hard hats and gloves, pulling levers of complicated machinery, straining singly or in groups to place a section of pipe, a caisson of steel, a run of cement. Among them ran water boys, an army of them, continuously feeding that precious liquid to workers who seemed to shed it as quickly as they drank it down.

Perhaps this struck her most, these thousands of sweat-glistened bodies, their right arms crossing their foreheads constantly to take the sweat off their brows to gain the vision they needed. Maybe because they *were* half naked, or their sweat made them look even more vulnerable, she sensed the juxtaposition of men against machinery of which Frank had spoken so often and his constant fears of small humans controlling forces so out of proportion to their own.

They had arrived at the railroad trestle and Frank drove slightly beyond it upriver. The Colorado was swollen, running at almost 72,000 cubic feet per second. Elle was hypnotized by that constant brown body glistening in the summer heat, and for the first time sensed its strength and its relentlessness and its utter silence, which made it as frightening as a jungle cat, immobile and poised for the kill.

"Here," Frank pointed downstream, "you can see the tunnel entries. There are four of them. See the Nevada side?"

"Yes," Elle said. "They're immense."

"And to the right you can see the Nevada spillway, which is almost completed."

Elle saw a huge basin already dug and being lined. "The day I turn the river," Frank said, and Elle noticed the very personalization of the statement, "we will dump rock off that railway bridge. There will be an endless column of trucks dumping rock, day and night for twenty-four hours, until I build a temporary barrier to force the river into the tunnels. Once I have the river turned I build my cofferdams. One where we're standing, another slightly below the tunnel entry."

"That," Elle said, "is a mystery to me."

"What?"

"Those cofferdams. If you turn the river into the tunnels, it will be out of the way."

"When I turn the river, Elle, I am depending on four fifty-six-foot tunnels and two huge spillways to keep the river at bay, and I grant you that if all our calculations are valid the tunnels should do the job. However," Frank too was staring at the Colorado, "I have learned on too many dams that I can't trust the lives of six thousand men to the cold figures of a slide rule or four tunnels. I use these cofferdams to form a box. That's what it's like, a box in which the men will work. Two cofferdams form two sides, the canyon walls the other two. Once I have this box then I get to bedrock and then I can build my dam. At that point I know that those stiffs working fifty feet below the river will survive."

"And what happens to those cofferdams when your real dam is built?"

"This one," he pointed, "will be submerged when the lake is formed. They'll probably name it after me."

Elle laughed.

"What's so funny?"

"Names are very important to construction men, aren't they?"

"I'd never really thought about it. I guess they are. I suppose you want to leave something behind so your kid can say, 'My old man did that,'" and before Elle could say anything, Frank put his arm around her.

"I'm sorry, honey," he said. "I didn't mean that to sound the way it did."

"I know that," Elle said. "I know it, Frank. I'd love to give you a son."

They embraced and a brakeman from a passing freight train waved his cap from the rear platform of the caboose; Frank took off his hat and waved in return.

"Let's get drunk," Elle said. "Let's go to Vegas, let's rent a room and do wonderful sinful things."

"Agreed," Frank said, "agreed, you vixen," as he headed the truck toward Las Vegas, threading himself between trucks and buses and passing cars of visitors like Barney Oldfield.

They drove to the Reno Hotel and rented a room. They drank hard gin in the hotel's dark bar mercilessly pierced by sunlight when patrons came in and out, and after drinking too much too fast, they climbed the stairs to their room and Elle suggested they take a shower together, which they had never done. Frank and Elle took great delight in soaping each other's slippery bodies. They spat mouthfuls of warm water at each other and tried making love in the shower, almost getting drowned in the process, and finally fell on top of the bed, wet, soapy, and sensuous. Almost the last traces of red had left the sky when they woke on top of the bed, neither at first understanding where they were and why, and both coming back into each other's arms, warm tender, and grateful for their love.

51

Although the Big Six Companies had easily been repaid their bond at the end of the first year, it was still a constant battle to collect monies due them for their labors. To justify payment by the government was one of the most disagreeable chores that Crowe had to perform.

He spent long hours with Wanke one September morning on that prickly item called "Measurements for Payments." This meeting concerned itself with quantity estimates for materials in the cofferdams, such stipulations as the size of aggregates (no larger than nine inches) to the mixture of silt, sand and gravel, down to the weight of the sheep-head rollers used for compacting earth.

Wanke looked over the specifications and mopped his brow. "I don't understand the boys in Denver," he said to Frank. "What the hell do they expect? Do they think God just has all this stuff lying around here like a commercial gravel yard? Nine-inch boulders, eight-pound rocks, Christ, we're robbing Peter to pay Paul."

"I know," Frank said sympathetically. "I know exactly how you feel, Tom, but you're just as aware as I am that no sooner do we finish one phase than the Bureau boys are here like buzzards trying to keep the 'long green' from coming to my office monthly."

"I know, I know, Frank, I've read the specs too. I'm wasting my time breaking twelve-inch rocks to nine inches. Shit!"

The door opened and Williams entered. He threw a copy of the Las Vegas *Age* on Crowe's desk.

"Read the headline," he ordered, and Crowe and Wanke picked up the paper.

HOOVER TO VISIT DAM SITE, the headline screamed.

"Accompanied by Secretary of Labor and Mrs. Lyman Wilbur, Bureau of Reclamation Chief Dr. Elwood Mead, and Mrs. Mead, and a large party from Washington, the President's Special will arrive in Boulder City at 7:30 Saturday, November 5. In an interview Mayor Hadley of Las Vegas stated that school children will line the trackage to the dam site."

"Don't say it." Tom Wanke spoke up first.

"I know."

"What do you know?" Williams asked.

"If I were Devere, that would be the night. Even the Wobblies read the papers."

Frank Crowe paced the room and nodded his head. "November 5," he repeated.

"November 5, we shall be ready for Mr. Devere."

"What about Hoover?"

"Fuck Hoover," Frank said. "I'll get Elle to take him around the dam site. I'm not building this dam for Hoover or for Franklin Roosevelt."

"Agreed," Wanke said, "but won't Devere smell a rat when neither you nor any of us is there to greet them?"

Crowe said slowly, "It will be nighttime. There'll be a lot of Secret Service. I'll have some of our own security boys. I'll find some tall son of a bitch and hand him my felt hat. Besides . . ."

"What?"

"I think Devere will have his hands full himself that night."

The lights burned long the evening of that same day behind Alma's fruit stand. Twelve men were seated around Devere's desk. He had held up the same newspaper bearing the same headline about Hoover.

When everybody calmed down Devere said, "Ever since Wayne's mysterious disappearance I've been afraid of November 3rd. I think

278

that stupid bastard got drunk and talked and neither Levy nor anyone else has seen him since. I think he squealed and they carefully buried him in the desert. Now," and he held up the paper, "Providence has played into our hands.

"The President, that rapist of Chile, is visiting the dam site on November 5th.

"That, gentlemen, will put Mr. Crowe out of commission and Mr. Williams, and Mr. Wanke, and most of the Boulder City police. That honorable asshole from Washington has given us a mandate, and we won't fail him. If his train remains overnight, as I expect, he will not only be able to admire the fruits of Crowe's labors, but his beady engineering eyes will gaze upon a smoldering concrete train, a carefully blown-up bridge, and probably the loss of another million votes."

"We could put a couple of sticks under Mr. Hoover's private car," Sinsky suggested.

"That's very smart," Devere said. "Very smart. Election Day is November 8. You'll make a martyr out of Hoover on November 5, and you'll have Curtis as your new president."

"You're right," Sinsky said. "You're really right."

"You bet your ass I'm right. Now let's see how right everything else is." He looked around the room.

"You've all checked your dynamite?"

Eight men nodded their heads.

"You check it daily?"

"Yes," they answered.

"Every stick is on the reservation. There are no floaters?"

"It's all there. The dynamite, the caps, the wiring."

"Good."

"Where will you be, Devere?" one of the blasters asked.

"I'll be right here, looking at my watch. At ten to eleven I'll walk into that cold desert night. At eleven-ten I expect to hear an enormous blast. At eleven-thirty I'll be at the Reno Hotel sitting at the bar. The only thing remaining in this room when the cops arrive will be crates of fruit. Alma's fruit stand will start to thrive. Mr. Roosevelt has promised us a New Deal."

52

There were hours, usually dawn hours, which Frank Crowe spent in his office alone. A signal to one of his staff engineers was sufficient to keep his door closed and his phone silent unless an emergency of sufficient magnitude arose to require his presence.

These hours were spent in thought and reflection. If one could observe Frank during these lonely hours one would see a man shuttling between statistics on the walls, maps on his drafting tables, specifications on his desk. One would see a man with his inevitable slide rule and his ever-present grease pencil. There were also hours when he simply stood or sat on his windowsill.

"A dam," one of his favorite professors at the University of Vermont had once said, "is not simply placing a wedge of cement between two rock cliffs. That is simply the frosting on the cake, the dotting of the 'i.' A dam, for most of its construction, is a matter of moving earth.

"If a dam requires diversion tunnels," Dr. Zenk had said, "then one must blast out thousands of tons of rock, but there must also be a place for that rock. If a dam requires cofferdams, material must be found to build them. If a dam requires concrete, materials for it must be close at hand in sufficient quantity. Earth must be moved for roads, and for trackage, and earth must be moved for storage areas, living quarters, water tanks. Canyon walls must be drilled for abutments and for cableways, an unwatered site must be cleaned to bedrock and *that* earth must be moved.

"It is one thing," that wise man emphasized, "to drill and cut and blast; the earth will give, and the mountains will yield. It is another to know what to do with that earth, with that rock, with that silt, and that mud. The engineer who builds a dam successfully must be a clairvoyant. He must think three-dimensionally both in space and in time. The engineer who will bring in a dam successfully will always be ahead of the drill bit, the shovel, the mucking truck, the cement mixers. Never forget that, gentlemen."

Frank had not forgotten. It was the week of September 11th, the heat still unbearable. Frank commenced work on a rock barrier jutting from the Nevada side downstream from the inner diversion tunnel. He used the rock coming out of the last excavation of that tunnel. This barrier would facilitate excavation for the base of the upper cofferdam. It marked the real beginning of the river diversion.

He looked at his wall and a projected schedule. This job was slated to begin October 1, 1933. He was slightly more than a year ahead of schedule. He left his office and Hans drove him to the dam site to inspect the concrete footings for runways for five cableways to span the river. Two of these, 2,575 feet in length, using three-inch cables having a capacity of 20 tons, were the longest cableways ever constructed in the world.

After this inspection Frank drove to his dam site aerie, where once more he closed the door and faced the river through his freshly washed windows. His eyes were fixed on the river, brown and languid. He felt like the Mexican peasant stopping at the altar of his local church. That gilded Christ, those soothing candles, those silken altar coverings, the lofty stained-glass windows might yet sustain him through a day in a dusty field and a night on a damp mud floor.

Frank Crowe stared at that river, and like a peasant wondered if the river heard, or if the river *felt*, or if the river *cared*. Even the textbooks, and the lectures, and the years of experience, had no answer. All a man could do was be prepared. One asked questions of the river, one cursed the river, one trusted the river, but the river, like Christ, was immutable.

53

At the sound of the noon whistle, on November 3, hundreds of grimy, ashen-faced men streamed out of the tunnels. In less than a year and a half they had built four of them, two on the Nevada side of Black Canyon, two on the Arizona side. Each tunnel was four thousand feet long and fifty-six feet in diameter, all of them lined with three feet of concrete as smooth as marble.

It was a Thursday and Jack Williams had requested the mess hall from Crowe for the party to celebrate the completion of the job. There was to be a feast of turkey and ham provided by the Six Companies for the men and their wives or friends.

"That was the fastest shift change I've ever seen," Williams said, standing at the portal of the Arizona Tunnel Number 2 as he and Crowe watched men stream out of the cavern.

"Ain't you going to the party, chief?" a number of them asked, and Williams waved and said he'd be there.

It had been a momentous job. Tens of thousands of tons of rock had been blasted out of these mountains, and tens of thousands of barrels of concrete had lined these tunnels. For almost a year the dust had never settled, the roar of dynamite had never abated, the sound of jackhammers had never ceased, and the mucking trucks had formed an endless parade in and out. Men had lived with poor air and scant light and constant noise and never-ending anxiety and fear of being buried alive or torn to shreds by dynamite. There were thirty men who had entered these tunnels at one shift or another during that year and a half who had not emerged alive, but now, this cool November morning, Crowe watched as one elderly man swept barely a dustpan full of sand out of the last few feet of the tunnel, like a local housewife sweeping her back porch.

Crowe watched the lonely man sweeping and Williams said gently, "That's good enough, Dad, get to the party."

It was probably the gentlest order Williams had given during the whole year. Once alone, Williams walked Frank through the tunnel. It was a ritual Frank had performed on previous dams. They walked in silence on the bottom of the giant tube.

Crowe said little as Williams pointed out an adit, a turn of direction, a setback for valves and controls.

It took forty minutes for the two men to walk the length of the tunnel. It was flawless and spotless and it was the way Williams built a tunnel. They watched the downriver exit grow larger and larger and finally emerged downstream into the weak November sun, the Colorado playing merrily through the canyon on its way to the Gulf of California.

Frank paused and ran his hands along the partly poured concrete lining.

"I've seen a lot of tunnels in my lifetime," Crowe said. "I've never seen a bigger one or a better one." He shook Jack Williams's hand, and Williams removed his hard hat and wiped off beads of sweat.

"I built it according to specs," Williams said, "but those were nice words anyway."

Hans was waiting to pick up the two men to take them to the mess hall. "God damn it," Crowe said, "I'd like to celebrate. *Really* celebrate, but now I've got to worry about that fucking Devere."

"When do you think they'll hit us?"

"I don't know," Crowe said. "I started that underpass three weeks ago. I got the trucks ready, I've got lookouts in the shithouse down below, the chief's boys are poised and armed. It could be tonight, tomorrow night, the night that Hoover gets here. I got to sit there and wait for the bastards."

"You ain't waiting alone," Williams said. "Tom and I ain't gonna miss that show."

Frank nodded his head. "It's one performance *I* could do without."

Hans drove Crowe and Williams to the mess hall, and the party was well under way. A great cheer went up as they entered and Williams, goaded by his men, finally rose and made a short speech.

He removed his hard hat and placed it on the table before him and he put down his mug of near beer. The room quieted down.

"Any man who works in a tunnel has got to be a fucking fool. Pardon me, ladies. Any man who supervises men who work in tunnels has got to be the biggest fucking fool. Pardon me, ladies. We started less than a year and a half ago with a pilot hole no bigger than my thumb and we finish today with the four largest tunnels in the world." There was a cheer.

"I know I was no angel in there, and if Nevada laws had allowed bull whips, I probably would have used them too, but you all acted like men, each and every one of you, and I salute you." He picked up his glass. "And I salute all the men who ended their lives in those tunnels. I'll drink to them, and hope they'll never see darkness again."

Frank returned to his office and spoke to the chief of police of Las Vegas on the phone.

"I'll need your help. When we get the bastards, you book 'em and keep 'em. No bail. Not yet."

"They got some tough attorneys," Pitt said.

"I know, but you'll have some pretty heavy charges. I'm going to leave it all in your hands. You can break the story, you can get the credit."

"Much obliged."

"Just be on call, every night, starting tonight. Keep one of your boys on the phone and awake."

"Got you, chief."

Crowe hung up the phone and Walker Young walked in.

"You all set, Frank?" he asked.

"As set as I'll ever be. You're going to have to explain my absence to Hoover. Elle will be there and a friend of mine."

"Who's that?"

"You'll find out."

"Didn't know you had any friends." Walker smiled slightly. "How many people are in on this?"

"Our security people, Vegas police, you, me, Tom and Jack."

"Good," Young said. "What if they succeed?" Young asked evenly.

"I'll lose a month rebuilding that bridge."

"And a couple of hundred men."

"Yes," Frank said. "A couple of hundred men."

At dinnertime Frank explained to Elle her role when Hoover arrived. "You won't be alone. Everybody from the Big Six is already arriving. You know Francesca, the others."

"I've never met a President of the United States. Do I curtsy?"

Frank laughed. "No. That's not necessary."

"I'll faint."

"You won't faint."

The doorbell rang and Frank rose to open it. It was Alan Payne, a hoist operator. He had worked on three dams with Crowe and their physical resemblance was striking. He was six feet two, gaunt, his face more weatherbeaten than Frank's, his nose more bourbon-speckled.

"Alan, this is my wife, Elle."

Elle rose and they shook hands.

"Would you like some supper, Mr. Payne?" Elle asked.

"No thanks, ma'am, already et."

"Well, Alan, I'll tell you why I sent for you. The President of the United States, as you know, is visiting the dam site Saturday night. For reasons I can't divulge now, you're going to accompany my wife that evening. You'll be wearing my suit and my felt hat and stay as much out of the light as you can.

"Once you're in Sequoia Lodge, your job is over."

"You mean I don't get to dance with your wife?"

"No, and you'd better not lose my hat or stain my suit."

"Frank," Elle said, "that isn't nice."

"Jesus," Alan said. "I get to shake the President's hand."

"He doesn't shake hands."

"Well," Alan said, "that ain't friendly. I voted for him."

"So did I," Frank said. "Would you like a drink?"

"No thanks." Alan stood.

"My driver will pick you up at six and bring you to the house. Just keep your mouth shut. You'll read all about it in the *Age* one of these days.

After Alan left Frank turned to Elle. "I'm going to have some long nights, honey. I'll be back here before dawn and then have Hans drive me to the office. I'll catch some sleep there. I'd like to keep a guard on the house but I can't spare any, so keep the doors locked and don't open them for *anybody*. You got that?"

"And if I tell you to be careful, what will that do?"

"I'm not aiming to get killed."

"Are you carrying a gun?"

"No," Frank said. "I'm more deadly with a pickaxe."

284

Frank noticed Elle shiver and he put his arms around her. There were tears in her eyes, and Frank kissed them, and her cheeks and her lips.

"I knew this night would come and I kept talking to myself. 'Don't cry,' I kept saying, 'don't cry.' Now look at me."

"I'll be all right, honey."

"I love you, Frank Crowe. Goddamnit, I love you."

Frank rushed upstairs. He took off his felt hat and donned a hard hat. Over his denims he buttoned his dark green poncho. He checked his flashlight and grabbed a pickaxe.

He said no more to Elle as he left the house and heard the dead bolt shut on his front door as he headed toward the railroad bridge on foot.

Devere's men, those who would perform the job, sat around his desk. They were all drinking whiskey tonight.

"Hoover will arrive at seven-thirty on Saturday. He should be in Sequoia Lodge by eight. I want you, Carl, to be lookout. When you see Crowe enter, give the signal to the boys. I can't wait for the shift change at eleven. We've got to work fast. Hoover will be in bed at ten. Those boys lead healthy lives. Just knowing Crowe is in that lodge will make me feel a lot better. A *lot* better."

Once more Devere went through the entire maneuver. Once more he asked each man if he knew where his dynamite was, how he would strap it to his legs. Once more he went through the wiring of the dynamite, the fusing, the men's entry and exit from the bridge. Outside their door, Hans Schroeder, on instructions of Frank Crowe, was burying two sticks of dynamite a short distance from the rear footing of Alma's fruit stand.

54

The terrain around the Arizona side of the railway bridge was stark and treacherous. There were huge boulders which had been pushed aside for the construction of that bridge, sheer cliffs, rolling hills heading toward the river. It was a moonless night as Frank had predicted, and the only illumination came from the construction taking place on the underpass, and even those series of two-hundred-watt bulbs were swallowed up quickly in the darkness of the canyon.

Crowe and a radioman spent most of the first night in the outhouse below the bridge, Williams sat in one of his sand-filled dump trucks, and Tom Wanke kept vigil at the Nevada side. Crowe trained his binoculars endlessly at the piers of the bridge, waiting for some movement, some sign of activity. By four in the morning he could see as well at night as he could during the day, and by early dawn he returned home. Devere had not struck.

The same fruitless vigil continued the following night and everyone grew testy, Crowe, Williams, Wanke, the security guards.

It was three days before the election on November 8, and Hoover's stop was to be his final journey West during the campaign. The following Tuesday he would go into a voting booth in Palo Alto and make a small dent in his massive defeat.

His train was long and impressive as it pulled into Boulder City. The train's boilers sparkled, the red-trimmed driving wheels steamed, even the well-pressed blue-and-white denims of the engineer and firemen were noted by the local press.

Chapman, Stein, Henderson, and Andrews, Mackenzie, Barnes, even Old Man Donner, and their wives, stood near the vestibule where Hoover would exit, as did Elle and Alan Payne wearing Frank's suit and his famous felt hat. They were in the second contingent with Walker Young and his wife. Secret Service men, young, short-haired wearing blue-and-white enamel buttons in their dark coat lapels, stared coldly at the roped-off crowds fifty feet beyond the car.

Finally Hoover emerged, tall, heavy-set, white-haired, his eyes like slits, his blue pin-striped suit well cut for a stocky figure, his black shoes gleaming from a valet's labors.

Hoover knew all the men from the Big Six on sight, and he knew Walker Young, and he *did* shake hands with Elle, who was feeling foolish next to the bogus husband at her side. There was little ado, and everyone climbed into limousines and drove through Boulder City to the Sequoia Lodge.

As the last of the party entered the lodge, the signal was given by one of Devere's men. This was a lookout above Sequoia Lodge. He saw dignitaries enter, he watched Hoover and Crowe enter, and when the door was shut he ran several hundred yards to the next runner. Within five minutes all of Devere's men had been given the signal to proceed. Each of them, in his hiding place behind a rock, a bush, an abandoned mine shaft, had five sticks of dynamite taped to his legs. Five of them were blasters from the tunnels; one was an electrician. There were Sinsky and O'Hara, their leader, an engineer on Crowe's staff. Their dress was identical to that of other men on the dam site, hard hats, denims; a few carried lunch pails, several of them held shovels.

They converged on the bridge separately from all sides. Crowe was staring through his field binoculars with red, sleep-robbed eyes. This was the third night and his back ached, cramped against the rough planking of the outhouse. On his left sat the radioman, half paralyzed from hours of confinement.

If Crowe had learned one thing in all those years of heavy construction, it was the rhythm of his workmen. Only self-preservation or a direct order made any stiff walk faster than his own leisurely pace. They were getting paid by the day, and the day was long enough. The "company" got just so many ergs from *any* man.

Crowe could not make out Devere's men around the pier of the bridge. They looked no different from other workmen nearby. He could not see them tape the dynamite to the piers, but he recognized a well-rehearsed performance, an unusual crispness of movement, a definite pattern of precision.

"That's it," he said quietly to the radio operator. "The bastards have arrived."

The operator closed the switch and alerted Williams in his dump truck on the bridge. There were ten trucks scattered about the area, some working on the underpass, others shuttling between Boulder and the dam site. Two of these trucks, filled with sand, moved toward the bridge. Williams was in the lead truck; a third truck moved toward the area of the piers.

The two upper trucks made equally well-rehearsed turns on the bridge and quietly backed to its edge. Crowe could hear the meshing of the gears as the truck beds slowly raised and the fulcrum of inertia was finally reached when eight tons of sand slid quietly and treacherously toward the saboteurs below. The sand was carefully screened and of the proper mesh to do its job. Wanke had seen to that. It came almost quietly, like a strong gust of wind, but it came relentlessly. Only one of the eight men had time to yell, "Look out. Jesus," before he too was swallowed up in the avalanche. It took less than ten seconds for the men to be encased in sand.

Crowe, now out of the outhouse, advanced toward the eerie scene. It looked like the mound of a freshly dug grave, and there was a sense of relief as he noticed that mound come alive, first an arm, a leg, then heads and torsos of coughing, spitting men, rubbing the sand out of their eyes, their ears, their mouths and noses.

Pitt's truck had stopped in front of them, its headlights blazing; his deputies arrived with shotguns, surrounding the sandpile filled with thrashing men.

"Get your fucking hands up," Pitt ordered. All the men complied

287

except Sinsky. He drew a revolver and aimed it at Crowe. The single shot missed Frank and ricocheted off the fender of a truck, hitting Williams in the shoulder. Pitt's deputies returned the fire and Sinsky fell to the ground.

Frank ran toward his friend. He commandeered a passing truck, pushed a dazed Williams into the cab, and ordered the driver from his seat. Crowe took off his shirt, folded it, and held it against the oozing wound.

"Push on this," Frank said, as he jammed the gear shift into low and rushed to the hospital.

Frank sat outside the operating room on a hard bench and faced the gleaming white hallway of the hospital corridor.

He heard Williams's voice, loud and clear: "Don't cut nothing off, or I'll kill you," and then he heard the deep ether-induced breathing and the sound of metal instruments being dropped into aluminum pans.

Maria and Elle, stunned and tearful, soon joined Frank. Finally the surgeon came into the hallway. His gloved hand held a hemostat. It was bloody and in its serrated tip was a .32-caliber bullet.

"Missed his jugular by six millimeters," the young surgeon said. "The luck of the Irish."

They watched Williams being wheeled from surgery and transferred to a bed in a private room, and they watched the saline solution dripping slowly into his pierced and taped arm.

"I'll be back," Frank said, kissing Maria. "He'll be all right."

Maria turned to Elle. "Watch my kids. I'm not leaving his side."

"I will, Maria. I will," Elle said, "God bless you."

Frank and Elle drove to their house in silence, and once inside he slumped into his rocking chair as Elle poured him a stiff drink, and then another.

"Bishops and queens," Frank said. "Who figured on a gun?"

Tom Wanke entered the room.

"I just saw the surgeon," Tom said. "He said Jack will be okay."

"Yeah," Crowe nodded. "Maybe he was right. Maybe we should have blown up Alma's fruit stand."

Elle stood and kissed Frank. "I've got to get to Maria's kids."

Frank watched her leave the house and the fatigue of the last three nights made him shiver.

"We got them all," Wanke said.

"How about Devere?"

Wanke looked at his watch. "Chief Pitt's boys should have his place surrounded now."

At midnight Elle returned to the house and saw Frank asleep in the rocker. She fetched a blanket and spread it gently over his long exhausted frame and returned to Maria's children.

It was the sound of Hans's engine that wakened Crowe at five-thirty. He rubbed his eyes with his hands; he was confused, sleep-dazed, but rose instinctively. He washed his hands and face and ran his wet hand quickly over his sandy hair. He knew now where he was, and who he was, and found his felt hat on the hall table.

The morning air felt good and clean in his lungs as he swung himself into the seat of the truck.

"Take me to the newsstand and get over to Hoover's train. Hurry!"

The engine was already steaming as Hans drove along the length of the Presidential Special. Secret Service men surrounded the car and Crowe ordered one of them to tell the President that Frank Crowe wanted to see him.

The Secret Service man returned quickly and asked Crowe to follow him.

Frank, wearing the same clothes he had worn for three days and three nights, his beard stubbled, his eyes bloodshot, was almost staggered by the elegance of Hoover's car. He noticed the beautifully varnished mahogany, the mint green of the velour seats and couches, the shiny brass and crystal tulip lamps, the gleaming handrails, the blue carpeting with the presidential seal woven into the fabric.

Hoover, shaven, wore gray pants, a gray vest, an immaculate white shirt, and a small-patterned foulard tie. He was seated alone at a small table gleaming with white linen and well-polished silver. A rose stood proudly in a crystal bud vase.

"Good morning, Frank," Hoover said. "Sit down."

"Good morning, Mr. President," Frank answered, handing Hoover the morning paper and slumping into a plush chair across from him.

Hoover read the headlines of the paper:

AMBUSH DAM SABOTEURS
AT RAILWAY TRESTLE
One Killed
Asst. Supervisor Williams Injured

"This," said Frank, pointing at the paper, "is why I missed the party."

"Nonsense," Hoover joked. "You'll do anything not to wear a suit," but he was still reading the story; finally he put down the paper.

"Have you read this yet?"

"No sir. I rushed right over hoping to catch you."

Hoover signaled a waiter and told Frank to order breakfast.

"I'll just have some coffee," Frank said.

"Who is Devere?" Hoover asked.

"The local head of the Wobblies."

"Well, according to the paper, he got away."

"Son of a bitch," Frank said.

Hoover wiped his mouth with a napkin and looked at Frank. "I was up at five and toured the dam site. You should feel proud, Frank."

"Thank you, sir."

"How far ahead of schedule are you?"

"Fourteen months and three days. I can handle the dam, sir," Frank said almost pleadingly. "It's all that goddamn labor shit. I was trained as an engineer. I wasn't trained to fight a war."

Now Hoover rubbed his eyes. "I see your problems. Look at mine. I've lived with them for four years. There's something missing in the fiber of this generation. Everybody's looking for a handout. Nobody wants to roll up his shirt sleeves. Hard work and confidence would shake this depression."

"I know, sir," Frank said. "I shouldn't bother you with my troubles."

"Your troubles are my troubles, Frank. I've been all over this country. If Roosevelt wins, the commies will be right behind him."

An aide appeared at Hoover's side. "We are ready to depart, Mr. President."

"We are like hell."

Hoover stood quickly and surprised Frank with his statement: "I'd like to see Jack Williams before I leave."

"That is a graceful gesture," Frank said. "I don't have a limousine. Just a truck."

"Well, Frank, we've ridden trucks before around here, haven't we?"

"Yes sir."

A mess boy held Hoover's jacket and he slipped into it and proceeded briskly down the aisle of his car and stepped onto the platform.

"This is my driver, Mr. President, Hans Schroeder."

Hans could scarcely believe his eyes as Hoover sat next to him in Crowe's seat and the supervisor sat in the back.

"Let's go to the hospital," Frank said, but Hans sat frozen staring at the President of the United States.

"Move, boy," Crowe ordered, and Hoover laughed.

Maria was half asleep as a nurse opened the door to Jack Williams's room.

"You have a visitor," the nurse said as Maria and Jack looked at her. "The President of the United States."

"Oh, my God," Maria said, instinctively patting her hair and propping Jack up on a pillow.

Hoover walked into the room, followed by Frank.

"Well, Jack," Hoover said, "goofing off again, I see," and then he moved in Maria's direction and shook her hand.

Even voluble Jack Williams was stunned. "Mr. President," was all he was able to manage at first.

"I saw your tunnels this morning. They're magnificent."

"Thank you, sir."

"Are you in pain?"

"No sir."

"Well, take it easy until you're healed."

"Don't worry, Mr. President. I'll be up on Tuesday. I can vote with my left hand as well as my right."

Crowe laughed. "That's how you sign your name, isn't it?"

"How?" Williams asked.

"With an X."

"Well, boys, I can see the spirit hasn't gone out of you."

"We are very grateful for your visit," Maria said dutifully. "Our children will never forget your kindness."

"I thank all of you for the job *you* are doing. I've got to go. Unlike Mr. Crowe, I'm unfortunately always behind schedule."

Hans and Frank drove Hoover back to his train and watched it glide gracefully out of the Boulder City yard. They watched as the presidential seal at its rear grew smaller and smaller, and all Hans could manage was, "Jesus Christ, the President of the United States."

On Tuesday in Palo Alto, Herbert Hoover placed an X in the same spot as did Jack Williams and Frank Crowe, but those three votes were not sufficient. That night Hoover learned that he had been beaten mercilessly by the man with the well-chiseled face, the jaunty cigarette in a holder, and the warm and genuine smile, Franklin Delano Roosevelt.

55

A full-scale meeting of the Big Six was to be held in the lodge the day of Hoover's departure, but Elle prevailed on Roger Stein to schedule it for the following morning.

"Frank has been up three days and nights," she pleaded. "You've read the papers this morning."

"I have," Roger said, putting his arms around Elle's shoulders. "I'll postpone the meeting. Leave it to me."

"Anything to get your hands around a pretty girl," Francesca said, smiling.

"How is Jack Williams?" Stein asked.

"He's feeling better than Frank."

"You may be right," Francesca said. "I visited him an hour ago. There was a sign on his door. It read, 'No visitors except the President of the United States. Signed X.' "

For once, Frank was grateful for Elle's intervention. He showered and she massaged his back with liniment, and he barely made it to bed. He was sound asleep at two in the afternoon and felt grateful for the respite as Hans picked him up the following morning.

Everyone attended the meeting at Sequoia Lodge; even Barnes arrived at the "ungodly hour of seven," as he put it. The mess hall provided coffee and doughnuts and everyone cheered as Jack Williams entered the room, his arm in a sling, his hair obviously combed by Maria. It was parted on the wrong side.

Crowe unfolded maps and tacked them to the wall, but Mackenzie spoke up first.

"Frank, we've all read the papers from yesterday and there's no need to tell you we're grateful for the way you handled that crisis."

"Thank you," Frank said.

"We are also finally aware of the fact that labor *is* giving you more trouble than any of us had expected."

Stein spoke up. "Mackenzie is right and I'm at fault to a great extent. Until last night I figured the Wobblies to be a no-account ideology. I never put much stock in their militancy. Until now. Ed suggested Frank Berman come up here."

"From the FBI?" Crowe asked.

"Yes. Would you object to his presence at the dam site? We feel you've got your hands full enough."

"I would welcome him, but I'll give him no autonomy."

"Agreed," Mackenzie said. "Now what have you got for us?"

"Saturday morning, gentlemen, I shall turn Big Red into the tunnels. I hope you'll all be back for that. On this map I have drawn areas where you might want to observe, but I must ask you not to use your cars or limousines to reach the railroad bridge. I need that road clear for twenty-four hours for my equipment."

"And a little of mine," Walker Young said wryly.

"And a little of Walker Young's," Crowe added.

"And a little of mine," Barnes added, and everyone laughed except Frank.

"Jesus Christ," he yelled, "I've got no time for levity."

"Keep going, Frank," Roger Stein said.

"I'm sorry for the outburst," Frank said, and Jack Williams said, "What's levity?" and once more the room broke up in laughter.

"I have one more request," Frank added. "I shall announce a twenty-four-hour shift in the mess hall at noon. I ask your permission to give the men next Sunday off with pay."

"Granted," Old Man Donner said, without consulting his partners. No one objected and Crowe had Hans drive him to the mess hall.

56

At 11:30 A.M. on Thursday, Jack Williams set off two blasts to clear the temporary barriers which had been built in front of Tunnels 3 and 4 and at 5:30 Friday morning the battle began.

There were 180 trucks of every size and description poised to make their first pass over the trestle bridge. Anything and everything in Crowe's and Walker Young's inventory that could carry and dump a rock was stretched out on the road.

It was a cold clear morning, and the roar of all these engines could be heard and felt in Boulder City, seven miles away. Hans drove Crowe along the column of trucks back and forth, as he checked tires and listened to the sound of idling motors.

He was at the Nevada side of the bridge when he took out his watch. Five thirty-four, it read, and he closed its cover and replaced it in his pocket. He raised his arm, and like a train conductor, lowered it and the column was started. Williams was on the bridge supervising the dumping, Wanke controlled the flow of rock which replenished truck after truck.

The air was blue with exhaust and quickly turned brown as the trucks crossed the bridge one by one, backed against the side and slid off their cargo.

Forty trucks had already crossed the bridge when the column was stopped by one balking truck. Its engine was running but it did not move. Hans drove Crowe to the bottleneck and Crowe looked up at the driver of a five-ton mucking truck. He was a heavy man, tall and blue-eyed, his arms were muscular, his blond hair waved in the early-morning breeze.

293

"Move, you dumb Swede," Crowe yelled, "move!" but the man did not listen to Crowe. His hands poised on the wheel, he stared straight ahead.

"Move your ass," Crowe yelled, jumping out of his own truck and up to the cab of the stalled vehicle. He was face to face with the driver and started to curse once more, when he realized the man was dead, his hands frozen at the wheel.

"Jesus Christ," Crowe said, and yelled at Hans. "Get up here. This man is dead. Let's get him out of here."

It was an unpleasant task to pry the hands from the wooden steering wheel, and it was difficult to move the driver, his body rigid. Several young engineers arrived and helped extricate the body from the cab and place it in the back of Crowe's truck.

"Drive this truck," Crowe ordered Hans, and though the boy hated to touch that steering wheel, he obeyed, put the engine into gear, and the column began to roll once more.

Again Crowe drove to the head of the column and watched truck after truck dump its load of boulders.

After the first pass of 180 trucks and the second, the pattern was emerging. A truck was loaded on the Arizona side, the driver got into position and drove across the bridge to dump its load. He was again loaded at the Nevada side and followed the same pattern on his return trip.

Twenty of Crowe's best engineers directed the dumping. Crowe wanted an even pattern of rocks and boulders laid down.

Tanker trucks rode along the column refueling, and mechanics made quick repairs on overheated vehicles, replacing hoses and plugs and tires and batteries. Workers wearing white hard hats and white armbands and carrying white batons regulated the traffic, but little was spoken.

Crowe kept one eye on the endless column of trucks, another on the river. The first load and the second load were simply ignored by Big Red. When the noon whistle blew, the rock barrier was barely a foot above the height of the river. A slight spray emerged as the river played with the rocks like a child finding a new toy.

Ten trucks at a time swung off to a siding, where Anderson's boys were dispensing hot lunches and cups of coffee, and any man taking more than five minutes to eat heard the profanity of his foreman.

At times Crowe would jump up alongside a driver and jump off where Williams was stationed on the bridge. His arm still in a sling, his face turned upstream, he could offer little comfort to Crowe. "Like trying to fill a whore's cunt with a kid's dick," Williams said, and Crowe nodded.

294

"Just feels like we're dropping the boulders in a hole," Crowe said.

"I know," Williams added, "a hole that goes all the way to Colorado."

The parade continued. After eight hours, men swung gracefully in one side of a cab and the previous driver exited the other side; not one shift of gears was lost in the process. At four in the afternoon the barrier had risen to four feet, and the Colorado rippled; there were white water and foam as the river surmounted the wall of boulders. It was neither deterred nor perturbed. The river kept to its age-old path through Black Canyon.

Barnes watched, so did Chapman, so did Mackenzie, and so did Andrews. Walker Young and his boys from the Bureau watched, but as the sun set most of the brass returned to Sequoia Lodge. It was getting chilly. Dinner would be ready, the bourbon would be uncapped. Crowe knew what he was doing.

Night fell quickly and drivers had to adjust to the never-ending glare of headlights. At eight-thirty, one of Crowe's worst fears was realized. A driver had failed to set his brakes. He raised the tilt bed of his truck. The boulders slid smoothly into the river, but the truck followed the momentum of the boulders and fell off the bridge.

Crowe was at the spot in minutes, as was Williams. Crowe called for safety men, a crane, some stretcher bearers. The traffic men halted the column. There was silence; all one could hear was the muffled engines and the sound of the river, and everyone held his breath as a giant crane bit into the cab of the truck and raised it sufficiently for the stretcher bearers to extricate the driver.

The man was hurt but alive, and quickly carried to a waiting ambulance.

"You want to salvage the truck?" the crane operator asked Frank.

"Dump it," he said, "let's go." With a sickening crash the truck was cut loose, Crowe gave the signal, and the column began to move again.

"Your average is pretty good," Williams said. "I'd figured we'd lose four trucks by now."

Crowe nodded. "How high are we?"

"Five feet. Six on the Nevada end."

After a hearty dinner of roast beef and apple pie, some of the heads of the Big Six Companies returned to the bridge site. Slowly their eyes adjusted to the darkness as they watched the columns of trucks roll through the night, like giant fireflies, they heard the endless splash of boulders into the water, the whoosh of air brakes, the grinding of gears, the sound of the wooden ties on the bridge abused and re-abused by a never-ending cargo, and they watched the Colorado flowing below them still steadily, still strong, and even more menacing at night.

At one in the morning Hans brought Crowe a sandwich, a cup of coffee. "I've been relieved," he said, and Crowe nodded and ate in silence.

Wanke watched his stockpile of boulders. It was half gone by now, but he had backup dumps if he needed them. His radioman gave him estimates of the stock across the river. He was satisfied but impatient.

Dawn came slowly on Saturday. The dark canyon walls turned gray, then faintly orange as a weak sun rose over the horizon. Headlights were switched off, men rubbed their eyes, and Frank looked at the river.

His barrier was at nine feet now and the river was confused. It made it over some sections of the barrier and was stopped by others. A tide effect began, as Crowe knew it would, and the tops of the newly formed waves crested over the barrier defiantly. Crowe was all over the bridge, as was Williams, but they said nothing to each other. They felt a surge of new energy with approaching day, trucks moved more briskly, loads were dumped more efficiently, the battle was becoming a siege, and each man felt the challenge personally.

At eleven o'clock a lookout yelled the one sentence Crowe had waited for for over a year.

"She's taking it at 3."

Crowe jumped into his truck and reached the tunnel portal in no time. He watched as the river placidly entered the tunnel. Williams was soon behind him, and they stood silently side by side looking at that brown river entering the huge tunnel. They were struck like a Texas farmer hitting a gusher.

"She's taking it at 4," another lookout yelled minutes later, and Crowe and Williams drove to the Arizona side to watch the spectacle repeated.

It took two more hours to reach the crest of boulders at ten feet. The river had been stopped. Not even the spray from Big Red's disturbed waves crested the barrier.

Crowe gave the order, "Final run!"

At one-thirty the last truck had dumped its load and left the bridge for the last time. The last driver gave a thumbs-up to Crowe and Crowe returned the signal.

Frank could hear the men roaring to Boulder City. He could hear the hoopla and the yahoos and the yippees disappear around the canyon road. Men were heading for home and bed or Vegas or Aunt Mary's, men were heading for a bottle or the cool hand of a woman on a forehead.

At one-forty-four, Frank Crowe was standing alone on his bridge. He had just looked at his watch and his frame slumped over the railing as he stared at the river, now calmly flowing through Williams's tunnels.

Roger Stein and Elle and Francesca stood under a tree on the Arizona side. They had been there all night. Elle was tempted to run to her husband, but Roger stopped her.

"Leave him alone," he said gently. "This is between him and the river."

Finally the three of them watched Frank slowly walk across the bridge. He walked straighter, more gracefully than he had before this thirty-hour job.

Elle and Roger and Francesca walked toward him and Elle finally could not contain herself. She ran ahead of Roger and Francesca and flew into Frank's arms.

Frank scooped up the girl easily and held her close, he kissed her for every kiss she gave him, and finally Roger and Francesca reached the couple.

Frank put Elle down and shook Roger Stein's hand.

"Well, mister," Frank said. "We got this job done. Let's build ourselves a dam."

"Don't I get a kiss too?" Francesca said. "I've been standing here all night myself," and Frank kissed Francesca.

As they walked toward Crowe's truck, Roger Stein stopped and looked at Frank and Elle.

"Would you say that I was an interfering director of the Big Six?"

"No," Frank said. "No. I wish they were all like you."

"Well, Mr. Crowe, as your boss, I'm giving your first order."

"What's that?"

"I want you and Elle on that train tomorrow and I'll expect you as my guests at the Mark Hopkins Hotel at seven in the evening. I want you and Elle to have three days in our city. There'll be no argument."

It was Elle who now kissed Roger Stein, and Frank sat in the seat of his truck and took off his felt hat and threw it on the floor.

"I never disobeyed an order yet. San Francisco, here we come."

Roger Stein and Francesca watched Frank and Elle roar toward Boulder City, looking very young and very fit.

"That's quite a man," Francesca said.

"Yes, quite a man."

"Not Frank Crowe," Francesca said.

"Who?"

"Roger Stein."

57

San Francisco, its narrow-frontaged wood-framed homes cascading down nine steep hills toward one of the world's most beautiful natural harbors, has understandably produced a most chauvinistic citizenry. Despite the frequent fog, the freezing winds, the crowding caused by its peninsular location, nothing has deterred San Franciscans from loving the city. Despite its humble beginning as a town of miners, shippers, merchants, and rogues, it had from the onset a strong spine of elegance, much of this concentrated in the large mansions on Nob Hill and all of it now pinnacled by the magnificent new Mark Hopkins Hotel, which Roger Stein not only built but partly owned.

To say that Frank and Elle were awed by the four-story lobby, thickly carpeted, with wood-paneled walls and shining brass, is certainly an understatement, and the little bellboy who opened the door to their suite took rightful pride in showing them the large parlor with overstuffed Louis Quinze furniture. It was a moonlit night, the bay had a dark-blue iridescence, and the white, red, and green lights of the traffic upon it made it such a spectacular sight that Elle had to whisper to Frank to come and tip the boy.

On an octagonal table stood a silver bucket filled with ice and a bottle of French champagne, a bowl of fruit covered in cellophane was next to it, and a chaste card saying, "Welcome to our Fair City. Roger and Francesca Stein. We shall call you at ten in the morning."

Frank walked to the balcony and drank in the sights and the sounds. He could hear the bell of a locomotive, the shrill short whistles of tugboats, the long low blast of a steamer entering the Golden Gate.

Across the bay he could see the lights of Sausalito, Tiburon, Berkeley, and Oakland, and he filled his lungs with that good salt air.

Elle joined him after having unpacked, bearing two glasses of champagne.

Frank put his arms about her, feeling her nakedness under the thin cotton garments.

"You know," he said, "until this minute I didn't realize how much I've missed the sea. Just smell that air."

"It's beautiful," Elle said. "Look at that city, that bay."

"It's breathtaking," Frank said. "No wonder the boys from the Big Six rarely get to Boulder."

Elle raised her glass. "To the supervising engineer!"

"And his lovely wife," Frank said.

Frank looked at Elle and he kissed her gently, and then his eyes returned to the bay. "I've got to get to that water."

"I hope it can wait until tomorrow."

"If you have something better in mind." Frank smiled and Elle walked inside and slipped into bed.

"They're silk," she yelled.

"What's silk?"

"The sheets."

Frank changed into his freshly pressed pajamas. He filled their glasses once more and, holding the bottle, looked at Elle, her long hair spread over the pillow as elegantly as an Oriental flower arrangement, her figure outlined and softened by the silk sheets.

"Everything fits," Frank said. "You, the bed, the silk sheets, the champagne, except . . ."

"What?" Elle said.

"Me."

"Come here," Elle said, and Frank noticed that she was naked under the sheet.

Frank reached for the light switch, but Elle said, "Don't turn off the light. . . . This is too beautiful, I want to see it and feel it all."

They made love for an hour, perhaps longer, and Frank finally fell asleep sprawled sideways across the huge bed. Elle got up and filled her glass once more and returned to the balcony.

She stood naked on the sixteenth floor of the Mark Hopkins Hotel, her skin alabaster in the full moon, and she too stared at the city and the bay and was aware that other eyes from other rooms might well be staring at her. She did not care, perhaps she enjoyed it.

She awoke at seven and there was a note from Frank by her bedside. "Just ran to the bay. Be back soon. Love, The Maharajah."

Frank had reached the marina at 6:30 A.M. and watched a lovely dawn slowly color the water of the bay. There were rows and rows of gleaming yachts, power and sail. There were those whose brightwork shone, whose teak decks were well-calked, whose lines were properly coiled, whose gear was carefully covered with canvas, and there were others showing signs of neglect, abuse, or disuse.

Although there were yachts exceeding one hundred feet in length, some with beams of over sixteen feet, it was one boat that caught Frank's eye. She was a Friendship sloop: thirty feet long, her hull painted dark green, her teak decks as pale as the marrow of a man; even her spruce mast mirrored the early rays of the sun. There was a FOR SALE sign on the cabin door, and finally a maintenance man from the St. Francis Yacht Club came down the dock and walked toward him.

"Morning," Frank said.

"Good morning. Good day for sailing. Wind's up to ten knots already."

"You know about this boat?" Frank asked.

"The *Wind Song.* Sure."

"How much they asking for her?"

"A thousand dollars," the maintenance man said. "A lot of money. But she's a lot of boat."

"She's beautiful," Frank said.

"Yeah. Charlie Anson don't never let the varnish dry, always working on her."

"Why would he want to sell it?"

"Lost his job."

"Yes." Frank nodded. "Doesn't seem right."

The maintenance man laughed. "Guess it don't. You should listen to the boys at the club. Now that Roosevelt has won, they figure they're all gonna lose their boats."

Elle was dressed in a navy-blue suit when Frank returned. She was sitting on a small love seat in the parlor of their suite; a clean pair of white gloves lay next to her.

"Well, here's my meandering boy," she said.

"Guess what I saw? A real Friendship sloop. You should see the lines on her."

"What's wrong with *my* lines?"

"Nothing, why?"

"Did it ever occur to you, Frank Crowe, that we're on vacation?"

"Yes."

"We could have made love at dawn?"

"You want to?"

"It's not dawn. It's nine-thirty. You'd better get dressed. Francesca will be here in twenty-five minutes."

Frank was still tying his tie when Francesca phoned the room and told Elle she was in the lobby.

Roger Stein's wife drove a Packard and she drove it well. She dropped Frank off on Sansome Street, where Roger had his office. "We'll meet at Fisherman's Wharf at one. Roger will take you," she said to Frank before she and Elle drove toward Union Square.

Roger Stein's office was large but unostentatious. A simple bronze sign on the door said simply, MACKENZIE-STEIN, ENGINEERING, and the two floors of a brick office building held drafting rooms, accounting offices, mail rooms, and small glass-enclosed cubicles for senior personnel.

Once inside Stein's private office, Frank thanked Roger for his kindness and remarked that he had never slept in silk sheets before.

"I'll tell you something, Frank. Francesca and I have been married twenty-five years and we go to the hotel ourselves sometimes. Silk does something for women."

"It doesn't exactly hurt a man's libido either," Frank said.

"Well put. Well put," Roger said. "Sit down. Frank," Roger said. "This is your vacation. I don't want to talk business for one minute these few days. While the ladies are shopping, what will be your pleasure?"

"I have one piece of business," Frank said. "I've got to speak to Barnes. It's not about the dam. It's about his son."

"Why, was he injured?"

Frank hesitated, then said, "Not physically."

Roger looked puzzled, and said, "I'll get him on the phone. When would you like to see him?"

"At his convenience, and yours."

Stein left the office and Frank studied the framed pictures of Francesca, several sons and daughters, pictures of past construction, a wall full of degrees and awards.

Stein returned and said, "He'll see you now. His office is just around the corner. I'll pick you up at twelve-forty-five."

Frank looked at his watch. "I'm much obliged."

Barnes behind a massive desk, half hidden by the smoke of a massive cigar, motioned Frank to sit in a stuffed leather chair. He opened a humidor.

"Cigar?"

"No thank you."

"Brandy?"

"No, it's too early."

"Never too early," Barnes said, as he poured a generous measure from a cut-crystal decanter.

"What I have to say," Frank started, "is not too pleasant. You can believe me, I'd rather not be here."

"What's up?"

"Do you recall when I invited you to Sequoia Lodge?"

"Sure do. What a redhead. I can feel her lips now."

"I had you on the dam site for a reason."

"What reason?"

"I knew that your son was being used by the Wobblies. They were after information. The exact day I would turn the river. I gave it to him that night."

Barnes put down his glass. He looked hard at Crowe. *"Why* would *my* son be in with the Wobblies?"

"A girl," Frank said. "A girl that . . ."

Barnes held up his hand.

"Don't say any more." He puffed on his cigar and watched the smoke rise toward the ceiling.

"That cunt-hungry little bastard. Just like his old man."

Frank was uncomfortable and said nothing.

"So you came to tell me you're gonna fire him."

"That was my plan," Crowe said, "but Assistant Supervisor Wanke, you know him . . ."

"Yes."

"He has children. I don't . . ."

"Go on."

"He said, 'Tell Barnes that firing him, that clearing him out, won't help that boy.' "

"What will?" Barnes asked. "He's already raped one of the Andover girls."

"Wanke suggested he use another name, not yours, work a different part of the dam, live on what he makes, no car, no apartment in Vegas . . ."

Barnes now paced the floor of his office. Finally he turned to Frank.

"I appreciate what you told me, Frank. I really do. You should have fired the little prick and I couldn't have blamed you."

"He doesn't have it easy on the dam site with your name."

"I guess not. I never figured."

Suddenly Barnes became pensive and sat at the edge of his desk looking at Frank.

"You got no kids. That's smart. I got three. Never been close to them. These days the only time I'm happy is when I'm out of that house and under the sheets with another woman. The older I get, the less finicky I am.

"But the boy is there and he's got my blood, and you tell Wanke to put him on under another name. I'll do what you say. I owe you men a measure of thanks."

"We'll handle it," Crowe said, anxious to conclude this session.

"How about a brandy now?"

"Now," Crowe said, "will be just fine."

"I heard that Roosevelt might change the name of the dam."

"To what?" Crowe asked, astonished.

"Roosevelt."

"He can't. They named one after Teddy."

"I know. Maybe Lucy."

"Lucy? Who's that?"

"A lady he's friendly with."

"Franklin Roosevelt?"

"Yeah. Not bad for a cripple, eh? Beginning to like that son of a bitch better already."

58

After a merry luncheon at Fisherman's Wharf, a crisp salad, freshly cracked crab, loaves of French bread barely out of the oven, the Steins left Frank and Elle on their own, and they returned to the marina.

Rarely had Elle seen Frank so ecstatic over anything material as over the little Friendship sloop. He carefully pointed out the merits of its rigging, the placement of the tiller, the walkaround space of the deck, the coziness of its small cabin forward.

"How much is it?" Elle asked.

"One thousand dollars," Frank answered.

"Buy it!"

Frank laughed. "What would I do with it in Boulder City?"

"Come down to the city once a month and sail it."

Frank shook his head. "Foolish," he said. "Just foolish. That boat is like a woman. It needs care. Daily care. I couldn't leave that up to someone else."

Elle smiled. "The only one that stops you from owning that boat is yourself. Not me."

"I know."

"If you've decided against it, the only lines I can offer you are my own. I'm sure that bed is made up."

Frank looked up from the marina and saw the Mark Hopkins Hotel, its nineteen stories gleaming in the afternoon sun. He contemplated walking, then yelled "Taxi" at a passing cab.

"Mark Hopkins," Frank said casually as the driver started his vehicle, and Frank looked smug and a smile passed his lips. A few lines of fatigue seemed to have vanished from his face already.

Although Roger Stein chose not to live on Nob Hill, his mansion in Pacific Heights was still impressive. It was Italianate and its square design was pierced by a well-lit courtyard. Their taxi stopped under a glass porte-cochere, and a Chinese houseboy wearing dark pants and a well-pressed white jacket, bow tie, and white shirt escorted them to the living room, flower- and book-filled, with a hearty fire in a marble fireplace, a lovely view of the bay from a large window facing north.

Francesca, well coifed, wearing a long black silk dress, looked lovely descending a graceful marble staircase, followed by Roger.

"Sit down, sit down."

Roger walked to a small silver tray and began mixing drinks.

"To our dear guests," he said after he had finished, and everyone raised a glass.

"This is a lovely house," Elle said. "It is the loveliest house I've ever seen."

"It is," Francesa said. "Roger built it."

"Yes." Stein smiled. "You can thank the Oakland Sewer System for it. I have a manhole cover framed in my study."

Crowe laughed. As Elle and Francesca left to tour the upper three floors he said, "I cannot tell you, Roger, what a wonderful time we're having."

"That's good."

"It's also been unsettling."

"Don't tell me you miss work already?"

"No. No," Frank repeated. "We own a small but lovely home in Salt Lake City. Big trees. Good yard. I always thought I'd be content to end my days there. I never knew how much I loved the sea. Today I spotted a Friendship sloop in your marina. Absolutely bristol. I don't know whether I want to live in a landlocked community anymore."

Roger looked up while fixing a second drink. "Frank," he said, "when the dam is completed, you will be a very rich man. You can choose to live wherever you wish."

"I've been a working stiff all my life. I wouldn't know how to handle that kind of money. Would you help?"

Roger was startled by the question. He looked at Frank steadily. "I could and I would, but I won't."

"Why?"

"It is something I have promised Francesca. I'll help you any way I can, Frank, but not in money matters. We're Jewish. I think you understand that."

"I respect it," Frank said, "but I disagree. I take no stock in a man's religion."

304

"Let me ask you a very brutal question, Frank."

"Go ahead."

"No offense?"

"My word."

"Why are there no Negroes working on the dam?"

"We don't hire Negroes."

"Why not?"

"None apply."

"Why not?"

"They know they wouldn't get hired."

"That's right. Don't Negroes starve like whites?"

"I guess."

"Didn't Negroes fight in the war? Aren't there black veterans?"

"Sure."

"Isn't this supposed to be a democracy?"

"They couldn't stand the heat. The pressure."

"Why not? Isn't it hot in Africa?"

"You couldn't get a white man to work next to a black man. We'd have a riot in no time."

"Agreed. But is that right?"

"Perhaps not right, but it's reality."

"You say you like this house?"

Frank nodded his head.

"It's one of the most expensive houses in San Francisco. Half my workers on the Oakland Sewer System were black."

"How did you do it? No riots, no race trouble?"

"None."

"I can't believe it."

"I had a hell of a supervising engineer. John Washington."

"I've heard of him," Frank said. "He's very good."

"Yes," Stein said. "And he's black as the ace of spades."

"You should see this house," Elle said, returning with Francesca. "You should see the books. *Thousands* of them. When do I get my library in Boulder?"

"Enough, enough," Roger Stein said. "This is Frank and Elle's vacation. I've been filling Frank with social crap; you're putting pressure on him."

"Dinner is served," Francesca said, taking Frank by the arm.

They sat under a beautiful chandelier, and dinner revolved around pleasantries and irrelevancies, and before Frank and Elle left Roger took Frank aside.

"About investing your bonus, Frank, talk to Mackenzie. That Scotchman has a better Jewish head than mine."

Frank slept little that night and Elle sensed it. "Let's go outside," she suggested, and they both stood at the railing of the balcony facing the city and bay.

"I know one thing," Frank said. "I love you. I'm sure of that. I know I know my job. I'm sure of that too."

"Then what's bothering you? You're so restless."

Frank looked at Elle. He saw the concern in her eyes.

"I am basically an orderly man," Frank said. "I try to solve problems in an orderly manner. Most of my problems are equations. If you plot the right coordinates, the equation will come out. But these last few days, I don't know. I just don't know."

"What's bothering you, Frank?"

"Nothing serious, really. I think about some of the social questions Roger has raised, I think about this city, that little lovely boat, I think about our living in Salt Lake City. . . ."

"You're thinking about choices," Elle said.

"Yes. Exactly."

"When you finish this job you'll have lots of choices."

"I know, Roger pointed that out to me too."

"Does that bother you?"

"Yes, in a very odd way. I have never lived like that. Every move I've made has been carefully planned. I think the unknown frightens me."

Elle put her arm around her husband. "What can I do to help?"

Frank put his large hands around Elle's beautiful moonlit oval face. He spoke more to himself than to Elle.

"There is an evenness to your cheekbones. They are the right height and the right width, and your eyes are a beautiful blue, vital. There is so much peace in your face. So much peace."

Frank kissed her warmly, tenderly. "Just let me look at your face."

There were tears in Elle's eyes and she didn't know what to say or how to help, but she knew that this strong, self-reliant man was troubled and it troubled her to see him like this.

"Where did you come from, Elle?" he said, almost reverently. "Where did you come from?"

He was restless on the entire train ride back to Las Vegas and genuinely happy to see Hans at the station. The boy had even brought his old hat, and Elle laughed as Frank ripped his necktie off.

"Here," he said, handing it to her. "Make some pen wipers out of it."

59

The headquarters of the IWW were in Chicago, a two-story red-brick building near the slaughterhouse district, whose disrepair, perhaps studied, well exemplified the purpose and militancy of its occupants.

Devere sat uncomfortably across the desk from Warner Strong, graying, in his fifties, still trim, his black eyes very alive. Devere handed Strong a worn canvas bag containing money, a black ledger accounting for spent funds.

Strong picked up the bag, felt its contents, and let it drop on the desk.

"Well," he said sternly, "I don't know what's left in here, but all the money we've spent at Hoover has been a waste. You fucked up the whole job." He looked at Devere, who said nothing.

"You fucked up because you forgot everything you've been taught."

"Such as?" Devere asked.

"I'm not going to chronicle it all now," Strong said. "I don't think you're a revolutionary at all, Devere. I think you're just a killer."

"We had it all down pat," Devere said.

"Sure, you had it all down pat. You put all your eggs in one basket."

"If that bridge had been blown, I would have *finished* Crowe."

Strong stood. His large frame towered over the seated Devere.

"You *didn't* blow the bridge. You blew seven of our guys into the penitentiary and the eighth to hell."

"I didn't know he had my gun."

"*That* was your first mistake. Now every one of those seven boys will face a rap for attempted murder. Your biggest mistake, however, was that you misjudged Crowe."

"That son of a bitch," Devere said.

"Sure, that son of a bitch. You thought you had the perfect day to pull that job. The day Hoover visited the dam."

"Well?" Devere said.

"If I were Crowe, I would have figured the same as you. The *perfect day.*"

"How did I know Crowe knew my plans?"

"In the first place," Strong said, "you stole forty sticks of dynamite. That was stupid."

"They used one hundred thousand sticks a day when they were tunneling. How could they miss forty lousy sticks?"

"The stuff was color-coded. Williams knew about every single stick in his arsenal."

"Well, you didn't send me any dynamite."

"I never figured you needed it."

"Look," Devere, now angry himself, said loudly, "there is only one way to stop Crowe."

"How?"

"With the river."

"You're right. But you didn't stop him."

"Not yet."

"Well," Strong mocked, "that river is flowing gently through Crowe's tunnels. How you gonna stop him now?"

"There are several ways."

"Go ahead. Tell me."

"He'll be building his cofferdams next. If the upper cofferdam fails, he'll never unwater the dam site, and he'll never pour a bucket of concrete."

"And how, Mr. Devere, do you propose to stop a cofferdam? I've seen the plans. It's a hundred feet high, earth and rock covered, with a six-inch concrete face. It would take all the dynamite in Nevada to blow it up."

"You don't have to blow up the whole dam. All you need is a good leak. The river will do the rest."

"*The river*, mister," Strong shouted, "*is flowing through the tunnels!*"

"That's right. It is now."

"What do you mean, it is now?"

"Tunnels can be plugged."

"How?"

"Dynamite."

"Dynamite. Dynamite. Jesus Christ. That's all you can think about. You were having some success in the Nevada tunnels. You followed the rules. Trucks broke down, air lines ruptured, cave-ins occurred, power went off. You're fighting a battle, Devere, not a war."

"With Crowe it's a war," Devere answered. "Everything's on his side. His spies, his guards, the federal boys, the Vegas police chief. There is no law on that dam site outside of Crowe."

"Are you trying to tell me that the odds are in favor of the capitalists? Jesus Christ, what do you think this struggle is all about? Just look at the Rouge. Do you want me to give up because Henry Ford has everything on his side? Of course he has. He's got the money. He owns the cops, and his boy Bennett has got a force larger than the U.S. Army. Does that stop me?"

"And how are you doing at the Rouge?"

"I don't have to answer to you, Devere. I'm just figuring whether to set you out to pasture."

"I made out a list of proposals," Devere said, taking a paper out of his coat pocket and handing it to Strong.

"Take it or leave it," he said, almost pathetically. "I can go on relief like the rest of the country."

"They don't give you whiskey money on relief," Strong said.

Warner Strong seated himself behind the desk and looked at Devere's list, then shoved it aside.

"Do you ever *feel* anything anymore, Devere?"

"What do you mean?"

"You killed two boys in Boulder with your fucking gun. Schroeder and Sinsky. You feel nothing?"

"Nothing," Devere said. "Nothing for nearly fifteen years."

Strong stared at Devere's groin.

"Do you still draw?"

"Not really."

"Too bad. You used to be a good artist."

"Thanks," Devere said.

"All right," Strong said. "I'm not going to ask for your card." He picked up Devere's list. "Some of this stuff is good. It might work. I'm going to send you back to Vegas. Only you ain't gonna be in charge."

"Who is?"

"Levy."

"The Jew lawyer."

"Yes. Levy, the Jew lawyer, and you call him a Jew once more and you *will* be out of a job."

"So that rat came right back to you."

"That 'rat,' Devere, was educated by the IWW. He came here to tell me you were fucking up. That was his job. Now you can join him in Vegas or you can get out of my sight."

"I got no choice. I'll go back to Vegas."

Devere passed Levy entering Strong's office as he left.

Levy sat down and Strong held up Devere's list. "He's down," Strong said, "but he isn't out. Better look this stuff over. I'll be sending him to Vegas in a few weeks."

"Does he know his role?" Levy asked.

Strong nodded. "He knows. If he doesn't stay in line, can him."

60

Black Canyon, that forbidding gorge chosen as the most feasible in which to build the dam, consisted of two sheer rock walls, 800 feet high, with a maximum width at the river level of 370 feet and a maximum width of 970 feet at the top of the gorge. It was both the geologic soundness of the rock and the narrowness of the gorge that made the site ideal for the dam, but its narrowness, its absolute confinement, made Crowe's work extremely difficult.

Now that the river was turned, he would have to build his cofferdams and get to bedrock in the unwatered site. The Bureau of Reclamation had projected an excavation of 100 feet to remove the silt and sand and loose rock deposited by the Colorado for eons. The specifications for the upstream cofferdam called for a height of 98 feet, a base thickness of 750 feet, and a length of 450 feet.

To accomplish these two diverse and immense jobs of engineering simultaneously took inordinate precision, for all that was available to Crowe was narrow winding roads, trackage so convoluted that even the Union Pacific refused to operate it, rolling stock and trucks which had to operate at peak efficiency around the clock.

It was the lack of room that gave Crowe his challenge. The area was only a quarter of a mile across. The closest site for Wanke's mixing plant was 4,000 feet upstream; aggregates for the concrete were dredged out of the river five miles upstream, transported by rail seven miles to a sorting and washing plant, and finally stored five miles from the dam site and the mixers. Structural steel and lumber were stored in Boulder City seven miles away; even the closest disposal area for canyon excavation was two miles away.

To accomplish all his goals, Crowe now had 5,000 men working three shifts. He had a fleet of trucks, trailers, power shovels, and tractors. He had 13 locomotives and 150 pieces of rolling stock. He had 10 cableways.

Daily he removed 22,000 cubic yards of muck and rock from the river bed, transported it by truck to a waiting train headed for the dam site, a train which would return with rock which filled another

310

column of trucks, dumping 120 loads an hour on the upper cofferdam, a load every 30 seconds, 24 hours a day.

As the cofferdam rose, the river bed was lowered, and it was all performed on those narrow winding roads, with those tortuous railbeds, and it was done with a precision marred only by collisions and rock slides and rainstorms and equipment failures.

Inside the canyon walls Jack Williams was blasting out the penstock tunnels. These would carry water for power production later. Upriver, men were building the foundations for the intake towers. Black Canyon was being attacked from all sides, and from its very core, and though each worker had for the most part a very simple or repetitive job— a run from Hemenway Wash to the canyon, driving a tractor along the cofferdam, loading a freight car, running a cableway—the aggregate of 5,000 such jobs called for orchestration which filled each wall in Frank's office with constantly changing data and graphs, and brought in a steady parade of young engineers, constantly redrawing, refiguring, revaluating these data, recording and projecting the massive construction taking place outside their doorstep.

And all of it not only made Frank think in three dimensions, trying hard to stay ahead of each disaster, but made him wish for Ouija boards, stargazers, voodoo, or magic, anything which would help him with his tables of probability.

61

Hoover did not invite Roosevelt to the traditional dinner at the White House the last night of his tenure, and spoke not one word to him during their long ride down Pennsylvania Avenue to the inaugural stand. At first Roosevelt tried small talk but finally gave up and took off his top hat and waved it at the crowds and bestowed his great smile.

Hoover found no relief listening to one of Roosevelt's finest speeches, in which he declared to the nation that it had nothing to fear but fear itself. And Hoover's greatest apprehensions about his successor were realized when Roosevelt received the most tumultuous applause for his proclamation that if Congress failed to provide adequate remedies for the depression, he would ask for "broad executive power to wage a war against the emergency as great as the power that would be given to me if we were in fact invaded by a foreign foe."

To Hoover this smacked of dictatorship, and he hurried to Union Station to depart. The last ignominy was the dismissal of the Secret Service protecting Hoover before he left Washington. It was Roosevelt's way of saying that the man who had for four years failed to protect his fellow Americans was hardly worthy of protection for himself. As Hoover, weary from the long day, leaned back in the velour of his seat, he recalled one of his own statements made not too long before, "Democracy is not a polite employer."

Hoover's fear of Roosevelt's dictatorial direction, his paranoia about change, even caused him to speculate about the coincidence that on March 5, the day after Roosevelt's inauguration, Hitler came to power. On February 27, the Reichstag had burned in Berlin and Hitler fanned those flames into victory, blaming the fire on Communists, Jews, and the Versailles treaty.

When Roosevelt, as one of his first acts as President, declared a four-day bank holiday making good his threat that the "unscrupulous money changers must be driven from the temple," Hoover likened the act to the burning of the Reichstag, but the country was in no mood to go along with Hoover anymore. Will Rogers turned Hoover's bitter remarks and said, "If Roosevelt burned down the Capitol, we would cheer and say, 'Well, we at least got a fire started anyway.'"

Although Frank was supervising engineer of the dam, he had to deal with other collateral supervisory personnel. There was Walker Young for the Bureau of Reclamation, but Frank's rapport with him had been tested on other dams. And there was Andell, head engineer of Babcock & Wilcox of Barberton, Ohio, who was overseeing his $11 million contract with the government.

Andell, a tall white-haired man, lean and short-tempered, was responsible for the shipment of 29 million pounds of plates and structural shapes requiring 1,000 flat cars. With this raw material he built almost endless miles of pipe from 6-inch to 30-foot monsters.

When Andell's steel-fabricating plant was finished upstream from the dam site, he gave Crowe a tour of his facility and Frank was impressed.

After the inspection, Frank sat in Andell's office, almost as austere as his own.

"Well, Andell," Crowe said, "I've got to admit that's quite a plant."

"Glad you think so. They told me you were a fast worker and I said, 'If the man needs his steel, I'll have it for him in the warehouse.' "

"It looks to me that you're ready," Crowe said. "What about security?"

"What do you mean?"

"You probably heard about the railroad bridge?"

"I did."

"Well, we foiled the Wobblies there, but they're not finished with us. I've been trying to outguess the bastards all along. I don't know where they'll strike next."

"We've had a lot of trouble in our plant in Barberton," Andell said. "My boys have been handpicked. I've seen them shove a white-hot steel bar right up a Wobbly ass. Not a pretty sight."

"I don't expect that kind of trouble," Frank said. "I don't think they'll try violence so soon again. But there are other ways to stop us, like sabotaging the manufacture of your steel."

"Perhaps there's something I have not shown you," Andell said. "Come with me."

They walked through the length of the steel plant and entered a large barren room containing a fourteen-foot piece of equipment.

"What's this?" Frank asked.

"An x ray machine."

"Jesus Christ," Frank exclaimed.

"Yup." Andell laughed. "I'm going to x-ray every piece of steel going into your dam."

"I've never seen one this big."

"You bet you haven't. It's the biggest in the world, and I expect your confidence. My company is the only one that owns one."

Frank liked Andell, and asked him to the Reno Club, where both men ate the usual hearty steaks and drank a goodly amount of bourbon. Finally Frank broached the subject which concerned him most.

"I'm almost finished with the longest cofferdams ever built. I think they'll take everything the river throws at us this summer—the tunnels and the cofferdams."

"They look pretty good to me," Andell said.

"But there'll come a day, maybe sooner than you think, when you'll put those gates on those tunnels."

"That's right," Andell said. "My specs call for a 2,400,000-pound gate."

"Will the gates hold?"

Andell rubbed his eyes and looked at Crowe. "I use the same careful tolerances on my steel as you use on your cofferdams."

"That makes me feel good."

"I'll tell you something you might not know."

"What's that?"

313

"I studied at Vermont, like you. Only I got out ahead of you."

"I'll drink to that," Crowe said.

"Tell me something, Crowe, what worries you the most, the Wobblies or the river?"

Frank, somewhat drunk, looked at his fellow engineer. "The river, Mr. Andell. That fucking river."

62

The following morning Frank was surprised by Mackenzie, Stein, and Barnes in his office.

"I must be seeing things," Frank said. "You boys must have been up all night. . . ."

"This isn't a social call," Barnes said, "although I would appreciate a chair."

Crowe opened the door to his outer office and asked one of his young engineers to borrow four chairs from the lady typists.

When all four men were finally seated, Mackenzie spoke up.

"I know," he said, "that from your vantage point the directors of the Big Six seem simply to be shuffling between our offices and Sam's Restaurant."

"Only *sometimes* do I feel that way," Crowe said.

"Well, we *do* have things to worry about, and last year you almost didn't get your river into those tunnels."

"Why?"

"Because the U.S. government and your friend Hoover decided to curtail government expenditures and cut our appropriation from ten million to six for the year. You would have lost nine hundred men on the dam."

"What did you do?"

"We sent Ed Chapman. He knows more people in Washington than all of us put together. A summer relief bill gave us all the money we needed."

"Why didn't you tell me?"

"We figured you had enough to worry about."

"Well, I appreciate your concern. But why *this* meeting?"

314

"Well," Mackenzie said, "we might have worked ourselves into a trap. Now that we're so far ahead of schedule, we've heard rumors that Ickes wants to channel some of the money to other projects."

"He can't," Frank said. "I've almost got the cofferdams finished. He can't stop us at this point."

"He *can* do anything," Barnes said.

"So why didn't you boys keep this stuff to yourself this time?"

"Well," Roger Stein said, "we *have* learned something which we know will disturb you."

"What's that?"

"Ickes is changing the name from Hoover Dam to Boulder Dam. We know how you feel about Hoover."

"The son of a bitch," Frank said viciously.

"Look, Frank," Roger said calmly, "what's done is done. The good old days in Washington are gone. You don't have to like it, but you'll have to accept it. We don't want this appropriation cut again."

"The gutless bastards," Frank said. "I rode down this river with Hoover ten years ago. If it weren't for him, we'd never have built this dam."

"To the victor belong the spoils," Barnes said, "so accept it gracefully, Frank."

"Too bad he couldn't call it Roosevelt."

"Yeah, his cousin beat him to it."

"They should have called it Colorado Dam," Mackenzie offered. "At least that's what we're damming."

"Let's hope we are," Barnes said, now standing. "Where have you got my son working, Frank?" he asked after the others had left.

"The print shop."

"What name did you give him?"

"John Bailey. I'd suggest you send for him or he'll have the same old troubles if his old man visits him."

"You're probably right."

"John Bailey at Boulder Dam," Frank said. "Shit. I should have stayed at sea."

"I know how you feel," Barnes said sympathetically. "There are times I wish I weren't this old. I'd like to join the navy myself."

"There," Frank said, "use my phone." Outside his office, Frank asked one of his engineers to remove those goddamned chairs after Barnes had left.

63

Frank had given Elle space for the Boulder City library in the basement of the Big Six administration building, and the use of two carpenters, who fashioned bookcases and tables and chairs for the austere room. But this bleakness soon vanished as case after case of books arrived and Elle and her volunteer helpers unwrapped each donation like a Christmas present.

Nightly Elle would expound on the heavy usage of the facility, and one evening told Frank that even Hans had shown up.

"He made a rather unusual request," she said.

"What's that?"

"He was quite sheepish, but finally when no one else was around my desk he said, 'I want some books so I can learn how to talk like the chief.' "

Frank laughed. "A lot of those words aren't in the dictionary."

"It's the others that he is interested in. I'm sure he *knows* the ones you're referring to. Have you ever wondered what will happen to Hans when this dam is finished?"

"I honestly haven't. He'll make out all right. He's a bright kid."

"Exactly. Wouldn't it be nice if you took some interest?"

"We don't have a lot of time for conversation during the day."

"Take some," Elle said.

Frank said "Yes," but she knew his mind was on other things.

The following morning he met with Wanke and Williams.

"I had a visit with Barnes and Mackenzie and Stein," Frank said. "The news wasn't very encouraging."

"What now?" Williams asked.

"They are afraid the new government might cut our appropriations. We're too far ahead."

"Son of a bitch," Williams said. "We got a penalty clause if we don't finish on time and now they're trying to penalize us for being ahead of schedule.

"What the hell are we going to do with all those men? I thought this administration wanted higher employment."

"I want a contingency report from both of you," Frank said. "I want to document to the government the *cost* of stopping or slowing the dam at this point."

Wanke paced the floor, and finally faced Frank. "How long do you expect your cofferdams to take?"

"Twenty-six days," Frank said. "Why?"

"That's twenty-six days that they could stop us. Once we start pouring the dam itself, there's *no* way to stop us."

"That's true," Frank said.

"I can give you some men," Wanke said.

"I could use them."

"How about a hundred?"

"That would take five days off completion."

Williams offered one hundred men himself. "My boys will be so glad to come out of the hole you'll never get them back in."

"That will take ten days off the cofferdam completion."

"Leaving us sixteen days," Wanke said.

"Sixteen days," Frank repeated. "I wonder how busy they are in Washington at this minute."

"They're plenty busy," Williams said. "I read that Harry Hopkins feller set up shop in the hallways. Said he didn't have time for the carpet layer. Men needed jobs."

"I read that too," Frank said. "Maybe we're worried about nothing."

"You two guys are the only ones worried," Wanke said dryly. "I voted for Roosevelt. Remember?"

"Yeah, well, you were always a little odd," Williams said.

"All right," Frank said, "we've got no time to argue politics. I'll get that cofferdam finished ahead of schedule. Next question: the reds."

Williams drew a piece of paper from his back pocket.

"Here," he said, handing it to Frank.

Frank looked at the document. It was a suit for damages against the Big Six Companies for $76,343 filed by L. F. Mulligan. Frank read aloud for Wanke's benefit. "Mr. Mulligan claims permanent disability resulting from exposure to carbon monoxide gas while working in the tunnels. He claims dizziness, headaches, edema of the brain, heart spells. . . ." Frank's voice trailed off.

"If I find the son of a bitch," Williams said bitterly, "he can add two broken legs, a broken nose, and a boxful of teeth to his complaints."

"Wait, Jack," Frank said. "Did you notice who the attorney is on this case?"

"No."

"Levy."

"Some Jew bastard," Williams said.

317

"Not some Jew bastard," Frank corrected. "Levy is the Wobbly attorney."

"Very clever," Wanke said. "If the dynamite won't work, try the courts."

"Exactly. This won't be the last suit."

"Well, you know the judges around here," Williams said. "We've been delivering enough booze and broads to them."

"This is a *federal* court," Frank said emphatically. "Those boys are appointed for life. You can't fuck with them; besides, those do-gooders in Washington will watch this case like a hawk."

Wanke looked at Williams. "How much merit in a complaint like this?"

"None."

"How can you be so sure?"

"I've inhaled more carbon monoxide than any stiff in my tunnels, and I could beat the shit out of any man in there."

"Looks like we've got a good witness for the defense," Frank said.

"Sure, but if those bastards are going to start suing one by one, I'll be spending my days in the courthouse instead of the tunnels."

"Just let me find Mr. Mulligan, Frank. When my boys finish him up, the second stiff is gonna think twice before filing suit."

Frank scratched his head, then looked at Williams. "Locate the bastard," Frank said, "but don't touch him. Keep your eye on him. I'll talk to the Big Six lawyers. That's an order." Then, turning to Wanke, "Well, Tom, you still proud to be in the liberal column?"

"I'm a Democrat," Wanke said. "I'm not a liberal, and not a red. There's no validity in bringing them all together."

"We'll see," Frank said. "We'll see. And you read where Roosevelt appointed Madam Perkins Secretary of Labor? A woman."

"So what?" Wanke said. "Do you think all women are liberals or reds? Do you think your wife is a red?"

"Meaning no disrespect," Williams said, "I think women are good for one thing only, and you know what that is."

The meeting was over and Frank was left alone and confused, and confusion angered him greatly. it was the next thing to stupidity.

64

It had taken Frank Crowe less than eight months to throw up his monstrous cofferdams and get to bedrock on the dam site. Six hundred thousand cubic yards of gravel and 100,000 cubic yards of sand and silt had been removed from the former Colorado river bed, and tens of thousands of tons of rock and earth and sand had built the cofferdams, their upstream face carefully covered with six inches of concrete like the frosting of a birthday cake.

It was a Sunday, June 4, and the heat was rising as fast as the Colorado, swelling from its tributaries. On Tuesday the boys from the Big Six would come up to witness the first pouring of concrete of the actual dam itself, but today Frank drove Elle to the site alone, and unrolled a very elaborate plan which had absorbed him for months on end in his study.

"Do you see those carpenters working on the canyon floor?"

"Yes," Elle said, "barely."

"That's over eight hundred feet down. They're building the first wooden form, fifty feet by sixty feet by five feet deep. That's how this dam will be poured. Those forms have a quarter-inch tolerance, which is better than the furniture from Monkey Ward."

Frank spread out his plan and Elle could see the ultimate shape of the dam, but also a very intricate system of numbered grids.

"When the dam is finished," he said, "it will all look like one solid mass of concrete, sculptured and awesome and graceful and beautiful."

Elle weighed his carefully chosen words.

"But," he continued, "it will not be poured like filling a cake tin with batter. It will be formed by 260 columns like 260 skyscrapers, interlocked vertically and horizontally and finally joined by grouting under pressure."

"Why does it have to be so complicated?" Elle asked.

"You see those buckets on those railroad cars? Each one of them holds eight cubic yards of concrete. I've got to pour 3,240,871 cubic yards, to be exact. To cool that much concrete would take several hundred years, which is longer than I care to wait for my bonus."

Frank smiled and continued. "Each form, like the one being built below, will be ringed with one-inch copper pipes and I'll cool it with ice water before I pour the next rise. I will have hundreds of heat sensors all over this dam. There'll be no mystery about the setting time."

Elle stared at the site and at the plans and at her husband.

"I'm certain," Frank said, "that you've heard countless people tell you that I'll never pour this dam as quickly as I intend to."

"I have," Elle said.

"Well, now," Frank said, "with all due modesty you'll understand why *I'm* building this dam. No one has ever cooled concrete in this fashion, nobody has ever tried it."

"You mean this is *your* idea?"

"Yes, it is."

Elle looked steadily at her husband. "Can I ask you a wifely question?"

"Go ahead."

"Will it work?"

"I am certain of the engineering, that's all."

"What is it that worries you?"

"The river. The river first. The reds, and Roosevelt."

"Three R's," Elle said.

"You're right. Three R's."

"I could add a fourth," Elle said. "Rest."

"There won't be much time for that, honey. We've got to pour concrete for years. Each layer before the previous one sets. We've got to pour and pour, twenty-four hours a day, until we're finished."

"Today is Sunday," Elle said. "You're not going to pour today."

"That's right."

Before Frank went to sleep he said to Elle, "You could add a fifth R to the list."

"What's that?"

"Romp."

Tuesday, June 6, 1933, was a historic day on the dam site. The first bucket of concrete would be poured, which represented the actual construction of the dam itself, and though Frank could appreciate the symbolism of the event and the celebration of the fact that he had come this far in so short a time, he had little interest in the officials, the heads of the Big Six, the government people who stood at a prudent distance from the wooden form both to witness it and have their picture taken.

Frank was not with them. He sat next to Charlie Bornstein in the control room of Cableway Number 4, his watch in his hand, his clipboard on his knee.

Wanke's mud was ready for Bornstein; three huge gleaming buckets festooned with red, white, and blue ribbon were poised on the track behind the cableway.

Frank looked at his watch and gave the signal. It was eight o'clock in the morning. A stiff-legged derrick gingerly picked up the bucket and brought it beneath the cableway. Bornstein, the chief operator, faced six steel levers, each a foot and a half long, the metal as shiny as a silver tray from Tiffany's. An array of gauges, white lettering on black, was at his left; a canted window gave him a view of the dam site. He sat on a metal tractor seat, an improvised pillow cushioning its perforated steel.

Behind the control room, whose ceiling was cooled by a piece of wet canvas as Stubbs had suggested, was the cable tower, filled with immense drums which played out and retrieved the massive three-inch steel cable which spanned the gorge. Below these cables ran the carriage which transported the concrete buckets.

Three men were involved in the operation: the hoist man in the control tower, a skip tender whose signals controlled the acceleration and deceleration of the load, and a signalman located in a lookout station perched on the edge of the canyon rim. The skip tender was the vital cog in the operation, since his instructions to the signalman and hoist operator were vital to the efficacy of the operation.

Frank listened to the radio of the skip tender, watched the first bucket traveling across the canyon until it reached the spot above the form, and then followed with his eyes the bucket as it descended eight hundred feet below. In the form two operators pulled a lever and quickly jumped aside. Eight tons of concrete, the *first* eight tons of concrete for Boulder Dam, had been poured.

"Right on the button," Frank said.

"Thank you," Bornstein said, but Frank was not finished. It had taken eight minutes for the bucket to leave the Nevada side until it reached the canyon floor on the Arizona side.

"These cables," Frank said, "are designed to carry your buckets twelve hundred feet per minute horizontally and three hundred feet per minute vertically. You should have reached that form in three and a half minutes instead of eight."

"Maybe that's true," Bornstein said. "But this is the first bucket and they got all that brass below me."

"To hell with the brass. From now on you and your boys will drop those buckets like cue balls in a corner pocket. Even if Jesus Christ emerges out of those forms, *dump*. Do you understand?"

"Yes sir."

Frank left the control tower and jumped into his truck. He closed the cover of his watch and said to Hans, "Well, let's go down to the brass. I hope none of them got any mud on their duds."

Assistant Secretary of the Interior Foster, a representative of Harold Ickes, a tall elegantly-dressed gray-haired man in his early sixties, shook Crowe's hand when he arrived at the dam site.

"The secretary," Foster said, "sends his congratulations and apologizes for his absence."

"Yes," Frank said, "he must be a very busy man changing names of government projects."

Stein, suspecting trouble between the two men, thrust himself between them and said to Foster, "I hope you'll join us for drinks, Mr. Secretary. We make the best martinis in the West."

"I shall be delighted."

Frank left the two men and walked to the form, where other buckets of concrete came down from the "sky hook," as the puddlers referred to it.

There were nine men in the concrete form during the pouring. Two of them were responsible for the unloading of the bucket while the others puddled and tamped the moist concrete. As soon as the first form was filled, plumbers stood by to ring it with fourteen-gauge, one-inch copper tubing, which at first circulated air-cooled water and finally refrigerated water from the enormous ammonia cooling plant which had been built downstream.

The sun was setting when Frank and Tom Wanke walked back to his office.

"Well, shall we join the boys at the lodge for a drink?" Frank asked.

"Why not?"

The party was noisy and drunken when Frank arrived at Sequoia Lodge, and one by one the directors of the Big Six managed to put their arms around Frank, offered to get him a drink; but Frank maneuvered his way toward Foster.

"Well, how are things in Washington, Mr. Foster?" Frank asked.

"Hectic."

"How so?"

"There are so many bureaus springing up, people are forever going to the wrong office."

"So I've heard."

"We've cut unemployment by two percent already."

"Just hiring in Washington, D.C., I suppose."

"No sir. Perhaps you don't get the papers up here but since March we've passed the Emergency Banking Act, the Economy Act, the Federal Emergency Relief Act, the Agricultural Adjustment Act, the Farm Mortgage Act. . . ." Foster stared at Crowe and continued, "We've created the TVA Act, the CCC, the National Industrial Recovery Act.

. . . We're regulating the stock market, the railroads, we've gone off the gold standard. . . ."

"I'll agree you've been busy," Frank said. "Do you think you're moving in the right direction?"

"We're moving," Foster said. "That's more than Hoover could ever claim."

Foster's speech reflected a meticulous education and his gray-blue eyes looked imperturbable. "Mr. Ickes told me before I left that I could expect antagonism from you, sir. He said that you and Hoover had been very close."

"That's true," Frank said. "Herbert Hoover is a great man."

"It is not our intention to belittle Mr. Hoover. Roosevelt has better things to do. You should spend a little time in Washington. I think you'd find it exciting."

"I've got enough excitement right here. How did you end up there?"

"I am by trade a physicist, Mr. Crowe, and I arrived at my post in Washington for two reasons: one, my stewardship as president of Princeton gave me a certain reputation for leadership, but foremost, I happen to believe in Mr. Roosevelt's philosophy."

"And what is that, exactly?"

"Well, unlike Hoover, Roosevelt does not believe that he can stop unemployment by telling Americans to roll up their sleeves and go to work. They can roll their sleeves up to their armpits, if there are no jobs, there are no jobs."

"And where do *you* find the jobs that Hoover couldn't?"

"We *create* them. Public works, for the most part, the CCC, farm subsidies, small business loans, scholarships. Maybe we can even make engineers out of some of your laborers."

"The great benign government."

"No, Mr. Crowe, not the great benign government. A government with vision, with a conscience, a government with eyes, and ears, and a nose. Do you realize Hoover rarely stepped out of the White House?"

"And what is to prevent all this largesse from turning democracy into a socialistic state?"

Foster looked at Frank. "That's rather a worn shibboleth, wouldn't you say?"

"Not in my book."

"Workingmen have dignity, workingmen pay taxes, they come out of the breadlines, and out of the hobo camps. The greatest breeding ground for Communists is stagnant men."

"A point," Crowe said almost grudgingly.

"The great immutable Hoover and his dear friends the Mellons, the Fords, the Carnegies, all played into the Communists' hands."

"While Roosevelt cruises on Astor's *Nourmahal*," Frank said.

"Ah," Foster said, "you have been watching." He put down his glass. "You have to understand that Roosevelt is a very complicated man. He *is* to the manner born. He is very much the squire of Hyde Park, but his social instincts are also very correct. He works eighteen hours a day, seven days a week, as does his staff, but when he plays, he'll play on Astor's yacht. He likes a good pheasant and he knows the vintage of a good champagne."

"It will be interesting to see Roosevelt's vision through those champagne bubbles," Crowe said.

"Mr. Hoover viewed the country through the well-cut prisms of Waterford crystal; no matter how you turned it, the view was distorted. . . ."

"What an elegant disciple," Elle said, joining Foster and Frank.

"This," Frank said, kissing Elle, "is Mr. Foster. My wife, Mrs. Crowe."

Foster bent slightly and extended his hand. "It is indeed a pleasure to meet you." Then, turning to Frank, he continued, "You know, Mr. Crowe, I am not on this dam site purely for this celebration."

"What is your mission then?"

"To study your operation. Your men are far better off than most of the workers in this country."

"I'll take that as a compliment."

"And so you should. . . ."

"Well, flattery will get you nowhere," Frank said.

But Elle softened that statement. "It won't hurt, Mr. Foster. Underneath that will of iron . . ."

Roger Stein joined the three of them.

"Well, Frank, have you managed to alienate the Department of Interior sufficiently to jeopardize our dam?"

Foster laughed. "Not at all, Mr. Stein. Engineers, like physicists, see life as an equation. Ideologies are hard to accept by men trained in absolutes."

Frank offered his hand to Foster.

"I have enjoyed this talk," Frank said. "Tell Ickes he sent a good man. I haven't bought all you've told me, but if you're right, I'll come to see you in Washington. If you're wrong, I could use a good physicist on the dam site."

Foster shook Frank's hand and Elle's. He looked at her. "I hope *I'm* right. Your looks would brighten the scene around the capital. We've got too many earnest thick-legged women running around Washington. Even Roosevelt mentioned that."

Challenged by Foster's solid logic, Frank waved Hans off outside the lodge and walked hand in hand with Elle toward their house.

324

The night was still warm, small hot zephyrs rustled the new-grown trees, there were sounds of a piano being practiced, a baseball game being broadcast, a Victrola being played.

As Frank sat on the edge of their bed he watched Elle, her head propped up on a pillow.

"And so I have a President who likes vintage champagne and long-legged women."

"And works eighteen hours a day, seven days a week," Elle said.

"That's true," Frank admitted. "If I remember correctly, Hoover always took a two-hour nap after lunch."

Elle smiled and watched Frank fall asleep.

65

Frank slept badly that night, not only because he was fighting the effects of the alcohol, but because he knew tomorrow could be a crucial day for the dam.

It was one thing, he knew, to trade ideologies with Washington people over a martini in Sequoia Lodge, it was another to deal with the cold, hard realities of a new and foreign administration.

Edward Chapman was pacing Crowe's office the following morning, waiting for a legal decision which both he and Crowe knew might be not only costly, but also dangerous.

Roosevelt had seated a new federal judge in Carson City, Nevada, whose first mission had been to prosecute a long-standing suit between Clark County and the dam site. Clark County had assessed the valuation of that project at $2,556,484 and demanded to be paid taxes for the period of 1931 to 1933.

In 1931 the attorneys of the Big Six had ignored the suit, claiming that the dam was built on a federal reservation and could not be taxed, and when this failed, they played a game of delay upon delay, hoping in some way to sway the then Republican judge to decide that the claim was without merit.

Since most of the men of the Big Six felt that Hoover would not be defeated, this laissez-faire attitude seemed prudent, but after Roosevelt's victory, a new judge was seated whose sympathies were not with management and whose patience did not match that of his predecessor.

Chapman paced Frank Crowe's office as the attorneys arrived from the courthouse and announced that the minimum figure the court would accept for taxes was $180,813 for the years 1931 to 1933, and that the judge ordered a settlement that day or he might very well entertain punitive damages.

It was a furious and sweaty Chapman who signed that check, looked at it, and waved it in the faces of the attorneys.

"You've had two years, *two years*, to settle this with a Republican, and you sat around with your finger up your ass, and now we have one of these do-gooders from Washington taking our money like candy from a baby."

"Who, Mr. Chapman, expected a Republican defeat?"

"In my business, Mr. Callan, you expect *everything*. What makes your business different?"

"If one could win every case, Mr. Chapman, one would not need attorneys."

"Bullshit," Chapman roared. "I've seen your bills. I hardly feel that the Big Six will feel kindly paying for defense which was useless."

"The levy might have been higher."

"The levy," Chapman said, still shouting, "is *illegal*. We're building a dam. We're creating employment. Where the hell would Clark County *be* without us? We've built roads and railroads and every visitor and gambler from the whole United States leaves some of their money in Clark County, and now the bastards want taxes. *Taxes* for what?"

"Lawyers do not make laws, Mr. Chapman."

"No," Chapman said. "Lawyers just make goddamned politicians, and lawyers become goddamned judges. Here," he said, "take this fucking check and find yourself a train back to the city."

Frank totally agreed with Chapman, both about the immorality of this taxation and the poor performance of the company lawyers. He stated this, but continued, "I don't like these shysters any better than you do, Ed, but unfortunately now we need them more than ever."

"Why?"

"The Wobblies have filed two suits against us already. Two tunnelers are claiming $100,000 for physical damages. As soon as news of *this* settlement gets out, there'll be no end of suits."

"I've watched this goddamned Roosevelt," Chapman said. "There are acts for the farmers and acts for the homeowners, and acts for the unemployed. Every ten minutes there is another act for all the bums in this country. Who in the hell does he think *creates* employment? Where in the hell does he think he'll find the jobs? What about us? What about the men who risk their hard-earned money to build projects like this? What does he do for *us?* Tax us. That's what he does. Tax us. I tell you, Frank, I tell you for your sake and for mine, this project better come in at a profit, because it's going to be a cold day before I venture any more capital to create employment for Mr. Roosevelt. This country is going to hell!" He still paced the floor. "Do you know that we defeated by only one vote an injunction to enforce labor laws on the dam site? *One* fucking vote. If that injunction had passed we could kiss any hopes of profit goodbye."

"I saw the decision," Frank said. "There will be more votes."

"I know," Chapman said. "That Roosevelt is riding high. Too high. I can't fight him with shyster lawyers."

"How do you fight him?"

"With votes, Mr. Crowe. Votes are the only thing that gentleman understands. Even Mr. Roosevelt will have to stand for reelection, unless he abolishes the Constitution altogether, and even that wouldn't surprise me."

The phone rang and Frank picked it up. His face turned white.

"What is it?" Chapman asked when Frank hung up.

"The scaffolding in the Nevada glory hole collapsed. Eight men disappeared into the tunnels."

"I'm going home," Chapman said. "There go eight more lawsuits," but Frank did not hear the last of Chapman's statement; he was already in his truck and yelled at Hans:

"The Nevada spillway. Hurry."

There were two giant spillways above the dam site, each large enough to float a destroyer. Drum gates would be placed on the river side of these spillways; should the lake building up behind the dam reach the level of these drum gates, they would revolve automatically and discharge the water into the spillways and into the outer diversion tunnels. The connection between each spillway and its diversion tunnel was a tunnel seventy feet in diameter running from the floor of the spillway to the diversion tunnel. The openings of the connecting tunnels were known as the glory holes. The one on the Nevada side was completed save for its lining. Eight men had been at work constructing a wooden form to pour that lining.

Crowe well knew the anatomy of the glory holes; it had taken a great deal of engineering because of the convoluted configuration and the steep slope toward the tunnels. He knew it would be difficult to build forms in this area since two-by-fours were not meant to go around parabolic curves, and expert carpentry was needed. Crowe had ordered safety nets, but arriving at the site of the accident he saw that his order had been ignored.

He had seen hundreds of accidents in his lifetime of heavy construction. There was always the combination of jagged broken wood, smudges and pools of fresh blood, torn jagged flesh, often limbs or bodies, adding the animate horror to the inanimate destruction.

The men had fallen one hundred feet into the Nevada spillway, the heavy form falling behind them. At this moment, what was left of them was traveling through those tunnels. The Colorado had not yet exacted the last toll from Crowe, he knew that.

"Where's the safety engineer?" Crowe asked Williams.

"Gone over the hill, that son of a bitch. Look," he pointed, "see those red hooks?"

"I see them."

"They were placed and tested yesterday. . . . There's the safety net unused." Jack pointed to the steel mesh lying at the side of the glory hole.

"Shit," is all Frank could say as he jumped into his truck and headed for the tunnel outlet.

Three carpenters, one with a broken back, one with a fractured leg, the third with a concussion, emerged from the tunnel, clinging to the form and painfully headed for the banks of the Colorado. Five others were less fortunate. Their remains were driven to the morgue after they were recovered from the river.

Frank had barely finished his supper, and Elle sensed his anger, when the dreaded whir of the emergency siren pierced through the night. Frank reached the night foreman by phone and waited. Elle watched him drum against the table nervously with his fingers, and after several minutes Elkins reported that the load line on 11 Cableway had broken. "A stiff was riding a pump from the canyon floor to the pump house. They dropped two hundred feet. Nothing left of him or the pump."

Frank slept little that night. Elle felt him tossing and turning. He rose before dawn and paced his study, occasionally stopping to make some notes.

Elle had risen and joined her husband, but he scarcely noticed her.

"This morning," he said, "is a good time to stay out of my way."

"I understand," Elle said, and returned to bed.

At lunchtime Frank rose from his seat in the mess hall. Men stopped eating, dropped their silverware, and turned their heads to face him.

"In the last twenty-four hours," Frank said, "we have lost six men. Five from drowning, one from a fall. Loss of life on a construction site is a tragic but valid statistic. *Needless* loss of life is not. All six men who died yesterday died needlessly." He paused and looked at the workers. "The five men who drowned would be sitting here if the safety net which lay twenty yards from the glory hole had been used. Supervisor Williams tested the hooks for that net only hours before the accident. The safety man did not place that net and he has gone south.

"The man who was buried rode a pump on the cableway. I have seen scores of you ride those buckets up and down from the canyon although I have strictly forbidden this. If you do this for thrills or to save time, I don't care, it is *forbidden!*

"I know that we have encouraged competition among you and have made generous donations both of cash and beer chits for outstanding performance. It is not my intention to stop rewarding hard work. However, starting this minute, since you bastards refuse to read signs or heed warnings, and want to gamble with the laws of nature, I am telling you that *any job*, any job performed which infracts even the most *minor* of safety instructions, will go without pay, and any safety engineer found derelict in his duties will not only be fired but prosecuted.

"This dam," Frank said sonorously, "will be rising now. Almost unnoticeably, like the hour hand on a clock, this dam will be rising. Night and day. Each new elevation will bring us closer to the completion, but each increasing elevation will make the dam more dangerous. Those of you working forty feet above the dam site now will be working four hundred feet above it in a year and almost eight hundred feet in two years." Frank paused. "This dam can be built safely if you follow orders, or it can be built foolishly and the Colorado will spit in your face. Whatever is left of it. The choice is yours."

Frank left the mess hall before the men sat down again. They finished their meal in silence.

Frank returned to his office, still angry, still upset by the events of the past two days. Reluctantly he opened his plans meticulously labeled September 20, 1934, and as he suspected, the same plan was spread before Devere, sharing a trailer in Vegas with Levy and three other hand-picked men from Detroit.

The atmosphere was more optimistic in that trailer this day, since Levy assumed that the legal defeat of the Big Six Companies in federal court was decidedly in his favor. The chance of his suits against the company, he felt, was immensely strengthened by that decision, and his strategy to bleed the Big Six in court seemed a wise one. Even the close vote of the labor board heartened him.

"We lost by one vote," Levy said. "One vote and we would have had labor laws on the dam site."

"We lost," Devere said, "that's what counts. We're no better off than we were before."

"There'll be another chance next year," Levy said.

"Next year, shit. Next year Crowe will have half that dam finished. There hasn't been a pay raise in three years now. Besides, what makes you think you'll win those court cases?"

Levy smiled. "The Big Six didn't figure on losing that tax suit in Clark County, did they?"

"Guess not."

"Of course not. Got fooled by a new, honest, hard-driving federal judge. Gilroy is his name. He'll be trying those tunnelers' suits, too. Good old Gilroy. If I just win *one* suit, I'll bring Crowe to his knees."

"And what if you lose?"

"Then we'll try it your way." He looked at Devere studying the plans of the dam site.

"Sure," Devere said. "Warner Strong said I fucked up because I put all my eggs into one basket."

"He was right."

"He *was* right, but you're doing the same thing."

"We've got a different climate now," Levy countered. "Roosevelt is getting so close to socialism I think we can pin a Wobbly badge on him soon."

"Bullshit. That crippled Groton boy. What does he know about working stiffs?"

Levy fixed Devere with an angry stare. "He knows about being crippled."

66

For two years now Crowe had become accustomed to seeing Hans wait in or near the truck, sometimes smoking, sometimes dozing, waiting to drive him to the next destination. It was to the boy's credit that Crowe never had to search him out, that his punctuality in the morning matched Crowe's own and that only rarely did the vehicle break down. Hans was not only a reliable driver but also an excellent mechanic. All this Crowe knew, appreciated, and simply accepted; but one morning, leaving his office to head for the dam site, he discovered two phenomena, one was Hans reading, the other was the boy wearing glasses. Suddenly Frank recalled Elle's concern about his driver, remembered her asking him to take an interest.

"Well, I'll be damned," Crowe said, "you've stopped picking your nose. What are you reading?"

"It's *Automotive Mechanics,*" Hans said, showing Frank the book.

"I thought you knew all *about* cars."

"I can fix 'em," Hans said, "but I don't really know what I'm fixing. . . . That damned gasoline engine is more complicated than I figured."

"So it is," Frank said. "What are your plans?"

"Work in a garage. Met a fellow in South Amana. Wanted to give me a job when I was coming West. Nice little town. All green. Thought he might remember me."

"You know enough now to be a good mechanic," Frank said. "Why don't you raise your sights?"

"Like what?"

"Go to college, study engineering. You must have learned something on the dam site."

Hans blushed. "I haven't been picking my nose, chief. I've been watching. Mostly you. There's nothing I'd like better than being an engineer. My old man always wanted that."

"What's stopping you?"

"First off, I'm too old to start college."

Frank laughed. "Too *old?* How old are you?"

"Twenty-eight."

"Hell, you're just a kid."

"There are other reasons."

"Such as?"

"Money—Terry is pregnant."

Frank was surprised but betrayed nothing. "Congratulations. When are you going to be a father?"

"Christmas."

"I told you once I owed you a favor, remember?" Frank said.

"You owe me nothing, chief."

"Let me decide that. We'll finish this job and we'll see about college. I talked to a fellow named Foster not long ago. Assistant Secretary of the Interior. He spoke about Roosevelt's plans for young men like you."

"I'm much obliged, chief," Hans said, "but I got to think about feeding mouths."

"I'll talk to Elle. I hear you been going to the library."

"Yes sir."

"I'll get some stuff for you to read. Just read it carefully and let me worry about money."

Hans reached into his pocket and produced a watch. It was exactly like Crowe's. The boy pressed the stem and the cover flew open. "We're going to be late," Hans said, looking from the face of the watch to Crowe.

Crowe looked at Hans and the watch, and he could not stop laughing.

"You're off to a good start," he said. "Once you've got a watch like that, you'll find you're always late."

67

It was another hot summer on the dam site. On June 30, 1933, Crowe recorded 124 degrees on the bottom of the canyon, where much work was now concentrated; he watched the water carriers, the exhausts of diesels, the wind gauges, and painfully recalled the admonition of the doctors who warned him he couldn't push his men too hard in this heat. He had no time to slow down, and less time for reflection.

Although he monitored the calls from the river watchers upstream, and took cognizance of the size of his tunnels, the strength of his upstream cofferdam, he nevertheless kept a steady watch on the swollen river as it entered the tunnels and played about the bottom of his cofferdam. At the height of the spring runoff, fifteen feet of his cofferdam was under water.

"Could set my watch the way you patrol this dam," Williams said, joining Frank on top of the precipice. "You must come out here four times a day."

"Right," Frank said, "and twice at night."

"Don't you have any faith in my tunnels?"

"I've got all the faith in the world in them, Jack, but I don't trust the river. I could think of eight tributaries right now that aren't flowing at crest tide. A good summer storm and this river will rise and rise."

"I'm only using two tunnels right now. You want me to open the other two?"

"No. Not yet. I'd just as soon test the integrity of this cofferdam."

"She's holding like a dollar condom," Williams said.

"I know. It better hold. I've got four thousand men working below this dam. . . ."

"You've got more than three hundred percent tolerance," Williams said. "That river's about as high as it will go."

"Look upstream." Frank pointed. "You see the Colorado bulge in the center, it's like a coiled rattler. . . ."

"Well," Williams said, "I've got my own troubles."

"Like what?"

"Like putting thirty-foot sections of pipe into thirty-one-foot tunnels. It's like putting a dick into a virgin."

Frank thought briefly about Williams's constant sexual metaphors, but let it pass.

"The tighter the fit the less grouting you'll need."

"You don't have to tell me that, but you're stealing my best hoist men for your dam."

"They're *all* green, Jack, even mine."

"But you can dump a bucket of concrete and miss, so what? I've got one shot at my tunnels. If they don't place it right the first time I'm in real trouble."

"Just take it slow," Frank advised.

"Slow, shit. The way your schedule runs I've got no time to take it slow."

"Do you need more time?"

"I'll outbuild you anytime, Mr. Crowe."

"Then stop bitching."

"I've stopped," Williams said. Once more he looked up the river. "Yup, the way that river is roaring down the canyon reminds me of a freight train without an engine." Williams laughed. "I'll comfort you like you comfort me."

But Crowe was more patient than Williams; he knew that pouring the dam was like a ballet. It was a continuous series of movements. The concrete mixers upstream poured four cubic yards of concrete every three minutes into huge buckets weighing over twenty tons and holding eight cubic yards of mud. Three of these buckets rested on flat cars and, once filled, were delivered to the dam site by electric locomotives; then hooks from the cableways lifted them and the hoistmen delicately delivered them to the forms at the bottom of the canyon, some eight hundred feet down.

Although there was a certain reliability and predictability in the machinery, the rolling stock, the mixers, the cableways, the men were still green. Movements were not yet instinctive, levers were still pulled with apprehension, uncertainty. The muscles were still untrained and the eyes were not all-seeing. There had not even been enough mishaps for them to gain experience; only time would help, and production rose in a curve, not unlike the one projected in Frank's office. In June he poured 25,000 cubic yards, in August he poured 149,000 cubic

333

yards, by October he exceeded 200,000 cubic yards, still using the same men, the same equipment. By October he was dumping a bucket a minute, twenty-four hours a day, which had been his goal. He gave out the beer chits and told his men that they could do better yet.

All was going well: the dam was rising eight to nine feet a week and Williams was lining his tunnels with the giant sections of steel pipes from Babcock & Wilcox as easily and steadily as slipping a wedding ring on a lovely girl.

But this period of calm and progress that graced the dam site, at least temporarily, did nothing to lessen the turmoil that had steadily been growing within Elle. It had begun when a girl named Elaine Haskell, the wife of one of the muckers, approached Elle in the library, asking for a book on wildflowers and ending up crying uncontrollably. Puzzled by the outburst, Elle held the girl close, trying to comfort her. Through the thin dress, Elle could feel the girl's bones protruding from her slight frame. Elle remembered that when she first met Elaine two years before she had been a robust, beautiful girl whose eagerness to make new friends had gotten her involved in all the social get-togethers. Yet Elle hadn't seen Elaine around for several months, and now she looked years older. Looking down at the girl's stomach, Elle noticed a slight roundness forming. Since she had two other children at home, Elle imagined the girl had little time to waste on social clubs.

"I didn't mean to act so stupid, Mrs. Crowe, honest. I just had to get away from the house and I thought a book with some pretty pictures might cheer me up some." Elaine was wiping the tears from her face, but her chin still quivered.

"Don't be sorry." Elle smiled at the girl, but avoided her eyes. They looked hollow and old. Instinctively, Elle put her hand up to her own face. "You have a right to cry if something is bothering you. Though, with another baby on the way, I'd think you'd have reason to be happy, too."

Elaine looked down at her stomach and her chin began to quiver even more. Elle realized she had said the wrong thing, and there seemed nothing to do but wait until the tears subsided again to find out what was wrong.

"It isn't his, the baby."

Elle tried not to seem shocked, but the suddenness of the admission caught her off guard. "Do you know . . . does your husband have any idea . . ."

"It's one of the men I sleep with from the evening shift that got me knocked up." Elaine said these words quickly and with determination, as if the strength of her reply could keep her from feeling shame under Elle's surprised gaze. "I'm what they call a *graveyard whore,*

334

Mrs. Crowe. I see my husband off for the graveyard shift and then I pick up a man at that same bus stop. He gives me a dollar." Elaine wiped her red, dry hands along her dress. "And then I give that dollar to my husband. There ain't no other way." Elaine turned around and ran out the door.

That night, and for several nights to come, Elle went down to the stop where the men came back from work and others were waiting to leave. Elle would keep her distance, pretending to be out for a stroll. She'd watch the women, just like Elaine, seeing their husbands off and then going home with other men. Some women even carried babies in their arms. At times Elle would see the husband looking back from the bus window, watching his wife as another stiff put his arm around her waist.

During the day, Elle felt she had begun to notice the women around her for the first time—women she had known for years, whose houses she had visited, and whose children she had played with. They now all looked ugly and wasted, growing old before their time, as if they were all graveyard whores. Elle cried for them, and for herself.

Elle heard the front door close and listened to Frank come upstairs and she looked at him perplexed, tears in her eyes, a perplexity shared by her husband watching his crying wife.

"What's wrong? What's wrong, Elle?"

"Nothing," she said, staring into space. " . . . Everything . . ."

"What does that mean?"

Elle turned her head, but Frank walked toward her and pushed her tear-streaked face to meet his eyes. "What is it, Elle?"

"You kept warning me. Over and over again in Salt Lake, I know. I know all that. You kept telling me how it would be."

"Well?"

"I guess I'm not as strong as I imagined."

"I don't know what you're talking about."

"You warned me that things wouldn't be pretty on the dam site. There'd be long hours, and I had to accept that without question. There'd be accidents and phone calls in the middle of the night. And that I accepted too. But finding out how the women are treated, that they are bought and sold . . . left to grow ugly . . ."

Frank grabbed Elle by the shoulders and made her look straight at him. "You're not making sense, Elle. What's going on?"

Elle freed herself from Frank's grip and went over to pour herself a drink, something she had seldom done before. When she spoke again, the hysteria had gone out of her voice and only anger and determination remained.

"While you're busy building your tunnels and your dam, have you ever looked at the women on this dam site? I don't mean the ones who have just come, but the ones who have been here for one year, two years—long enough for the sun to start drying out their skin, making them look old."

Frank shook his head, still confused. "What does this have to do with you, Elle?"

"Because this dam is destroying me and every other woman around here." Elle put down her glass and looked up at her husband. She saw that her words had hurt him. She wondered how much she meant them. But she couldn't stop now.

"Have you ever watched those girls during the shift change at eleven o'clock? They're not seeing their men off. They're waiting for other men from the swing shift to come back from the dam. They sleep with them, Frank. For a *dollar. One dollar.* That's less than Aunt Mary charges. They *need* that dollar. Most of them do it with their husbands' permission."

"How do you know all that?"

"You told me there are no secrets on the dam site. You were right. Only it took me a little longer than most to see the truth. Maybe I didn't want to know."

Frank pushed back his hat and took Elle's hand in his.

"I'm sorry for those women. And I'm sorry you had to find out about them. It's never happened on a dam I've worked on before. But a lot's different this time."

"You mean you *knew!*"

"Yes, I knew, Elle. You just said it yourself. There are no secrets."

"And you let it happen."

"There's one thing I learned a long time ago in construction, Elle; you can tell a man to blast, or to work or to gamble with his life, you can tell him to work overtime, you can kick his butt to work harder, but there's one thing you never tell a man. You don't tell a man what to do with his pecker."

Frank walked out the front door, leaving a confused and frightened Elle staring after him. An hour later, Elle heard the same door open again. Neither said a word as Frank took Elle in his arms and they embraced.

After a few minutes, Elle broke the silence. "I didn't mean what I said, Frank, not about the dam destroying me. I was just angry, and I felt so helpless."

Frank brushed her hair back and kissed her softly on the cheek. "There's a lot that shouldn't be happening on this dam, Elle. There's a lot that makes me angry and helpless, too. It's a feeling you've got to learn to live with—or walk away from."

The next day Elle went to visit Elaine Haskell, and to take her a book on wildflowers.

68

Las Vegas, which had been rescued from obscurity by construction of the Boulder Dam, had never used its new-found prosperity wisely. A scant twenty-three miles from Boulder City, which by law and inclination was developing into a moral, well-tended small community, Las Vegas as it had in its inception flourished only from the exploitation of man's weaknesses: gambling, prostitution, alcohol, and narcotics. There were honest payrolls, to be sure; the railroad yards employed hard-working men, the hotels and casinos were staffed by underpaid and overworked waitresses, chambermaids, bartenders, and musicians; but those in power—the sheriff, the mayor, the men who dealt in gambling, in real estate, men who could have influenced a city approaching a population of ten thousand—had no urge to shape a community, no desire to invest any part of their huge income for the public good.

Services were inadequate, fire protection was ludicrous, even the few schools which the city fathers grudgingly built cost only a fraction of a new casino, a fancy Western bar, a new Creole-style "house" whose women wore red and yellow garters, and that's all.

Two men who were well aware of the state of affairs in Las Vegas, Nevada, were Frank Crowe and Tony Gallino from Detroit, whose huge brick house, surrounded by an awesome ten-foot wall garlanded with broken glass, sat on a knoll three miles from Fremont Street.

For Crowe, Las Vegas was both a necessity and a headache. He needed the railroad for his supplies, and his men needed the town for diversion. He had built other dams where men had the same needs, and while those other sites had also been near small towns which contained bars and houses, these establishments were restricted to a few well-regulated square blocks; they were neither the lifeblood nor the sole enterprise.

Gallino, almost fifty, stocky, of Sicilian descent, had made his mark early in Detroit, reputedly killing a number of men by drowning, garrote, gun, and axe, and by the time he had reached the age of thirty he was so expert at his craft that an execution could be ordered and performed in less than eight hours.

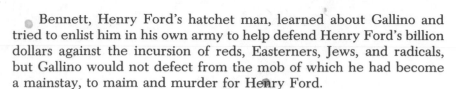

Bennett, Henry Ford's hatchet man, learned about Gallino and tried to enlist him in his own army to help defend Henry Ford's billion dollars against the incursion of reds, Easterners, Jews, and radicals, but Gallino would not defect from the mob of which he had become a mainstay, to maim and murder for Henry Ford.

It was a wise decision, no doubt, for the mob sent Gallino west. They did not want a confrontation with Bennett, whose army and monies were greater than theirs, but Gallino, like a bullfighter, was surrounded by an ever-increasing bunch of awed hoodlums, whose nerve did not quite match that of this cold-blooded perfectionist killer. Gallino was the kind of man who'd get ideas.

"We'll give you one-half the action," the mob's attorney had told him, "and we will pay spot cash for any 'deliveries' we make to Las Vegas."

Gallino had heard of Las Vegas. Reared in the shadow of the Rouge, he had listened to the tales of sunshine and fast cars, and swimming pools and an endless parade of naked, willing girls.

He accepted the challenge and left Detroit for the West.

Gallino was no fool; he took a businessman's view toward the workers from the dam. On payday, those who were gamblers or thirsty were welcome in Vegas, and there, with a curious mixture of benevolence (free lunches, free cigars, generous measures of inexpensive booze), with willing girls and well-paid musicians, the men were easily parted from their pay checks.

Men that got boisterous, men that went broke, were collared by Gallino's "boys" and delivered to Pitt's jail. All this was legal. Gallino could easily maintain his image of master killer by keeping saloon owners and madams and whores and pimps in line; if any of them found it too tempting to keep part of his cut, they were found dead as punctually as mortgage bills, and the variety and imagination of their demises supplied endless material for national tabloids. He was the darling of the *Police Gazette*. Gallino, it was said, spent his entire summer naked in his swimming pool, keeping one eye on the "operation" in Vegas, the other on an endless parade of naked girls who floated around his pool on brand-new inner tubes. When drunk, he was known to deflate those inner tubes with expertise, using either a German Mauser complete with silencer, or a small stiletto which was put in his drink by his butler.

Crowe sat on the edge of his desk and faced Pitt, who had been summoned from Las Vegas.

"I know, chief," Pitt said respectfully, "why you've asked me out. Gallino."

"That's right," Crowe said. "Gallino. You're on the take."

"That's true," Pitt said. "I'm doing you enough favors and I have to work with Gallino. Nobody has roughed up your boys, not in my jail. And you get them out for a song."

"Right," Crowe said, "and I appreciate that. I didn't ask you up to lecture you."

"What then?"

"You were police chief in Vegas before I got here, before my boys got here. We've made Vegas a rich town, we've no doubt made you and lots of others in your city rich men. Don't you boys have any civic pride? Why don't you build roads and hospitals and theaters and parks? All your money goes into more houses, more casinos, sleazy hotels, greasy spoons. . . ."

"You don't know Vegas," Pitt said. "You came in twenty-seven. You saw it. We were being swallowed up by the desert. All we had to offer was a decaying Block 16 and a few bars and a couple of lodges for the railroad men. That payroll was dwindling every month. . . . Another year without the dam and Vegas would have been finished."

"But that has changed."

"Sure it has. We got a new payroll. Yours. Bigger payroll than anybody ever saw in the Southwest. So the locals are getting rich, sure, only there's more traffic than even the locals can handle. We got us Gallino." He looked steadily at Crowe. "If it weren't for Gallino, it would be another punk. I got no men to stand up to those bastards. We breed them tough in the West; they breed them like animals in the East. . . . They say he blinded his sister with a poker 'cause she danced with a nigger in a speakeasy."

"We are a *free* country," Frank yelled. "We've got laws, and a constitution and representatives in the House, and men in the Senate and men on the bench. *One* prick, one degenerate punk like Gallino can terrorize you, and me, and thousands of my men?"

"The way I heard it, chief, Gallino gave ten thousand dollars in cash to Hoover's campaign, and the same amount to Roosevelt. He gave two thousand dollars to each senatorial candidate of Nevada and five hundred dollars to each House member. . . ."

"And they all took it?"

Pitt nodded his head.

"They all took it," Crowe repeated. "Shit," Crowe yelled. "Shit. Why am I busting my ass, why are my men busting their asses slaving in this fucking territory to save the Imperial Valley, to light up some gangster's tennis court in L.A., to fatten up the purse of the Barneses, to grease the palm of one more crooked politician? *Shit*—that's all I can say."

"What do you want from a goddamn small-town police chief? Your dam will be finished, your payroll will end, and Vegas once more will drift into the dust of the desert."

"It will," Crowe said. "You bet it will, and that's where it belongs. Not *one* of *you*, not one *single* one of you in that fucking town, has one ounce of altruism in you."

"I don't know what that means."

"Even if I explained it to you, you still wouldn't know what it means." Crowe headed for the door of his office. "I've got work to do," he said, and left.

He rose in the mess hall that day, and his men, knowing he did not deal in irrelevancies, put down their utensils and listened.

"I know that every time I stand up and make these goddamned speeches I treat you men like children. I plead with you to take salt tablets, I swear at you to obey the safety laws." The men well remembered all these speeches.

"I'm talking to you today about something which is none of my business. Las Vegas." He looked around the room. "You men work hard. You can quote me. You sweat your balls off in the summer and you freeze them in the winter. It is not easy pay for any of you. And when you get your money from the bull cook on Friday, you can do any goddamned thing with it you want. A lot of you go to Vegas. It's a free country and I'm not a minister.

"But Vegas is not as honest as your labor. The dice are crooked, the wheel is loaded, the booze is watered, and the whores are hungry.

"Every Monday I bail out scores of men for drunk and disorderly, for rape, for unpaid chits, for assault and battery. . . .

"A handful of men," Crowe said, "a *handful* of men sitting in their pools, in their air-conditioned parlor suites, with hot and cold running whores, are getting rich on your hard-earned goddamned money.

"I cannot tell you what to do! I cannot go through your wallets as you leave the gates of the reservation, but I am also not powerless.

"As of this minute, I am legalizing Bingo in the Rec Hall in Boulder City. Bet your heart out, but the games will be honest, I can assure you of that.

"I cannot legalize prostitution on the dam site, but I can tell you younger men that I've never heard of a case of rape in a town like Las Vegas."

There was muffled laughter in the room.

"Before you fornicate, take off your clothes, and those of your partner, fold them carefully and place them ten feet from the bed. . . .

340

No one will scream rape, I assure you, and *no* cop will ever arrest you.

"One last word," Crowe said. "Among you are two reporters from the august Vegas press. I am saying this for them as much as I am saying it for you. I am telling it to that scum Gallino.

"If anything I say today will have an impact on you . . . then it will hurt Gallino, and it will hurt Las Vegas.

"And if that gentleman, so well versed in murder and brutality, and that community so expert in evil, cares to retaliate, then I say to them: We are six thousand men strong. . . . We have enough dynamite to blow them to hell, enough power shovels to pound them into eternity, and enough work-hardened fists to drive them into the dust from which we pulled them."

The men understood and the women of Boulder City understood it better than the men, but this speech was the first one to cause men to get up from their benches and cheer and raise their fists.

The reporters of the two Vegas papers almost collided on the Boulder Highway trying to get Crowe's speech into print, and when the papers reached the town the following morning a chain reaction began.

No one in the "mansion" had the nerve to show the story to Gallino, but it took only an hour for him to see the paper. He laughed. But Las Vegas recorded the lowest volume of business for any weekend in months and the local chamber of commerce met in emergency session.

Devere had also read the paper and without checking with his new boss, Levy, embarked on a mission which he hoped would put him back in the good graces of Warner Strong. He paid a call on Gallino. He was impressed neither by the size of the house nor by the reputed orgiastic behavior of Gallino's women. He strode purposefully to the corner of the pool where the heavy Sicilian had spread his hairy arms, letting his legs and genitalia float obscenely in the blue still waters of the pool.

"I'm Devere of the IWW," he said.

"So?" Gallino said coldly.

"We've got common business."

"State it," Gallino ordered.

"I can't talk, looking at a man's balls."

"Why not? Jealous?"

"Maybe," Devere said. "I gave mine to the Kaiser."

Gallino respected this honesty and stepped out of the pool. He was short, stocky, and square. He was so ugly, a Grosse Pointe socialite once told him, it was erotic; and he had always believed her. His valet handed him a robe and the two men headed for Gallino's study, his pride, since it was finished in rosewood, and its walls lined with precious leather-covered classics, none of which Gallino had ever read. He was illiterate.

Gallino at first was embarrassed then livid at finding two lesbian whores on his couch, tongue to vagina. Gallino listened to their muted groans for a minute, then pressed a button. In seconds a giant young man appeared at his side.

"Those two cunts are screwing on my llama-hide couch. You know nobody's allowed in here."

Suddenly the girls looked up, and terror was quickly visible in their faces.

The man hit the girls quickly across the face, then picked them up like sides of beef.

"What you want me to do?"

"Kick their asses in."

"No," the girls yelled. "Jesus God."

Gallino walked over to the couch and gently straightened the delicate leather.

The bully left the study with the screaming girls and Gallino seated himself at the desk. "When he's through with them they couldn't interest a railroad conductor. Want a drink?"

"Sure. Whiskey."

Gallino walked to a bar and poured Devere a stiff drink in a cut-glass goblet.

"What's on your mind, Devere?"

"You read the papers this morning?"

"I have."

"What do you think of Crowe?"

"What kind of a dumb-ass question is that?"

"We're willing to pay for Crowe's death."

"Who is *we?*"

"The IWW."

"Who is that?"

"The Industrial Workers of the World."

"Very interesting. How much?"

"Eight hundred dollars," Devere said.

"You're joking."

"Why?"

"Eight hundred dollars for a *major* hit?"

"That's all we've got," Devere said.

"You must be some piss-ass outfit," Gallino said.

"Yeah," Devere said, "I guess to you we are." Devere rose, half drunk. He extended his hand. "Sorry to bother you."

342

"No bother. I like Frank Crowe just where he is. Building a dam. Employing stiffs. He's doing just fine. They'll all be back. They ain't gonna play Bingo long."

Devere looked jealously at the impressive library and took out a volume of drawings by Goya.

"What a beautiful book," he said.

"Let me see it," Gallino said, and Devere showed him the stark charcoal drawing.

"Naked ladies," Gallino said. "Son of a bitch. I thought all these books just had words in them."

69

It was seven o'clock in the morning and the cool gray light of dawn barely lit the large but sparsely furnished office of Secretary of the Interior Harold Ickes. Not unlike Crowe, he was a man who knew no hours, and Foster, his well-tailored assistant secretary from Princeton, accustomed to the gentlemanly hours of academia, saw little sense in this ungodly schedule of the New Deal, but was slowly getting used to rising in the dark and shaving by the light of a forty-watt bulb over his sink in Georgetown.

"I saw your report about Boulder," Ickes said, ignoring all amenities. "What did you think of Crowe?"

"I was impressed," Foster said.

"How?"

"He's not your average construction engineer."

"How does he differ?"

"He's more intellectual than he lets on."

"I got a memo from the boss," Ickes said, tapping his desk with a pencil, referring to FDR. "He wanted me to assess the employment factor on that dam." He handed Foster a manila folder. "We figured for each man working on the dam two others throughout the country were employed. Figuring six thousand men on the dam, you're talking about eighteen thousand nationally, really."

"That's very impressive."

"It is and it isn't. All of this is temporary employment. The way

343

Crowe is moving he'll have that dam finished before the next election. That means eighteen thousand men once more unemployed before Roosevelt's next campaign."

"That dam," Foster said, "is being built by private enterprise, the Big Six. The earlier they complete it, the more money they'll make."

"I understand that," Ickes said. "We're stuck with this arrangement, thanks to Mr. Hoover."

"I know," Foster said. "But are we gearing the upswing in the economy to an election timetable?"

Ickes looked at Foster sternly. "We've got less than four years to get this country out of this slump."

"You're saying we've got four years to make Roosevelt look good."

"I don't need your sarcasm, Foster, at seven in the morning. If we are going to continue our crusade, it is essential that Roosevelt be reelected. That should make sense even to a Princeton man."

"Political sense, sure."

"Look," Ickes said impatiently, "I don't want to argue about the ethics or morality of practical politics. I want to know about Crowe. I think these dams are a good thing, but not the way this one is being built. Most of the money goes to the Big Six, private enterprise, and most of the money once it's built will go to Southern California Edison, another private enterprise." He said these two words as if they were venomous.

"You're forgetting the increased taxes we'll generate from a fertile Imperial Valley, the savings in flood control for the federal government," Foster added.

"I'm forgetting nothing. We're stuck with Boulder Dam, but new dams, bigger dams, can be built by the Bureau of Reclamation. They've built dams before, Arrowrock, Deadwood, Tieton—all good dams."

"All built by Crowe," Foster said.

"That's right. For the government. The question, Foster, the question now is whether Crowe would return to the government. I hear he has a piece of Boulder."

"I honestly don't know. Why don't you ask him?"

"I will," Ickes said, "when the time is right, but I need to know more about the man. Is he building that dam just for the money?"

"I've had a twenty-minute conversation with Mr. Crowe. I didn't go into his motives."

"I understand that," Ickes said, "but you must have gotten some impressions."

"Well," Foster said reflectively, "he's a New Englander. Probably still has the first dollar he ever made. He's got an extremely pretty young wife. . . . I'd say he was the kind of man who gets what he wants."

344

Ickes placed another folder in front of Foster.

"What's this?"

"Crowe's curriculum vitae from the Bureau of Reclamation."

"What does it divulge?"

"He's received every commendation the government can bestow."

Foster returned the folder unread to Ickes. "I don't like these things. I feel it indecent to look into a man's life."

Ickes laughed. "They've got one started on you right now."

"Well," Foster said, "you can put down my dislike of this practice."

Ickes looked at his watch. It was seven-twenty. "I've got better things to do. . . ."

At the Bohemian Club in San Francisco, Barnes brought up Frank Crowe's speech in the mess hall. The story had had enough impact in Las Vegas to merit coverage in the San Francisco *Examiner*.

"I wish," Barnes said, "Crowe would keep his nose out of Las Vegas."

"I don't blame him," Andrews said. "That town is a hell hole, run by a bunch of mobsters. . . ."

"I still say it's none of our business."

"It's none of *our* business," Andrews said, pointing to the partners of the Big Six. "Crowe is running the job. They're *his* men, not ours."

"As long as they don't ask for a raise," Barnes said.

"Well," Mackenzie added, "you saw how close that court decision was on allowing unions. They're not through with us yet."

"The way Crowe is pouring that concrete," Barnes added, rubbing his hands, "old Frank will have that dam finished before their next meeting."

"You hope," Mackenzie said. "That dam is far from finished. Crowe said something about the Department of Interior snooping around the dam site."

"What the hell do *they* want?" Barnes asked.

"Who knows? With this goddamned Roosevelt, there'll be three inspectors for every working stiff."

"Creating employment," Andrews said.

"Creating employment, shit. The way things are going a goddamned laborer is going to ask for five bucks a day. How in the hell you gonna run a construction company with those kind of wages?"

A Filipino waiter came by delivering another round of drinks.

Barnes held up his martini in a frosted tumbler. "Look at this," he said. "Thirty-five cents for a goddamned martini. I can make a better one at home for eight cents."

"That's true," Mackenzie said, "but who the hell wants to drink at home?"

"You're right, Bill, you're right. It don't come cheap today to keep your sanity."

The men rose for lunch and the talk returned to construction.

"We're looking in South America," Barnes said, "Mexico, the Amazon . . . There's still a lot of places on this earth where you can get labor for nothing."

"We've been making the same projections," Andrews said. "There's nothing left in this country for us."

"Let the CCC and the WPA build their dams."

"They can build them," Barnes said, "but I wouldn't want to live below them."

"Ain't that the truth?" said Andrews. "We've got some nose picker painting a mural in the post office on Clement Street. Can you imagine, a *mural* in a post office? . . . I asked the guy what he was doing, he said he was with the WPA Artists Program. I said, 'No kidding, what the hell are you painting?'

"'The story of Sir Francis Drake,' he said.

"'I never heard of him,' I said. 'If the taxpayers are paying all that money, why don't you paint some naked ladies on the wall? Might help you sell stamps.'"

"What did he say to that?"

"Just gave me a dirty look. Murals in post offices. Shit. The beginning of the end."

Barnes shouted at the waiter, "What do you mean you're out of finnan haddie?"

"The chef said we're out, sir."

"I've had finnan haddie at this club for fifteen years. Every Friday. You tell that son of a bitch in the kitchen I'm gonna send him over to that Jew club—the Concordia. Those bastards don't care *what* they eat on Friday."

"Relax," MacKenzie said. "The beef shank is real good."

"No finnan haddie, if that don't take the cake."

The heat abated in October and Frank Crowe was unaware of all the attention surrounding him. He had other problems, for no sooner were his men getting the rhythm of pouring the concrete, of handling the unwieldy buckets, of operating the cableways efficiently, of shunting railway cars with dispatch, than the inevitable carelessness set in.

Hans, who had been meticulously studying the books suggested by Crowe, *Elementary Geometry, Weights and Measurements, Basic Physics,* wrestling with endless problems posed at the end of each chapter, daily watched Crowe as they traveled from the gravel plant to the lo-mix plant to the cableways and to the canyon floor. He watched and listened as Crowe ordered pulleys rehung and guy wires installed and admonished men for working motors at speeds exceeding their limits and scolded others whose safety belts were worn. He put a level on forms which would receive the concrete, and heaven help the carpenter whose work did not place the bubble in its rightful place. He checked wind velocities and hygrometers and resistors and took readings of heat sensors and monitored panels of his ammonia plant. He would feel the texture of a batch of unpoured concrete like a courtesan shopping for a velvet coat.

And since Crowe had only two eyes and eighteen hours a day to check his project, events occurred which might have been prevented, but which happened anyway. Locomotives simply quit and had to be repaired. Trucks ran off the road and broke through bridges. Cranes and shovels spun wide and sent power lines to the ground, steam shovels dug too deep and callously uprooted carefully marked air and water lines. Men fell, men slid, men were trapped, men got hit, men got run over.

"Watch this," Frank said to Hans. They were four hundred feet above the canyon floor. A hard-hatted worker below them carried a four-by-twelve piece of lumber. He had it well balanced on his shoulder and traveled easily down a path. When he reached the canyon floor he continued toward the rising dam. Someone called the man's name. He turned as did the piece of lumber on his shoulder; its end swinging wide from the turn hit another man in the eye.

In minutes a first-aid man was at the worker's side and a small crowd gathered.

"I could have predicted that," Crowe said. "He's got no red tag on the end of his load, he didn't follow orders to look ahead and look ahead only when loaded. That dumb son of a bitch will cost the company four hours and may cost that other stiff an eye."

"You can't be everywhere at the same time, chief."

"That's right, but I've got two hundred engineers on this dam to teach these stiffs how to obey orders." He watched an ambulance arrive and turned his head from the tragedy.

"Take me home," he said to Hans. "When I was younger, I'd go right down to that spot and punch the foreman in the nose."

Five dams, he recalled. Each man has five dams in him. This was his sixth. Perhaps there was more validity in that statement than he was willing to believe.

He was fifty and fit as a man approaching forty. He could take it all, the heat, the cold, the dampness, the hours, and yet lately he felt a certain resignation, a lack of will for those constant confrontations, which were the heart and substance of supervision, and as he saw his house loom on the hillside, he thought about Elle and *her* fears and *her* rebellion of late, and he wondered whether life was still the equation he had always believed in, whether hard work and intelligence would ultimately triumph. He was still wondering as Elle handed him an ice-cold martini.

"I got a phone call from Mrs. Otis, my former boss in the library in Las Vegas."

"What did she want?"

"They fired her and closed the library. She said as a result of your speech the city had to cut down on services."

Frank laughed. "Of course. How natural. The first thing the bastards would close is the library. None of them can read in the first place."

"It's not funny for Mrs. Otis," Elle said.

"I'm not laughing at her plight, honey. Tell her to call me. I'll get her a job on the dam."

"Doing what? She's a librarian."

"I know," Frank said. "I'd like to have my papers put in order."

Elle kissed Frank. "Hard day?"

"You bet. I wonder about *our* library. Half the guys on this dam can't read, either. Oh, Jesus, Elle, sometimes I'd like to have a fucking whip."

70

Frank Gilroy was forty years old, a graduate of Hastings School of Law in Berkeley, a fine attorney and a man with civic instincts. He had practiced in Reno for ten years and prospered, but tiring of endless divorce cases, bootlegging defenses, mining claim disputes, he turned to politics. He had worked hard for Roosevelt as county chairman, feeling sometimes that he was a lone liberal in that conservative island, Nevada, but his labors bore fruit when Roosevelt was elected, and Gilroy was named to the federal bench in Carson City. He was one of the youngest judges so appointed, and since his jurisdiction included Las Vegas, that hotbed of vice, his actions were closely watched both locally and in Washington.

He was in chambers at seven-thirty in the morning, and there was still frost on the lawn of the courthouse outside his window when the phone rang. It was the Secretary of the Interior, Harold Ickes, from Washington.

"Good morning to you." Ickes said. "I understand you are trying Moolan *versus* the Big Six today."

"That's right," Gilroy said, surprised. "How did you know?"

"We know everything in Washington," joked the secretary.

"I see," Gilroy said, perplexed.

"I saw the attorney general at the Japanese Embassy last night. . . . We talked about this case," Ickes said.

"I didn't know it was so elevated."

"It could be," Ickes said. "I'll come to the point."

"Yes?"

"The government wants Moolan to lose."

Ickes expected silence and his expectations were right. Finally Gilroy said, "Why? Since when is the New Deal fighting for big business?"

"We're not."

"But you said . . ."

"I know what I said. The government is interested in Frank Crowe. If Crowe loses this case, there'll be no end of suits. . . ."

"What if Moolan's suit has merit?"

"I am sixty years old, judge," Ickes said. "To keep *this* ship afloat I do my share of compromising, believe me."

"Mr. Secretary," Gilroy said, "I shall do my best . . . and give my regards to the attorney general."

"I shall do that, judge," Ickes said, then paused. "This conversation is between us."

"On that you have my word," Gilroy said.

"Thank you. I shall be at the dam in the spring. I hope to meet you, sir."

"It will be my pleasure."

Ickes hung up and looked at the barren trees outside his window, crossed off another name on his list, and picked up his receiver.

Frank Gilroy looked at his freshly ironed black robe across the room. They had not taught him *this* in law school, he thought as he donned it.

The courtroom was quite empty as Gilroy entered. There was no jury, and after being sworn in Moolan was on the stand first. He was a short man, thin, his emaciation emphasized by faded denims, a pair of worn half boots, a short almost military haircut. Gilroy noted the man's appearance and doubted Levy's wisdom in instructing a plaintiff to testify in this dress, which no doubt he'd done. But Levy was smooth in his interrogation, establishing the number of years the man had worked (one), the number of years he had been disabled

349

(two), the number of children he had to support (five), and a full and detailed account of the witness's ailments.

Gilroy listened to the recitation, noticed the way Moolan savored his newly learned medical terminology (silicosis). The room was quiet save for Levy and Moolan. Gilroy said nothing; neither did Abernathy from San Francisco, defending the Big Six Companies. When Levy had finished with his client, Gilroy looked at Abernathy.

"Do you wish to cross-examine the witness, counselor?"

Abernathy, tall, slender, gray-haired, well tailored in a blue pin-stripe suit, stood and said, "No questions, your honor."

The next witness was Dr. Bellem, short, dapper, wearing a suit too tight for his spreading frame. Levy questioned him carefully about Moolan's visits to the doctor's office, his diagnosis, his treatment, his prognosis. When this was finished, Abernathy rose to the challenge and asked a question.

"Dr. Bellem, what kind of doctor are you?"

"I'm a chiropractor."

"You're not a doctor of medicine?"

"It's the same thing," Bellem said.

"I beg to differ."

"We're all doctors."

Abernathy took his eyes off the witness and faced the judge. "Would you like me to differentiate, your honor?"

"There is no need."

"That will be all, *Dr.* Bellem."

Bellem was confused and hurt as he stepped down, and Levy appeared restless.

Jack Williams took the stand and Abernathy established his position on the dam site.

"Mr. Williams, how many men did you have in those tunnels during construction of the diversion tunnels?"

"Six hundred," Williams said, "consisting of three shifts."

"Have any of those six hundred men complained of unsafe working conditions?"

"Not until now."

"And where are all those six hundred men today?"

"Still working. Just different tunnels."

"I see," Abernathy said. "That will be all."

Levy rose and faced Williams. He was thirty and good-looking, with a very pale skin, a very dark beard despite a close shave, myopic eyes, a penchant for perspiration.

"Did you, Mr. Williams, obey all the safety laws of the State of Nevada?"

"No sir."

"Why not?"

"The State of Nevada has no jurisdiction on the dam site."

"Who does?"

"Frank Crowe."

"And who is he?"

"The supervising engineer."

"Is he a safety engineer?"

"He's a civil engineer."

"And Mr. Crowe makes arbitrary rules regarding safety on the dam site?"

"Mr. Crowe *never* makes arbitrary rules."

"In *your* opinion?"

"In my opinion," Williams answered, getting angry.

"How many men were killed in your diversion tunnels?" Levy asked.

"Twelve," Williams answered. "All accidental."

"I did not ask you *how* they were killed. Isn't that a very high death rate, Mr. Williams?"

"One man, Mr. Levy," Williams said, "is a high death rate."

"Ah, a philosopher," Levy said, beginning to rattle Williams, and Abernathy objected.

"Sustained," Gilroy said.

"Is there not another suit pending, Mr. Williams?"

"You tell me, you're filing them all."

"You are not answering my question."

"Yes, there is another suit pending."

"And you do not know how many men are diseased and disabled from your laissez-faire safety rules."

"Objection."

"Sustained."

"Well, you don't know, do you, Mr. Williams?"

"No, I don't know, Mr. Levy."

"That is all."

Williams left the stand, angry, threatening, but Abernathy ignored this and called another witness.

"Will Dr. Morton take the stand?"

A young gray-suited man rose and placed his hand on the Bible. He was red-blond and slightly freckled. He had good long square hands, Gilroy noticed.

"What kind of doctor are you, Dr. Morton?"

"I am a doctor of medicine."

"Where did you graduate?"

"Stanford University."

"Dr. Morton," Abernathy asked quietly, "what do you make of your colleague's diagnosis of the plaintiff?"

"Chiropractors," Morton said, "are not my colleagues."

"Objection," Levy said.

"Sustained."

Abernathy took a few paces, then returned to the witness.

"I'll rephrase that. What is your professional opinion of Dr. Bellem's diagnosis?"

Morton faced Dr. Bellem and the plaintiff.

"If Mr. Moolan indeed had silicosis . . ." he paused, "then he would not be testifying here today."

"Why?" Abernathy asked.

"He would be dead."

"Objection," Levy shouted. "Objection," but Judge Gilroy was rapping his desk with his walnut gavel.

"The court," he said, "will take this case under advisement."

"Your honor," Levy said, almost pleadingly.

But Gilroy said sternly, "If the medical testimony of Dr. Morton proves accurate, then this case is dismissed."

"Your honor," Levy shouted.

But Gilroy gaveled him down. "If there is any question about Dr. Morton's testimony, the clerk will inform you about resumption of this trial." Once more he banged his gavel. "Court adjourned."

Gilroy returned to his chambers and removed his robe. He sat in his squeaky wooden armchair and placed his feet on his oak desk. There had been no need for Ickes's call, he thought. He pressed a button and a clerk answered.

"Take this testimony to the Clark County Medical Society."

"Yes sir."

"And have them call me tomorrow."

"Well," Devere said, quite drunk already. "How is Clarence Darrow?"

"The judge took it under advisement," Levy said.

"Did he now? Waiting for the payoff . . ."

Levy sat down, weary, sick. "You're probably right."

"Still had that faint glimmer of hope that justice would prevail?"

"Yes," Levy said, "I did."

"Jesus, God almighty. Haven't you ever heard of Sacco and Vanzetti? The Scottsboro boys?"

"Yes, I heard of them."

"Didn't that tell you *something* about American justice?"

"Not enough," Levy said.

"All right," Devere said, "now we're getting somewhere. If you're poor, you ain't got a chance; if you're red, you ain't got a chance; if you're black, you ain't got a chance."

"All right, Devere," Levy said testily. "You've made your point. We'll try it your way."

"Yeah, kid." Devere said. "Forget all that law shit."

"Law shit," Levy repeated mostly to himself. "Law shit. Give me a glass of whiskey."

"Gladly, comrade," Devere said, "gladly," and he poured another tumbler and handed it to Levy.

"To the revolution," he said, raising his glass.

"Yeah," Levy answered.

At the dam site Williams reported the day to Crowe. "Looks like we got 'em beat," he said.

"That's good."

"That Jew lawyer was beginning to get under my skin though."

"That's what he gets paid for."

"I suppose."

"Now that they've failed in court," Frank thought aloud, "I wonder what they'll have in store for us next."

"I don't know," Williams said. "I'd still like to blow the whole bunch to kingdom come."

"I know how you feel, Jack. So would I."

71

Although, to the innocent visitor observing from the rim of the canyon, erecting a dam seemed nothing more than filling an endless procession of wooden boxes with concrete, the process was far more complex and precise.

Each wooden box known as a form was five feet deep and measured fifty by sixty feet on its sides. These wooden forms required extreme precision in construction and they in turn were lined with corrugated steel, which would form the expansion locks, later to be filled with grouting. After the forms were completed and inspected, a thin layer of grouting (wet sand and water) was sprayed over the surface of the preceding block to clean it and facilitate a bond. Nine men entered a form, including a foreman and a signalman who guided the bucket

353

to its destination by radio. When the circular seven-foot monster descended from the sky, two workmen tripped the safety latches on the bottom of the twenty-ton bucket, and the signalman instructed the cableway operator six hundred feet above him to release the concrete.

Each pour had to be worked in place, and with all the sophisticated machinery surrounding this form, nothing was as effective in placing concrete as workmen tamping it in place with their rubber-booted feet. When Crowe said once that his "entire dam will be built by hand," he was right, although his appendages were wrong. Once the form was filled to capacity, grouting pipes and cooling pipes were installed, and after a set of twenty-four hours, the forms could be removed and placed at the succeeding rise.

Each form required air, water, and electricity. There were carpentry and pipe fitting and welding and masonry, and though all of it looked effortless because now it was routine, Crowe impressed on his engineers, his foremen, the importance of constant integrity in each single rise. "Think of it as *your* house," he said, "and take pride." When a rise was finished it was inspected, and when approved, work continued on another rise, and Crowe moved one grid ahead on the map on his wall.

A number of galleries (or tunnels) were built into the dam, some for permanent use, some for temporary inspections. The main gallery, however, was an eight-foot vertical slot in the center of the dam, which received all the cooling tubes from the setting of the dam. It was here that the flow of cooling water entering and leaving the dam was monitored, and endless copper pipes converging at this juncture gave the slot the appearance of a giant umbilical cord. It was a crucial juncture of the dam and all of its anatomy was drawn in red on Crowe's plans, as it was on Devere's map in his trailer.

"It's here," Devere pointed out to Levy, "right here, where I can hurt the bastard. That's the vital spot in the dam."

"And where in the hell are you going to get enough dynamite to blow this up?"

"I won't need dynamite. All I need is the best hoist operator on the dam."

"What can he do?"

"He can dump one bucket of concrete right into this slot, and it will be curtains for Crowe."

"And what is the operator going to do after that?"

"Go south. We'll give him a trip to Mexico."

"And who is 'him'?"

"That's gonna be your job."

"I see you're still giving orders."

354

"Forget it," Devere said. "We're all in it together."

Levy stepped back from the plan. "It will cause havoc, but it won't stop Crowe."

"That's right. But it will give him time to think. We'd better have our demands ready. If he doesn't meet them, he'll know we'll keep harassing him."

"I know what you're saying, Devere. I just wish . . ."

"What?"

"There's got to be a better way."

"You going soft?"

"I'm not going soft."

"If those cocksuckers," Devere said firmly, "won't negotiate, we'll *force* them to the table."

"We're not the only ones after them. The unions, the Trotskyites, the Socialists, the New Deal," Levy recited.

"Sure, and all they do is talk, and Crowe's boys just stall, and keep building all along. Talk won't do nothing with these guys. . . . They'll finish that dam right from under us. . . ."

"All right," Levy said. "I'll start hanging around the clubs in Searchlight. That's where those hoist operators drink."

"Yeah, but don't order those Jew drinks or they'll spot you right off."

"What's a Jew drink?"

"Lemonade, sarsaparilla . . ."

"Fuck you, Devere. Fuck you."

The atmosphere was more pleasant in the mess hall on December 5. Frank Crowe decided for once not to exhort his men every time he stood up, but instead brought a bottle of bourbon and a glass to the table. When lunch was almost finished he rose and filled the glass with liquor.

"I have some very good news for you men," he said. "Just before lunch I received a message on the radio that the Eighteenth Amendment has been repealed. For those of you who are not conversant with the law, the Eighteenth Amendment meant Prohibition."

A great cheer went up in the mess hall. When the room quieted down, Frank continued. "This is a great victory for the workingman, and since all of you have meticulously lived up to the spirit and the letter of that law, mostly the spirit, I have the pleasure to inform you that, despite the white ribboners, the preachers, the Salvation Army, you men may now legally take a drink of hard liquor."

The room rocked with laughter.

Frank raised his filled glass. "And so a toast to you and a toast to our leaders who have finally restored a measure of our liberties to us." He drank his drink and sat down and listened to the applause in the mess hall.

Elle was aware of Frank's unusual good humor, she was aware of his politeness.

She noticed that Frank took it gracefully when Hans asked him to be godfather to their newly born son and even followed her suggestion to buy that boy a good warm sweater, though it might be a year before the infant could wear it. Perhaps the greatest surprise awaited her Christmas Eve when Frank arrived at the house, ran in and fetched her. She followed him out to his truck, which was laden with new skis, poles, boots, and parkas. A small hand-lettered sign on the hood read, YOSEMITE OR BUST.

"I can't believe it, Frank. You did all this?"

"I think it's time for a little rest."

"You're going to leave the dam site?"

He opened his watch and looked at it sternly. "In precisely fourteen minutes."

Elle threw her arms around him and kissed him. "I threw you off schedule, didn't I?"

"I have a tolerance of several minutes."

She kissed him again. "More tolerance?" she asked.

"That's it." He slapped her fanny and pushed her toward the house.

"Oh my God," Elle said.

"What?"

"What will we do with the Williamses? They won't catch us 'in flagrante' Christmas Eve."

"'In flagrante,' indeed. Maybe I should lay a fire and keep the lights on."

Christmas at the Ahwahnee Lodge in Yosemite had been traditional for old-line San Franciscans, and it was only through the good offices of Roger Stein that Frank was able to obtain a lovely room at the inn. The festive mood began for Frank and Elle once they entered the gates of Yosemite Park. The sight of snow-capped mountains, waterfalls, dark green foliage was a welcome relief from the barren plains, desolate boulders, the treeless, endless horizons of Nevada.

The lodge was festive, garlanded elegantly with pine wreaths and boughs, liberally graced with wide red silk ribbons. The same man laid the fires in all the great stone fireplaces of the inn, and they burned and crackled crisply. The large dining room, baronial in scope, its tables set in white and red, was rivaled in elegance by the views of the snow-capped ranges framed by the sixty-foot-high windows.

Christmas was traditional and English at the Ahwahnee Lodge,

356

complete with yule log, the arrival of St. Nick, and the distribution of small but elegant gifts to all the children present, who despite years of depression, years of breadlines and hobo camps, were still flawlessly dressed in gray flannel suits with Peter Pan collars or little jumper dresses in tartan plaids.

Frank and Elle sat with Roger and Francesca, the Wertheimers from San Francisco, the Strausses of Levi Strauss, and the conversation was as warm as the hot buttered rum, and as piquant as the goose, served simply under glass.

Although neither Frank nor Elle had skied since leaving Vermont, this inherent skill, like swimming, had not left them, and Frank delighted in watching Elle gracefully schuss down the mountains of Badger Pass and stayed right alongside her as they traversed the powdered spines of the Sierras, still, white, and brilliant in the winter sun.

They ended each night in front of their own fire, Frank's eyes caressing Elle's silhouette against the flames. Their last night, after having made love, Elle faced Frank in bed.

"You've changed," she said.

"How?"

"I don't know exactly. You've become warmer, younger, more fun."

"Who knows," he said. "If I continue to get younger I might be the right age for you yet."

"That's always been *your* problem, Frank, never mine."

"I know, Elle, and I love you for it."

"You better get some sleep, honey. Tomorrow is a hard day."

"Back to the salt mines."

"I didn't mean that."

"What did you mean?"

"You're going to have to pay the bill for this bacchanal."

"Bacchanal indeed," he said, grabbing her fanny. "I'll take you once again, you wench. . . ."

"I'm all for the taking," Elle said, facing him.

The moon appeared from behind a cloud. Life was very full.

72

If New Year's Day of 1934 was an omen for the year to follow, it would not be a good year.

For several days Crowe had been receiving warnings from his river watchers, his meteorologists upstream, and he had asked Wanke and Williams and Walker Young, and Andell of Babcock & Wilcox, to his office at three in the afternoon. He pointed to a map of the Colorado and showed the storm center approximately three hundred miles east.

"Every report I get is worse than the last one. The whole Colorado system is getting drowned out. They say the Grand Canyon looks like Dante's Inferno."

"We've got a light shift working," Young said somberly.

"So do we." Crowe turned to Williams. "Round up every man jack you can find in Vegas. I want all three shifts on in three hours."

"It's New Year's Day, Frank. You know the kind of shape those boys will be in?"

"Never mind. That rain will sober them up in no time."

He turned to Andell. "You got any pipe lying around?"

"Tons of it."

"Secure it. I can't have steel flying all over the place."

"Shut down your mixers, Tom. We won't be pouring for a couple of days, and get those mules under cover. I want to shut off the third rail. I'll have stiffs crawling all over this dam site in no time."

There were no questions and each man left the office with his individual mission, leaving Frank and Walker Young.

"Big Red's revenge," Frank said. "God damn. Would strike on a holiday. . . ."

"We'll handle it," Young said calmly.

"We'll try," Frank said. "God knows we'll try, and now I've got to get on the phone and justify the overtime, can you imagine that?"

"No. I can't and I wouldn't. Fuck them, Frank, I'll back you up if they give you any shit."

"Fuck them, you're right, Walker. You're goddamn right. Oh, Jesus, there are times I wish I were back with the Bureau. I'm sick of building a dam with an accountant looking over my shoulder."

Walker Young laughed. "You should hear Ickes on that subject."

"Ickes, yes," Frank said. "I keep hearing more and more about him. What kind of man is he, anyway?"

"Do you remember when we took the launch down this river over fifteen years ago? You, myself, Hoover, Elwood Mead?"

"Sure."

"Well, Ickes is the only guy in that Roosevelt crowd you wouldn't mind having on board."

"Ickes, eh? What's his first name?"

"Harold."

"Harold Ickes. We'll charge the overtime to him."

"Not on your ass," Walker Young said. "I'm even billing you guys for the gas in my trucks."

"Thanks a lot, you bureaucrat . . ."

"I don't go skiing at Yosemite on *my* holiday," Young said sarcastically. "I can't afford that."

"I could answer that, Walker, but we've got better things to do."

And so they did. Frank and Hans sat in their truck on a mound overlooking the dam site and the river. Using his binoculars Frank watched the sky turn from blue to white to dark gray. He felt the wind picking up and he was startled by the first bolt of lightning, which struck a power pole thirty yards away from them.

"There go the lights," Frank said.

Thunder followed the lightning, angry shattering thunder, and more lightning and more thunder, and finally the sky broke like a shattered chandelier, rain so solid it almost choked a man, so driven with wind it tore asphalt to shreds, flooded everything in sight in minutes.

"Let's get out of here," Frank said. "We'll be buried in mud in no time. Let's get to the spillways."

Hans spun all over the road as did other vehicles. "It's like driving on ice," he said.

"Just take it easy," Crowe said quietly.

He met Williams at the Nevada spillway, and watched its floor covered with water.

"You want me to open the other tunnels?"

"You better," Frank said, and Williams disappeared into the rain.

Crowe watched electricians bringing emergency generators, and he guided men in the placement of lights. His eyes were on the river and on the upper cofferdam, and he watched tree stumps, barn sides, docks, and fences run down the Colorado, crashing ultimately into the cofferdam.

"Find Williams," he said to Hans, and they drove in the direction of the tunnels, but Williams met them halfway.

"Christ, Jack, it looks like half of Utah is coming down the river. We can't let all that stuff go into the tunnels."

"I'm way ahead of you, mister. I'm covering the portals with mesh."

"Where the hell you getting mesh?"

"The fence from the ball park."

"Good thinking."

Three young staff engineers joined Crowe.

"Shut off the water for Boulder City," he ordered. "That settling basin can't handle this. We'll all get cholera."

"Get me Wanke," he ordered the second engineer. "Bring me a tanker full of fuel oil and two hundred water bags," he told the third.

"Yes sir."

"Oh, Rick?"

"Yes?"

"Bring ten more boys up here. Move!"

The sky was so dark and leaden, the rain so relentless, no one noticed the arrival of night.

Four more engineers reported and Crowe identified them with his flashlight.

"I want two cranes on top of the cofferdam and two crane operators. Get me a convoy of twenty mucking trucks. . . . Waldo?"

"Yes sir."

"Spot those crews fifty feet off shore and pick up this debris. It's going to raise hell with the tunnels."

Wanke appeared, and ducked under Crowe's makeshift canvas top.

"You turn off your mixers?"

"No."

"Good."

"Don't tell me," Wanke said. "Bury some pumps at the tunnels."

"Right."

"They're already buried," Wanke said, "and they're pumping."

"Good."

Walker Young appeared out of the turret. "I just got word, Harper's Ferry broke loose."

"Oh, Jesus, that's going to knock the shit out of my dam."

"Stretch a cable," Young yelled.

"If I got time . . ."

Three more engineers appeared.

"I want a three-inch cable across the river four feet off the river. Smith, Illwell, do it!"

Crowe turned to Young. "Got any other good news?"

"Sure. Aunt Mary called up. Said she'd have a ranch breakfast for the boys, on the house."

"I hope we got enough boats to get there."

The river came hard and came fast, and the rain persisted, but finally day dawned at six-twenty and brought the sun. It had been twelve hours since Hans had driven Crowe to the river and it felt like fifty. As Crowe stepped out of his truck, he surveyed the dam site below him. Everything was the color of mud. The earth, the dam, the portals, the trucks, the cranes and cableways. A lone duck was calmly floating down the river. The Colorado was smooth and placid and laughing like hell.

Frank stretched and pulled his arms toward the middle of his chest. He looked at the area around his truck. It was littered with six dead flashlights.

"Jesus Christ," he said for the seventh time, "they don't even know how to make a flashlight anymore. . . ."

"Take me home, Hans. I want to get a shower."

"I want a three-inch cable, Smith, four feet off the river," the younger engineer imitated Crowe. "Just like that." He took off his shoes.

"Well, we got it up."

"Yeah, just in time. Boy, did you see that ferry come tearing down that river?"

"I saw it, Henry. I was on the other end of the three-inch cable."

"That's right, you were."

"It went halfway through that ferry before it stopped her."

"Yup. But it stopped her."

"Never learned that trick at school, did you?"

"No," Smith said. "Did you?"

"No, but I did last night."

Smith crawled into his sleeping bag. "At least the man could say please."

"He's probably writing you a thank-you note right now."

"Oh, shut up." Smith raised himself on one arm and looked at Illwell. "He's got command, I'll grant you that . . . but has he got the right to take my flashlight?"

"You shouldn't be an engineer, Smith."

"No? What do you think I should be?"

361

"A florist."

"Shit."

Illwell dodged the boot that Smith threw at him. It was ten in the morning.

73

June 6, 1934, marked another milestone on Boulder Dam, the pouring of the two-millionth bucket of concrete, and though this proved another tribute to Crowe's efficiency, it was the visual impact of this event that was so staggering. No one, at this point, could quite predict the final shape of the dam, since no structure that size had ever been built before; however, past the halfway point, the mass of concrete presented a sight which no one would ever forget. It looked like a very tall, windowless city confined to a very small area. Almost no two columns were of the same height; some soared over four hundred feet, others were at the two-hundred-foot level; their similarity was their identical proportions; and the uniformity of the color of the concrete. There were really only two materials visible, that gray-white concrete and the spattered lumber which preceded further construction. Simple wooden ladders ran between rises and hundreds of workmen labored at various elevations, their clothes quickly taking on the color of the dam.

And, as Frank looked at this monstrous arch, he was satisfied that he had finally put an end to the most popular myth about the dam, namely that it was filled with a number of trapped and buried men. Endless newspaper reports had made it appear that it was neither steel nor cement that kept the structure intact, but rather human bones. Crowe had invited the syndicated columnist Al Houston from the *New York Times* to visit the dam site and asked him to spend a day in one of the forms which was being poured. It had taken Houston only half a day to convince himself that no man could be trapped in each successive five-foot rise. At lunch at the Reno Club Houston assured Crowe that he would put an end to this stupid legend once and for all.

"I am much obliged," Frank had said. "I've got enough *real* troubles without these phony stories cooked up by the newspapers."

"I can see that, Mr. Crowe. This is not the first construction site I've covered. I think you're doing an admirable job. Just leave it to me."

Houston had not only written eloquently and truthfully about what he saw on the dam site, but had reaffirmed Frank's belief that he was still a good judge of men.

Mario Veneto was one of Crowe's best hoist operators. He had both the brains and dexterity to possibly have become a fine engineer, but his love of gambling—dice, horses, tokens—made him a slave to Las Vegas and a trial to his family. As other men calculated the odds against them in the casino, Veneto measured his memories of winning nights, of hundreds of dollars made in minutes and more often than not spent on debauchery in a few hours afterward.

Veneto was well known at the Lucky Seven Club, and occasional deficits were cheerfully carried by the house until the next payday. But a long streak of losing, an *unusual* streak of bad luck, left Veneto further and further in debt to Gallino, and when that figure reached $1,000, Veneto ceased to be an unlucky stiff, and became an easy mark.

Two men, whose only attributes were height and weight, appeared at Veneto's house at eleven in the morning in Boulder City. When Veneto, still sleepy from the graveyard shift, opened the door, he could see only a vast expanse of cheaply dressed flesh. He had never seen such massive men, even on the dam site. One of them bent forward slightly and picked up Veneto by his pajama collar.

"You owe the boss a grand," the hood said.

"I know," Veneto said, half choking.

"You're gonna pay it back."

"I know."

"Tonight!"

"Tonight?"

"Yeah. Tonight."

"I can't raise a grand by tonight."

"Well," the tall man said, still dangling Veneto easily, "you'll be off shift at midnight . . . and we'll expect you at eleven tomorrow with the grand, in cash."

He lowered Veneto to the ground.

"Ifen you don't come up with the scratch there won't be enough left of ya to put into a Chesterfield tin. Got it?"

"Look," Veneto pleaded, "there's got to be a way to work it out. . . ."

"There is. . . . We just gave it to you. Twenty-four hours. You're

363

a gambler. Place some smart bets. What's a grand?"

"It's nothing to you. It's a lot to me."

"That's what Gallino said. It's nothing to Veneto. It's *my* grand. See ya tomorrow."

Veneto closed his door and watched his wife, dressed in a cheap cotton robe, frying eggs.

"Who was that?" his wife asked.

"Nobody."

He walked to a kitchen cabinet and took out a bottle of bourbon and took a hefty swig.

"Kind of early to be boozin' it up," his wife said.

"Shut up."

Veneto walked to his bedroom and put on the same denims that he had shed only a few hours ago. He laced his boots and put a baseball cap on his head.

"Where you going? Breakfast is ready."

"Out," he said, and walked into the heat and slammed his front door.

He drove to the Wobbly trailer in Vegas. He knew where it was. He had been there before at Levy's invitation, but today he spoke to Devere.

"Well, Veneto, looks like we're finally going to do business."

"Yeah, it does."

"What do you owe Gallino?"

"How do you know I owe Gallino?"

"Don't ask stupid questions."

"Twelve hundred dollars," Veneto lied.

"That is a lot of money."

"Look, commie," Veneto yelled, "I don't need your fucking lectures. . . . What do you want?"

"A hot head," Devere teased, "a real hot head . . ."

"Screw you, I got my own troubles."

"Well, that's too bad, we all got troubles."

"Lay off," Levy said. "Tell him what you want."

Devere shot Levy an angry glance but proceeded. "How good are you with the levers?"

"Why don't you ask Levy? He's been hanging around the hoists for months."

"He's good," Levy said.

"All right," Devere said, standing and walking to a table which held his drawings of the dam. "You know the slot?"

"I know the slot."

"I want one bucket right down that slot. Right down the center." He pointed to it in the plans. "I want to knock out every pipe and header in that dam between elevation two hundred and four hundred."

"That's gonna take some fancy aiming," Veneto said.

"That's right. And you're asking for a pretty fancy price."

Devere covered the set of plans and sat down behind the desk. "Well, you mull it over for a while."

"I've got no time to mull it over," Veneto said. "I've got to do this tonight."

"Gallino's really got his hooks into you, hasn't he?"

"It's tonight," Veneto said, "or forget it."

"Tonight it is."

"Good," Veneto said. "I'll need the money in advance."

"I bet." Devere laughed. "I'll give you half now, and I'll deliver the rest to Gallino if you do a good job."

Devere reached under his desk and pulled out a black metal box, reached in his pocket for a key, and opened it. He took out five one-hundred-dollar bills. "There's half," he said.

"I told you twelve hundred dollars," Veneto said.

"I know you did." Devere smiled. "Gallino said you only owed him a grand. Maybe you didn't hear him too good."

"Maybe I didn't," Veneto said, leaving the trailer, sweating, and debating whether to go to the Reno Club. It would only be two rolls of the dice. One to double $500 and he'd have the money for Gallino. One to double the grand and he could repay Devere and be $500 ahead.

It was still quiet at one in the afternoon at the Reno Club and Veneto stood in the shadows watching the three crap tables under the glaring overhead lamps. There was little action, the dealers talking to each other, the only play by shills, whose alternately stacked silver dollars and lack of excitement marked them easily. He could detect no run at any table and grew tired of the looks of the security cop.

Finally he strode to the middle table, placed $500 on the line and took the dice from the stickman. He turned them carefully, looking for worn edges, for markings, but finally satisfied, let them loose in his cupped hand, wound up his arm and shot the dice against the backboard. Before his scream of "Come on seven" was out of his throat, the dice came to an immutable dead stop and two sixes loomed large and ominous.

"Crap, twelve," the dealer yelled, picking up the money and moving the dice to the next player.

Veneto walked from the table; he heard the casino manager yell, "Want a drink on the house, buddy?" but he got into his car and headed toward the dam site.

Veneto had been a gambler for a long time. He had run into

strings of bad luck before, but this last string was peculiar. He almost felt that Gallino, or perhaps Devere, had conspired to put him in this spot. There was nothing he could do about it now.

He had two choices: he could run now, but to get out from under Gallino was practically impossible; he could pull the job and Gallino would get $500 from Devere. He had half a chance that Gallino would give him more time for the rest of the money.

Frank Crowe was sound asleep when Veneto began his graveyard shift. The hoist operator had eaten nothing all day. He swung easily into the cab of Number 4 cableway and gave a cursory wave to Olsen, the man he replaced. The six levers over the past year had become extensions of his own fingers, and his accuracy in handling buckets of concrete had almost made him a legend on the dam site, but tonight he was shaky. He knew this would be his last shift. Veneto placed six buckets without any trouble and felt some relief that his experience overcame his trembling. At three o'clock in the morning he decided to make his move.

He easily picked up a bucket on the freight car behind him and swung it along the cable over the dam site. He could hear the crackle of the radio of his lookout man, but ripped off the headset. Slowly the bucket reached the center of the dam, and Veneto waited carefully until the sway of the bucket stopped. He was directly over the slot. It took only one lever, the furthest on the right, to lower the bucket, and Veneto pushed it full force. The bucket hurtled down at twice the speed intended for the cables and entered the slot.

Veneto's aim was perfect. The twenty-ton concrete-filled missile tore out massive staging, it broke eleven sets of headers and finally landed at elevation 211, burying and killing two pipe fitters. Veneto picked up the binoculars lying beside him and his eyes ran down the illuminated slot. Water poured from either side of the dam like blood from a man riddled with a machine gun. He lowered his binoculars and saw the jagged torn stagings, and then he heard the siren and he watched men with shovels attack the mountain of concrete.

He ran on foot through the desert night. He knew he could never get out of the reservation by car. He had killed a man, maybe more than one. This had not been in the cards, not for him, much less for Devere. At three-twenty the phone rang in Crowe's house and at three-thirty-five he was at the bottom of the slot.

Whether it was superstition or fear or a religious feeling with the crews, Crowe knew no work would continue on the dam until the men were found under the shattered bucket, under the mountain of slowly setting concrete, and though he did not remain to watch the final exhumation, he called a meeting in his office after he had inspected the damage done to his dam.

Wanke, Williams, a platoon of other engineers crowded around the map and listened as Frank, pointer in hand, went from elevation to elevation. "We've got to block everything from elevation 210 to 415. What we can't cool internally we'll have to cool externally. Anson," he said to an older, balding man, "you'll have to keep your boys going around the clock, ripping out damaged pipe, replacing it, fitting new sensors. . . ." He looked at Wanke. "We can pour around the slot. I'll have to refigure the pattern. As soon as we have one rise ready we'll keep pouring." Frank scratched his head. "If that son of a bitch had tried, he couldn't have done a better job."

Williams seemed impatient and after the meeting was concluded only he and Wanke remained. Williams could barely contain himself.

"Look, Frank," he said, "I've had almost all I can take. You know whose work this is."

"I know."

"Let me take ten of my boys and put an end to it."

"Take ten of your boys," Frank said grimly, "and a hundred sticks of dynamite. I won't argue with you anymore, Jack."

"Now you're talking," Williams said, rubbing his hands, and left Frank's office quickly.

"I don't understand the Wobbly mentality," Wanke said.

"They're trying to bring us to our knees," Crowe answered.

"How? By killing our men?"

"No, I don't think they expected any men at the bottom of the slot. With a murder rap over their heads I doubt if Williams will even find them."

"Have they made any demands?" Wanke asked.

"Who?"

"The Wobblies."

"The same demands they all make. Higher wages, fewer hours, drying rooms in the tunnels."

"And do we ever *give* in?"

"No. You give 'em an inch and they'll want a mile."

Wanke looked at Crowe. "They got a mile last night. . . ."

"I know, damn it, you don't have to rub it in."

Williams and his men, ten hard-hatted, colorfully tattooed tunnelers and muckers, surrounded Devere's trailer quickly, and Williams and two of his foremen entered the shabby interior. They could see unmade beds, books strewn about, a very drunk Devere sitting behind a cigarette-scarred old desk, a glass and bottle of whiskey in front of him, a pistol, a note pad.

"Stop right there," Devere said, pointing his pistol at Williams, and Jack stared at the man venomously, sitting there in a torn white shirt, unshaven, unkempt, obviously drunk. . . .

"If you don't make no mistakes," Devere slurred, "you can take me without a fight."

"Go on," Williams said.

"Tell Crowe he won," Devere said.

"Won what? You killed two of our men."

"That was not in the plan."

"What was?"

"What *was?* You an educated man stand here and ask me a dumb question like that."

It was only Devere's pointed pistol that kept Williams in check.

"Three dollars and fifty cents a day, that's what you pay your stiffs. *Three* dollars and fifty cents working in that hell hole in the summer, in that freezing abyss in the winter. Three fifty a day. Day and night while you and Wanke and Crowe and the Big Six get *fat.* This is 1934, Mr. Williams, and even that goddamned Roosevelt senses what's wrong." Devere wiped his brow. "We've tried strikes, and we've tried placards."

"And you tried to blow up our bridge," Williams said.

"Hell yes, because none of you will *listen.*"

"Our pay is better than the national average."

"Sure, because the national average is *shit.* Here, Mr. Williams," Devere said. "Here is my gun. You can shoot me now or you can put me in jail. I don't give a damn anymore. About you, or the dam, or the Wobblies or anything. I have run all my life, and I'll tell you something ironic, Mr. Williams."

"What's that?"

"I was born in this country. I fought for it." He waved his hand in disgust. "Hell, I'm sick of making speeches."

Williams looked at the pathetic creature sipping his whiskey.

"Take him in," Williams said. "Have him booked for murder." He threw Devere's pistol to one of his foremen.

Pitt's car pulled up and he entered the trailer with two deputies. They handcuffed Devere and placed him in back of the police car.

Williams watched the entire scene. Then he picked up Devere's half-empty bottle of whiskey, took it out and handed it to Devere. Devere looked at Williams, but said nothing.

Pitt drove off, sirens blaring, and Williams looked at his foremen. "I don't know what the hell is wrong with me. Going soft in my old age."

74

It had taken Frank Crowe almost two months to repair the damage done by Veneto and his errant bucket of concrete. Of course he continued to pour his dam, but his slide rule rarely cooled off as he figured and refigured a new pattern of construction which would allow the dam to rise despite the sabotage.

And, on a very cold and windy December 5, Frank Crowe, fully two years ahead of schedule, poured the three-millionth bucket of concrete, and the ultimate curvature and majesty of the dam's structure was becoming apparent. Frank could see that men going off shift, men who normally numbly headed for a seat on the double-decker buses for Boulder City, would take off their hard hats, wipe their brows, and look back at the dam, almost at full height now, monstrous, almost frightening, and feel a sense of pride.

For months now Williams had been plugging the outside diversion tunnels, and the lowering of the giant bulkhead gate at the inlet of the Arizona tunnel marked the beginning of Boulder Lake behind the dam. For Walker Young, for Frank Crowe, even for Harold Ickes, that moment was critical because from then on the waters from the Colorado not only would cease to be a hazard to the Imperial Valley, but the same water would soon become an economic asset: irrigation and electricity.

But there was another side to the accomplishment felt by the inhabitants of Boulder City. Christmas, 1934, had a flavor and a tone unlike any of the preceding holidays. Men who had carefully painted their small homes, women who had devotedly cultivated the desert soil for flowers and vegetables, mothers who had spent hours working on safety committees, all of them knew that the rising dam, as magnificent a monument as it might be to the genius of Frank Crowe, also represented perhaps the world's greatest single tombstone. When it was topped off in less than six months with a highway, its very being would, for the most part, mean the end of employment, the end of Boulder City, its clear water, its clean streets, its crimeless atmosphere, its decent schools, its camaraderie. Families and friends this year not only wished each other Merry Christmas, but most of them would say, or think, "I wonder where we'll be next year. I hate to take the kids out of school. I just about got that desert cooler working good. We'll never even see that first crop of strawberries we've planted."

Norton's Notions and Gifts noticed the atmosphere, as did Wenhardt's Clothing Emporium. Al Cashman found the sales of new cars down, and even Aunt Mary spent less money gifting her patrons and her benefactors. A climate of fear spread through the town. The uprooted farmer from Imperial was not so certain about returning to his parched land in El Centro, and the dusted-out Okie felt little enthusiasm for loading up the Model T to return to the heartland of America.

Harold Ickes arrived without fanfare on December 12 and was put up at Sequoia Lodge. Unlike other cabinet officers, who traveled with a retinue of servants and sycophants, Harold Ickes came alone. His luggage consisted of a small valise and a series of cardboard boxes and leatherette folders. Once ensconced in the comfort of the lodge, he phoned Crowe's office, and when told that the supervising engineer was busy on the dam site, he said simply, "Tell him that I am here and that I would be happy to see him at his convenience."

Perhaps it was the modesty of his message which helped Frank's attitude toward Ickes; at any rate, his meeting with the man became quickly amicable.

It was four in the afternoon when Crowe received the message from Ickes and he phoned him immediately.

"Mr. Secretary?"

"Yes."

"Frank Crowe."

"How are you, sir?"

"Apologetic. I had no warning about your early arrival."

"Neither you nor I, Mr. Crowe, are on a pleasure trip. I would like to see you at your convenience."

"I can be right up," Frank said, "but I'll make no excuses for my appearance."

"I've brought my own gin," Ickes said, "and I haven't shaved since I left Washington."

They shook hands when Crowe arrived. Ickes stirred a pitcher of martinis and poured into a chilled glass for Frank. He paced the ample expanse of Sequoia Lodge.

"You know," he said, "this living room with its Spanish Moorish furniture reminds me of the Boca Raton Club. Have you ever been there?"

"I'm afraid not."

"It's nothing to be apologetic about. I'd never frequent the place myself except for government business. It is privately owned by some

370

idiot who even during the depression has a waiting list of suckers eager to pay five thousand dollars to mix with other idiots in a totally prejudiced environment."

"It is a world I know little about," Frank said.

"You may say so," Ickes observed, "but the Boca Raton Club is just as much of an anomaly in the Florida swamp as this debauchery in the Nevada desert."

"The Sequoia Lodge, Mr. Secretary, was not my idea either."

"That," Ickes said, "I believe."

"You do, Mr. Ickes, make a good martini."

"Thank you," Ickes said, refilling Frank's glass. He paced the room. "I have not, as you may have noticed, asked for a tour of your dam site, not because I am not interested, but because I have been on top of it almost as closely as you have."

"Yes?"

"You've done a superb job."

"We're moving along," Frank said.

"Yes. Two years ahead of schedule."

Frank Crowe was not a man who liked accolades, nor was he a man impressed by public figures.

"Mr. Ickes," he said, "I appreciate the kind words, and I am enjoying your martinis, and just as carefully as you have probably studied my dossier, so have I perused your public career. It is—and for a Republican this is a hard admission—impressive. However, I do not think that we are watching the sun set on another day in the Nevada desert to pat each other on the back. We are both too busy for that."

"Quite true," Ickes said. "You are by profession an engineer, and I am by profession an attorney. My approach may be more circumlocutory than yours, but I hope as effective. First of all, Mr. Crowe, let me lay to rest the Boulder-Hoover controversy."

"I wish you would."

"This was the President's idea. He does not feel public-works projects should be named after living people. He turns down proposals weekly which were slated to carry his name. I know I've gotten the blame for this, but that's part of my job."

"I see," Frank said. "I've always felt that Hoover had a proprietary interest in this dam. The name seemed a proper tribute."

"I've speculated about this myself, Mr. Crowe. I wonder really whether Hoover built this dam as an engineering exercise rather than a work-creating entity."

"You will admit that Hoover made a very humanitarian record for himself after the Great War."

"Even *that*, Mr. Crowe, is debatable. I think at the time the man was a good administrator." Ickes laughed. "He had to have *some* talents

371

or he wouldn't have become so rich so young."

"So tell me about Roosevelt, and Washington, and the New Deal, Mr. Secretary."

Ickes refilled their glasses and looked at Crowe. "You have heard that I am the most progressive member of the Cabinet, but perhaps you don't know that I am not a Democrat. I'm an Independent, and it might equally surprise you that like you I have often fought the administration to create a hard-nosed public-works program, fiscally sound, meaningfully conceived, and carefully executed—unlike my colleague Harry Hopkins."

"A basic question, Mr. Secretary."

"Go ahead, Mr. Crowe."

"Where does the U.S. Treasury find the funds for all these projects? When Hoover left Washington the Treasury was on the brink of collapse. Banks were failing daily."

"A good question. Perhaps Roosevelt's first master stroke was the declaration of a National Bank Holiday. The country survived that and the catastrophe did not occur. Of course I've heard that Hoover meant to do the same thing, but he didn't."

"Reopening the banks did not enrich the Treasury."

"That's right. What enriched the Treasury was the government printing office. We printed so many dollars we had to use ten-year-old plates to do it. So everyone went around and said the dollar wasn't worth anything."

"Right."

"So Roosevelt went off the gold standard and I'll agree that the dollar still isn't worth a hell of a lot, but if a man has enough in his jeans to buy a cup of coffee, a doughnut, a pound of meat, an overcoat, he really doesn't give a dam what that piece of paper is backed with; he only cares whether the merchant will accept it."

"So a lot of it is illusory."

"No, not a lot of it, Mr. Crowe. A certain amount. People who work *pay* taxes, that's better than welfare. We lend money to small business *if* they create jobs; we lend money to farmers and we control the marketplace for crops. . . . We are even telling big business that if they pay their workers a respectable salary, that worker may become a consumer. . . ."

"You are priming the pump," Crowe said.

"*True*," Ickes yelled, "but we are getting more than well water, we're getting some confidence, some hope. You haven't traveled this country the way I have. I watched it during those last years of Hoover. Pellagra in the South, beriberi, malaria, high infant mortality, tuberculosis, crowded mental hospitals, hobo jungles, Hoovervilles . . ."

"I've seen some of it," Crowe said. "Right here in Vegas."

"Things had to be *done*."

"Well, I'll agree you are doing things—and from the men that have come here I'll say that Roosevelt must be quite a charmer to get such loyalists."

Ickes parted the velvet drapes to watch the Nevada sunset. He did not face Crowe as he said, "He is that. He is brilliant, devious, warm-hearted, steely. He is a very wide-gauge man." Ickes let the curtain drop and walked to the dining room. He found the large tubular map case, opened it, withdrew a six-foot-long drawing and spread it over the polished dining room table.

When Ickes had the long drawing secured at the edges he said to Crowe, "Come here, I'd like you to see this."

Frank faced the table and a beautiful rendition of the Grand Coulee Dam. He withdrew calipers from his shirt pocket, a pencil and paper, and totally oblivious of Ickes he measured the drawing, recording the dimensions: *Three-quarters of a mile long, thirty stories high, five hundred feet thick, spanning the upper Columbia.*

"Right on the nose," Ickes said, seeing him write the numbers.

"How far from Spokane?" Crowe asked.

"One hundred miles west."

Crowe put away his tools and backed away from the table, not taking his eyes off the drawing.

"I've heard this dam was going up. Who engineered it?"

"David at the Bureau," Ickes said.

"Tell David," Crowe said, "that it is not only ingenious, but beautiful. Extend him my congratulations and best wishes. It will be the largest dam in the world when it is finished."

"David," Ickes said, "cannot continue building that dam."

"Why not?"

"He is losing his sight."

"God damn it. No one should build that dam but David."

"He totally agrees with you, Mr. Crowe. I just saw him in Denver. He said only one other man can complete this dam. Frank Crowe. Now you know why I am here."

Crowe took one last look at the drawing, then returned to the parlor and his drink.

"Hoover, pardon me, Boulder, is my sixth dam, Mr. Secretary. I fully intended it to be my last. I thought it would be the biggest dam in the world."

"It still will be the highest," Ickes said, almost apologetically.

"Yes, the highest," Crowe said to himself.

"If you should accept my offer to finish the dam, Mr. Crowe, I'll have to ask you to rejoin the Bureau of Reclamation. This dam is not being built by private interests like Boulder. I have reorganized the

373

Bureau. There will be three regional directors. You would be one of them. Your pay would be less than you are making now. It would be the same as mine."

Now Crowe rose and faced Ickes. "It is true," he said, "I left the Bureau before this dam because I felt I was underpaid. After this dam I'll have all the money I'll ever need. Frankly I miss working for the Bureau. The money is not an issue."

"What is?"

"There are several," Crowe said. "One," he said, "is that dam," pointing to the dining room. "It is the most beautiful dam I've ever seen. I wish I'd never laid eyes on it."

"And you and your boys would do a hell of a job finishing it," Ickes said.

"I have no boys, Mr. Secretary. I am an engineer. I am not a scoutmaster or a politician looking for votes. I am really getting sick and tired of all this social crap I keep hearing. I haven't finished this dam and everybody's worried about *my* boys, about Boulder City, the economy of the Colorado Basin. *That's your* job, Mr. Secretary, you and your geniuses in Washington."

"A valid point," Ickes said. "What next?"

"Next," Crowe said, "is simply the fact that I don't know whether I have the guts or the drive to tackle another dam. A bigger dam. Sometimes I question my abilities on *this* project."

"What is there to question? You're two years ahead."

"I'm two years ahead and ten years older."

Ickes looked at Crowe. "I am sixty years of age," he said, "and I work eighteen hours a day, and when I get home I can't sleep. . . ."

Crowe looked at Ickes with true compassion. "There is another reason. My wife."

Ickes nodded his head.

"I have a lovely young wife, Mr. Secretary. She has opened a wider world for me. I am not sure that I want to collapse in her lap."

"That is a reason I can respect," Ickes said, rolling up the plan and replacing it in the leatherette tube.

"Mr. Foster, the assistant secretary, has told me about her. He was quite captivated. Do I get to meet her?"

Frank hesitated, then said, "No, Mr. Secretary. You boys from Washington have taken a good lesson in charm from your boss. I think this is a decision I would like to make all by myself."

Ickes extended his hand. "The loss is mine, but I understand your answer."

"Good night, Mr. Secretary. You'll be hearing from me."

"Good night, Mr. Crowe. Here," he said, "take along this drawing. I have more copies in Washington."

Frank Crowe laughed and put on his hat. "I bet you have."

Frank had Hans drive him to his office, where he stored the plan. He resisted looking at it once more and decided to say nothing to anyone about the proposal, not even Elle. The first decision, he knew, he would have to make himself, and all the reasons he gave Ickes were valid.

Ickes knew he had intrigued Crowe, and felt that his chances were about even that the man would accept the challenge, but he wondered now, facing another night of insomnia, whether he was proud of this charm of which Crowe had spoken. Looking down at the dam site at midnight, watching this massive project, so well illuminated and so highly organized, he wondered whether a man like Crowe did not really deserve some peace and some rest. It had been a life well spent, there was no doubt of that.

75

In San Francisco, the final days of 1934 already showed some signs of an improving economy. The street corners of Post and Powell reverberated with the bells of the crowded cable cars and the bells of the pale Salvation Army maidens; the mood was one of holly and cheer. The Christmas tree in the rotunda of the City of Paris rose seventy feet and awed all who saw it, festooned with gold and silver ribbons and hundreds of glass balls in red and gold and silver. The windows of Gump's displayed jade and Buddhas and kimonos, reminding shoppers of their geography on the edge of the Pacific Basin.

Barnes and Stein, Mackenzie, Henderson, and Chapman were also downtown the day of Christmas Eve, and their table at Sam's had held a reserved sign since the restaurant's opening. Well dressed in heavy woolen suits, they shed their light raincoats after entering the restaurant, and soon held cold martinis at the stand-up bar and nodded or spoke to their fellow San Franciscans this foggy festive day.

Once seated, each man placed a small bundle of well-wrapped, expensive-looking gifts in front of him and ordered dark ale and cracked crabs to begin the holiday quietly and relaxed in the company of men and peers before the onslaught of children and grandchildren who would noisily dictate the next two days.

Chapman was the first to raise his glass. "A toast," he said, "to our rising dam."

And they all clinked glasses and downed their ale.

"And may it be finished next year," Barnes proposed, and once more the ritual was respected.

"My boys in Washington tell me," Chapman said, "that Ickes is building another big one."

"I know," Mackenzie said, "the Grand Coulee near Spokane."

"That's right," Chapman said. "My boys said it will be three times as big as Boulder."

"It's Ickes's dam," Henderson said. "He'll have the Bureau of Reclamation build it."

"They can't build it all," Chapman said. "It's too big. They'll need outside contractors before it's finished."

"I wonder if Crowe knows about it?" Roger Stein asked.

"Wouldn't surprise me. I heard that Ickes was up at the dam site not long ago."

"I wonder if Crowe would take on another dam?" Mackenzie asked, wiping his lips with a well-ironed white napkin.

"I'm not so sure," Stein said. "I figure his bonus at almost three hundred thousand dollars."

"Pretty close," Barnes said. "We've figured the profit ourselves."

"I bet you have," Mackenzie said. "That goddamned bookkeeper of yours probably figures daily."

"Hourly," Barnes said, good-humoredly, and then added seriously, "I always *thought* it was a mistake to give Crowe a percentage. Right from the start."

"And if we hadn't where in hell do you think we'd be right now?" Stein asked. "Halfway through the tunnels? You name me another man who would have us two years ahead of schedule."

"It's not just the money," Barnes said. "He might retire. Say we got in on Grand Coulee, then what?"

"Then you *are* admitting Crowe played a role," Mackenzie prodded.

"I won't take anything away from the man," Barnes said.

"Well," Mackenzie said, "*you're* an engineer. Would *you* like to be supervising Grand Coulee?"

"I think I'm a little old for the job."

"Old, hell. You can't be more than a year older than Crowe."

"He's in better shape."

"You bet your ass," Mackenzie said, looking at Barnes. "When was the last time you worked a slide rule?"

"Lay off," Barnes said. "It's Christmas, for Christ sake."

Frank Crowe, Wanke, and Williams were well aware of the mixed emotions that occupied the residents of Boulder City this Christmas. Though they faced a more secure future than their men, they too would miss the hard ritual they had performed side by side for so many years. Frank, it was true, had the plans for Grand Coulee safely locked in his office, but he suspected that both Wanke and Williams had caught wind of that project, and just as carefully as he avoided the issue with Elle, so he kept the dam to himself with his friends. He suspected that each of them was going through his own turmoil.

Frank and Elle made the rounds this year. They took presents to Hans and Terry, they visited the Williamses, the Wankes, they paid their respects to Walker Young and his wife, and even Elle noticed the solemnity in the air.

They sat by the fire Christmas night sipping hot buttered rum, which Elle had concocted from the *Community Cook Book*.

"When do you think the dam will be finished?" she asked.

"This year, honey, that's all I can say. It could be September if all goes well, it could be next Christmas. I spend as much time rescheduling as I do scheduling on this dam. The clouds are building up again. There'll be storms, perhaps more storms than we've ever had. There's talk about the All-American Canal. I'll have men quit on me in droves if they start hiring before I'm finished."

"And what about Ickes?" Elle said. "You've never talked about your meeting with him."

"He's a fine man. We beat the Wobblies in court because of him."

"Did he tell you that?"

"No. I just learned it from a reporter in Vegas. Ickes won't give me any trouble on the dam."

"That's good," Elle said. "You've been so quiet lately."

Frank drew Elle closer to him. They were sitting on the floor, her back on his chest.

"How about your library, honey? Are you going to miss your library?"

"Yes," she said. "I'll miss that library and that lovely card catalogue your boys built and the worn-out children's books, the monthly shipments. . . ."

Elle turned and faced Frank. Her robe opened and the navy-blue piping of the collar framed her lovely breasts. Frank bent down and kissed her, his eyes on the fire ahead.

"Maybe we could go to Hawaii for a while," Elle said, her eyes reflecting the flames. "We could lie on the beach and swim and you could fish and sail. . . . I've always wanted to see Hawaii."

"Where does a little girl from Vermont get an appetite for Hawaii? Now tell me that?"

"The *National Geographics*. I couldn't wait for them to arrive at the library. I devoured those magazines. Constantinople, Venice, Manaus, Nepal, there is so much to see in this world. I'd like to see it all."

Frank was kissing her breasts.

"You're not listening to me at all."

"I'm listening. Hawaii," he mumbled. "Constantinople. I wouldn't even know how to get to Constantinople."

"You say yes, and I'll work out the itinerary."

"*You* say yes, and I'll work out the itinerary," Frank said, unbuttoning her robe.

"You don't need permission, Frank, and you know your way around the territory pretty well."

"Not true," he said. "There are untold mysteries in you I've never probed."

She kissed Frank deeply.

"I wonder how our aspens are doing in Salt Lake City."

"I wonder," Frank said, but that was not what he was wondering about at all.

76

The tunnel gates held and operated as flawlessly as the mainspring of a railroad watch. Andell, the supervisor of Babcock & Wilcox, appeared in Frank's office, leaving his valise outside the door.

"Mr. Crowe," he said, extending his hand. "I'm leaving the dam site."

"So soon?"

"Yes. We have all the steel you've ordered in the warehouse. I'll keep a standby crew until you've finished the dam. I've ordered the dismantling of our main plant, and we'll be shipping our facilities out as quickly as I can get the flat cars."

"I'm sorry we haven't had more time with each other," Frank said. "You and your men have performed flawlessly. I'm deeply grateful."

"The admiration is mutual, Mr. Crowe. Perhaps our paths will cross again."

"Perhaps," Frank said, "perhaps," thinking of the plans in his cabinet. "Are you heading home?"

"No. I'm off to Denver, to check some plans at the Bureau, and then I'll head for Washington and a conference with Secretary Ickes. Should I give him a message?"

Frank scratched his head. "As a matter of fact yes. Tell him to send me his formula for a dry martini."

Crowe walked Andell to his waiting car. They shook hands once more and Crowe patted him on the back. "Well done, sir. Expected no less when you told me you had attended the University of Vermont."

"That's right," Andell said. "The bastards did teach us something."

Crowe waved and returned to his office. Goddamned Ickes, he thought. Was he taking everybody for granted?

The pouring of the dam continued around the clock. Dumping a bucket a minute had become routine, and record was piled upon record. Storms came down the basin, but this year Crowe was more prepared, continuing to pour despite the rain, stretching huge canvas covers over the form being filled. No storm, no flood would threaten the dam. When Andell had dropped his 2.4-million-pound gate in Tunnel Number 4, the Colorado, thus far diverted, was finally yoked. It had been a big day for Crowe.

Perhaps one of the greatest problems Frank faced was the ever-increasing number of tourists who were flocking to the almost-completed dam. They came by day and by night and clogged his roads and littered his observation points. At times at night the dam site resembled a Bedouin camp. They had doubted from the beginning that that great yawning chasm called Black Canyon could ever be filled with concrete, but all their doubts were dispelled as the dam rose foot by foot, day after day, week after week.

Frank Crowe, forever the tight-fisted New Englander, prepared to deal with the problems as he assembled his engineers and foremen before him.

"Gentlemen," he said, "as you know we are reaching the sunset hours of construction, and though it is bad luck in this business to pass out accolades before the project is finished, I can say to those of you who will be leaving us soon that you have all performed with skill and dedication, and these words will be reflected in your severance reports when you receive them. I think those of you who will be leaving us early can proudly say, 'I've worked on Hoover Dam.'"

There was laughter in the room.

379

"Well, it's Hoover Dam to me, call it what you will."

Crowe continued to speak, outlining his instructions for dismantling the dam site. When he finished, the men began raising their hands with questions.

"Go ahead." Crowe nodded to a young engineer.

"How soon after severance, chief, must we vacate Boulder City?"

"You will receive one month grace on your rent to give you time to relocate."

Another older man raised his hand. It was River Joe. "Where you building the next dam, chief?"

Crowe looked at the white-haired laborer. "I don't know whether I'll be building another dam. Haven't you had enough, Joe?"

The old man stroked his chin. "I ain't no souvenir yet," and the room filled once again with laughter.

Another engineer raised his hand.

"Go ahead, Statler."

"All we hear is rumors, chief. Rumors. Rumors of that dam in Washington, rumors of a big canal through California. I can't feed my family with rumors."

This was the dreaded question Crowe knew would come up.

He looked at Statler, at the other men. "This is a new administration, a new Department of the Interior, a new Bureau of Reclamation. I suggest you turn to them for that answer."

"I've tried," Statler said seriously. "Not one of them has an office in Vegas."

Crowe thought of the Grand Coulee and hated to be evasive.

"I shall call Secretary Ickes and inform him of this. If there is one word that scares hell out of those boys in Washington, it's unemployment. I'll do this today. You have my word."

Crowe left the meeting and had Hans drive him to his office. He closed the door and looked at the telephone he dreaded using; he knew what would be asked of him if he called Ickes and he knew he did not have an answer, and yet he had to honor his word and call the man.

When the call had gone through, Ickes's first words were, "Eight parts gin, one part vermouth, and run a cut lemon around the inside rim of a chilled glass."

Crowe smiled. "I have that written down."

"Are you planning to open a bar or build me a dam?"

He was as blunt as all that.

"Mr. Secretary," Frank said, "I have not reached a decision. However, the men on my dam, those that face imminent severance, are getting anxious about future projects."

"How many men are you letting go?"

"Several hundred now. The figures will increase the closer we come to the end."

"I see," Ickes said. "I can't announce any future hiring schedules for Grand Coulee until I have an answer from you, sir."

"I know this is a compliment, Mr. Ickes, but both of us know that I'm not the only man who can finish that dam."

"David thinks so."

"You are putting tremendous pressure on me."

"No more than I get from my boss every day."

"That's true, I'm sure," Crowe said, "but you are not my boss."

"Not yet," Ickes said.

"There'll soon be thousands of men unemployed up here," Crowe pleaded.

"Ah," Ickes said. "Now who's playing politician? Didn't you distinctly tell me that was *our* problem in Washington?"

"Yes, I did."

"So you care more about *your* boys than you are willing to admit?"

"I could use one of your martinis right now."

"I bet you could. Well, what do you say?"

"I will not make a commitment until this dam is finished, Mr. Secretary."

"All right," Ickes said. "You're still a free man."

"I wish that were true," Crowe said.

"I shall make a concession, Mr. Crowe," Ickes said. "We will be going forward with the All-American Canal. I will put a hiring office in Las Vegas. I just hope to hell it won't siphon off your best men."

"That's a risk we'll both have to take," Crowe said.

"Yes," Ickes answered, and there was silence.

"Mr. Secretary," Frank asked after several minutes.

"I'm on the line."

"I thank you."

"That's quite all right. Mr. Crowe?"

"Yes."

"I'm going to ask you a question I have no right to ask you. With your permission."

"Go right ahead."

"Why don't you ask your wife?"

And now there was silence on Crowe's end. Finally he said, "I do not resent the question, Mr. Secretary, but I do not have to answer it."

"You're right, Mr. Crowe. It's been nice talking to you."

"Goodbye, Mr. Secretary."

77

After Devere's successful attempt to disrupt the rigid schedule for the dam it was understandable that Crowe's apprehension increased, and though he felt that the threat of Devere and the Wobblies would be minimal now, he could not dismiss Gallino, Vegas, a town full of misfits, disgruntled workers about to be laid off; in short he knew he was *so* close now, and he was *so* close so soon, his fears were only heightened. Where before he would fill in the slot in the middle of the dam in two-hundred-foot rises, he now closed that gap in twenty-foot increments. He had guards with shotguns at all vital points of construction with orders to shoot without asking questions. All this was against his nature, but now he was driven. Like a sculptor who puts his chisel once more against a bust, so Crowe was finishing his dam meticulously, purposefully, and with a measure of awe. The slightest opening was grouted and re-grouted, the curvature of its face was checked and rechecked, and as he ran his hand across the face of a newly poured rise he would say to the foreman, "I want this as smooth as a baby's ass" or "as velvet as a virgin's thigh," depending on the time of day.

Elle sensed this tension in her husband, but blamed it on the climactic phase of construction. She did not realize how much other pressures were working inside the man. She came home nightly from the library and talked of changes in the town, the men, but steadfastly made plans for the life ahead. She continued to ask Frank about a completion date for the dam, but he continued to evade that question, pleading in all honesty the fact that he could not predict contingencies.

Even this close to completion accidents never ceased. Ladders collapsed, heavy machinery fell hundreds of feet, cableways frayed and broke, buckets collapsed, cranes toppled, trucks slid off roads, gondolas were derailed and men were killed, maimed, electrocuted, drowned, and Frank's weekly visits to the hospital were more frequent than ever, since he knew that it would be hard and so painful to have come so close and end the job as a cripple.

78

In March and April Frank Crowe spent most of his hours at his dam site office fitting in the last pieces to complete the dam as carefully as a dowager completing an elegant puzzle. Each day saw the completion of one more rise, and all the millions of buckets of concrete were finally coming together in one massive congruous arch.

On Memorial Day, a bronze plaque was erected. It read, IN MEMORY OF OUR FELLOW MEN. THEY LABORED THAT MILLIONS MIGHT SEE A BRIGHTER DAY, and engraved on the plaque were eighty-nine names. Walker Young spoke:

"This project, because of its awesome natural setting, has been fraught with hazard, and loss of life in its construction was not unexpected. That more lives were not lost is evidence of the effort made to avoid accidents and speaks well for the caliber of the workmen themselves, since each one's safety of necessity depended not alone upon his own actions, but upon the actions of his fellow men. I wish on this occasion to pay tribute, not only to those in whose honor we are gathered, but to all who have had a part in construction. I wish to express, on behalf of your government, deep sympathy for those of you who have suffered the loss of a relative or friend. May this dam stand as a lasting monument to his courage."

The whistle blew at two o'clock and work resumed on the dam site, and Crowe was relieved to have this necessary ritual behind him. He remembered Elle's sensitivity to the subject of death and now wondered how truly callous he was about the matter himself. Standing in his office, looking at the dam site below him, he knew every spot and every detail of where a man was killed and why, and though he knew that he fought disaster as vigorously as any working superintendent, he also knew that part of those men's lives had been in *his* hands, and even with orders and edicts and platoons of safety men, their deaths in some measure rested on his shoulders, and he would always have to live with that fact.

"To hell with that," he yelled at a startled young engineer in his office. "We don't need to buy any lumber *now*. Are the boys too tired to pull out nails from used lumber?"

"Some of it is warped, sir."

"Then steam it straight, for Christ sake."

The boy left, and Crowe was chagrined. He knew he was venting anger unrelated to the event.

The following morning Crowe drove to Las Vegas and stopped at the hiring office for the All-American Canal. He did not enter but watched a good number of men he knew and respected from the dam in line to see the hiring officer.

He returned to the dam and called for a meeting with Wanke and Williams. After their arrival he seemed truly disturbed, pacing his office.

"I figure three weeks, maybe a month," he said finally, "and we'll have it topped off."

"I got five weeks concrete ready," Wanke said. "We're figuring about the same."

"I'm lining my last penstock tunnel," Williams said. "I'll beat you to the draw."

"You know about Grand Coulee?" Frank asked bluntly, surprising his friends.

"Yes," Wanke said.

"Sure," Williams added.

"*Everybody* seems to know about Grand Coulee."

"You can get the whole set of plans from the Bureau for five bucks."

"And you sent for them just for academic interest?" Frank said, still pacing.

"I sent for them to wallpaper my outhouse," Williams said.

"And *I* sent for them because of my never-ending quest for engineering know-how," Wanke said jokingly.

"Shit," was all Crowe could say.

"Well, Mr. Supervisor," Williams said, "I suppose you know *nothing* about Grand Coulee. Ickes came up here just to play poker?"

"Yes, I know all about it. David designed it. It's a masterpiece."

"But David won't finish building it?" Williams asked.

"No. He's losing his sight."

"And they've asked you to take it over?"

"Yes."

"And what did you tell Ickes?" Wanke asked.

"Nothing."

"I see," Williams said.

"Well, what have *you* guys decided?"

"We're keeping our options open," Wanke said.

"What does that mean?" Crowe asked.

"It means if you can't tell us what the fuck is going through your head, why should you demand anything of us? In two months, Frank, I can pat you on the back, and I can pat Tom on the back and say, 'It's been nice knowing you boys, see you around.' "

"I had that coming," Frank said. "I sure did."

"Is that all there is to this discussion?" Williams asked sourly, picking up his hard hat.

"No," Frank said quietly. He looked at both of them. "If you remember, seven years ago we drove up here in a pickup truck. We talked about the fact that each man has five dams in him. Well, now we've got six."

"We blew the hell out of that myth," Wanke said.

"Yes, and no," Crowe said. "The thought never left me all these years. For seven years I've fought that river, Devere, Barnes, the heat, the rain. . . . There were more days than I'd like to admit when I felt that saying had a lot of merit in it."

"Meaning what?" Williams asked. "You're afraid of Grand Coulee?"

"That's part of it," Crowe admitted.

"What else?" Williams asked.

"I haven't discussed it with Elle."

"Well, *discuss* it," Jack said adamantly.

"Hold on, Jack," Wanke interceded. "That's neither your business nor mine."

"The hell you say," Williams shot back. "You know goddamned well that Frank's decision is important to us. Since *when* do the *women* do the deciding around here?"

Crowe looked at both his friends. "I appreciate the fact that my decision makes a difference. I've got those goddamned plans in my desk and they've been tantalizing me since Ickes first unrolled them. I've tried to ignore them, I've tried to think they didn't exist. It's stupid. I know that. All the men I've severing are looking at me, saying, *What* now? *Where* now? What do we do, Mr. Crowe? Some of our best boys are going to the All-American Canal. I was down in Vegas this morning and watched. Everybody seems to know about the new dam. Elle *must* know. She has ears. They might even have a set of plans in the library."

"Well, *ask* her, for Christ sake," Williams half shouted, but Wanke interceded.

"Wait, Jack, hold on. Don't do this to Frank."

"Do what?"

Wanke looked at Williams. "Don't force him to give an answer before he's ready."

"I know, I know," Williams said, "but I've got crews too, just like you, and God knows why they'd want to work for me again the way I treat them, but I get questioned too. Just like Frank."

Frank rose to full length and faced both his friends.

"I've listened to everything you've both said and you have the right to say all that. As long as you've known me you can't accuse me of being a procrastinator." He pointed out the window. "If half that dam collapsed right now I'd have three contingency plans to shore it up again. I *will* make a decision, and I will tell you as soon as I have, you have my word. *When* that will be I cannot answer, nor can I tell you *what* my answer will be."

Frank left his office, almost relieved at the set of problems facing him that morning, almost anxious for some challenges which would push his personal crisis aside.

The dam still rose in five-foot sections, and although it was almost completed, it seemed that each rise now took more time than ever, and though the men worked as furiously as they always had, Crowe's impatience was evident all over the project.

He could see warehouses being dismantled, and trackage being pulled up, and at the railroad yard he watched the endless loading of trucks, and tractors and cranes all headed back to the respective headquarters of the Big Six.

Sunday night he left the dam site early and found Elle at home sorting out clothes, books, furnishings.

"You're getting ready to leave?" Frank asked.

"Just getting ready," Elle said, matching up socks and rolling the matched pairs.

He walked to the kitchen and made two martinis, put them on a side table in the parlor, and called Elle.

"Be right down, Frank," she said, and finally appeared, crisp and bright as usual, in a neatly pressed pair of slacks, a freshly laundered peasant blouse.

"Sit down," Frank said, and Elle complied.

He looked at her and watched her composure and the strength and calmness of her features. He watched her eyes, her lovely deep blue eyes, open and alive and unafraid.

"Secretary Ickes has asked me to take over the Grand Coulee Dam. I've seen the plans. It will be the most beautiful dam in the world and the largest."

"I know," Elle said.

"How long have you known?"

386

"You told me once a long time ago that nothing that goes on on this dam site stays secret for more than an hour. That's true."

"Then you've known for *weeks?*"

"Yes, I have."

"And what *else* do you know?"

"I know that you want to tackle that dam more than anything in the world."

Frank stood and walked around his parlor. He noticed the absence of vases and ashtrays and doilies and pictures.

"And you've been afraid to ask me," Elle said.

"Yes," Frank admitted openly.

"I've been dreading the question too," Elle said. "Because the answer I will give you as a woman and as your wife will be one that you won't like."

"What is your answer?"

"Sit down, Frank," Elle said. "I told Maria once that I've loved you from the first letter you ever sent me. That love, Frank, has only grown. I have watched you now for four years. I've watched you wrestle with every physical problem, and wrestle with nature, heat, storms, I've watched you wrestle with each emotional problem. For the latter, I'm mostly to blame, but I won't apologize for that. You're not the man I married. You're not the man I thought you'd be. You're *twice* that man. You are brilliant and tough and warm and sensual and fallible. No one could ask for more than that."

"Then why. . . . ?" Frank asked.

But Elle continued. "What right do I, Elle Crowe, age thirty-three, what right do I have to stop you from running your life the way you want to? What right do I have to deny a man, *my* man, the ultimate challenge in engineering when his whole *life* has been a series of challenges." And now Elle rose and stood in front of the unlit fireplace.

"I do not have that right, Frank, I know that."

"You do," Frank said.

"No." Elle shook her head and there were tears in her eyes. "But I have a right, maybe a duty as your wife, to say no. No, goddamnit, Frank Crowe. *Enough.* It's enough. Enough sweating and freezing and enough nights with four hours' sleep or no sleep or nights of turning and tossing. I have that right. When you were ill I finally went to Maria's across the street. She thought I was sleeping, but I wasn't. I was on my knees, Frank, praying that you would make it, that you would breathe and walk and make love to me again.

"We don't need the money from that dam, you know that. You don't need the glory from that dam. You don't need the danger and I don't need the fear."

"Elle," Frank said.

"Wait, Frank. Wait. I am telling you only that I want you *alive*, I want you at my side, I want you in my bed. I want to be your last challenge. I have a right to say that, but I'm not sure I will."

"Thank God you said that, Elle."

"Why?"

"Because all you've said, and said so well, is everything that's going through my mind.

"I cannot live with myself, Elle. I detest myself for all this indecision. I know that Grand Coulee is an indulgence. I know that goddamned project, its scope, its challenge are dangled in front of me like a diadem. I love you, Elle, I love you so much, perhaps even *you* can't fathom its depth. I never knew love before. None. Not physical, not emotional. You've taught me all that. And *still*, still with all that, with all that knowledge of the kind of life we could have, the peace, the warmth, the security, with *all* that, that fucking dam looms over my head like a frightening, fascinating thunderhead."

He looked at Elle. "I don't know what's my right either. I know only that I have made the decision within myself. I cannot sit in a rocker in Salt Lake City knowing that goddamned dam is rising above the Columbia without me."

Elle came over to Frank and sat next to him. She wiped her eyes and put her arms around him.

"I'm going home," she said. "I'm going to our house in Salt Lake City. I'm going to sleep in our bed and I am going to look at the bannister you built and I am going to look at the shingles you placed and the spout you fashioned, and I am going to think, and be alone.

"I am not leaving you, Frank. I want to go home for a week, and I'll return."

"I understand that," Frank said, kissing Elle on the cheeks. "I am glad *somebody* in this family can make a decision."

Hans drove Elle to the station in Las Vegas in the morning, helped her with her small valise, and looked puzzled as she waved from the olive-green coach after she had boarded the train. They had made a silent trip from Boulder City, but Hans tactfully did not ask questions he knew were none of his business. This tact even extended to Terry. He told her nothing about Elle's departure, feeling it was a matter between the chief and his wife and not one for idle gossip.

Frank paced his office waiting for Hans to return; he instinctively gave instructions to engineers, foremen, inspectors who rotated in and out of his office; his mind was not on the dam, but by his watch he knew when Elle would depart and how much further away she was with each passing hour.

He hardly slept the first night; his bed seemed painfully empty, and Elle's clean pillow looked pristine and sacred next to his own. He rose at four to respond to a fire at a substation and was almost grateful for the involvement. They contained the blaze at noon but he did not go to the mess hall for lunch. Hans noticed Crowe's frenetic pace, driving from the tower portals to the upper concrete plant, from the Boulder office to the dam site, listening to endless curt commands, constant admonitions, even lengthy harassments. Frank ate dinner at the mess hall, using the small room reserved for brass, but neither tasted nor smelled the special steak they cooked for him; even the tapioca pudding he loved he left untouched.

Once more he returned to the dam site at night. All blocks except L and G were topped now. He was running further ahead of schedule than he had anticipated. He finally retired at ten, but unable to sleep, he lay on the couch wondering about Elle now in Salt Lake City, in their house. He could see her, her lovely arms, her smooth back; he could visualize her in her white slip with the lace border and her shoeless, stockinged legs so long and lovely. Only the gin by his side let him doze off, but he rose at dawn feeling tired and acid.

The highway linking Nevada and Arizona was being built in sections as the dam reached its ultimate height, and Frank watched the grading and the pouring of asphalt. He checked and rechecked the contour of this roadway and spotted some workmen on either side sculpting a railing of concrete. He strode quickly toward the men carefully carving stars and hexagons and flags and eagles with delicate trowels and considerable talent.

"What the hell are you doing?" he asked angrily.

"What's it to you?"

"Do you know *who* I am?"

"No, mister, I don't know who you are and I couldn't care less."

"This is my dam," Crowe shouted.

"Ain't that something," one of the sculptors said, smiling at his co-worker.

"Who told you to put this crap on my dam?"

"Look, mister," the sculptor, a young good-looking man said impatiently, "these are my orders. They're signed by Walker Young."

"Well, get that shit off that railing. This dam is rising in one long curve. I don't need that whorehouse trimming at the top."

"I just got my orders," the sculptor said, continuing his work, and Frank reached down, pulled the trowel out of the man's hand, and knocked off the ornamentation.

"I am Frank Crowe," he said. "I am supervisor of this dam. You take this fucking drawing and tell Walker Young to shove it up his ass." He tore up the blueprint and signaled to Hans.

"Take me back to my house," he ordered, and Hans whipped

389

his truck around and headed toward Boulder City. The sculptors had hardly had time to comprehend the scene; they scratched their heads watching Crowe's truck roar out of the canyon.

They walked toward an asphalt worker and said, "Who the hell is Frank Crowe?"

"The chief."

"No kidding? What is he? Loco?"

"You better watch your mouth, mister."

"Just came up and tore our plans to shreds."

"I've been watching you guys myself," the dirt-stained worker said. "Do they really *pay* you guys to diddle with that shit?"

It was mid-morning when Frank reached his house. It took him five minutes to don a fresh pair of denims, to pack a toothbrush, a razor, and a comb, and to take a poncho off the hall tree. He had not even removed his hat, and he jumped back into his car.

"I've got to make the ten o'clock out of Vegas. Step on it," he said to Hans.

He saw the train starting to leave the station as they arrived at the terminal, and he did not bother with buying a ticket but ran along the train until he found an open vestibule, swung himself on board quite expertly, watched by an aging conductor who looked at him suspiciously through his gold-rimmed glasses.

"You got a ticket, mister?" he said skeptically.

"No," Frank answered, "but I've got cash."

"You better show it to me or I'll toss you off in Searchlight."

Frank reached for his wallet and took out a bill. The conductor finally focused on Frank and said, "Ain't you Frank Crowe?"

"That's right."

"Well, I'll be damned. You've aged a little since the last time I had you on this run. Bet you don't remember."

"Son of a bitch," Crowe said. "I *do*. Did you ever buy some land in Vegas?"

"Sure did. Much obliged. Hear you're almost done with the dam."

"Yeah," Crowe said. "Almost. Here's my money."

"Forget it," the conductor said. "If you won't tell Union Pacific, I sure as hell won't either."

Frank laughed for the first time in three days and put his hand on the aging conductor's shoulder. He found an empty leather sofa in the men's room and lay down. He lowered the green shade to keep the sun out and pulled his hat over his face. He loved the sound of the accelerating steel wheels on the junctions of the tracks and could almost feel Elle in his arms before he fell asleep.

At Colonnade Junction, four hours out of Vegas, he was sound asleep and unaware that scarcely two feet away from him, for a brief minute, was Elle, on the westbound run for Vegas. At six that night he opened the front door of his home in Salt Lake City, and after several minutes of frantic searching, he found it empty, their bed made, her valise gone, only a moist bar of soap attesting to her recent presence.

79

Elle had cried herself to sleep on the train to Salt Lake City. She had been aware of a couple of salesmen watching the progress of her skirt as she reclined in the velour of her seat, and she had been grateful when the conductor kept an eye on her and the strangers ahead of her. She had taken a cab in Salt Lake City and asked the driver to open the house, which he did after receiving a quarter tip.

"You want me to turn the lights on, ma'am?" he asked.

"Just in the hall."

The cabbie switched on the light and said, "Anything else I can do?"

"No, thank you. Good night."

"Good night."

Elle shut the door and switched on more lights, in the living room, the kitchen, the stairway leading upstairs. The house smelled musty and warm and she noticed a thick coating of dust on covered furniture; the carpeting was frayed; even the lovely bannister was chipped, its paint peeling.

She ran upstairs; there was an iron cot in their bedroom, and the ticking of the mattress had a large hole exposing the cotton batting like an open wound. She opened the windows and brushed some cobwebs out of her hair. She found a blanket in the linen closet, and a pillow and removed her navy-blue dress, took off her shoes, and fell exhausted on the unmade bed, finding slight solace from the warmth of the rough woolen blanket, reaching out instinctively for the man she had left in Boulder City.

The morning proved worse, for not only did she find the house a shambles, linoleum burned and torn, drapes frayed, cabinets broken, but even the lovely yard had almost totally gone to weeds.

She was angry and feisty. After showering she walked across the street to the Walkers', who had been paid to maintain the house after the tenants had left. She rang the bell and waited for a heavy-set middle-aged woman to open the door.

"I'm Mrs. Crowe."

"That's right," Mrs. Walker said. "Been a long time. Why don't you come in?"

"I'd rather not. I want to know about our house."

"What can I tell you."

"It's a shambles. My husband's been paying you good money to take care of it."

"Well, the folks you rented it to left it a mess."

"I rather doubt that," Elle said. "It doesn't look like anybody's been in it for months."

"Oh, we've had the boys sweep it regular."

"What about the yard? It hasn't seen a drop of water."

"Well, if that ain't something," Mrs. Walker said. "Here you come from Boulder City, where I been hearing all kinds of bad stories from the church, 'bout all the drinking and gambling and whoring, and you come here to this God-loving house telling me how to behave."

She started to slam the door, but Elle's foot prevented that.

"We'll see you in court, Mrs. Walker. I shall retain an attorney this morning and leave it in his hands. He will inspect the damage before the sun sets on Angel Moroni. Goodbye."

She did engage an attorney, and he inspected the house, the grounds, and after he left Elle set about scrubbing and polishing and waxing and mending. She almost collapsed at sunset, and realized she had not eaten for twenty-four hours.

She made up a proper bed that night, but she could not sleep any better than Frank in Nevada. She tried to relax, and unable to do so, tried desperately to find some peace which would allow her to make a sound judgment. But neither reason nor logic came to her that night, and a long walk through the tree-lined, well-swept streets of Salt Lake City did not make her feel that she was home.

That night she *did* think and tried to sort out her motives. This house in Salt Lake City was not the haven she had thought of these past years. Though it could be restored to its original beauty, she felt alien here. She missed the camaraderie, the sharing, the sorrows and humor of Boulder City. Perhaps now, for the first time, she could understand Frank's and Tom's and Jack's desire to live on a construction site, and she remembered how a report from the *New York Times* had described the project as a ship. Now, ashore, she missed that voyage, the movement, the drive. She was also aware that she was being selfish.

What would Frank do in Salt Lake? He was too young really to
retire. He was in good shape, in his early fifties, not a man bent very
much on pleasure. . . . Did she have the right to end his career, or
try to end it?

She had read about the Columbia River. It was big but not as
ferocious as the Colorado. Washington was green and more seasonal
than Nevada. They could ski in the winter, and perhaps she could
get Frank to buy a boat for the summer. She remembered that little
Friendship sloop in San Francisco. But most of her thoughts were
about Frank. She missed his strong, lean hands on her breasts, she
missed his back, his strong arms about her waist. The only way she
could go to sleep finally that night was to pack her small bag, to lay
out her traveling clothes, to know she'd be on that train to Vegas in
the morning and in her husband's arms that night.

She boarded the train at seven in the morning and not once looked
back at Salt Lake City, its trees, its Temple, its Tabernacle. Nothing
would be more welcome than the dusty, brown, treeless geography
surrounding Boulder City, and nothing she missed as much as Frank
or the hall tree which held his poncho, his slicker, his goddamn felt
hat.

80

Frank Crowe sat down in his living room and noticed the damage
done to his house, and he noticed Elle's attempts to remedy it as much
as possible, but it mattered little to him. He tried the phone in the
hallway and knew it would be disconnected, and ran toward a filling
station with a pay phone. His first call was to the Bureau of Reclamation
in Denver.

"Frank Crowe here," he said. "Who's in charge?"

"Alfred Smith," an operator said.

"Connect me with him, please."

"Yes sir."

"Smith here," Frank heard.

"Frank Crowe here."

"*Mr.* Crowe, congratulations."

"Why?"

"I hear you're just about ready to top off Hoover."

"You must be an old-timer."

"You don't recall me," Smith said, "but I worked for you on Deadwood."

"Redheaded guy, face full of freckles?"

"The red has turned to gray, but your memory is good. What can I do for you?"

"I have a personal problem, Mr. Smith. Is there a Bureau plane leaving Salt Lake tonight, tomorrow?"

"Let me look at my schedule," Smith said. "The Secret Service is coming in at nine tonight. They'll be leaving for Vegas in the morning. They're checking security for Roosevelt's arrival."

"Splendid!" Frank said. "Can you get me on that flight?"

"I'll kick off anybody but the pilot, sir."

"I won't forget the kindness," Frank said. "What time are they scheduled to take off?"

"You name it, Mr. Crowe, and I'll set the time."

"Do you think five A.M. would be too early?"

"I think five o'clock should give those boys from Washington plenty of time to enjoy Salt Lake City, eat dinner, and have three hours' sleep. Consider it done, Mr. Crowe."

"I owe you," Frank said, "the best martini ever made and Harold Ickes gave me the formula."

"Well, Mr. Crowe, I shall be there with Roosevelt and I shall accept it."

"Good night," Frank said, "and thank you."

He reached into his pocket for more change and phoned the number of his house in Boulder. It mercifully took less than two rings for Elle to answer the phone.

"Frank . . . where in the hell are you?"

"In Salt Lake . . ."

"I couldn't wait a week," she said.

"Neither could I," he answered.

"I know. The phone doesn't work."

"I'm in a service station, Elle. . . . Elle?"

"Yes, darling."

"I'll be home . . . *our* home in Boulder tomorrow."

"I'll be at the station."

"No," Frank said. "I'm flying in."

"Flying?"

"Yes. Get Hans to the airport at six and tell him to wait. . . . I'll be there at seven."

"In the morning?"

"Yes. Don't go to work. I've got good news for you. . . ."

394

There was silence and finally Elle said, "I've got good news for you too, Frank. *Eat* something."

"Eat?" he said.

"Yes, *eat.*"

"All right, angel, I'll eat. Good night."

"Good night, Frank. I miss you."

When Frank retired that night he set the same alarm clock Elle had set but he bothered neither to undress nor to unpack. That lonely cot felt like the ones in the men's rooms of the Union Pacific's parlor cars, but he thought he detected the smell of Elle's hair on the pillow.

He was at the Salt Lake City airport at four-forty-five the following morning. The terminal was a small wooden building, its coffee shop still closed. He could see the windsock hanging from a pole outside; the wind was coming from the west. At five o'clock the pilot, dressed in leather, entered the stark building.

"Mr. Crowe?"

"Yes."

"We're ready."

"Let's go."

He followed the pilot across the field to a twelve-seater, the plane filled but for one seat with sleepy or disgruntled Secret Service men, their hair cut short, their suit coats draped over them. No one spoke; some of the men were sleeping and his welcome was far from warm, as he had expected, but Frank cared little. He heard the pilot close the door, he heard one engine being started, then the next, and he felt himself jostled as they crossed the rutted runway.

He heard the Fairchild engines being revved up and he caught stroboscopic reflections of the first rays of the sun on the aluminum propeller blade outside his window. He could feel the pilot release the brakes and roar down the field, making a respectable takeoff into the Utah dawn.

Elle, dressed in white shorts and a navy-blue shirt, had gone with Hans to the airport in Las Vegas, arriving at six o'clock in the morning. They made small talk, waiting for Frank to arrive, and Hans spoke of the possibility of a federal scholarship at the University of Washington. Elle asked him to remind her to see if Frank might have some weight to help him obtain it.

At six-thirty-five the small fragile plane started to lose altitude, and at six-forty-five it came to a stop in front of the Las Vegas terminal, even more primitive than the one they had left in Salt Lake City. Frank rushed out of the cabin after thanking the pilot and flew into the open arms of Elle, who had run to meet him. He would never forget the feel of her slender body pressed into his, and he knew that their tears commingled as they stood alone and exposed in the middle of the runway in the Nevada blue-gray morning.

At seven-fifteen Hans arrived in front of the Crowe house and Frank and Elle walked together back into their house and again they embraced for a very long time.

"You've got the answer, Elle," Frank said finally. "It was right here. I'm not going to build that dam. I'm not going to ever let you leave my side. Ever, ever. I've been absolutely out of my mind, alone."

Elle stroked Frank's head. She could feel the stubble of his beard.

"I went berserk myself, darling," Elle said. "I hated our house, the yard, Salt Lake, the *good* people of the neighborhood. I wanted to kill the Walkers the way they had neglected us."

She looked at Frank, her blue eyes calm now. "I want you to build that dam, Frank."

"Why?"

"I don't want anyone else to build that dam."

"Elle, I haven't thought about that dam since the minute you left."

"*I have,*" Elle said. "The way you make love, Frank, I can hardly put you in a rocking chair."

"I could do it in a rocking chair. You want to try?"

"I was very selfish, Frank. I want you to forgive me."

"But you may be right, Elle. Have you thought of that?"

"I *may* be. I've thought about that a lot, but it finally came down to one thing over and over again."

"What's that?"

"I married a dam builder, I had my eyes wide open when I did this, and I'm still married to a dam builder."

Frank turned and pulled his wife into his arms. He buried his face in her lovely long blond hair.

"I want you to be *sure*, Elle," he said quietly. "I want you to be absolutely *sure*. No concessions, no compromises."

"I'm *sure*, Frank."

"We'll have more than twice the crew on that dam than we've had here. We'll have twice the dam and twice the crises. There'll be nights without electricity and days without water."

"But there'll be our bed," Elle said, "this bed, and I've learned to heat a flatiron on the stove, and I can credibly press a pair of denims. I've learned how to keep a stew simmering for hours and still make it edible."

"I love you, honey," Frank said, and once more she looked into his eyes.

"I thought of two men these last three days. You and David who

396

designed that lovely dam. It is a strange fate that he would go blind at this point, isn't it?"

"I've thought of that too."

"It's almost as if you'd been rehearsing all these years to complete that dam. We're not religious, Frank, either one of us, but I could not help thinking that some higher power has destined you for Grand Coulee. You're not doing it for me. I want you to believe that."

"I want to, Elle, I really do."

"It's done," she said.

"It's done," Frank echoed. "I need an hour's sleep. I haven't slept in days."

"And, by the sound of your stomach, you haven't eaten either," but Frank was out already.

The sun was streaming hard into the bedroom window when he finally rose. He could smell bacon cooking; he heard activity in the kitchen. He washed and shaved. He put on the clean denims Elle had hung over the chair by the bed and came down in his stocking feet, startling Elle as he circled her slim body from behind.

"Looks good," he said, "smells good."

"You scared me. Breakfast will be ready in a minute."

"I wasn't talking about breakfast."

"You're terrible, Frank Crowe. Go read the morning paper."

"I thought I'd survey the rocking chair. It couldn't be too hard."

"Get out of my kitchen," Elle said, feeling his freshly shaved face. "Kind of liked that beard. Maybe you can grow one in Hawaii."

He slapped her fanny. "Hawaii," he said, going to the parlor, but he said it without rancor.

81

He left the house at noon feeling warm and fulfilled, bypassed his office and drove directly to the dam site. For weeks now he had noticed that the volume of traffic was *leaving* the dam, truck after truck now hauling lumber, pipe, tools, machinery, and though all this was going according to his plans he felt regretful since each turn in the road, each cliff, each boulder, each ravine held a memory; every inch of road leading to the dam had been a part of him for over four years now.

Hans made the final turn and there was the dam, raw, gray, still garlanded with headers, tubing, and wooden casing, but fully asserting itself with its base thickness of over 600 feet, its length of over 1,280 feet, its arch as graceful as the first drawing he had ever made of it on the back of a menu at Lisa's Café across the street from the Bureau of Reclamation in Denver.

He met Wanke on the Nevada side of the almost completed highway crossing the dam. He got out of his truck and shook Tom's hand.

"We're short four rises," Tom said, "B Block, G Block, L Block, and E. Today is June 3rd. We'll top off June 5th. I'll have two hundred buckets left over."

"That's pretty close figuring, Mr. Wanke."

"Well, we also used slide rules at the University of Colorado."

"Evidently," Crowe said, watching the diminished crews laboring below him. "Of course those two hundred buckets will be deducted from your bonus."

"Agreed," Wanke said, "and I certainly hope you didn't draw a day's pay while you were gone."

Frank laughed.

"I'll tell you what, Frank. I'd like to encase that goddamned book-keeper of Barnes's. Do you think that's possible?"

"Not until he's paid us."

"Agreed."

"How do you want him buried? Vertical or horizontal?"

"With his adding machine up his ass."

"Done," Wanke said, leaving, and Frank spotted Walker Young on the Arizona side and had Hans drive toward him.

"Walker?" Frank shouted.

"Yes?"

Frank jumped out of the car.

"I'd like a minute." He grabbed Walker Young and walked to a quieter part of the dam.

"I owe you an apology," Frank said.

"You surely do. What did you do? Go plumb loco?"

"That's right, Walker. Plumb loco. If you can find those men I'd like to apologize in person."

"No need," Walker said. "The more I thought about it the more I agreed with you. The beauty of this dam is its size and its shape. It needs no gewgaws on the top."

"I'm glad you agree," Frank said.

"Subject closed," Walker said. "Can you come to my office for a minute?"

"Of course."

Walker Young's office was as sterile and meticulous as Frank Crowe's: maps neatly rolled, stored in well-made cubbyholes; a solid drafting board; well-polished glass-covered mahogany desk; a wall covered with books and government reports. There *was* a difference. The room contained chairs.

Walker said, "Sit down," and Frank did, facing his friend.

"First thing on the agenda, Frank, is that I'd suggest you'd call me *Mr.* Walker from now on."

Frank looked perplexed.

"Secretary Ickes phoned me yesterday and asked whether I'd head up the Bureau of Reclamation."

"Son of a bitch." Frank rose and extended his hand. "They couldn't find a better man."

"Thanks, Frank. My wife agrees with you."

"I'll hand it to Ickes, he knows how to pick 'em."

"I'm glad you think so," Walker said, betraying nothing.

He reached behind his desk and pulled out a drawing.

"Order Number 1," Walker Young said. "Grandstand to be built for President Roosevelt arriving Boulder City July 2."

Frank studied the plan, noticed a provision for a ramp for Roosevelt's wheelchair, the three rows tiered, each to contain twenty chairs.

"Order Number 2," Walker continued. "We expect a short speech from you, after Roosevelt and Ickes have spoken. You'll be expected to wear a suit."

"Shit," Frank said. "I knew you had something up your sleeve."

"Order Number 3. There will be a short reception at Sequoia Lodge following the dedication. The President will depart Las Vegas by train at six in the evening. . . . I have drafted a memo which I shall have printed if you approve." He handed it to Frank, who read it.

"Sounds right to me," Frank said, handing it back.

"Initial it," Young ordered.

"Boy, you're going to be some bureaucrat, Walker."

"*Mr.* Young."

"*Mr.* Young."

Frank stood. "Is that all?"

"That's all."

Again Frank extended his hand. "My heartiest congratulations again, Mr. Young."

"Thanks, Frank. You can call me Walker."

There were really two celebrations to commemorate the finishing of the dam: the official one with the President and high government officials who were going to arrive in Boulder to reap whatever political dividends could be earned from a project of this magnitude, and an unofficial celebration, which Crowe discussed with Arthur Anderson in his office.

"In two days, Mr. Anderson, we will pour the final concrete on the dam. I shall make an announcement in the mess hall at the noon meal that we will be placing a hemlock on the top of the dam at five o'clock that evening.

"At six o'clock I want you to open the doors to the mess hall and I want a *feast*. I mean a *feast*. Ham, turkey, steaks, pies, well, you know your business.

"The Big Six will provide the beer, Las Vegas will provide the music, and you will provide the tolerance. There *will* be drinking. Do you understand?"

Anderson, more portly, more bald than he had been four years ago, looked at the chief.

"We have differed these past years," Anderson said, "but I must admit that you have been a very honest man to work for. If you should build another dam I'd be pleased to put in a bid."

"Anderson," Crowe said, "I hope you do. I have to admit that you've delivered everything you promised. You only failed to make a Mormon out of me."

"Just give me time. Just give me time."

Sequoia Lodge was filling with all the directors and their wives on June 4. Their cars and limousines crowded the modest street around the complex, and the commissary trades which supplied the kitchen brought more cases of booze than cans of butter.

The directors and their wives joined Frank and Elle at the Crowe home for cocktails that first night. After Roger proposed a toast to the imminent completion of the dam, two years ahead of schedule, he reached into his coat pocket for an envelope.

"As treasurer of the Big Six Companies," he said formally, "I present to you, Mr. Supervisor, a check for $312,674.67, representing ten percent of the profits realized by the Big Six Companies, in no small measure due to your dedication and engineering skill."

It was a gray check, ten inches long and three inches wide and bore the careful calligraphy of Barnes's shirtsleeved bookkeeper.

Frank studied it and said, "I decipher a slight tremor in the writing. It must have been a difficult check to make out."

"I'm sure it was." Roger laughed, and watched as Francesca fished for another envelope in her purse.

400

"To welcome you to the realm of capitalists," Francesca said, giving Elle the second envelope, "the directors have instructed me to give you this small token of their affection."

"What is it?" Elle asked, looking suddenly very young.

"Open it," Frank said, and Elle opened the envelope and saw two tickets, colorful and officially stamped.

"Cabin 112, S. S. *Lurline,* The Matson Shipping Company. Departing San Francisco September 1, arriving Honolulu September 6."

Elle was crying and threw her arms around Frank, around Roger, Francesca. . . .

"I don't know what to say," she cried. "I bet you were behind all this, Frank Crowe."

"Hawaii," he said. "Where the hell is Hawaii? And I suppose I'll have to wear a tie for dinner."

"Every night," Roger Stein said, "except luau night."

"Every night," Crowe repeated like a schoolboy, "except luau night. Jesus Christ."

They followed the Steins to Sequoia Lodge after the handshakes and backpatting of the other directors. Frank had even asked Hans to join them and bring Terry, and watched as this lovely young girl in a neatly ironed cotton dress was carefully embraced by each director. And he watched their wives, some skeptical, some amused at the never-ending magnetism of a young beautiful girl, a fact of life that Elle had almost gotten used to in the past four years.

After lunch the following day, June 5, 1935, Frank Crowe rose in the mess hall.

"Gentlemen," he said, "because of your labors and the labors of those who are no longer here, we shall pour the last block of concrete at three o'clock this afternoon. At the five o'clock whistle I want every man, woman, and child at the downstream side of the dam as we place a hemlock at elevation 727.

"Because of your hard work we are accomplishing this two years and five days ahead of schedule."

A roar went up in the mess hall.

"Tonight at five o'clock that dam will be finished and it will forever belong to the American people. However, if those of you who have worked so hard on this dam feel it is yours, then, for once, you'll get no argument from me, because I also feel this dam is mine.

"After the ceremonies, this mess hall will be open and Mr. Anderson has promised me a feast and the directors of the Big Six Companies have promised me a tank car of beer. Thursday, June 6, will be a lay day on the dam."

Frank sat down, but the cheering continued.

401

Tom Gam, a young tunneler, finally rose and the men quieted down.

"Me and the boys . . ." he said, frightened.

"Speak up," several men yelled.

"*Me and the boys,* chief, got you a little present and," he faltered, "well, you know how we feel."

"Give him the present," someone yelled.

"Oh yeah, the present."

The boy handed Frank a large box and Frank carefully opened it. It was a brand-new felt hat.

Touched, Frank said, "I've worked on six dams now, and this is the sixth new felt hat I've received. I want to thank you, and if you're ever in Salt Lake City, stop by Crowe's Hat Shop." He waved the hat and sat down, and the cheering continued.

82

Frank returned one evening to find Elle sitting at their dining-room table. An open letter was in front of her, as well as a drink in her hand, which was unusual for Elle.

"Hi, Frank."

"What are you doing?"

"I am thinking, and the more I think, the angrier I get."

"What's upsetting you?"

"A letter," she paused, "from my father. He saw my picture in the paper from a story about the dam completion. Here, read it."

Frank picked up a ruled sheet of notebook paper and noticed that the handwriting was unpracticed and difficult.

Dear Elle,

It seemed a bit queer to see your picture in the newspaper the other day. Me and your brothers didn't know where you were. Looks like you're doing real good. We often talk about you since we buried your mother and I think she forgave you in the end. Your youngest brother Mike left and we don't know where he is. Things have been hard around here with the factories closing and I could sure use a good job, and it looks like your husband could give me one.

I wouldn't have enough money to come west but you could mail me a check to P.O. Box 12, Camden, Maine, and I'd appreciate it. If you ever see Mike tell him he owes me fifty dollars.

Your Father

Frank looked at Elle, who was teary-eyed. "I was a child when they threw me out. Not *once* did they wonder *where* I was, how I was. None of them except Mike, God bless him . . . . and he left. I'm happy about that."

"What do you want to do, Elle?"

"About what?"

"That letter."

"I want to light a fire with it, Frank. Does that make me seem cold?"

Frank shook his head. "No," he said, "it makes you human. Do you want to send him some money?"

"Not one dime, Frank. Not one cent, and if he showed up at that front door tomorrow, I'd have the marshal throw him off the reservation."

Frank put his hand around Elle's neck.

"I tried it once," Frank said, "years ago. I tried going home. There is no home. There never was."

Elle kissed his hand stroking her face.

"I'd put it all in the past, Frank. Sometimes I'd wonder where Mike was. I loved Mike. I thought it was all sealed off, and then something like this letter pries off the lid again."

"Forget it, Elle." He pointed at her drink. "Do you have a monopoly on the liquor in this household?"

"I'm sorry, Frank." Elle jumped up.

"How about dinner at the Rainbow Room?"

"The *Rainbow* Room. That's expensive."

"Who cares," Frank said. "I'm a rich man."

Elle laughed now, and Frank did too. He was a rich man. In more ways than one.

One could sense the diminishing payroll of the dam project at the Rainbow Room in Las Vegas. Captains and waiters whose principal benefactors had been high rollers and gangsters in the town suddenly found tips smaller, tables empty, and a need once again to try to be courteous to ordinary customers. Few in that gaudy room, with tables sheathed in satin, and set with real silver and cut-crystal goblets, knew Frank Crowe. He had rarely frequented the place and he was happy that he and Elle were isolated in a booth which faced neither the bandstand nor the dance floor.

403

"I didn't need that letter today," Elle said. "Boulder City is depressing enough. Every day I see friends come in the library saying goodbye, everyone hoping we will all meet again."

"I know. I have the same thing in the office. I've had some damned fine engineers up here. Lots of good young ones, too. . . ."

"I'm going to miss our house, Frank."

"Which one, the one in Salt Lake City?"

"No, the one here. I'd like to sell the house in Salt Lake. I couldn't bear to see what they did to it."

"I agree, Elle. I'll call a real-estate broker and list it."

"Hey," Elle said, "you're supposed to be cheering me up."

"That's right. Waiter!"

"What kind of house do you think we'll have at Grand Coulee?"

"Well, as regional director of the Bureau of Reclamation—we call that S-1 in the service—I should be entitled to a pretty fair spread."

"You didn't tell me all that."

Frank continued. "If I remember, S-1 status entitles you to a twelve-room house, a housekeeper and groundskeeper, a government car, and a thirty-foot flagpole."

"A housekeeper! My God, what will I do with a housekeeper?"

"As the wife of a regional director of the Bureau you will be expected to be gracious, and adaptable, and constantly available."

"For what?"

"The regional director."

"You *have* come a long way in five years, Frank Crowe. Do you expect me to spend all my time in bed?"

"Not all, just most."

Elle heard the band strike up and watched guests at neighboring tables rise to go to the dance floor.

"Wouldn't you think that a regional director should be able to dance?"

"That may well be a requirement. How are you coming on the mending of my denims?"

"Don't dodge that question, Frank. I've offered to teach you. My God, a twelve-room house should have an elegant parlor."

"I might take you up on that offer."

"I know, when I'm not in bed panting."

"I'll tell you something, Elle. I used to look at *National Geographics* too—when I was a kid."

"I bet for different reasons than mine," Elle said, smiling.

"Yes. I always thought all ladies' breasts were black."

Elle shook her head.

83

Only the dedication loomed ahead. Already the President and his party had boarded in Washington, D.C.

Ickes, occupying one of the suites in Roosevelt's opulent private railroad car, could see the endless miles of track lined by millions of Americans who were paying tribute in some way to a man who these past two years had given them jobs or hope, and certainly restored a good deal of dignity. Although a conservative, unlike Hopkins, Ickes was perhaps the most liberal and practical man in the cabinet.

They were traveling through Idaho when Roosevelt called Ickes and the two of them huddled in the far corner of the parlor car, watching the lovely verdant countryside roll by.

"I'm having trouble with my speech for Boulder," Roosevelt said, handing Ickes a note pad. "No doubt yours is finished and superb, as usual."

"It is finished," Ickes said, "but I don't know about its merit."

"You're a natural, Harold. I wish I had your writing talent."

"You are being very kind, Mr. President."

"Now," he said, pointing at the note pad in Ickes's hand, "what I am trying to get across in this speech is the fact that this dam is not only an example of what big government can do—there's no way to deny that, when you look at that monster—but I'd like it to be a précis of what's ahead. I'd like to capitalize politically on these big projects. What about Grand Coulee? Can I put that in my speech?"

"I rather wish you wouldn't Mr. President. Not specifically."

"Why?"

"I am awaiting word from Frank Crowe whether or not he will complete it. I haven't received an answer so far."

"That's the one who built Boulder?"

"Exactly."

"Is he *that* vital?" Roosevelt asked.

Ickes thought. "We shall proceed with Grand Coulee no matter what; however, if Crowe were in charge it would be one project neither you nor I would have to concern ourselves with after he took over. You are dedicating Boulder two years ahead of schedule."

405

"I've heard that," Roosevelt said. "Amazing. And Crowe has been approached?"

"Yes sir. By me. I feel he will do it, but I know he must make his own decision. Any pressure from you or me would work against us."

"I understand," Roosevelt said, "but could we hint at other projects like Boulder in this speech?"

"I can manage that, I'm sure."

"You know, Harold, I've given a lot of thought to Hoover since my election. He had everything going for him. He had the looks, the intelligence, the breeding, perhaps even the instincts. You know what his downfall was?"

"You, Mr. President."

And Roosevelt laughed. "No, I didn't mean that. His downfall was that he never got out to meet his countrymen. He neither looked nor listened. He didn't feel, or smell, or touch. I think Americans in number frightened him."

"I think that's a very astute analysis, sir," Ickes said.

"Politics, politics," Mrs. Roosevelt said, pulling up a chair. "How are you, Harold, are you comfortable?"

Ickes rose. "Very," Ickes said, "thank you. How about you?"

"I feel like a queen," Mrs. Roosevelt said. "You should see how I travel alone. I'm sure I've set the world's record for dressing and undressing in a lower berth, at least among first ladies."

"That's a very provocative statement," Roosevelt said.

"It is a great tribute to you, sir," Ickes said, "half the country lining the track on our way west. You have accomplished a lot."

Roosevelt smiled gently. "You've all done a lot. Eleanor, you, Harry, every one of you."

It was a performance that Ickes could not deny, and he didn't. Perhaps all these millions that Hopkins had put behind those useless brooms *had* served a function. Hopkins's WPA program, his free-wheeling spending, had always gone against Ickes's grain, but if he was to help this President, then he must practice tolerance. The cause was bigger than the man. Perhaps Hopkins felt that. At least Ickes hoped so.

They say a President never runs out of conservative neckties and schoolchildren waving small American flags, and they were there at Boulder that day. It was a big day, no doubt. Governor Richard Kirman had proclaimed it a school holiday, the post office had created a commemorative stamp, which went on sale that morning in the Boulder City post office, and when Roosevelt arrived at the dam site, a crowd of over twenty thousand people covered the roads, the hills, the boulders surrounding the dam.

The President was welcomed by the directors of the Big Six Companies and by Elwood Mead, director of the Bureau of Reclamation. He shook the hands of seven governors of Western states, of Frank Crowe, Jack Williams, and Tom Wanke, and he shook the hands of all wives present, and had a personal word for each of them.

"Mr. Crowe," he said to Frank. "I hear you have two precious qualities."

"I didn't know."

Roosevelt smiled broadly. "Yes. One is impatience, and the other is a pretty wife." He shook Elle's hand as did Mrs. Roosevelt.

She said to Elle, "My husband has great appreciation for performance and beauty."

After the introductions the President's limousine crossed the dam and stopped at the newly built observation point on the Arizona side, and while Walker Young explained the intricacies of the dam, Frank Crowe escorted Mrs. Roosevelt and Harry Hopkins to a cable car which traveled along the face of the dam.

At ten-fifteen all the distinguished guests returned to the speakers' platform to the sounds of "Hail to the Chief" played by the Las Vegas high school band. Secretary Ickes gave the first speech, calling particular attention to the conservationist aspects of the dam and the role of the President as a conservationist. He spoke of Swing and Johnson and other politicians who should reap glory from this project; and he seemed to Frank to pound the name Boulder, Boulder Dam, irrevocably through that microphone to all those around him and to millions of listeners throughout the land. After his well-received speech he introduced the President. Roosevelt stood, in a blue suit, his short hair tousled slightly by the breeze, his chest erect, his shirt gleaming, his gold-rimmed glasses reflecting the summer sun.

"Ten years ago the place where we are gathered was an unpeopled, forbidding desert. In the bottom of a gloomy canyon, whose precipitous walls rose to a height of eight hundred feet, flowed a turbulent, dangerous river. The mountains on either side of the canyon were difficult of access, with neither road nor trails, and their rocks were protected by neither trees nor grass, from the blazing heat of the sun. The site of Boulder City was a cactus-covered waste. The transformation wrought here is a twentieth-century marvel.

"We are here to celebrate the completion of the greatest dam in the world. . . . The people of the United States are proud of Boulder Dam. With the exception of the few who are narrow-visioned, the people on the Atlantic Seaboard, the people in the Middle West, and the people in the South must surely recognize that the national benefits which will be derived from the completion of this project will make themselves felt in every state. They know that poverty or distress in a community two thousand miles away may affect them, and that prosperity and higher standards of living across a whole continent will help them back home.

"Today marks the official completion and dedication of Boulder Dam, the first of four great governmental regional units. This is an engineering victory of the first order—another great achievement of American resourcefulness, skill, and determination.

"That is why I have the right once more to congratulate you who have created Boulder Dam and in behalf of the nation to say to you, 'Well done.' "

It was a long speech, a careful speech, a good political speech, Frank thought, particularly for a man who had had nothing to do with the conception of the dam. So engrossed was he in these reflections that he was impervious to his introduction, and to the cheers of the crowd before him, cheers which exceeded even those for the President. Elle prodded Frank and he rose slowly. Carrying his notebook, he stood at the microphone at midday, a warm sun overhead and many, many faces he knew around him.

"Mr. President, Secretrary Ickes, Commissioner Mead, Honorable Senators and Governors, gentlemen of the Big Six Companies, my inclination today is to say, 'Welcome to my dam.' I don't make that statement lightly, since for more than the last four years every stick of wood and every nail, and every ton of cement or bar of steel which has emanated from *some* part of this country filtered through my drafting board and was finally placed, hammered, drilled or cursed into place. Perhaps I'd like to call it my dam because you gentlemen in Washington have been equally busy designating this structure, resulting in most folks now calling it *'Boulder, Hoover, whatever it is.'* "

Everyone laughed, and according to Elle later, no one laughed louder than Roosevelt.

"So much for levity," Frank continued, "for this dam was by no means a lark. As you sit or stand here today before this great and graceful structure, I know you'll think it has all the sophistication of a nail. Here we have Black Canyon," and Frank pointed toward the abutment walls of the dam, "and all you do is fill those age-old granite walls with a plug of cement.

"It was not as easy as all that, and what you see before you is much more complex than you might realize. We had nothing in Black Canyon to begin with. No electricity, no roads, no railroads, no drinking water. We had no housing, no mess hall, no hospital. We had no trees, no streets, no lawns, no shade.

"We had heat. We had merciless heat for merciless months, day and night, and we had cold, and we had winds, and we had rain. We had snow, and we had hail, and foremost we had the Colorado

408

River—Big Red, crafty, forceful, never-yielding adversary until we yoked it barely a few months ago.

"The sun would set before I could name all the heroes who built this dam and all those men who died attempting. You worked well, you worked fast, and you worked with skill. No supervising engineer can ask for more.

"There were four people on this project without whom I could not have accomplished this job. Supervisor Williams and his tunnels, Supervisor Wanke and his flawless concrete, Mr. Walker Young and his endless assistance with his men from the Bureau, and lastly my wife, Elle, who has asked me to announce that there are still three hundred books overdue at the Boulder City library. God bless you all and thank you."

Frank Crowe sat down and Elle kissed him. The President shook his hand, as did Secretary Ickes and Harry Hopkins, and Frank, now perspiring, was anxious to join everyone at the Sequoia Lodge for a stiff drink before his knees buckled.

Never in its four-year history had Sequoia Lodge had so many visitors and so much liquor, and it was difficult at first for Frank to isolate Secretary Ickes, but he finally managed to draw him aside.

"Mr. Secretary."

"Yes, Mr. Crowe?"

"I have decided to accept your offer to complete Grand Coulee Dam."

"That makes me very happy, Mr. Crowe," Ickes said, pumping Frank's hand. "The President on the way over here from the dedication said, 'Put that man on the payroll, Harold. He got a bigger ovation than I did.'"

Frank smiled. "I have a request, however."

"I know," Ickes said. "You want the biggest house on the dam site."

"No sir, that's not it."

"You want ten percent of the profits."

"No, no, not that either. I have a driver, a young man named Hans Schroeder. He's applied for a federal scholarship to the University of Washington."

Ickes said, "And what makes you think I can do anything for him?"

"Well, any man that can order a federal judge around . . ."

"So you know about that."

Ickes took out a notebook and a gold pencil. "How do you spell his name?"

"S-c-h-r-o-e-d-e-r."

"Fine. Now if you don't mind, I'd like to get back to your wife before Roosevelt monopolizes her."

Frank picked up another drink and fell in and out of the arms of every director of the Big Six, of Walker Young and Elwood Mead, and finally rounded up Wanke and Williams.

"Let's take a walk."

"With all this free booze flowing?"

"We'll be back," Frank said. "They won't run out."

They made a curious sight, all dressed in their Sunday best, blue suits, white shirts, neckties, and polished shoes, as they rode together in Frank's truck.

Frank drove silently through Boulder City toward the dam. Hundreds of visitors who had come to watch the dedication, most of them on foot, were returning on this same road. Finally Crowe made a turn, ran his truck up a sharp incline, and shut off the engine.

"From here we walk," Crowe said, and the other two men, as uncomfortable as Crowe in their suits, followed him as he led them up a path. It was the same path he had chosen in 1927, and soon they were standing at the same spot where Crowe had first shown them Black Canyon.

Despite the festivities, the band music, and the cheering which had taken place earlier that day, all was quiet in this spot. The Nevada desert spread out before them in the summer heat was as desolate and as quiet and foreboding as it had been eight years ago. All was gray or sand color. The sky was a leaden blue broken by lazy clouds; the walls of Black Canyon looked as austere and impenetrable as before. No trees had grown here, no vegetation relieved the eye; even the river, the raging, dancing Colorado, had disappeared below them.

And there was the dam, all 727 feet of it, all 6 million tons of it, and despite its immensity, its awesome height, the structure, it occurred to all three men simultaneously, *belonged*. Its color fused into the colors of the desert; its curvature, graceful and distinct, seemed like an extension of nature; and above all, that eerie stillness that had awed them eight years ago still prevailed. The men themselves were silent for a long time.

"She's in," Frank said, looking at neither Tom nor Jack.

"She's in good," Wanke answered.

"Yup," Williams said. "She's in good."

Frank reached into his pocket and brought out two envelopes.

"This money is yours," he said. "You've more than earned it," handing his friends each a check for more than $60,000, "but giving you this money is not meant as absolution for my appreciation."

He shook Tom's hand earnestly, and that of Williams. "We stood here eight years ago," Frank said, "and I asked you boys whether it could be done. You said, 'Yes,' and your appraisal was correct. No supervisor building today or any other day could have expected more and received as much as I did from you. I am deeply grateful."

"Well," Williams said, "those are kind words."

"Indeed," Wanke added, "but I think we've had enough speeches for one day."

"Once more you're right," Frank said. He pulled out his watch and opened it. It was four-thirty-two. "I'll be starting Grand Coulee on November 12. I'll see you at seven o'clock."

"You wouldn't want to make that seven-fifteen?" Williams said, now laughing.

And Frank looked at Williams, and at Wanke, and he looked at the dam and the dam site below it. Somehow, he missed the Colorado River. He remembered the sounds and the ripples and the color of that river, and then he turned abruptly and walked down the little path toward his truck. He opened his collar button and pulled off his tie.

239   246